THE STRONGEST HEART

Book Three in The Clan Donald Saga

REGAN WALKER

THE STRONGEST HEART

Paperback ISBN: 978-1-7354381-4-6

PRAISE FOR REGAN WALKER

"The writing is excellent, the research impeccable, and the love story is epic. You can't ask for more than that."

—*The Book Review*

"Regan Walker is a master of her craft. Her novels instantly draw you in, keep you reading and leave you with a smile on your face."

—*Good Friends, Good Books*

"Ms. Walker has the rare ability to make you forget you are reading a book. The characters become real, the modern world fades away, and all that is left is the intrigue, drama, and romance."

—*Straight from the Library*

"Walker's detailed historical research enhances the time and place of the story without losing sight of what is essential to a romance: chemistry between the leads and hope for the future."

—*Publisher's Weekly*

"...an enthralling story."

—*RT Book Reviews*

"Spellbinding and Expertly Crafted...Walker's characters are complex and well-rounded and, in her hands, real historical figures merge seamlessly with those from her imagination."

—*A Reader's Review*

ACKNOWLEDGEMENTS

I am indebted to photographer Alex Trowski for his magnificent photograph of the Three Sisters of Glencoe that provided the background for the cover, the same photograph on the book's page on my website.

The wonderful talent of illustrator Bob Marshall is shown in the map he did for *Summer Warrior* and *Bound by Honor*, updated for this story.

I must also thank Dr. Katharine Simms, author of *Gaelic Ulster in the Middle Ages*, for her invaluable assistance in helping me to understand the history, customs and players in Ulster at the time of my story. She graciously engaged in an email correspondence with me that provided much useful information and shed light on the guests who would have attended John Mor's wedding.

As he did for *Bound by Honor*, Ian Ross Mcdonnell, author of *Clan Donald & Iona Abbey: 1200-1500*, helped me with many historical details, including the story of the Green Abbot, Finguine MacKinnon, and Iona Abbey, the *"Cathedral of the Isles"*. It is Clan Donald's legacy, which the Macdonalds built, protected and maintained as their ancient ecclesiastical capital. Ian graciously engaged in an extensive email correspondence with me that provided valuable information. I thank him for his kind assistance and sharing his wealth of knowledge, and for his comments on the final manuscript.

As always, I cannot forget my beta readers. In Canada, Liette Bougie, one of my readers, has a fine eye for detail.

The Clan Donald badge is used with the gracious permission of Clan Donald's High Commissioner.

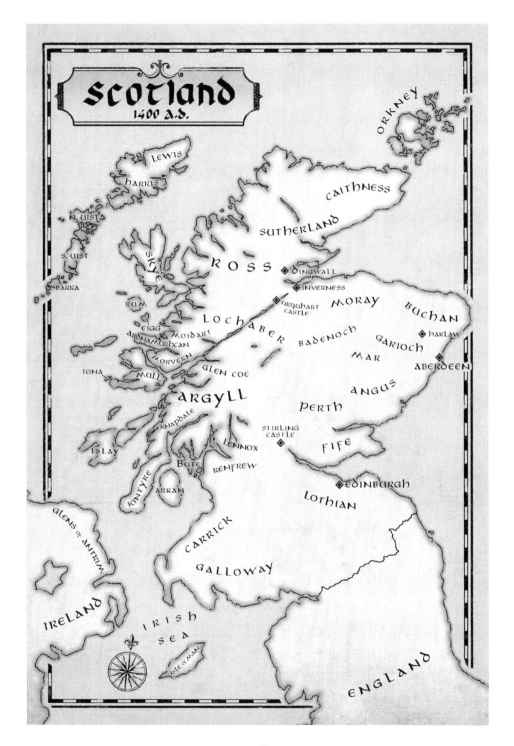

CHARACTERS OF NOTE

DONALD MACDONALD of Islay, grandson of Robert II, King of Scots, from 1386 he was Lord of the Isles, chief of Clan Donald, and eventually Earl of Ross.

RANALD MACDONALD, half-brother to Donald, son of Amie MacRuairi of Garmoran

ALEXANDER ("Alex") MACDONALD, First of Keppoch, Lord of Lochaber, Donald's brother, younger son of John of Islay

JOHN MOR MACDONALD, Donald's brother, son of John of Islay, eventually Lord of Dunyvaig and the Glens

JOHN MACALISTER, Donald's cousin and lifelong friend, Rector of St. Comgan's Church at Kilchoan on Ardnamurchan, then Prior of Iona and eventually Abbot of Iona, the Lord Spiritual on the Council of the Isles

MARIOTA LESLIE, also called MARIOTA ROSS, sister of Alexander (who became Earl of Ross), and wife of Donald Macdonald, eventually Countess of Ross

LACHLAN MACLEAN, chief of the Macleans and Steward of Donald's household

HECTOR ROY MACLEAN ("Red Hector"), eldest son of Lachlan, succeeded his father as chief of the Macleans, Donald's nephew and Lieutenant General of the Isles

ABIGAIL (Abby), Mariota's handmaiden

EUPHEMIA, Countess of Ross, Mariota's mother

ALEXANDER STEWART, Earl of Buchan and Lord of Ross (until 1392), son of Robert II, King of Scots, Mariota's stepfather, aka the Wolf of Badenoch

ALEXANDER STEWART, Earl of Mar, the Wolf's illegitimate son

ROBERT STEWART, Earl of Fife, eventually Duke of Albany and Regent (governor) of Scotland while James I was held captive in England

SIR THOMAS GOODSELL, knight in the service of the Countess of Ross, who becomes the head of Mariota's guard

GWYN KIMBALL, Welsh bowman from Ross who accompanies Sir Thomas

FERGUS BEATON, Donald's physician

MALCOLM CAULDER, Donald's constable at Ardtornish

MALCOLM BEG MACKINTOSH, chief of the Mackintoshes

FINGUINE MACKINNON, Abbot of Iona

EWEN MACKINNON, chief of the MacKinnons

JOHN DONGAN, Bishop of the Isles (until July 1387)

MICHAEL, Bishop of the Isles (as of July 1387), previously Archbishop of Cashel

ALEXANDER MACDONALD ("Sandy"), eldest son of Donald and Mariota

RICHARD II, King of England and Lord of Ireland

WILLIAM ("Willie") THORPE, Donald's "spy" in London, a friend from Oxford, and a follower of John Wycliffe

HENRY IV, King of England and Lord of Ireland

JAMES I, King of Scots held captive in England

ANGUS DU MACKAY, Chief of the Mackays of Strathnaver

Some of Donald's chaplains over time:
BEAN MACGILLANDRIS, chaplain and secretary to Donald, and by 1397, Bishop of Argyll

DAVID MACMURCHIE, chaplain and secretary to Donald, who became Archdeacon of Lismore

JOHN LYON, chaplain at the time of Harlaw, who became chaplain to James I and then Archdeacon of Teviotdale

THE CLAN DONALD SAGA

Their roots were in ancient Ireland with its high kings, in the Isles where the Norse settled and in ancient Dalriada, the Kingdom of the Gaels. They were the great sea lords, plying the waters in their longships and galleys, ruling the western Highlands and the Hebrides for four hundred years.

From Somerled, the first Lord of the Isles, to the Macdonalds who fought both with and against Scotland's kings and, later, at Culloden for freedom, to those who came to America to help win her independence, they were known for their courage, honor and constancy.

These are the tales of their chieftains, men of great deeds, and the women they loved. Their stories are worth remembering. In bringing them to the world of historical fiction, I write about my own clan, my own heritage, hoping to inspire my fellow Clan Donald members and my readers who love all things Scottish.

THE STRONGEST HEART

In the late 14th century, the Kingdom of the Isles was under assault from the ambitious Albany Stewarts, who were taking advantage of Scotland's empty throne to increase their power. Jealous of the Macdonald lordship to the west, the ruthless Robert Stewart, Duke of Albany, thwarted Donald of Islay, Lord of the Isles, at every turn.

A man of keen intelligence, strategy and faith, educated at Oxford and a frequent guest of England's kings, Donald did not intend to allow a traitorous royal thug to rob him of his legacy. The Earldom of Ross was the buffer he needed to keep the Isles safe. Not unmindful of all that was at stake, he took as his bride Mariota, heiress to the Earldom of Ross.

What he could not achieve through diplomacy or marriage, Donald was prepared to claim by right of the sword. In the greatest battle Scotland has ever seen, he would demonstrate the power of the Isles to become the Hero of Harlaw.

It is no joy without Clan Donald,
It is no strength to be without them;
The best clan in the world;
To them belongs every goodly man.

The noblest clan ever born,
Who personified prowess and awesomeness;
A people to whom tyrants made submission;
They had great wisdom and piety.

A brave, kind, mighty clan,
The hottest clan in the face of battle;
The most gentle clan among women;
And most valorous in war.

A clan who did not make war on the church,
They feared being dispraised;
Learning was commanded;
And in the rear were
Service and honor and self-respect.

A clan without arrogance, without injustice,
Who seized naught save the spoils of war;
Whose nobles were men of spirit;
And whose common men were most steadfast.

~ Gaelic lament by Giolla Coluim mac an Ollaimh,
a MacMhuirich bard
Book of the Dean of Lismore, 1493

CHAPTER 1

Castle Tioram, Loch Moidart 1386

"ARE YOU CERTAIN?" Donald looked into the eyes of his half-brother, blue like his own, trying to discern Ranald's true feelings. The eldest of John of Islay's sons by his first marriage to Amie MacRuairi, heiress of Garmoran, Ranald had aged much in the last year and was unwell, but his mind had not lost its edge.

"'Tis what Father wanted, Donnie," Ranald said in a calm voice. They sat across from each other in front of the fire in the great hall of Castle Tioram. "It is what he prepared you for, educating you at Oxford and insisting you follow in his steps, building a relationship with England's kings. Has not Richard the Second treated you like a 'Prince of the Isles' to this day?"

Donald nodded, for it had been at his father's urging that he had cultivated a relationship with England's king, who had given him a safe conduct lasting six years to attend Oxford, not as a mere student but as a *clericus*, a man of high status.

"You may yet need your Oxford learning and the support of King Richard to defend our Isles."

Donald sat back in his chair. "I might need my sword more. Our father, at times, led the lordship into battle as did our grandfather, Angus Og Macdonald, in support of his friend King Robert Bruce."

"Aye, I'll not deny it. You might."

"It is not enough to know Father wanted this, Ranald. I must know your support is freely given, for I would have no bad blood between our heirs and our kin. That is why I have come."

Reclining in his chair, pale from his sickness, Ranald sighed. "The MacRuairi lands Father settled upon me will serve my five sons well, and my brother, Godfrey, as Lord of Uist, should have no complaint. Besides, the torch can be passed to no other, for King Robert's royal charter, by which he gave lands to our father, provided the heir to the lordship must be the eldest of the king's grandsons born to his daughter, Margaret."

Donald was proud of his royal heritage, bestowed upon him as a result of his father's second marriage to Princess Margaret of Scotland, and all it meant for the lordship, yet Ranald was Steward of the Isles and well-liked by the people. "As eldest son, you are the feudal heir. Will the clan's leaders consent to another leading them now that Father has passed from this life?"

"Aye, they will. You are only in your second decade but you have a strong heart, which the clan will need to keep the Stewarts at bay. While you were in England, Alexander Stewart, one of the king's many sons, constantly plagued Lochaber, making it a frontier our father had to continually defend."

"My brother, Alex, has told me of those battles and how the earl earned the name the Wolf of Badenoch for his robberies and incursions."

Ranald's gaze drifted to the fire, as if in contemplation, and then back to Donald. "Now that Father lies with our forefathers at Iona, I have called for a meeting of the Council of the Isles. It will be a sennight from now at Kildonan on the Isle of Eigg, one of my own territories." Donald's uncertainty must have shown on his face for Ranald added, "The chiefs and the clergy will come, and once they are assembled, I will put your name forward, reminding them that our father leaned heavily upon you as his health failed him. You will be called to the position of chief, and I will hand you the scepter myself. Your right to the title Lord of the Isles will be unquestioned."

Donald felt the heavy weight of the lordship descending upon him, but he could find no fault in his half-brother's plan. "Very well, it shall be as you say." He rose, met Ranald's unwavering gaze, grasped his forearm and wished him well.

As Donald sailed back to Morvern, his thoughts were on what lay ahead after the installation ceremony was concluded.

BY ANCIENT TRADITION, the ceremony whereby a new chief of Clan Donald was named, and the Lord of the Isles installed, took place at the lordship's seat at Loch Finlaggan on Islay. The ceremony was followed by much gaiety and celebration with the families present. But this one, per Ranald's plan, would occur on the Isle of Eigg and, given the circumstances, likely would not be accompanied by women and children.

A small but significant isle, Eigg was a favorite gathering place of the clans and the place where Donan, an Irish priest and missionary, had constructed a monastery in the seventh century only to be killed by the Picts he had come to save. Kildonan, the place Ranald proposed they meet, was named after the martyred priest.

The sun was directly overhead when Donald's crew pulled his galley over the white sand beach to rest alongside many others, each bearing a pennon identifying the clan. Flying from the mast on Donald's ship was the black galley on a saffron background with furled sail, the symbol of the Macdonald.

Donald stepped down from his ship, his boots touching the beach at Kildonan. Flanked by his younger brothers, John Mor and Alexander, and accompanied by his cousin and good friend, John MacAlister, rector of St. Comgan's Church at Kilchoan on Ardnamurchan, he strode up the beach toward the chiefs, who had gathered on a knoll. Like Donald, his brothers were fair-haired though Alex's hair was even fairer, almost flaxen.

Halfway up the beach, Ranald met him, one hand outstretched while leaning on a staff with the other. "Welcome to Eigg."

Donald returned Ranald's smile and shook his hand.

Sweeping his gaze over Donald's attire, Ranald said, "It is good you have dressed the part."

Donald had taken care with his appearance, knowing he had chiefs to win who were older than him by decades and who might not have chosen him as their next lord. His finest crimson tunic, which he had last worn to meet with England's king, was embroidered with gold and silver threads, his cloak drawn together with a golden brooch. He wore no armor or mail, but at his gilded belt hung both sword and dirk. He had trimmed his chestnut-colored beard and mustache and confined most of his long blond hair at his nape.

"I made sure he looked the lord he would become," said Donald's cousin, John, the smile on the priest's face giving proof of their easy rapport, "and the chief he will soon be named." John was the great-grandson of Alexander Macdonald, brother of Angus Og, Donald's paternal grandfather. Both brothers had been Lords of the Isles. John, although of the nobility, was a humble man of God who, though a rector, at times served as Donald's scribe. He wore only the simple black habit of a Benedictine monk.

Ranald's gaze shifted to the men who stood watching them from the knoll. "They have all come, Donnie. Of course, Lachlan Maclean of Duart and his eldest son, your nephew, Hector, are here. Also Malcolm Beg, chief of the Mackintoshes. With them are the Macleods of South Uist, the MacKinnons, the Macduffies of Colonsay, who have come with their recorders, the MacQuarries of Ulva, the MacMillans of Lochaber, the MacKays from Kintyre, the MacEacherns, the MacNicols, and the Camerons. And more besides. They have been arriving for hours."

Donald was gratified so many had come, but did they come to oppose or support him? "I assume they know why they have been invited."

"Aye. They know. The Bishop of the Isles and Iona's abbot are here as well, necessary to install a new Lord of the Isles. Come, let us join the chiefs."

Save for the half-dozen years he'd spent at Oxford, Donald had known these men all of his life. Most recently, they had been present for his father's burial on Iona, a solemn affair that lasted eight days, allowing them time for conversation and shared meals.

Squaring his shoulders, he walked with Ranald up the slope, his brothers and Rector John following.

Ranald leaned in. "The ceremony will be in the stone church just beyond where the chiefs are gathered. I have brought our father's sword, the scepter and a white tunic for you."

Donald studied the faces coming closer. Not all bore smiles. "Is there much opposition?"

"Some, but I doubt they will speak against you. I have told them you are not only Father's choice but mine. There are no others to challenge you."

Donald moved into the crowd, greeting each chief as he went. Ranald, Rector John and his brothers went with him. A few chiefs came forward. Among those were Lachlan Maclean, chief of the Macleans of Mull, who had married Donald's half-sister, Mary. His eldest son was Hector, whose head of dark red hair and his red beard had won him the nickname "Red Hector" to distinguish him from his uncle, Hector Maclean of Lochbuie. Hector stood nearly as tall as Donald, several inches over six feet, and was already proving to be a master with a sword.

"Uncle!" exclaimed Hector, his smile wide, his handshake firm. "I, for one, am happy to be here to swear my allegiance to you."

"'Tis an auspicious day," said Lachlan, the Maclean chief, "a new beginning for the lordship."

"It is good to see friendly faces," said Donald.

Spotting John Dongan, Bishop of the Isles, speaking with Finguine MacKinnon, Abbot of Iona, Donald excused himself and strode to meet them. "Bishop…Abbot," he said, inclining his head to each man. "Thank you for heeding Ranald's call. We could accomplish nothing here without you."

"I would be obedient to John of Islay's decision to name you the next chief," said Bishop Dongan resplendent in his official vestments, mitre and ring.

"And I," said Abbot Finguine. "As he lay dying, he told me to see to it." The abbot wore the black habit of the Order of St. Benedict, which Donald expected, but he had added to that a black woolen mantle with a bejeweled golden braid flowing down each side and circling the wide sleeves, more expensive and ornate a costume than Donald remembered from his father's burial.

"We are missing the stone that contains the depression into which the new chief would set his foot," said the bishop. "That remains on Islay. But Ranald has made sure the sword and scepter are here."

Donald thanked them for their support and for coming prepared to accomplish the task of installing a new chief. Saying he would see them shortly, he moved into the crowd to speak with others. If Donald were to follow in his father's footsteps, he must know well the chiefs and their concerns.

His father had shown leadership in times of war but he gained the title "good John of Islay" for his devotion to the church and the spiritual needs of the lordship. He had maintained many chapels and houses of worship and endowed lands for Iona's abbey to secure its future.

As he left the Macduffies, Donald's friend, Rector John MacAlister, came alongside him. Handsome with his dark tonsured hair and full beard, and no wrinkle in his habit, he said, "When today's ceremony is concluded and you are Lord of the Isles, we must speak about the clergy on Iona."

Donald glanced into the expressive brown eyes of his friend. "If you mean Abbot Finguine, I am curious to know what feeds his aberrant opulence."

"There is much you do not know, much that concerns Iona's abbey your father did not have time to deal with before he died."

Donald remembered the week he had spent on the isle to bury his father. Nothing had struck him as amiss at the time, but then he had been in mourning along with the chiefs and their families, for John of Islay was much loved. Before he could reply, Ranald's voice boomed across the assembled group of men. "I have asked you to gather here because it is time we install a new chief, a new lord. Consistent with the wishes of my father, John of Islay, Lord of the Isles, and my own, I believe the next lord should be his son, Donald, grandson of Angus Og Macdonald and King Robert the Second."

Ranald gestured toward the stone church set on the nearby rise. "Let us remove to the church where the ceremony can be performed."

Mumblings came to Donald's ears as they walked toward the church. At his side, Ranald said, "Those who would object urged me to take my place as feudal heir. I have assured them I will not. My age and illness disqualify me under the old tanistry laws as not being 'king fit', and adding to that our father's wishes, they were persuaded to allow you to ascend to be chief."

"Thank you, Ranald. In time, I hope to gain their trust."

"It was the right decision for all. You will be a great chief, Donnie. Of that I have no doubt. Now, you must don the white tunic."

In a small alcove off the main chamber, Donald slipped the white tunic over his own, the garment that represented his innocence and integrity of heart and assured the clans he would be a light to the people and maintain the true faith.

Light streamed through the windows of the church as the men filed in, the sun's rays falling on the altar where Donald stood with Ranald and the bishop.

When all were inside, Ranald addressed them again. "I nominate my brother, Donald, to be our next chief and Lord of the Isles. I have discussed my reasons with many of you. Donald is a man of distinguished abilities, educated and equipped to take on this position. As his strength failed him, our father leaned upon Donald. I believe he will be a great chief."

There were a few frowns but when no objections were raised, Donald faced them. "I know I am young and, in your eyes, untried as either a warrior or a leader, but my father began preparing me for this role when I was a lad. Sending me to England to study at Oxford and spend time at the English court were only parts of his plan. Binding the lordship to the Royal Stewarts was another, but that bond has disadvantages as well as advantages. At times they are our friends—at times, our enemies. The challenges that lie ahead are many but with God's help, and your support, I would dedicate my life to the lordship, to protect our Isles and to maintain our independence and honor."

To Donald's great relief, many heads nodded.

The ceremony proceeded, led by Bishop Dongan. He nodded to Donald, who freely gave his oath. "I vow to walk in the footsteps and uprightness of my father and his forbearers."

Ranald handed him the white rod of kingship, indicating he had the power to rule, not with tyranny and partiality, but with discretion, sincerity and purity.

The bishop then placed John of Islay's sword in Donald's hand, signifying that his duty was to protect and defend the lordship from its enemies in peace or war. Donald glanced down at the shining steel, knowing it might one day take him into battle.

Lastly, the bishop prayed for Donald, asking God to give him wisdom.

O Lord, show Your servant, Donald, Your ways.
Teach him Your paths. Lead him in Your truth.
Give him courage to face our enemies.
For You are the God of our salvation, our strength.
On You we wait all the day.

Donald was aware his success as chief, as was true of his predecessors, was dependent upon God's favor, and he silently vowed to seek the path of righteousness.

After this, the chiefs offered prayers for Donald's success and the chamber grew quiet, but only for a moment before cheers erupted, echoing off the stone walls.

Among the loudest was that of his nephew, Red Hector. "To Donald of Islay, our new chief!"

Donald was asked to sit in a chair and the chiefs came forward, each making his oath of fealty with bowed head and hands between those of their new lord. If Donald thought some did so with less than enthusiasm, he did not mention it, but he looked long into their eyes to discern their true feelings.

Ranald had brought wine to celebrate and no one left before lifting a goblet in toast to the new lord. After several drinks, Donald found himself in a small group with his brothers, the rector and Ranald.

"Now that you are Lord of the Isles," said Alex with a grin, "you must consider an heir."

"First a marriage," put in the rector.

"Aye," said Ranald, "and there is a bride identified already. Lady Mariota Leslie, the betrothal Father arranged for you when you were a child."

Into Donald's mind appeared the image of a young girl with unusual green-gold eyes and braids that hung to her waist. "The daughter of Walter Leslie? I know little of her."

"If she is anything like her mother, she will be obedient to the king's wishes," said Ranald. "Her father, Sir Walter Leslie, the Earl of Ross, died four years ago while you were gone. However, the betrothal agreed to between him, and our father, and the king, who was then the High Steward, still stands. Our father believed Lady Mariota and Ross might one day be key to the future of the Isles."

Donald nodded. He could see the reasoning behind his father's actions. Ross was a large province and a buffer between the Isles and the rest of Scotland.

Alex said, "Months after Walter Leslie died, the Wolf of Badenoch married his widow, Euphemia, and the king, his father, named him Earl of Buchan. Though the countess had given Leslie a son who would inherit the title, the Wolf has asserted control over the countess' lands that now include not only Ross and Dingwall, but also the Isles of Lewis and Skye."

Donald looked at the faces before him. "I see much happened while I was in England."

"Aye and all of it hostile to the interests of the Macdonalds," said Ranald. "King Robert may be your grandfather, but his actions have undermined Clan Donald. After all, Lewis has been a part of the lordship for over two score years and we also dominate Skye."

"The chiefs did not mention this at the burial," muttered Donald.

"They would not have wanted to cast a dark shadow over an already sober gathering," said Rector John.

Donald let out a deep breath. "I see the lordship is mired in a tangle the king has allowed in order to benefit his many sons, most troublesome of which is the Wolf of Badenoch."

"Aye," said Ranald. "Our father would have spared you the shadow that looms over the Isles. But if you are to be chief, you must know the truth."

"For that, I thank you," said Donald. "I would not live with lies."

CHAPTER 2

Ardtornish Castle, Morvern

THAT EVENING, as the day drew to a close, Donald ate and drank with his companions in the warmth of Ardtornish's great hall. Outside, the sun had set, leaving the autumn sky a pale salmon color and the waters around the point, where the castle stood guard over the Sound of Mull, a shimmering light blue.

Donald favored this time of day when he could settle before the fire with his hounds and a goblet of wine to ponder the day's events. At Oxford he had kept company with the sons of English nobles. This night, his company consisted of his brother, Alex, and his cousin, John MacAlister, the rector. His brother, John Mor, had excused himself, Donald assumed, to visit some young woman.

"The wine Ranald was kind to provide was much appreciated," he said, remembering how the installation ceremony concluded on Eigg.

"And much needed," said Alex. "It helped to soothe the ruffled feathers of a few chiefs."

Donald turned the half-empty goblet of wine in his hand, feeling the cool silver on his fingers. "It is a beginning at least." He studied his cousin's calm face. "Do you think those who were discontent with the result will rise against me?"

"It is difficult to say at this point," said John, looking very much the priest in his black robe. "Though, in the end, I thought it went well."

"I would not trust some of them," put in Alex. "They still might challenge you—not for Ranald's sake—but for their own, to gain more territory or more power."

"I can only wait and hope that, in time, they will become content with my leadership," said Donald. "A first order of business requires me to allocate lands to our family. Alex, if you agree, I would make you Lord of Lochaber. It was part of Mother's dowry and you have fought for it alongside our father. It is an important part of the lordship and includes Morvern, Ardnamurchan and Moidart. Those lands and Keppoch Castle should be yours. What say you?"

Alex smiled. "I would be pleased to have them and Mary will be happy to have a more permanent home of our own."

"For our brother, John Mor, I was thinking of the castle at Dunyvaig on Islay, together with other lands on Kintyre, which were part of our mother's dowry."

"Our mother might disagree with the dispensation of her dowry lands, but I should think John Mor will accept that," said Alex. "They are some of the best lands in the lordship."

"And mine to give to whom I will," said Donald. "Though I may have to contribute to the dowries of my sisters." There was a moment of silence and then Donald said to his cousin, John MacAlister, "I would see you have a position in the church that serves the Isles and not just a rectory on Ardnamurchan."

"I do not seek a higher position," said John. "It is enough to be your occasional counselor and clerk."

Donald smiled as he considered his cousin's words. John MacAlister was the great-grandson of Alexander Macdonald, Lord of the Isles before Donald's grandfather. Still uneasy about his unusual rise to become chief, Donald recognized that his cousin John was still eligible within the old Celtic laws to be selected as leader. "Though you are a senior family noble, you remain humble, choosing to serve the church, as many in your place would not have done. Thus, it is with pleasure I will welcome you into a greater role as you faithfully serve God and the lordship."

Donald paused for only a moment to catch the look of approval on his cousin's face. Then, reminded of their conversation on Eigg, he said, "There was something you wanted to tell me about Iona's abbot."

John heaved a sigh, as if his next words pained him. "Had your father not been distracted with building the priory on Oransay and improving the chapel at Finlaggan, he would have tended to the matter, for he loved Iona."

"He gave much to see it secure," said Alex, "confirming lands for the abbey on Mull that stock many cattle. "And he established the school of stone carving on Iona."

"In recent years, the situation at Iona has worsened," said John. "You noticed Abbot Finguine's elaborate cloak. It is a reflection of his priorities. He entered the abbey by reason of succession rather than devotion. From what I have learned, he is robbing the wealth of the abbey, allowing it to fall into disrepair and decay. Were it to continue, the abbey would be impoverished."

"Why would he do that?" demanded Donald.

"He milks Iona's endowments of their tithes, rents and resources for the enrichment of his family, his concubines and their many children."

"Concubines?" Donald said in shock. "I saw no concubines when I was there."

"When you were on Iona for your father's burial, you would not have seen them," said John. "They would have been kept out of sight along with the abbot's bastards."

"It is not unheard of for noblemen of the church to have concubines," said Alex.

"I agree," said John. "However, in this instance, Abbot Finguine, is a 'green abbot', one who was never a monk. He has dowered his daughters by the concubines with largesse from the goods and revenues of the abbey. Without intervention, it will never be allowed to return to its pristine state. You might not have noticed the new monument the abbot has erected—for his own glory, not that of God's. I expect the abbey paid for it."

Donald felt his temper rise as his friend spoke. Iona's abbey and church were the spiritual legacy of his family and of the lordship, erected by the Macdonalds and maintained by them for generations to God's glory. "I am reminded of the words of one of the masters at Oxford, a priest and a scholar named John Wycliffe. I oft attended his lectures. He questioned the privileged status of the clergy and their extravagant living, something you would doubtless agree with, John. He believed many were motivated by temporal gain and used their power in England for their own position and status rather than to bring the gospel to the people they had vowed to serve. I was much persuaded by his words."

John nodded. "I have heard of Wycliffe and his views and agree with them. As the clan chief and Lord of the Isles, heir of the abbey's founder, the son of Somerled, it is your responsibility to make inquiry into the situation at Iona to assure the abbey's proper maintenance and provision. You must be the one to ensure the conditions of the lordship's endowments are met."

Donald squeezed his hand around his goblet so tightly his knuckles turned white. "A duty I do not shrink from."

"A new chief would be expected to visit all the Isles," offered Alex. "Why not do that and begin with Iona?"

"A good idea," said Donald. "John, I would ask you to come with me and my brothers, at least to Iona to examine the abbey with me and then you could stay to review the abbey's accounts."

"Abbot Finguine will not be pleased, but if it is your request, he cannot refuse."

That night, before he retired, Donald spoke to his brother, John Mor, about the lands he intended to give him. His brother was not receptive to Donald's plans.

"The lands you would give me are nothing compared to the ones you hold."

"But those are lands I hold for the lordship. The chief must hold the greater share. Aside from that, I need you to protect Kintyre against a Stewart incursion."

John said no more but his expression told Donald he was not pleased. "Will you sail with me to Iona? I am thinking of asking Rector John to review the accounts. If you are willing, I would leave a galley for you and him to sail back to Ardtornish when the review is accomplished." Donald did not speak of the concerns about Finguine MacKinnon, known as a "green abbot". He would rather have his brother's impressions without influencing him.

Clearly reluctant, he finally nodded. "Aye, I will go."

Isle of Iona, spring 1387

AS THEY NEARED the shore of the small isle off the west coast of Mull, the wind rose as it always did in this place, but the good weather held. Donald's crew pulled on the oars, bringing the red stone abbey and church closer. His heart soared to see again the stately edifice that dominated Iona's shore. The most sacred place in the lordship.

They left the galley on the shore, and pressed on to the abbey, walking amid an abundance of wildflowers and passing the small stone building with the slate roof that was St. Oran's Chapel. It was built by Somerled to hold the bones of his male successors, lying close to the saint's. South of the chapel is *Reilig Odhrain*, the burial ground named after the saint. It is the final resting place of isle chieftains as well as Norse, Scottish and Irish kings.

Donald had been formulating an explanation for why he and his brothers and their cousin had come. If Abbot Finguine was guilty of sins toward the church, he would not look upon Donald's visit with favor.

The abbot met them at the door of the abbey. "To what do we owe this honor, so close after your father's burial?"

"Now that I am chief, Abbot Finguine, I am traveling to all the lands of the lordship to greet the people with my brothers and our cousin, John MacAlister. I am beginning at Iona because of its significance."

With a forced smile, the abbot said, "I see." The black robe he wore over his cowl was gilded and bejeweled as Donald had previously observed. New, however, were the jeweled rings on his fingers. On his chest, hanging from a thick gold chain, lay a gold pectoral cross also set with jewels.

The abbot's gaze drifted over Donald and his companions before he gestured them ahead. "Let us retire inside where a warm fire and good meal await."

The abbot served them a dinner of roast beef, the source of which Donald was certain was the cattle grazing on the Ross of Mull just across the sound that separated that isle from Iona. It was one of seventeen land grants that the Macdonalds had endowed the abbey to assure its financial security. And now, the grants on Mull were being usurped by the MacKinnons.

Forcing the beef down with a drink of his wine, Donald explained to the abbot that he wanted to tour the buildings and review the accounts. "My father died before there was time to do this with him. It falls to me to discharge my duty of care toward the abbey and its church."

That the abbot took umbrage at this was clear from his furrowed brow and downturned mouth. "If you feel you must."

Donald chose not to respond to that. Instead, he said, "I have asked Rector John to undertake the task of reviewing the accounts. He and my brother, John Mor, will stay behind when I depart for other Isles."

"Of course," said the abbot before pressing his lips tightly together.

Donald gazed around the dining hall. "I understand you have concubines. Are we to meet them?"

The abbot hid his surprise well. "If you would like." Turning to one of the monks attending them, the abbot whispered in his ear. Donald exchanged a glance with Rector John.

A few moments later two women appeared in the elegant gowns of noblewomen and curtseyed before Donald. Both were comely which was not surprising given their role in the abbot's life. Donald thought them to be in their late thirties. They were several years younger than the abbot yet old enough to have grown children. It was difficult for him to imagine how a Benedictine vow of poverty allowed the abbot to clothe these women like daughters of a king.

The abbot said, "Only two of them and some of their children are here just now. Allow me to present Ailis from Mull, and Joan from the Isle of Harris."

Donald inclined his head to the women. "And your children?"

"Ailis has two daughters and Joan is the mother of my sons, as well as a daughter."

Donald's cousin had told him the abbot had children from his concubines, but he wanted the abbot to acknowledge the daughters he generously dowered from abbey monies. He wondered how old their children were and why there had never been any mention of them before this. A son of his name might be expected to follow him as abbot but that was not at all decided in Donald's mind. As his friend, the rector, would remind him, a bad tree could not bear good fruit.

Dingwall Castle, Earldom of Ross, 1387

MARIOTA FELT the pleasant pull on her scalp as her mother ran the brush through her long hair. Her handmaiden, Abby, could have done it but her mother enjoyed the task and so did she. It was the time when they talked of more intimate things than the castle's household and the lands of the earldom. On this day, Mariota's mind strayed to her stepfather, Alexander Stewart, Earl of Buchan.

"Mother, you have been married to the Earl of Buchan for five years yet I never see him. Not that I mind, you understand. He is a dreadful man, nothing like Father."

"Your father was a knight of renown and a gentleman. The Wolf of Badenoch, as the Earl of Buchan is called, is not. When he is not ravaging the countryside with his rough band of caterans, he is with his mistress and their large brood at Lochindorb Castle in Moray. Which is surrounded, I am told, by water. We are best free of the man."

"Why ever did you marry him?"

"He was not my choice any more than was your father. My second marriage was King Robert's choice; the first was King David's, a reward for your father's service on crusade. Immediately after the wedding to the Wolf, based on my lands in Buchan, King Robert made Alexander Stewart the Earl of Buchan. The Stewarts, you see, wanted Ross."

"And will Buchan have it?"

"Not unless he outlives your brother, Alexander. And even if he does, you would hold the senior claim to the title Countess of Ross. You are elder of my children."

"Then I hope my brother lives for a very long time."

"I have given Buchan no children so he has no heirs to inherit the earldom. In fact, I have been thinking of complaining to the pope about the empty nature of our marriage. Your father's friends have encouraged me to seek a divorce, but mayhap the pope will give me an annulment."

"I think you should pursue whatever gives you your freedom," said Mariota.

Finished with the brushing, her mother said, "Do you wish me to plait it?"

"No. Today, I would take up the sides and let the rest hang free."

"You have such lovely hair, golden in the sunlight, like mine was at your age. Now mine is threaded with silver."

"Doubtless due in no small part to the last man a king foisted upon you." Mariota loved her mother and knew the Earl of Buchan had brought her both grief and embarrassment, a wife neglected and abandoned. "Still, you are only in your forties and beautiful."

"I am glad you think so, Daughter, even if I know better. Speaking of the king's marriage arrangements, you remind me of yours. 'Twas made when you were but a child. The king and your father met here at Dingwall with John of Islay, Lord of the Isles, to betroth you to Donald, his eldest son by Princess Margaret. Now that you are entering in your second decade, it is time. Some would say past time."

Despite that truth, Mariota was in no hurry to wed. Her life at Dingwall was pleasant. "I vaguely recall a ceremony and a boy with fair hair and blue eyes. What do you know of him?"

"Nothing save his parentage, which speaks well of him. He and I share a grandfather, Angus Og Macdonald, whose daughter, Mary, married my father the fifth earl of Ross. That relation was dealt with in the betrothal."

Mariota had a vague recollection of having heard that before. "I assume it required some sorting out by the church."

"Yes, but permission was given."

"I do not worry for that. I just don't like the thought of being carted off to some island away from you and Dingwall to live under the rule of a stranger." At that moment, Mariota determined to find out what she could about him.

"You will have time. He has only just succeeded to the lordship and is likely taken up with affairs in the Isles."

Pursuing her earlier thought, Mariota said, "If you agree, I would send one of our guards to the Isles to learn what he can of this man."

"I am not opposed to it. I should have done the same when I was told I would wed the Wolf. But choose the man you send carefully, someone you trust, someone discreet."

Her hair finished, Mariota rose and turned to hug her mother. "Thank you."

On her morning ride, she was only vaguely aware of the sunlight on the green hills and the wind in her hair. Her mind was focused on the man she would choose for her errand and what she would tell him.

Later, she summoned to the solar the one she had decided upon.

His fist over his heart, the dark-haired Sir Thomas Goodsell bowed deeply upon entering. "You asked for me, my lady?"

She had noticed Sir Thomas when he first came to Dingwall, brought by her father. His erect stance, massive shoulders and well-muscled arms spoke of his prowess with a sword. As well, she had observed him on the practice field bettering other men-at-arms. When men who served her father drank in the hall late into the night, he often stood aside, as if keeping watch.

"I did. If you are willing, Sir Thomas, I would propose to send you on an errand to gain information about a certain man. My mother, the countess, is agreeable."

He returned her an expectant look. "Whatever you ask I will do."

"Your loyalty is admirable. The man is Donald Macdonald—*the* Macdonald—chief of his clan and Lord of the Isles."

The knight's expression told her the name and title impressed him. "What would you learn about him?"

Taking a deep breath, she said, "He is new to his role of chief. I want to know if he is intelligent, if he is wise, if he is kind. Do the other men look up to him? Or, is he ignorant and cruel and despised? Does he have a lover, a mistress? Is he frequently drunk? His speech crude?"

She could see his resolve was clear by his set jaw. "Where will I find him?"

"He rules over the Isles and some of the mainland so he could be anywhere. I am told his ship flies the black galley that is the symbol of the Macdonald but, as the chief, he commands the fleet of the lordship."

"How much time do I have?"

"I set no time limit but would ask you to send me word within three months of what you have learned and how much longer you might be. I will see you have coin enough for such a journey. Be discreet. Dress to blend in with the Islesmen. If you need to, you are free to take a position among the men serving the Macdonald."

"Very well."

"As I recall," she said, "you have some relations in Argyll."

He nodded. "Distant cousins on my mother's side."

"That being so, visit your family there first. It may prove informative. Take a man you trust with you, one who might come to me with your messages. Tell our constable to see me if he would know more of your mission."

Sir Thomas bowed, as if to leave, and then said, "My lady, may I ask, who is this man to you? A friend or an enemy?"

"That remains to be seen. He is my betrothed."

Ardtornish Castle, Morvern 1387

DONALD HAD COMPLETED his visit to the Isles and his lands. He had called upon his mother who was in Argyll with some of his younger siblings, a visit that was more formal than he would have liked. He and his brother, Alex, had spent Christmas at Finlaggan, the seat of the lordship on Islay. Now that spring had arrived and the Isles were in bloom, they were returning to Morvern where they had agreed to meet their cousin, John.

It was on this return trip that Donald learned Ranald had passed from this life. A melancholy came over him at hearing the sad news. "I expect we have missed his burial on Iona."

"Aye," said Alex, his blue eyes thoughtful. "But we can pay our respects at his grave after we meet with our cousin."

"Yes, and I may have need to speak to Abbot Finguine after I hear from the good rector. 'Tis but a short sail to Iona."

Donald's visits to the chiefs had gone well. He had made suggestions and offered help where he could assist with work they had underway. He signed charters his father or Ranald had left undone and saw to the business of the lordship. When he asked for help in guarding their lands against the Stewarts, the chiefs had willingly offered men-at-arms. In all this, Donald viewed his role as facilitating whatever made the lordship stronger and whatever encouraged the faith of the clans.

His father's true son, he never forgot the church. No chapel or church would be allowed to fall into disrepair. His chaplain and secretary, Bean MacGillandris, a man of solemn presence in his black robes, had accompanied him and participated in the observance of Christmas at Finlaggan in the chapel John of Islay had finished.

As he met with the chiefs, Donald had also gathered information on where their enemies might attempt an assault. He was aware the Stewarts, particularly the Wolf of Badenoch, were pushing ever westward. He learned of the Wolf's movement into Glen Mor, the Great Glen, that cut a diagonal path across the Highlands from Inverness on the Moray Firth in the northeast to Loch Linnhe in the southwest with Loch Ness at its center. It was an increasingly important artery in the waterways plied by the galleys of the lordship, and Donald knew he must be diligent to keep the waterways free.

A light rain was falling as the crew pulled the galley onto the beach at Ardtornish. Rector John, was waiting for Donald, along with Donald's hounds, as he and Alex strode up the beach.

Glad to be inside, they left their cloaks with the servants and went to stand before the fire, their hands outstretched to the heat of the flames.

John was the first to speak. "Before you ask, John Mor wanted to remain on Iona, knowing you would be back to collect him."

Donald nodded. "What did you find in the abbey's accounts?"

"Discrepancies. Less income accounted for in the receipts from Mull, Tiree and Colonsay than should be. No sums expended for needed upkeep and repairs of masonry and timber."

"'Tis not surprising," said Donald. "I saw for myself the repairs that were left wanting before I sailed."

John's demeanor turned serious. "The explanations the abbot and his servants gave me for work undone and sums not accounted for were not satisfactory. When I asked about revenues, they could not account for all the rents, tithes and gifts the abbey would have received. And they could not show all expenditures."

Donald frowned. "So the abbot has betrayed the trust the lordship placed in him."

"Sounds like a nest of vipers has crept into the church at Iona," added Alex.

"There is one thing more," said Donald's cousin. "I am loath to mention it, and I cannot help but wonder if it is some scheme of the abbot and his daughter."

Donald and his brother fixed their eyes on John.

"John Mor has taken up with one of the abbot's daughters, a young woman named Christina. It is why he asked to remain behind."

Knowing John Mor's ability to charm women and his proclivities that rarely saw him sleeping alone, Donald raised his brows, waiting to hear more.

"The abbot certainly did not discourage it."

Donald shook his head. "No, he would not, for if I should fall in battle without an heir, John Mor would be the one to take up the scepter for he is the next oldest."

"I can well imagine the abbot would eagerly embrace such a possibility," said Alex.

Donald said, "Then it is good I mean to return to Iona. In the course of paying my respects to Ranald, I will deal with the abbot."

"Tread carefully, Donnie," said his cousin, "the abbot is wily. My presence has put him on his guard. Do not forget that his brother, Ewen, is the MacKinnon chief and your Marischal and Standard Bearer. A very powerful presence lurking just across the narrow Sound of Mull. He is used to getting his way on Iona by stint of their hereditary family possession."

The Isle of Iona

WITH HIS BROTHER, Alex, beside him, Donald knelt before Ranald's grave, their pale hair blowing in the breeze. The earth was still damp and the grass disturbed from the burial. Despite the hundreds buried in the ancient graveyard, Donald had no trouble finding his half-brother's grave.

The carved slab was the newest stone laid to rest in the burial place of the MacRuairis near the chapel, reserved for the immediate family of the chief. At the top was a foliated cross with vine and leaf scrolling carved in the stone. A galley with furled sail followed and, beneath that, the inscription, "Here lies Ranald Macdonald". At the top of the plant scroll two lions stood rampart, their tails becoming the vine that continued on. The craftsmanship was exquisite and reflected the grave slab of their father, John of Islay, except their father's displayed the sword of state and a stag hunt with his Irish wolfhounds.

"A fitting tribute for such a fine man," said Donald.

"Aye," said Alex, "Iona's artisans and master masons worked long and hard on this."

Donald lifted his gaze to St. Oran's Chapel, the small stone building in the distance where the Lords of the Isles were buried. Had

Ranald not been faithful to the wishes of their father and the king, he would have been buried there. Donald lamented the loss of his mentor who had unselfishly guided him to the chief's position.

"I am sad at his passing," said Donald, "but I rejoice that he is not here despite what the stone says. He is in Heaven with our Lord and the best men of the Isles. We will see him again, for he was a man of faith." Donald got to his feet. "It is time I deal with the abbot." The wind blew his cloak behind him as he strode toward the abbey, preparing himself for the confrontation that awaited.

Abbot Finguine, his dark tonsured hair just showing beneath his hood, met them at the door. "You have been to Ranald's grave." It was a simple statement, devoid of sentiment.

"I have. I was sorry to miss the burial."

"It was well attended. Many mourned his passing." Donald detected a note of condemnation. The abbot paused as if to say goodbye. "Did you wish to come in?"

"Yes, if you would. I need to speak to you about the abbey and its church."

Without a word more, the abbot turned and walked ahead. Donald and Alex followed. Once seated, Donald got quickly to business. "Abbot Finguine, I am not content with what I see here. You must agree the buildings are not being repaired or kept in order and the grounds are not well-tended. Further, based on Rector John's review, the accounts do not always show all of the abbey's rents or how the money is spent."

"To the contrary, I am certain all is in order."

"That being the case, I assume you will agree with what I intend to do. Except for the benefices, which are yours and the prior's, I will collect the abbey's endowed incomes myself and, after paying the abbey's expenses, buy the timber and hewn stone and hire workmen and artisans to repair any damage and restore this sacred place."

The abbot glared at Donald. "That is unprecedented!"

"Unprecedented you say? Only your waste of the abbey's endowments and the largesse of your gifts and dowries for your women and children are unprecedented."

"The abbey is my responsibility!" the abbot shouted.

"But you have failed to meet that responsibility. If I allowed this to continue, you would have the abbey decaying with a large part of the chapter and choir in ruins and the poor monks going hungry." Then, narrowing his eyes on the abbot, he said, "Perhaps you have forgotten this was a religious endowment, feudal in nature, which makes me your liege lord. It was my family that founded this abbey, provided the lands to secure its income and the artisans to make it what it should be. I will not allow your concubines and children to benefit off the backs of my clansmen. In God the Almighty's name, I will see this is rectified!"

The abbot leaped to his feet. "This is outrageous!"

Donald was unfazed. In a calm voice that belied his seething anger, he said, "I will send my factor and lay bailees each month to collect the funds. See that they are properly accounted for as well as any expenditures on the abbey's behalf."

With that, Donald rose, along with Alex. "If you would call our brother, John Mor, we will depart."

ONCE THE CHIEF'S galley had sailed away, Finguine turned to his concubines, Ailis and Joan, and his son, who was the Iona prior, also named Finguine. "We must rid ourselves of that man or he and his rector will be the end of us and the MacKinnons."

"I would not underestimate the rector, John MacAlister" said his son. "He is of their nobility, the great-grandson of Alexander Macdonald, the Lord of the Isles slain by the MacDougalls."

"I know a way, my lord," said Joan. "The Macdonald chief's brother, John Mor, is enamored with our daughter, Christina. We need only convince her to seduce him and encourage him to rebel against his brother. Already my daughter tells me he complains that the lands Donald of Islay would give him are inadequate for his status."

Finguine paused to consider this for only a moment. "Yes, encourage her, and I will speak to my brother. An invitation to John Mor from Ewen, chief of the MacKinnons, to visit him at Castle Findanus on Skye will surely not be declined."

CHAPTER 3

Ardtornish Castle, Morvern

DONALD AND ALEX had sailed back to Morvern with John Mor sulking most of the way. Whether it was due to his leaving the daughter of MacKinnon's concubine or his displeasure with his inheritance, Donald could not say.

A week later, his brother was still in a pout but was suddenly cheered when he received an invitation to visit the MacKinnon chief on Skye. Donald ruminated on what was behind the invitation and John Mor's sudden happiness. Surely it was not merely the possibility of seeing Christina, the daughter of the MacKinnon abbot, though Donald had no doubt she would be present.

"It cannot be good," said Alex. "Some plot is afoot else why would a chief call our brother alone?"

"I suspect you are correct, but I can hardly restrain John Mor from such dalliances. He is fully grown, after all."

That morning, a message arrived for Alex from one of his captains. Reading it, he remarked to Donald, "The Wolf moves closer. He has gained lands at the head of Loch Ness from the Earl of Moray.

Now he threatens the Great Glen."

"Neither the king, the Wolf's father, nor his elder brother, John Carrick, have restrained him or his caterans from plaguing the country," said Donald. "It appears we will have to increase our forces defending the eastern borders against Buchan's earl."

"I am recruiting more men into my retinue," said Alex. "You might want to do the same."

"I agree. Even before that message arrived, I asked my constable to add fighting men to my guard and galloglass to the lordship's galleys."

SIR THOMAS DECIDED to take his Welsh friend Gwyn Kimball with him to Argyll and thence to the Isles. Gwyn was good with a bow and had proven himself in the service of the Earl of Ross. Mindful of Lady Mariota's instructions, Thomas knew him to be trustworthy.

They had stayed but a few days on the Scottish coast and were packing up while talking about where to go next. "I had hoped my relations could tell us something about the Macdonald, but we didn't learn much," he told Gwyn.

"No, but then I do not think your cousins knew much. Donald is too new in his position of chief. He is young—younger than we are. Only time will show his character, if he be true or false."

"We did learn something helpful to our mission," said Thomas, as he attached his bedroll to his saddle. Word had spread that the Lord of the Isles and his brother, Alexander, Lord of Lochaber, were recruiting men to add to their retinues. "We know there is an opportunity to serve the chief and his brother."

"If we enter the service of Lord Alexander to guard his eastern border from Alexander Stewart, Buchan's earl," said Gwyn, "we may not see as much of the Macdonald as we would like."

"Agreed. Therefore, I propose we go directly to Morvern and seek out the Macdonald's constable. To gain the information Lady Mariota desires, we must be close to the chief."

Gwyn nodded. "Besides his constable, he will have a captain of his guard and a man who captains his galley."

With that in mind, they bid farewell to Thomas' cousins and set their horses toward Morvern.

EXCITEMENT ROSE in John's chest as he cast his gaze on the fortified hill house rising from a rocky promontory jutting into the sea inlet of Loch Slapin on Skye. The sun shone on the stone walls of Castle Findanus, the seat of Clan MacKinnon.

His anticipation arose from the fact the invitation had come to him, not his brother, causing John Mor's mind to be full of questions. Was the invitation from the MacKinnon chief intended to draw their clan closer to the Macdonalds? Did the chief have in mind some business of trade? Or, might Ewen be concerned about John's intentions toward his niece, Christina? John had openly engaged in a relationship with the abbot's seductively lovely daughter. Though he had no intention of marrying her, he happily accepted what she freely gave.

The man who approached, dressed in finery befitting someone who served the chief, bowed before him. John thought he might be the castle steward. "Chief Ewen awaits you in the great hall. If you would follow me, my lord, I will take you to him. Your crew will be seen to."

John motioned to the two guards he brought with him in addition to his crew, and the three of them proceeded up the winding path that led to the top of the promontory. Surveying the stone walls surrounding the castle, he could see it was built for defense. From the parapet around the three-story tower, guards stood at attention, looking out to sea.

The huge wooden door at the arched entrance to the tower swung open. Just inside, stood Ewen, the MacKinnon chief. "Welcome, Lord John."

In addition to light from the windows, the great hall was ablaze with torches set in sconces. Hanging from the wooden roof were wrought iron cartwheels holding many candles.

John offered his hand in friendship, motioning his guards to remain by the door. "I thank you for the invitation. We have met before at Finlaggan and most recently on Iona for my father's burial and then on Eigg for my brother's installation as chief."

Ewen MacKinnon was, like the abbot his brother, a man of middle years with strands of gray in his dark hair and beard. His face had a harsh appearance except when he smiled, which he did now. Gesturing to two chairs set before the fireplace, he beckoned John to sit.

The fire burning steadily smelled pleasantly of pine. Wine was quickly served in elegant goblets and a plate of cheese and bread placed between them on a small table. "I trust you can stay for dinner?"

Seeing no traces of anger on the chief's face, John was inclined to accept. The days were long at this time of year and, even after dinner, there would be sufficient light to sail. "That is gracious of you."

"I am hoping we will soon be allies in a great cause."

John inclined his head. "A great cause?"

"Aye. One that may see you as chief of the Macdonalds."

John was taken aback. "But there is a chief...my broth—"

"Yes, I know. But he has treated you badly in the allocation of lands. A paltry bit of ground for the brother who would reign in his stead should anything untoward befall him."

"'Tis true I am not happy with the allocation Donald proposes. But to rebel against him..." His voice trailed off as he realized the MacKinnon chief's intriguing thought appealed. "What do you have in mind?"

"For now, it is enough to say that the MacKinnons and certain other clans agree that if we have our way, you would rule in Donald's place."

John sat back prepared to hear more. The chief went on at some length, elaborating on the MacKinnon history going back to Somerled's time and their role in bringing Robert Bruce to power. "As you see, we are an old clan with deep roots in the Isles. Moreover, for decades, the abbot and prior at Iona have been MacKinnons. Your brother, Donald, would propose to interfere with that long relationship and dictate terms of service to us."

This was new to John. What was Donald up to?

By the time the MacKinnon chief finished recounting his displeasure at Donald's meddling in what Abbot Finguine considered "matters of the church", John had downed two goblets of wine and, lulled by the warmth of the fire, was feeling most agreeable. "What do you propose?"

"Nothing at the moment. I wanted to sound you out. If you agree, we will move to gather allies to the cause. There were some chiefs who were not in favor of Donald becoming chief. It will be a small thing to seek them out. And, of course, we have ties already with the Macleods and Macleans."

Ah, thought John. The concubines. "Very well. I assume you will contact me when you have more to say."

"Of course." The chief summoned a servant and whispered an order. A few minutes later, Christina appeared in a revealing crimson gown that clung to her curves. Her long dark hair glistened in the firelight. Jewels dangling from her neck drew his gaze to her generous bosom.

"John!" she exclaimed. "I had heard you might be coming to visit my uncle. Are you to stay the night?"

He had not planned on overnighting at the MacKinnon castle, but the thought of running his hands over Christina's supple body changed his mind. "If Chief Ewen asks me to stay, I would be inclined to do so."

Ewen MacKinnon smiled, softening his harsh countenance. "But of course."

ARRIVING AT ARDTORNISH, Thomas was reminded of why the Lords of the Isles and their clans located castles where they did. Ardtornish sat on a headland projecting into the Sound of Mull. A stone fortress with a view down the sound both east and west would never be taken by surprise.

Thomas approached a guard and asked for the constable. Before he could explain why he and Gwyn had come, the guard said, "More recruits for the lord's new men-at-arms?"

"Why, yes." Thomas said and then introduced himself and Gwyn.

"A knight? By your surname I presume your father is English."

"He was," said Thomas.

"Well, that will please the Macdonald. He is a friend of King Richard." With a glance at Gwyn, who Thomas had introduced as an archer of some skill, he said, "Archers are always welcome. You should meet those from the MacInnes clan. They are the lordship's hereditary bowmen."

Gwyn's expression brightened.

The guard took them to the constable who seemed pleased to greet them. A man of two score years with a battle-hardened demeanor, he said, "Lord Donald is on Mull visiting the Macleans." Looking behind them to where their horses stood, he added, "I am taking a galley to meet him. You can leave your horses here with the groom and sail with me."

The voyage down the Sound of Mull to Duart Castle was a short one. The good weather held with white clouds drifting in a clear blue sky and a breeze blowing them on. The rhythm of the crew's chanting lulled Thomas nearly to sleep. Being unused to the roll of the ship, Thomas and Gwyn had to hold on to stay upright. "We will have to become used to traveling over water rather than land," Thomas said to his companion.

Before Gwyn could reply, the constable approached, seemingly unaffected by the movement of the ship. "The crew you see chanting to the pull of the oars are all good swordsmen."

Thomas' gaze shifted to the weapons stored in the center of the galley. "Yet they prefer to be crew on Lord Donald's ships?"

A smile spread across the constable's face. "They prefer to be with Lord Donald and much of the time he is traveling by galley with several ships. Were they to stay on land, they would be guarding his castles and manor houses. On the Macdonald's own galley, larger than this one, many of the crew are galloglass warriors. It has been so since the time of Lord Donald's great-grandfather, Angus Mor."

"I have heard of the galloglass," said Gwyn. "They are famous in Ireland."

"Aye," said the constable. "And in the Isles where they originated.

They fought with Lord Donald's grandfather for King Robert Bruce at Bannockburn. The Macdonalds have ever been closely tied to the Irish. Lord Donald's grandmother was Áine O'Cahan, an Irish princess."

Thomas made a mental note of Donald Macdonald's Irish connections and the loyalty of those who served him.

The massive stone edifice that was Duart Castle rose from a high crag on a peninsula jutting into the Sound of Mull. Thomas had always thought Dingwall Castle in Ross an impressive sight, but it lacked the setting of the glistening blue waters that surrounded Duart.

On the wide swath of green in front of the castle, a large crowd had gathered. Men shouted encouragement to two swordsmen facing each other with targes in their left hands and swords in their right.

"Ah, Red Hector is at it again," said the constable, shaking his head.

The two men who stood poised with raised swords wore mail but no helmets. In addition to their swords and targes, each had a dirk secured at his belt. In appearance, except for their height, they were very different. The one Thomas assumed was Red Hector sported long hair and a beard, both dark red. His bold even features rendered him quite handsome. The other was fair, his hair and beard flaxen blond.

The constable walked closer and the surrounding crowd parted to allow him to pass. Thomas followed in his footsteps, curious to know what was happening.

Between the two men, poised to fight, was another with his back to the constable. He turned at the constable's approach. "Malcolm! You have finally arrived. About time."

Thomas noted the one who spoke, despite his youth, had a deep voice and was as tall as Hector, several inches over Thomas' six feet. His coloring was a mixture of the two combatants with long blond hair pulled away from his face and a well-trimmed dark red beard.

"I tried to talk them out of it," he said to the constable, "but with no luck. The Norwegian, it seems, is a knight of some renown in his country and insists on proving his skill by mortal combat—a duel to the death. I have urged him to seek only first blood but without success. My nephew, unsurprisingly, is willing to accept the challenge."

"This is what comes of Hector's many successes, my lord," said the constable to the one Thomas now assumed was Donald, Lord of the Isles. "Every knight of any reputation wants to measure weapons with him in an attempt to claim victory for bringing our champion down."

The Macdonald turned to the Norwegian. "Are you sure about this?"

"Ja," he said, nodding vigorously.

Lord Donald backed up to where the constable stood and shouted for a priest named Father Bean MacGillandris.

"His chaplain," explained the constable.

When the priest arrived in his black robe, the Macdonald said, "Please pray for their souls, Bean. 'Tis mortal combat."

The chaplain, stoic but capable and obedient to the call, spoke to the two men in a voice loud enough for those pressing close to hear. "One of you will soon meet his maker, the God of Heaven. Therefore, I urge you to repent of your sins and accept His gift of salvation." With that, the chaplain bowed his head and in a low voice Thomas could not hear, began to pray.

When he finished, he stepped back to join the constable.

Lord Donald said, "Very well, let it begin."

Judging the two opponents, Thomas could not have said which had the upper hand. But something about the Macdonald's demeanor told Thomas the Lord of the Isles was not worried about his nephew.

The Norwegian came on strong, thrusting powerfully. Red Hector, surprised, leaped backward, slapping the Norwegian's blade aside. Circling his opponent, Hector appeared to be sizing up the foreigner's style.

The crowd, rooting for the Isleman, began to shout, "Hector! Hector!"

The Norwegian shifted from foot to foot, taunting Hector with his targe. "You fear my blade, eh, Isleman?"

A small smile crossed Hector's face but he said nothing. Clearly, he was enjoying this. With a sudden strike, so fast Thomas could barely follow his sword, Hector brought his blade down on the Norwegian's right arm, not piercing the mail but likely bruising, and therefore weakening the man's sword arm.

The Norwegian struck back in anger, cutting downwards from his right. Hector raised his targe just in time to block the blade aimed at his side. Turning in a tight circle, he swung his sword across the Norwegian's unguarded neck. It was not enough to take off the man's head but it left a deep cut gushing blood.

The Norwegian dropped his targe and pressed his hand to the cut, trying to wield his sword with his right arm despite his weakened state. Snarling his anger, he mumbled words of protest and swung at Hector, nearly connecting with his face.

Thomas had the impression Hector was now toying with his opponent. He exuded confidence gained from what, Thomas surmised, must have been many sword battles.

In a flourish of battling blades, the Norwegian made a last effort to bring down the Isleman, striking left, then right, but Hector was stronger, cutting and thrusting relentlessly.

"Finish it!" shouted the Macdonald. And Hector did with a clean slice across the Norwegian's neck. His flaxen hair now soaked with blood, the man dropped to the ground, his pale blue eyes staring blankly up at the sky.

Loud cheers erupted from the watching crowd. Hector smiled at his admirers and raised his bloody sword in triumph.

The chaplain advanced and, saying words that would see the man's soul to Heaven, touched the Norwegian's forehead and crossed the air in front of him.

Lord Donald called to his nephew. "See that he is properly buried in sacred ground. He was a brave warrior."

"Aye, my lord," said Hector, turning from his admirers to attend to the duty.

The constable drew near to Lord Donald and spoke to him briefly before beckoning Thomas and Gwyn to him. "My lord, here are two more for your new fighting men, one a knight and the other a bowman."

Lord Donald studied the two of them for a brief moment and

then offered his hand. "Welcome." Thomas was struck by the intense blue of his eyes, the warmth of his smile and his strong grip.

Accepting his hand of friendship, Thomas said, "We understand you are looking to increase your fighting men, and offer what skills we have."

"Your surname is English."

Thomas would not lie to the Macdonald, especially given he was Lady Mariota's betrothed. But he would not mention he had served the Earl of Ross. "My father was English. He died in the Crusades. I was squire to a knight who came to Scotland after that time. But he, too, is dead. My mother's people were from Argyll."

"A worthy background," said the Macdonald. Turning to Gwyn, he said, "And you are Welsh, I'm told."

"Yes, my lord. The bow is my weapon of choice."

Lord Donald nodded and then turned to his constable and whispered a few words to him. Turning back to Thomas, he said, "I am planning a visit to King Richard either this spring or next. It would be good to have a knight of English origin with me. My entourage will be large enough so that you, Sir Thomas, and your archer friend are welcome to accompany me."

Thomas said, "We would be most happy to do so."

"That being the case, you can add yourselves to my guard until we depart for England."

THOMAS HAD BEEN serving Lord Donald for several months and was now accustomed to travel by galley as the Macdonald chief was always moving. The year had turned and Lord Donald was now at his manor house in Kilcummin on the west coast of Islay where the beautiful beach at Machir Bay welcomed his galleys.

Thomas had observed the young lord with his siblings, his men and his chiefs. With all, he had an easy rapport. There were women, too, in the castles and even in his manor house on Islay but Thomas never saw any behavior that would suggest one of them was a lover or a mistress. It seemed to Thomas that Lord Donald was a man of devout faith, often accompanied by clergy. One in particular, Rector

John MacAlister, was a close companion.

One evening as he sat at a small writing table in the bedchamber he shared with Gwyn, Thomas pulled out a piece of parchment and dipped his quill into a bottle of ink. "It is time I write Lady Mariota. I am overdue."

"Shall I take the message to her when you have finished?"

"Yes. It was what she intended. There will be a galley to Ardtornish where we left our horses, but do not linger in Ross as Lord Donald will depart in a month for England."

Thomas began to write.

To Lady Mariota of Ross from Sir Thomas Goodsell, her humble servant,

> *My Lady,*
>
> *I apologize for the lateness of this message, but I wanted to be able to write to you with some confidence.*
>
> *To begin with the superficial, the first thing I noticed about Lord Donald was his height, well over six feet. He is fair in coloring but with a short auburn beard, very striking in contrast to his pale blond hair.*
>
> *As to his character, he has a presence all remark upon and maturity beyond his years. He speaks well but then he was educated at Oxford and is often found reading. Although his manner is decisive, he is always willing to listen.*
>
> *The lordship is a great burden he willingly carries. The men—his guard and the crews of his many galleys—accept his orders without question. I have never seen him display cruelty. I have observed him drinking with the men upon occasion, but he is never drunk. The chiefs of the clans who are subordinate to him, so far as I can tell, respect him.*
>
> *He is quick to laugh but can turn serious when the matter calls for it.*
>
> *He is often accompanied by clergy and frequently visits the kirks of his kingdom. The only time I have seen him lose his temper is when a church has not been well-tended, and then he has harsh words for those who failed in their duty.*
>
> *Women smile at him, as they consider him attractive, but I have*

seen no signs of a lover or mistress. He scarce has time.

He is royal Irish by his grandmother, an Isle lord by his father and grandfather, and a Stewart by his mother. But he is not like any Stewart you have ever met. More like his father, who they called "good John of Islay" for his love of the church.

The Macdonald's heart is firmly in the Isles he loves.

He is planning a visit to King Richard and has asked me and Gwyn to be a part of his retinue. If you agree, I would like to accompany him.

MARIOTA READ THE letter and looked up at her mother, who was waiting patiently for news. "Would you be willing to let Sir Thomas and Gwyn, the Welshman, leave your employ for that of the Lord of the Isles?

Her mother's brow wrinkled. "Whyever would they?"

Mariota handed her mother the letter. "You'd best read what Sir Thomas has to say. It appears they have fallen under his spell."

CHAPTER 4

The Lord of the Isles' manor at Kilcummin on Islay's west coast, summer 1388

DONALD STARED at the pale blue-green waters rushing onto the beach at Kilcummin, pondering what he must do. With him were his brother, Alex, and John MacAlister, his cousin. Voicing his worry aloud, he said, "The situation in Scotland grows worse."

His grandfather, King Robert the Second, the first Stewart to sit on Scotland's throne, was in his seventies and a weak ruler. Four years before, he had lost control of the country to his eldest son, John, Earl of Carrick, who had renewed the conflict with England, precipitating border skirmishes between the two countries.

"Aye," agreed Alex. "Carrick has failed in the essential task of reining in his brother, Buchan's earl, the Wolf of Badenoch. Worse, Carrick's accident with his horse has rendered him physically incapable of governing Scotland."

Turning to his companions, Donald eyed his cousin, who spent less time as a rector these days since he'd joined Donald's court. John said, "Carrick's younger brother, Robert, Earl of Fife, has been quick to step into the breach."

"Another Stewart uncle of mine," Donald said with a smirk. "And that one is known for his contriving and manipulation."

"He has made himself Guardian of Scotland," said Alex, "wasting no time assuring his place in the kingdom."

"At least he has promised to rid the north of the menace of his older brother," said John.

Donald shrugged. "The Wolf is the king's favorite son. He will attempt to shelter him, but for how long, one cannot say. My grandfather is ailing."

"Many nobles want the Wolf's band of wicked outlaws reined in," said John. "They rape and pillage across the Highlands with impunity, including the Wolf's own lands and the properties of the church. For that, the Bishop of Moray has a grudge against him. The Wolf's method is to allow his caterans to raid until they cause a loss of revenue. Then, he steps in and transfers the land he does not control to himself, including the lands of the church. The bishop will help Fife."

"How?" Donald wondered aloud.

"Well, to begin with," said John, "the Wolf has ignored his marriage to Euphemia, Countess of Ross, and lives instead with his mistress in his bleak castle of Lochindorb. Though he has other castles, not the least of which is Euphemia's castle of Dingwall, it is from Lochindorb that he conducts his reign of terror."

"A despicable creature," interjected Donald, running his hand over his bearded chin. "I have heard that between his mistress and his other women, he has sired forty children, all bastards."

"Ah, but importantly," put in Alex, "the Countess of Ross has given him none."

"Which is what his brother, the Earl of Fife, and the church will use to deprive him of Ross," said John. "All it will take is for Rome to grant Euphemia a divorce. Then Ross will again be solely hers and, in time, her son's."

"Ah, Ross," said Donald upon reflection. "You remind me I am betrothed to the countess' daughter. It is time I claim my bride, but first, I must call upon King Richard. With the Earl of Fife taking control, our alliance with England is more important than ever, and I have delayed my trip overlong.

FROM HIS CASTLE of Dunyvaig on Islay, John Mor sailed north to Iona where he was to meet again with Ewen, the MacKinnon chief, this time joined by the man's brother, Finguine, Iona's Abbot. Christina would be there and had sent John a message saying she wanted to see him.

As the white sand beach came nearer and Iona Abbey loomed ahead, it occurred to him that an abbey seemed a strange place to plot a rebellion. But John did not have the convictions of his brother. He was willing to meet the MacKinnons anywhere for the chance to enlarge his lands and his title. Christina had assured him that Donald would be sorry he had treated him in a miserly manner.

Batting away the midges, he entered the abbey and was met by a small gathering of men standing with the MacKinnon chief. A few men-at-arms from the chief's guard stood with him, as well as Abbot Finguine and senior men he recognized from the Macleod of Harris and Maclean kindreds.

Ewen MacKinnon gestured to an arched doorway in one of the abbey walls. "Come, let us sit and share some wine."

They retreated to a chamber where a wooden table stood surrounded by chairs. A narrow window cast light into the small chamber. On the table sat flickering candles and a tray of silver goblets. As the men took their seats, Christina appeared carrying a pitcher. She smiled at the men. "Allow me to serve you." Circling the table, she poured the wine.

"My daughter," explained the abbot to the men, whose expressions told John they admired Christina's seductive beauty.

It had been several months since John had been with her. She looked different somehow, more rounded in the face. And then he saw what could not be hidden. She was with child!

As Christina poured the wine into John's goblet, she bent her head to his ear and whispered, "Our child will be a son. I just know it."

John was unsure of his feelings. On the one hand he was glad the babe growing in her belly was his. If she were correct, he would be John's first son. But the child's appearing would change little between them, and she must know it. A mistress' child would be a bastard, not an heir.

She tossed him a smile as she left.

John gazed at the faces of the men staring back at him. None showed any sign they thought it significant that Christina was pregnant, nor did they inquire as to who was the father.

"We have come to an agreement to support your claim to the lordship," said Ewen MacKinnon. "After all, you are deserving. Then, too, we assume when you are chief, you will dispense lands generously to those who have aided you."

John nodded. The suggestion seemed only fair.

The Maclean, who was not Lachlan, their chief, said, "We are prepared to bring Islesmen and mercenaries to the fight that will ensure your success, and thus ours."

To those words, the man from the Macleods added, "There were those who were not pleased to see your brother elevated over Ranald, but he is gone, and we need one of our own to govern the Isles, one who understands our needs." John had not recognized this man at first. He was a relation of the chief but not his eldest son, John.

The MacKinnon chief had never discussed their needs with John except to object to Donald's rules concerning Iona's abbey. The church and the clergy had always been more important to Donald than to John. If these men wanted more lands, what of it? He only cared about the lands he would gain in the bargain.

The abbot smiled contentedly, his hand circling his silver goblet. "The abbey will support you and the ones who rise against your brother. We are hoping to take him by surprise."

"You will not harm Donald?" When he thought about what this change in leadership would mean for Donald, he thought of banishment not death.

The MacKinnon chief was quick to answer. "Of course not."

"We need to discuss timing," said the Macleod kindred, his voice and manner displaying his impatience.

John had not touched his wine, for he did not find the company relaxing. Straightening in his chair, he said, "It will have to wait until I return from England. My brother has asked me to accompany him to visit King Richard. We leave shortly."

The men shared looks with each other that told John they were uncertain of whether he should go.

"It seems to me," interjected the MacKinnon chief, "it would be good for John to have the support of King Richard." Then, turning to John, "As your father and brother have enjoyed the favor of England and its kings, so should you. It may be important once you become chief."

The senior man from the Macleans agreed. "Yes, by all means, go. By the time you return, we will have raised a large contingent of men-at-arms to fight for your cause."

AT SUMMER'S ZENITH, Donald sailed south from Islay with a large retinue and a great number of galleys. King Richard had granted him a safe conduct to enter England with eighty horse.

Among Donald's company were his constable, Malcolm, his guard and additional men-at-arms, as well as servants to attend both men and horses.

His traveling companions included his cousin, John MacAlister, and Father Bean MacGillandris, his chaplain and secretary, wearing their black Benedictine robes. His physician, Fergus Beaton from Mull accompanied Donald, and his brother, John Mor. Donald's half-brother Godfrey, Ranald's brother, had also come at his invitation. Alex had agreed to stay at Ardtornish to govern the business of the Isles and keep an eye on Iona's abbot.

Before he left, Donald had discussed with John MacAlister and his brother, Alex, his reasons for taking John Mor and Godfrey with him.

"King Richard will be pleased to meet Ranald's brother and to know there are good relations between the two families of John of Islay," Donald said to Alex. "As for our brother, John, I want to show him the partnership we could have if he would cease from dwelling on what he does not have and be thankful for all that is his as my partner."

John MacAlister steepled his fingers over the cross he wore on his chest. "Finding joy in life often begins with being thankful for what God has given us."

"Wise words, John," said Alex. "But our brother has shown no indication he has come to that understanding."

"Mayhap he will in time," said Donald. "It is my prayer."

A week later, Donald and his companions departed Islay where he kept most of his fleet. Two days after that, they arrived at Bristol on England's western shore. The Isles traded fish, including salmon and herring, cattle and hides from Bristol's harbor, so Donald knew the area fairly well.

Above them gray clouds hovered. Donald was relieved there was no rain to make unloading the horses more difficult. The process took some time with so many of them. People stopped to watch; children were especially curious.

While Donald's constable supervised the unloading, one of the king's men approached, accompanied by guards wearing the king's livery displaying the white hart.

"My lord," the man said, bowing to Donald from his horse, "His Majesty, Richard, King of England, sent me ahead to escort you to London and to show you to your lodging."

"The king is gracious," said Donald, swinging into his saddle. "Is the manner of address to England's king new?" Donald had only heard Richard the Second addressed as "my lord" or "my lord king" before.

"His Majesty is King Richard's preferred address as of a short while ago."

Donald had heard the young king had been at war with some of his nobles and parliament concerning taxation and the king's finances. His recent assertion of authority must be driving the new address.

With Donald leading the long procession, they rode east with the king's men. After overnighting along the way at an inn, they neared the outskirts of London. The crowds began to grow in number, as did the wretched smells from the Thames where waste was routinely dumped.

Once in the city, the people overflowed the streets. Traders and artisans spilled out of their workshops to speak to their customers, some of whom dressed in velvet and damask, a stark contrast to the peasants. Taverns disgorged their patrons to mingle with the crowds. Harlots, soliciting customers, leaned against the buildings, their breasts all but exposed. As the Islesmen passed, they shouted, encouraging them to turn aside.

Donald's brother stared at the women openmouthed. "I have never seen the like of this."

"The sins of the city are on full display," said John MacAlister.

"London is an old city and its port older, still," Godfrey said to John Mor. "I was here once before in my youth and was amazed as you are. Be glad your home is in the Isles." Godfrey had Ranald's dark coloring but now in his fourth decade, his hair was laced with gray as was his beard. Donald had been pleased when he consented to come with him to London.

The stench rose as they reached the city center. The sewers on each side of the road were merely open gutters running with waste from chamber pots, butcher shops and horses.

As the sounds rose to a tumult, memories of Donald's time in England flooded back to him—the hordes of people, the noise, the dirt and the smells that made him wince.

Donald's father had encouraged him to seek an alliance with England's young king, which he believed would be to the lordship's advantage, and Donald had done so.

As he thought of King Richard, Donald recalled the time that thousands of men had marched on London to protest the introduction of a poll tax by the king's regent. The rioters murdered government leaders and members of the royal household. King Richard, then only fourteen, had bravely met the protesters, made promises to them and led them from the scene. But he did not keep the promises he made to the mob that day. Donald only hoped the king would keep any promises he made to him.

But the man Donald remembered the best, the one who had influenced him the most, was John Wycliffe, the Oxford master who had died in the year Donald returned to the Isles. He had disapproved of clerical celibacy, pilgrimages, the selling of indulgences and praying to saints. He believed many monasteries were corrupt. It had been Wycliffe's words that came back to him when he learned of Abbot Finguine's treachery.

Drawing up beside Donald, his constable said, "I had forgotten how dirty this city is."

Donald smiled, "You must remember, Malcolm, as Godfrey said, it is very old and its problems made worse by thousands of people. Even so, its trade manages to thrive. By day, the quays are kept busy with ships bringing goods from the Baltic and Mediterranean."

From behind Donald, John MacAlister said, "I am told London is home to some great churches. I am hoping to see Westminster Abbey while we are here."

"I will make certain you do," said Donald. "It is grander than Iona Abbey but no better loved."

The crowd parted to let them pass as they followed the king's men down the wide street leading to the palace. Donald pointed out the abbey that stood next to it. Everywhere, people stared at them, seeing, Donald knew, tall Highlanders and Islesmen—many with long hair and beards—in fine tunics and cloaks with swords and dirks at their waists mounted on horses walking in a long procession accompanied by clergy. The men who were new to his guard, the knight and the Welsh bowman, with their shorter hair and somewhat different appearance, made for an interesting addition.

"It is not a sight the people see every day," the king's lead man remarked. "Even mounted, your Islesmen are intimating for their size, much taller and larger than most Londoners."

Donald remembered his days at Oxford when he was the tallest in his college and his dress and hair different then as they were now. "But the king is only a few inches shorter than I am," said Donald.

"Yes," said the king's man, "but he is a Plantagenet and has their greater height."

That afternoon, once they had settled into their chambers in the palace, Donald asked to be shown to the king. A short while later, with John Mor, Godfrey, John MacAlister and his guard, he was led to the throne room.

King Richard was younger than Donald, though both were in

their twenties. Since Donald, his brothers and his other companions were taller than Richard, he was glad the king was seated on his throne as they entered the great hall. Beneath a bejeweled golden crown his hair was a reddish-yellow, his round face fair and rosy, and his beard scant. His attire was opulent, even for a king, with an ermine cape over his gilded dark green tunic and crimson velvet robe lined with ermine.

Surrounded by his court, but missing his queen, Anne of Bohemia, who must have been with her women, the king beckoned Donald forward.

A loud voice from behind announced him. "Donald of Islay, Lord of the Isles."

Leaving his guard at the door, Donald stepped forward with his companions and bowed before the king.

King Richard said, "Lord D-D-Donald. We are glad to see you. How was your j-j-journey?"

Donald recalled that the king stammered when he spoke and hastened to put him at ease. "The fair weather held as we sailed south, Your Majesty. It was very kind of you to send an escort who eased our entry into London and assisted with our lodgings."

The king cast a glance at Donald's companions. "Who have you b-b-brought with you?"

"My brother, John Mor, Lord of Dunyvaig and Kintyre, my half-brother, Godfrey, Lord of Uist, and my cousin, John MacAlister, who is also a rector and a close friend. There are others in our party who are not here at the moment."

Each bowed before the king. Donald hoped the youth of their party made the king comfortable. He had heard Richard was often in disagreement with his older advisors and nobles.

King Richard might have been born in France but Donald knew him to be at ease with the Gaelic culture and language, perhaps more so than the English he ruled. Thus, he interpreted the king's evident pleasure at their arrival to be genuine.

"You have c-come a long way," said the king. "Tonight we c-celebrate your arrival. T-tomorrow to business, for we have much to d-d-discuss."

THE DINNER THAT evening exceeded Donald's expectations. King Richard was known for his elaborate meals, and this was surely one of them. Roast beef, lamb and pork were set before them on large trays. A swan with its feathers still intact graced one end of the table. Roast crane was also served along with other fowl. Spices, some Donald had never tasted, flavored every dish. For the last course, there were individual custard tarts with nutmeg and pears boiled in sweet wine sauce with ginger.

Sitting on the king's right was Queen Anne, a lovely woman of regal appearance. Her crown was set upon her flowing veil, leaving her long blonde plait hanging down her back.

At one point, the king leaned over to Donald, sitting on his left. "Last year, I had a collection of recipes p-p-prepared from a banquet I held with my uncle, the Duke of Lancaster."

"Your Majesty would not be trying to outdo the French, would he?" Donald asked with an amused smile.

The king shrugged. "We acknowledge France's contribution to f-f-food, but we think our collection of nearly three hundred recipes will amaze even them. As well, we wanted to instruct our people in how to make common p-p-pottages and meats and prepare extravagant dishes for special occasions."

It was an unusual feat for a king but then Richard was unusual in many respects. He wanted peace with France while some of his advisors would have preferred war.

The king had invited Donald to bring others in his retinue to dinner, including his constable, his chaplain, his physician and his guard. From their expressions, Donald could see that Godfrey and John Mor were impressed by the feast laid before them. John MacAlister, like Donald, would have preferred simpler fare such as they served at Donald's court, but such an elaborate meal was to be expected when dining with England's king.

As the dinner slowly unfolded, they were entertained, first by musicians of considerable talent, and then by the king's favorite poet, Geoffrey Chaucer, who held the high position of Controller of Customs and Justice of the Peace. Donald knew of Chaucer's works from his days at Oxford but he had never been treated to the poet's own reading.

"What have you for us t-tonight?" asked the king.

Chaucer, his thin face graced with a graying beard of scant pro-portion, bowed deeply. "For you and your guests, Your Highness, I would propose to read from something I am working on now. It is a collection of tales told by pilgrims on their way to Becket's shrine at Canterbury."

"Do you write in French?" asked the king.

"English, Sire. And the one I have chosen to read from is *The Knight's Tale*, although I caution, it is not yet finished."

"Very well, you may p-p-proceed."

At the king's gesture, the poet took the floor and thence began to tell the story of a heroic duke named Theseus, who was Lord of Athens. Returning from a successful battle, he encountered a group of noble ladies, widows whose husbands had been slain by Creon, the cruel King of Thebes, who had desecrated the bodies and denied them a proper burial.

Theseus gave comfort to the widows, swearing his oath as a true knight to wreak vengeance on Creon so that all Greece would speak of how well he had deserved his death.

With his banner displayed, Theseus then rode forth, his host marching on beside him. At this point, the poet read,

"With Creon, who was Thebes' dread lord and king,
He fought and slew him, manfully, like knight,
In open war, and put his host to flight;
And by assault he took the city then,
Levelling wall and rafter with his men;
And to the ladies he restored again
The bones of their poor husbands who were slain,
To do for them the last rites of that day."

There was a great deal more to what the poet read, including a story of two knights who were passionate in their love for the same woman, but before the tale was fully told, the poet broke off, declaring he had yet to finish it. "It will be a long story with many parts."

Frowning, the king glanced at his queen who nodded. Shifting his gaze to the poet, the king said, "You must r-return with more of it, for my queen and I would hear the end."

So, it was agreed that Chaucer would return as soon as he had more written. Before he departed, Donald begged leave of King Richard to ask the poet for a favor, which leave was granted.

The next morning after breaking their fast, Donald was summoned to the king's presence. He took with him Godfrey, John Mor, John MacAlister and his chaplain, who was also his secretary for these would be serious discussions.

"Sit you d-d-down," said the king, "for we would speak to you of Ireland."

Donald had his own matters to discuss with the king but he was not against Richard's raising Ireland as the first issue. In fact, he had anticipated it for the lordship had many interests in Ulster.

"What h-h-happens in Ireland is of great importance to us," began the king. "We fear it may take our p-presence and an army to quell the rebels who th-threaten our English colony there. In the meantime, much can be done to c-check Scottish expansion in the northern Irish Sea."

By Scottish expansion, Donald knew the king meant the Scottish Crown's expansion, which was essentially Stewart expansion. It was, in fact, Donald's issue he intended to discuss with the king. "It seems we are of one mind, Your Majesty. What would you have the lordship do?"

"We w-w-would that you use your many galleys to s-s-safeguard the trade routes and seagoing passageways around Ulster. Moreover, we would that you had a greater p-p-presence in Ulster itself, aligning your Isles with the Bissetts in the Glens of Antrim. They stand against the S-Stewarts, who are allied with the O'Donnells against us. We know that your father, John of Islay, had c-considerable interests in Ireland and his alliances with the British Crown helped protect the Earldom of Ulster."

"That is so," said Donald. "In fact, my father intervened with King Edward the Third on behalf of the Bissetts so that they regained their lands taken by Edward the Second. Hence, our families enjoy a warm relationship. As for the patrols you suggest, we will gladly undertake them. And we will seek a greater role in Ulster. One of my sisters has married Robert Savage, brother of the crown's Seneschal of Ulster."

The king smiled. "Yes. We are aware and the matter p-pleases us, Lord Donald. Now, is there something you would discuss with us?"

"You have touched on it, Your Majesty. The ambitions of the Stewarts concern me. They already harass my eastern border in Lochaber and now threaten the Great Glen, which is critical to our access to the Highlands."

"Are you not a S-Stewart by your mother?" asked the king.

"I am, but I am also my father's son. John of Islay loved the Isles and our lands on the Scottish coast. He wished to protect them from those who would seek to possess them, whether from Ireland or Scotland. My grandfather, King Robert, has had many sons and gives away lands like honey at harvest time, though they belong to others."

The king nodded. "I am glad you have s-spoken of this. We will assist where we can. Meanwhile, you have our approval to r-r-resist their intrusion with force if need be."

JOHN MOR HAD listened attentively to all that was said, astounded by the respect the English king had shown his brother and their easy rapport. The next morning, Donald was summoned to a private meeting with the king. Before he left, Donald had arranged for a tour of Westminster Abbey for John MacAlister. Invited to go along, John supposed he might see this grand abbey everyone talked about.

"The king is completing the construction on the nave begun by Henry the Third," said their guide. Benedictine monks strode through the abbey as the guide drew the visitors' attention to the arched ceiling high above them. "It rises one hundred feet above the floor. King Edward rebuilt the abbey to be not only a great monastery but a grand place of worship, drawing man's attention to God."

John raised his gaze to the gilded vaulted ceiling, illuminated by light from windows set high in the stone walls, trying to imagine how the setting might call attention to God. He admired the stone arches that, if nothing else, gave testimony to the wealth of England's kings.

"Kings have been coronated here since William the Conqueror," said the guide. He then pointed to the shrine of St. Edward the Confessor, rising high above the floor, plated with gold and encrusted with jewels. "And most of England's kings are buried here." John had never seen the like.

Directing their attention to the walls, the guide said, "Do take time to note the brilliant paintings."

As John MacAlister veered off to see a painting of a clergyman, John followed, watching the priest's black robes move as he walked.

Catching up with him, John asked, "What did you think of my brother's meeting with the king yesterday?"

Without turning his attention from the painting, John MacAlister said, "The king wants close ties to the Macdonalds and our help in Ireland. I thought it a good token of his respect for the Lord of the Isles to desire such an alliance."

John Mor reflected upon his cousin's words. "He treated my brother like a foreign monarch."

"King Richard may well consider him as such. To be Lord of the Isles is no small thing, even were he not the grandson of the King of Scots. Donnie reigns, if you will allow the word, over the Kingdom of the Isles and has at his command a great army of Islesmen and Highlanders as well as a fleet of hundreds of ships to carry them. With the king's interest in Ireland, it is not surprising he would want to hold your brother close."

When he was chief, thought John, he would have those men and ships at his command and King Richard would call *him* friend.

CHAPTER 5

Ardtornish Castle, Morvern, end of summer 1388

FROM BRISTOL, DONALD had sailed first to Islay. At Dunyvaig, he had left John Mor with some of the horses. Then, he dispatched a galley to North Uist to return Godfrey home. Rounding the isle, he sailed to Kilcummin where he left most of the remaining horses. Now, he had returned to Ardtornish, tired but pleased with all he had accomplished in London.

Standing with his companions in front of the castle looking out on the Sound of Mull, Donald watched the rays of the setting sun dancing on the water. The tension he had carried for weeks subsided like a halyard gone slack. "It is good to be back," he said. Beside him, Alex ran his hand through his flaxen hair. He appeared to be nervous, as if hiding something of importance. Whatever it was, he did not begin with it.

"The meeting with King Richard went well?" he asked.

"It did. I believe we have gained his trust. At our first meeting, he wanted to discuss Ireland and his concern for the English in Ulster. The next morning, the king asked me to meet with him again, this time just the two of us. He wanted me to be a party—as England's ally—to the treaty he is negotiating with France."

"He shows you great favor in this," said John MacAlister. "Scotland will undoubtedly be allied with France, and King Richard wants you and the Isles allied with him and England."

Donald acknowledged as how that might be so. "If it pleases King Richard to have the Isles with him, so be it. The king also gave his approval for our resisting the Stewart incursions. Which is to say he will not interfere if we oppose the aggression of King Robert's many sons." He glanced at John, his cousin and friend, who nodded his agreement. "Ireland is Richard's cause at the moment," continued Donald, "and it serves our interests to meet his requests to protect the fishing off Ulster's northern coast and to become more involved in Antrim."

"Meantime, it is good you are home," said Alex.

A smile came to Donald's face as he considered what next he would do. "I am hoping to turn my attention to Ross. It is time I claim my bride." In truth, he had thought of her many times while he was in London.

Alex pressed his lips together. "You may want to delay your trip."

"Why?"

His brother looked around them as if to be sure no one was listening. The guards were not close and their cousin John's strong features bore no sign of alarm beneath his tonsured brown hair. Donald patiently waited for Alex to explain.

"While you were gone," he said, leaning in, "rumors came to me of a plot to rob you of your title, mayhap your life, and install John Mor in your place."

Donald drew back, disbelieving. "Our brother? Can this be true?"

"You asked me to keep an eye on Iona, Donnie. I made a brief trip there with one of your factors who was collecting rents. A monk drew me aside while Abbot Finguine was otherwise occupied and told me of a conversation he had overheard."

"Why would he tell you this?" asked Donald.

"You think it might be a trap?" asked Alex, his blue eyes inquiring.

"Possibly. I put nothing past the abbot."

"I am not surprised Abbot Finguine would conceive such a plot," said their cousin. "He does not like the changes you have made."

"They were necessary, John, if Iona's abbey is to be preserved."

"I agree most heartedly but MacKinnon continues to resist. The care of the abbey and its lands are not foremost in his mind except as they may serve to enrich his family."

"That is the problem with green abbots," said Donald. "They were never monks, nor are they elected but serve by hereditary lineage or appointment. It is not surprising they are known to alienate church property and use it for personal gain." Donald turned to his brother. "Do you know who is involved? Is John Mor a part of this?"

Alex nodded. "The monk observed him meeting with the MacKinnons and a few other men."

Donald sat back, considering the news, and a heaviness settled over him. "They are using my brother and his discontent, hoping to get from him what they could not get from me."

Alex said, "I think John Mor was seduced to the abbot's cause by his daughter Christina, who, by the by, the monk tells me is carrying John Mor's child. She freely tells all who will listen."

Donald shook his head. "John Mor never could resist a comely lass." To Alex he said, "I assume Abbot Finguine's brother, the MacKinnon chief, must know of this?"

"Aye, he leads the brood of vipers. According to the monk I spoke with, the MacKinnons are aligned with the Macleods of Harris and some of the Macleans. They met on Iona with the abbot and John Mor."

"The Macleans! How can that be? Their chief, Lachlan, is my brother-in-law, and I have just agreed to give him a charter confirming him in his lands and Duart Castle, making him First Laird of Duart."

"Lachlan was not mentioned," said Alex. "All the monk knew was that a Maclean attended the meeting. The MacKinnons were apparently to gather forces while John Mor was with you in London."

Donald stared into the water of the sound. In his mind, he pictured the battle to come. Even before his time at Oxford, he had been adept with a sword. No son of a Highland chief, much less the son of the Lord of the Isles, would fail to be trained in weapons and war. But he did not wish to fight against his younger brother. He was certain John Mor had been seduced to the MacKinnons' rebellion. Donald let out a sigh of resignation. "Then we must raise an army to meet them."

"I have already begun," said Alex. "I have sent word to those I know to be loyal to you, those who live on the abbey's lands on the Ross of Mull, who resent what the MacKinnons have done. Also, the Macleods of Lewis, the Mackintoshes, the Mackenzies, the men of Urquhart and Glen Moriston near Loch Ness, the Glen Coe MacDonalds, and the MacNeils of Barra. As well, I have spread the word to my own people in Lochaber, including Donald Dubh, the chief of the Camerons. But it would mean much if you were to visit those you would summon."

And so Donald did. In the days that followed, his galley could be spotted in the waters around the isles and lochs of the lordship and on Argyll's coast, as he, Alex and John MacAlister set forth to raise an army to put down the rebellion to come.

"WERE YOU SURPRISED how eager they were to join you?" asked Alex as they returned to Ardtornish weeks later.

"Given how I began, yes, I was surprised," said Donald. "Their quick agreement to defend my position as chief has cheered me immensely. They are good men, loyal and true."

"They have observed you as chief these past two years, Donnie, and they like how you lead. You have been generous with them, confirming lands, dispensing others, using your galleys to come to their aid when need be and defending the Isles against the Stewarts, your own relations. You have won them and, to a man, they will stand by you."

Donald breathed a sigh of relief. It had been the result he had sought from the beginning.

The rebellion of John Mor and the MacKinnons began in earnest as the heather bloomed and the leaves changed in the forests and glens from summer's green to autumn's red and gold. There were no large battles, only skirmishes, as Donald's army, greatly outnumbering the forces arrayed against them, forced the MacKinnons and their allies south. Autumn turned into winter with snows falling in the forests, yet the pursuit continued, sometimes on horses and sometimes at sea.

Dingwall Castle, Earldom of Ross, December 1388

"WELL, THAT EXPLAINS it," said Mariota, looking up from the letter she had just received from Sir Thomas.

"What?" said her mother, who was asking a servant to add another log to the fire. The castle was cold these days for winter had come with early snows.

"Lord Donald returned from his visit to England's king only to discover one of his brothers has risen against him, seeking a larger share of their inheritance it seems."

"Oh, dear," said her mother. "Not another struggle for power. Surely Scotland has seen enough."

"Sir Thomas says Lord Donald has raised a great contingent of Islesmen and chiefs to oppose his brother. Our knight is confident the Lord of the Isles will prevail."

"I do hope so if you are ever to have a husband."

"Did you know Donald's mother, Princess Margaret, married John of Islay when she was fifteen? The Lord of the Isles was in his fourth decade."

"I seem to recall she was young; it was his second marriage."

Mariota added the years in her mind. "You and she must be near the same age."

"That is so. Margaret and I are both in our forties."

Mariota, in her early twenties, did not mind the delay in her marriage, particularly if it kept her from being in the middle of a pitched battle. "I would not want to marry as young as Princess Margaret. My years alone have made me stronger."

"The Lord of the Isles will need a strong woman by his side. He may have the favor of priests, but a woman's wisdom will be helpful to such a man, and I do not believe he will receive it from his mother. I understand he is at odds with Lady Margaret for dispensing land to his brothers, particularly Kintyre, which she thought was hers."

A meddling mother-in-law did not appeal to Mariota. "I have hope that you will again be Countess of Ross, Mother, unencumbered by the Wolf of Badenoch. Are you encouraged that your husband, Alexander, has asked the Bishop of Moray to end your marriage?"

"It would spare me asking the pope for the same relief," said her mother, "but the bishop is not likely to agree to Alexander's demand. I am told he and the Bishop of Ross will order my husband to return to me. Alexander may agree, but I do not believe he will comply, for I know him better than the bishops. He will give lip service to their demands but he will not return to my bed."

"Doubtless a blessing," said Mariota, mindful of the man and his misdeeds.

"When I first met Alexander, I was a young widow," said her mother, staring into the fire. "Younger than you." She turned and Mariota saw a look of nostalgia cross her face. "He was handsome and mysterious, tall and dark with long black hair and fierce dark eyes. Naively, I thought him exciting. I even thought his courting sincere. Your father had been a renowned knight, a man of war but a gentleman and much older than I. When he passed, I was open to the courting of the younger Wolf. Alas, I knew little of him. Now, I consider he was merely doing the biding of his father, King Robert."

"What do you think will come of his defiance of the bishops should he do as you believe he will?"

"It is likely the Bishop of Moray will excommunicate him. It is the way of the church when defied. And then, we can only hope the Highlands will be spared the wrath of the Wolf."

Galloway, spring 1389

BY THE COMING of spring, Donald had chased his errant brother and his allies, the MacKinnons, to Kintyre and from there to Galloway, the lands of the Earl of Douglas. Sir Archibald Douglas, dubbed "the Grim" by the English for his countenance in battle, was accustomed to war, for his lands were near the English border.

As Donald's galley approached Galloway's western shore, Donald said to his brother and his constable, who stood with him on deck, "John Mor will find no shelter at the castle of Galloway's lord. Mayhap our brother has forgotten that my nephew, Hector Maclean, who fights with us, is married to Douglas' daughter. We will land our forces on Galloway's coast and Hector can pay a visit to his father-in-law, who doubtless is aware of the unwelcome MacKinnons treading upon his lands."

JOHN MOR WIPED the dirt from his brow as his horse bent his head to nibble on the new grass where they had stopped on a hill above the sea. Spring in Galloway had brought much rain, creating mud that splashed to the horses' stirrups. The MacKinnon chief, sitting astride his horse next to John had changed in the last several months. His graying dark hair, once well combed, was always in disarray and his face was harsher in appearance.

The rebellion had not gone well.

A scout rode up to Ewen MacKinnon. "The Lord of the Isles' galleys have been sighted off Galloway's coast, just north of here, my lord."

Ewen nodded. "Tell the men to be prepared to move."

"Yes, my lord." Turning his horse, the scout galloped away.

"I had hoped Donald would turn back when we came here, but he is relentless in his pursuit."

"I remember Donald in our youth," said John. "He was always determined. Relentless describes him well when he is roused to a cause."

Ewen said, "We do not have sufficient men to defeat his army. I did not believe he could raise the numbers he did. Too, I thought to take Donald by surprise, but it seems he anticipated our plans. If he has pursued us this far, he will not stop."

"No, I do not imagine he will," said John, voicing what he knew to be true.

The MacKinnon chief was a picture of defeat, his countenance downcast, the lines in his face more pronounced than when they had begun. "It may be best if we disperse in different directions."

"I agree," said John. Trying not to speak words of condemnation, he added, "It seems clear our plan has failed." John recalled his conversation with his cousin, John MacAlister, in London and all he said of Donald's power. Apparently, the MacKinnon chief had underestimated him. And so had John.

Raising his gaze to the west, he looked across the northern Irish Sea. In the distance, he saw a dark shadow of land. Ulster and the Glens of Antrim lay a mere twenty miles away. John could not return to Dunyvaig, for his brother would find him there and his life would be forfeit. He supposed it would be a fitting end for the rebellion in which he had willingly played a part.

Watching the coast of Ulster, he remembered his meeting with Donald and King Richard. It seemed so long ago. England's king had wanted the Macdonalds to be more involved in Ulster, to stand with the Bissetts against the Stewarts, who were allied with the O'Donnells. Could he find a future there and please King Richard in the process? Surely, he could avoid his brother's galleys for the time it would take to cross that narrow stretch of water. It was not the future he had envisioned but mayhap it was the best he could hope for.

DONALD AND HIS CHAPLAIN, Bean MacGillandris, were at prayer when Red Hector, newly commissioned as one of Donald's generals, returned from his meeting with Archibald Douglas, Lord of Galloway.

Finished with his prayer, Donald rose and greeted his nephew. "Hector, what news have you from your father-in-law?"

"He was aware of the rebels invading his lands and was none too pleased, but before he could send men to chase them away, they disbanded and have ridden off in different directions."

Donald glanced at Bean. "Our prayers are answered. There will be no battle." Donald did not want to encounter his brother in such a fight, nor did he wish to take the lives of Islesmen who merely followed orders.

Alex must have seen Hector arrive, for he came to join them.

"It is over," Donald told him.

"Aye," said Hector. "The villains run like rats before a deluge."

"Now, there is the matter of dispensing justice," said Donald. "We must capture the MacKinnon chief. He will be tried by the Council and if he is found guilty, as I assume he will be, he will hang. Other leaders of this misbegotten venture will be punished."

"What about Abbot Finguine?" asked Donald's chaplain. "You cannot hang him surely."

"No. We cannot take the life of a man of the church, though he be found unfaithful in his duty toward God. Rather, I think it fitting that he should be imprisoned for the rest of his life, perhaps on Iona where he conceived of this evil." For some while, Donald had been thinking of the abbot's penalty should he be captured. "We cannot allow him his freedom to plot treason again."

"Since he was the instigator," said Alex, "it is only right. But what of our brother, John Mor?"

"John is a more difficult case. He may have been deceived, but he went along with the MacKinnons' plan. Once he is captured, I will determine what is to be done with him."

FROM GALLOWAY, Donald returned to his manor at Kilcummin on the west coast of Islay, where he lingered, content to enjoy the warm summer days and blue skies, midges notwithstanding. The MacKinnons had been taken as they fled, but his brother was still at large.

At Kilcummin, he discussed with the chiefs who had been loyal to him what he proposed to do. "Should you agree," he said to them, "I am inclined to call a meeting of the Council of the Isles after the August harvest to dispense justice and to celebrate our victory."

"Aye," said Hector Maclean. "A celebration with games of skill and feasts would be most welcome."

"You did well helping me put down the rebellion, Nephew. A celebration is warranted."

The chiefs gladly gave their assent.

"Very well," he said, "it will be done. Plan on a gathering at the end of September before Michaelmas."

From his youth, Donald remembered the gatherings of the chefs at Finlaggan, the seat of the Macdonald clan on the two islands in the loch in the center of Islay. They were festive times that drew the chiefs and their families together. This, he vowed, would be such a time when they would gather in peace. After dispensing justice, he could show his appreciation and speak of happier times to come.

"You could invite your betrothed," suggested John MacAlister, who had sailed to Islay to join them. "It would be an appropriate time to introduce her to the clans and to present to them the woman who will soon be their new Lady of the Isles."

"A good idea," said Donald, "which calls for a trip to Ross, don't you think?"

"She would appreciate that," said John.

"Who should accompany me?" asked Donald.

"Take John," said Alex. "A priest makes a good chaperone."

"Yes, John should come. And Chaplain Bean. But I would take you as well, Alex. She might as well meet the men of the family, at least those who are here."

They did not speak often of their brother, John Mor, though rumors had come to them he was in Ulster and Donald had sent men to find him.

"Once she is here," said Donald, "she should meet the women of the clan. Our sister, Mary, as the wife of the Maclean chief, can introduce her."

"Mary Macdonald of Duart Castle would be a good choice," said Alex. "She knows everyone and will be a help to the younger Lady Mariota."

"May I suggest a letter?" said John. "One that would tell your betrothed of your desire to fulfill your pledge."

Donald warmed to the idea. And so, that very day, he sat down and applied his quill to parchment.

Donald of Islay, Lord of the Isles, to Lady Mariota of Ross,

My lady, I greet you with all respect and affection. It has been long since we were betrothed, but it is time, I think, for us to wed. I hope you agree. With that in mind, I propose that you should make a trip to the Isles after harvest to join the gathering of the clans at Finlaggan on Islay. There, I can present you to the chiefs of the Council and their wives. If you are agreeable, you have only to advise the man who carries this message, and I will send word as to when I will come to escort you. There will be two priests to act as chaperones.

Having sealed the letter, Donald said to his constable, "Give this to Sir Thomas and his companion, the Welshman, Gwyn Kimball. Ask them to take it to Lady Mariota at Dingwall Castle. I am certain they know the way."

"My lord?" asked Malcolm. On his face was a perplexed expression.

"Do you recall that when they joined my guard I asked you to keep a watch on them?"

"Aye," said his constable, "and I did. I noticed nothing amiss."

"Did you not think it odd...the timing of their coming? I may be wrong but I suspected then as I believe now that they are from Ross and serve Lady Mariota as well as me." At his constable's aghast expression, Donald said, "I do not complain as their service has been commendable. I believe the Welshman is the courier, for he is sometimes gone when Sir Thomas is present."

"A sick mother..." said his constable.

Donald raised his brows at that. "More like, a mistress eager for news." Smiling, he added, "Spies? Yes. Treasonous? No."

With a shocked look, his constable accepted the letter and walked off shaking his head. For his part, Donald concluded he was to marry an intelligent and canny woman.

Dingwall Castle, Earldom of Ross, August, 1389

MARIOTA WAS WITH her mother in the solar enjoying the pleasant evening when Sir Thomas arrived and bowed before her. The candles and the fire were casting shadows on the stone walls and tapestries.

Outside, the sun was setting behind the hills of Dingwall.

"Countess, my lady," he addressed each of them. Reaching his hand toward Mariota, he said, "This is from Donald, Lord of Islay."

She took the parchment from his hand, noting the seal impressed upon it, the galley of the Isles prominently embossed upon the red wax. "He asked you to deliver the message?"

"Yes, my lady."

"You may leave us Sir Thomas. I will send for you later."

He bowed and left.

Mariota shared a glance with her mother. "He knows."

"Mayhap he does. Donald is not a stupid man to be easily fooled." With an anxious look, she asked, "What does the letter say?"

Mariota broke the seal. The letter was not long and got quickly to the point. "He thinks it is time for us to wed and he bids me come to the Isles where his Council will meet after harvest on Islay."

"*Before* you are wed?"

"It would appear so. If I agree, I am to convey my approval to Sir Thomas, and Lord Donald will make plans to fetch me."

"Himself?"

"Yes."

"Well, that is a good sign," said her mother. "He does not treat you like so much baggage to be carted around by his servants. Do you think he expects you to marry him there?"

"He does not say so." She looked up from the parchment to meet her mother's thoughtful gaze. "I would have the wedding here in Ross, and I expect he knows that. From all I have heard, Donald is a man of decorum. Any man who comes to visit his betrothed with two priests in tow will observe the proprieties."

"God bless him for that. I would not be deprived of the pleasure of planning a wedding for my only daughter."

"You shall have time while I am gone. Or, did you want to go with us?"

"No. I will stay at Dingwall and begin your wedding plans. I imagine when you are wed, I will meet your new kin."

That evening, Mariota summoned Sir Thomas and told him she approved of Lord Donald's plans. "Whatever he asks, do not lie to him. He knows you serve me."

"But I have said nothing, my lady."

"I did not think you had, but Lord Donald has discerned the truth of it nonetheless." Meeting the gaze of her concerned champion, she said, "I do not think he is displeased, Sir Knight, or he would have dismissed you and he has not."

CHAPTER 6

Dingwall Castle, Earldom of Ross, September 1389

DONALD AND HIS men slowed their horses as they came to the top of a small hill. Mist lay in the valley below and, in the distance, the towers of Dingwall Castle, surrounded by a curtain wall and a moat, rose from the grassy plain. "John," he turned to his cousin, "what do we know of Dingwall Castle?"

A keeper of Scottish history, John lifted his dark brows and, staring ahead, said, "Dingwall is an old castle, first built by the Norse in the time of our ancestor, Somerled. It has been added to, of course, since then. More recently, it was from here the Earl of Ross led his men to fight with your grandfather for King Robert Bruce at Bannockburn. As a reward, the king granted the earl the lands of Dingwall."

"Lands coveted by many ever since," said Alex, sitting on Donald's other side.

John said, "That large body of water northeast of the castle is Cromarty Firth. It provides merchant ships access to the east coast of Scotland."

Donald had sailed north from Morvern, between Skye and the mainland, with four galleys, fifty-five men and horses sufficient for the main contingent. Beaching the galleys on the northern shore of Loch Carron, they set out for the two days' ride across Ross to Dingwall. What he observed on their journey reminded him how extensive were the lands of his future wife's family. Fertile soil, wide swaths of green forests and beautiful rivers and lochs had led him and his party to the green plain before him. "'Tis a fine land, Ross."

"Aye." said Alex, drawing his nearly white hair from his face. "It was what our father had in mind when he betrothed you to Lady Mariota. The charter, made before her brother Alexander, was born, was clear in its language that heirs female could inherit."

"Sir Thomas," Donald called to the knight. "Ride ahead and let the countess know we will soon be at her door."

"Yes, my lord." Turning his horse, the knight rode down the hill.

Donald led his retinue forward, his mind full of questions about Lady Mariota of Ross. She had consented to his plan to bring her to the Isles in advance of their marriage, which he considered a good sign. It was his hope she would be wooed by the Isles and their people as well as by him. He had brought her gifts he hoped would appeal to her, for he planned to use this time before their marriage to gain her affection.

Granted passage by the guards, they arrived in the bailey to find two women and a young man awaiting them with servants on either side. Though there was a score of years between them, the countess and her daughter resembled each other, tall, stately in posture and dressed as the noblewomen they were. Both wore gowns of silk brocade. Only Mariota wore her hair free, long and gold in color. If she were to age as her mother, he would have a beautiful wife for many decades.

Walter Leslie's son, Alexander, a tall and slender youth, had golden-colored hair like his sister and the beginnings of a beard.

Dismounting, Donald handed his reins to a groom and bowed before Countess Euphemia. "I am Donald of Islay, my lady."

"Greetings, Lord Donald. I am Euphemia, Countess of Ross and Buchan. This is my daughter, Mariota, and my son, Alexander."

At the countess' smile, Donald turned his eyes to his betrothed and bowed over her offered hand, noting her long slender fingers and ivory skin. "Lady Mariota." The faint scent of flowers wafted to his nose. "I apologize for the time it has taken me to honor our fathers' pledge. I am now anxious to do so."

Mariota's eyes sparkled. "Lord Donald, we are pleased to welcome you and your company to Dingwall. You need not apologize for the delay. We have used it wisely."

For what? He wondered but did not ask. Beneath arched brows and long lashes, her large eyes were green and gold. Ringed in dark green, the color turned gold toward the pupils. Unusual eyes in the Highlands. All the more surprising, for the eyes of her mother and brother were blue. Her lips were full and inviting and, just now, bore the hint of a smile. Donald was certain with what he already knew of her, he had won a great prize. Mayhap, too, a great challenge.

He was keenly aware of Mariota's unwavering gaze as he turned to her brother. "Alexander," he said, acknowledging the younger man. "I, too, have a brother named Alexander." He gestured to Alex, who had dismounted to join them. "Meet Alexander, Lord of Lochaber."

Alex inclined his head to the ladies and shook the lad's hand.

"Also among my companions," said Donald, "is our cousin, John MacAlister." He turned to acknowledge John. "His great-grandfather was Lord of the Isles before my grandfather. More than a priest and a rector, he is a good friend and trusted counselor." John was as tall as Donald and Alex but heavier in build, more like a galloglass, except for his black robes and tonsured hair that marked him a member of the Benedictine order. His manner, however, spoke of his noble breeding.

"Countess and Lady Mariota," John said with a small bow for the two women. "We would have come sooner—as was Lord Donald's desire—but we were waylaid by rebels for nearly a year."

"I trust the matter is in hand?" said Lady Mariota, a look of concern on her face.

"Yes," Donald said, "well in hand, though there is still the matter of my younger brother, John Mor, who was involved in the rebellion and escaped to Ireland."

Donald then introduced Chaplain Bean. He would have to find the priest a church one of these days, for it was clear he did not like to travel. Two days on the road had turned him dour, though he rose to the occasion to greet the countess and her children.

Surveying the men with Donald, the countess said, "You must be weary and thirsty. Refreshments await in the hall." Then to Donald, "Your men, servants and horses will be seen to."

Donald stole a look at his intended, who was watching him with her knowing eyes. He detected no shyness, only assessing curiosity, and wondered if she was disappointed in the man others had chosen for her.

Inside the castle, the great hall was impressive. Not since his mother's effect on Ardtornish had Donald seen a stark stone keep transformed into a place that was warm and inviting. Persian carpets in red and blue graced the floor; tapestries hung between sconces holding flaming torches; and over the large central fireplace, a crimson shield bearing three silver lions rampant was proudly displayed—the arms of the Earl of Ross. Beneath the shield hung a sword with a bejeweled hilt.

Several groupings of small tables and chairs with padded cushions were scattered about the large chamber making the high ceiling seem less formidable.

His eyes were drawn to one wall where shelves of books and parchments, typically confined to a solar, made a grand statement. While his cousin and his chaplain spoke to the countess, and his brother occupied young Alexander Leslie, Donald drew aside with Lady Mariota.

"Whose books are these?" he asked her.

"They began as my mother's, but now many are mine and Alexander's."

A servant passed a tray of goblets before them. Donald took one and found it contained a very good red wine. Tearing his gaze from the vast array of books, he asked. "Do you enjoy reading, my lady?"

"Yes, very much. And you?"

He nodded. "I brought many cases of books with me when I left

Oxford but with the pressing matters of the lordship, I have had little time to consider them until now." He might have added "Or you," but his absence was evidence enough of that.

Bringing her own goblet to her lips, she sipped, and then asked, "What do you like to read?"

"Many things, my lady. Histories in the main, including those that tell of wars and the lives of prominent people. Books for the soul—the psalter and Scripture. Anything by John Wycliffe, one of my masters at Oxford. And poetry." Watching carefully for her reaction, he said, "I brought you something to read."

Her eyes lit up. "You did? Tell me." Not since he had seen his sisters given jewels had he observed so much delight in a woman's eyes.

"Are you familiar with the works of the poet Geoffrey Chaucer?"

"Yes, generally."

"While I was visiting King Richard, Chaucer read to the king after dinner one evening from a new work, a series of tales told by pilgrims on their way to Canterbury. When I later spoke to the poet, he allowed as I might have a copy of the prologue. I thought you would enjoy his introduction to the stories to come. It is my hope we can secure copies of them as Chaucer writes them."

Again, her lovely eyes flashed. "What a wonderful gift! I shall treasure it."

THE NEXT MORNING Mariota's handmaiden delivered to her another gift from her betrothed, a long package wrapped in wool. "Lord Donald thought you might want to open this with your mother, Mistress."

Her young handmaiden hesitated, her eyes fixed on the package. "Thank you, Abby. You can go, but please ask the countess to come to my chamber when she is free."

Abby curtseyed and slipped out the open door.

Mariota laid the long parcel on her bed, intrigued. It was heavy but she was certain it was not metal or wood. She untied the ribbon that bound it. The cloth fell open and she gasped. The most exquisite silk she had ever seen lay before her, a deep shimmering blue like none she had in her wardrobe. What kind of a man gives the woman he is to marry such silk?

Her mother came up behind her. "Oh, my. Ultramarine silk!" She reached out her fingers to unroll a bit of the fabric. "A very fine quality. From Italy, most like, but the ultramarine dye is from the Orient. This blue symbolizes purity. Artists use the color in paintings of the Virgin Mary."

As Mariota lifted the fabric from the wool that had bound it, a folded parchment and a smaller parcel fell to her bed. She opened the parchment, sealed by the same galley of the Isles embossed in the red wax, and read the message aloud, "I look forward to seeing you wearing a gown made of this blue silk." Inside the smaller parcel, she found a long golden metallic band decorated with tiny pearls, about three inches wide, enough to go around a skirt hem and bodice. "For trimming the gown?"

Her mother inclined her head. "Most likely. The blue silk and the golden edging would make a lovely wedding gown."

Still admiring the silk, Mariota said, "Do you think that is how he meant it? There is only his note. He did not bring the silk himself but had Abby deliver it to me."

"It would obviously please him to see you wearing a gown made from this silk, even more should you choose it for your wedding. Perhaps he did not want to influence you by insisting. If so, he is a rare man who allows his bride to choose."

Mariota thought of her betrothed as she gazed at the silk fabric, the deep blue shimmering in the candlelight. He was a handsome man with his fair hair and short dark red beard. His deep-set blue eyes, together with his high cheekbones, gave his face a look of strength. "What do you think of Lord Donald?"

"What I have seen I like. He is well spoken and gracious. As we dined last evening, he made easy conversation and intelligent remarks. His face speaks of his character. The boy I met briefly all those years ago has grown into a man who I believe may be worthy of my daughter. I see now that John of Islay prepared Donald for you just as I have prepared you for him. You would appear to be well-suited. But the important thing is what *you* think."

"I like him, too, what little I know." Mother and daughter shared a look of understanding. "However, it is not his face that persuades me that I could love him. It is his thoughtfulness."

After breaking their fast that morning, Mariota thanked Lord Donald for his gifts. "The silk will make a lovely gown for a special occasion."

"I was hoping you would think so. When I saw it, I thought of you."

They did not linger at Dingwall but set out for the Isles that morning. Lord Donald had told her he was anxious to return to Islay where his chiefs would soon be gathering.

"We have business to dispense with before we can celebrate, but the chiefs will be most anxious to meet you."

She took with her only her handmaiden, their two horses and her gowns and jewels. "I am an experienced rider," she told Donald, "so you need have no worry for me, and Abby is young but strong and will keep pace."

His only reply was a smile that told her he did not find her words surprising.

She said, "I expect to enjoy the two days it will take us to reach the coast." Mariota looked forward to the chance to get to know the man she would marry and to the adventure of seeing his home she would one day share. "I have been east to Edinburgh but never so far west as the Isles."

"I have brought tents for the night we will be camped," he said. She would bring her hooded fur-lined cloak against the rain and cold she expected they would encounter at some point. "There is room in the wagon for all you wish to bring."

"You plan ahead," she said. "Most commendable."

Again, he just smiled. She could hear her mother saying, "Of course he plans; he was raised to lead thousands."

Except for that first morning, when they had a shower of rain, the day was fair and clear. The hills wore the last of summer's green overlaid by a cloak of heather, rendering the glens a splendid sight. It was cold in the mountain passes, and Mariota was glad she had worn her warm hooded mantle.

Lord Donald remained by her side as they rode west. Her hand-maiden rode with his brother, the priests and Sir Thomas. The main body of Lord Donald's men including Gwyn, the Welsh bowman from Ross, rode with the wagon, loaded with tents, food, clothing for Mariota and her handmaiden, and other goods. The wagon slowed their progress but was necessary for the journey.

It was afternoon and she had just asked Donald to tell her of his days at Oxford when a thunder of hooves sounded behind them. She turned her head toward the sound as the pounding grew louder.

"Caterans!" hissed Lord Alexander and drew his sword.

The word sent chills up Mariota's spine, for she had heard tales of their burning, rape and looting.

Immediately, Lord Donald drew his sword and began shouting orders. "Sir Thomas, Alex, John and Gwyn stay with the women!" Turning to the main body of his men, he yelled, "To me! To me! Bring the wagon close."

Galloping toward them from both sides were men who looked to be outlaws, unkempt ruffians brandishing weapons but wearing no livery and carrying no banner.

Shouting war cries, they came closer.

Mariota's heart was in her throat. She gripped the reins of her horse tightly.

Abby cried, "Save us!"

Sir Thomas slid his sword from its scabbard and held it ready. The priests—unlike any priests she knew—drew long, wicked-looking dirks from their robes. Gwyn nocked an arrow in his bow.

"Hired mercenaries, my lady," said Lord Alexander. "We will deal with them." By now, Mariota and Abby were surrounded by the men Lord Donald had assigned to protect them, their weapons poised to fight off the attackers.

Mariota grabbed the bridle of Abby's horse to keep it under con-trol for her handmaiden sat frozen in her saddle.

Lord Donald continued to order his men with cool precision. Dividing them into two groups, they met the threat head on. The caterans matched his men in numbers but, to her mind, did not match them in skill. Of course, the Islesmen were galloglass, trained to fight from their youth.

The clang of swords and shouts of men erupted all around her.

Arrows flew from Gwyn's bow in rapid succession.

Mariota's heart raced.

With his sword held high, Lord Donald broke from his men and rode hard for what looked to be the outlaw leader, the one shouting orders. Two caterans rode toward Donald, one on either side, as if to try to stop him.

Mariota inhaled sharply and held her breath.

With a slash of his blade to one side, then the other, Lord Donald cut down the two caterans. To the leader, he shouted, "In whose name do you attack?"

"Great Alexander, the king's son!"

Mariota was shocked. *The Earl of Buchan?*

Lord Donald reined in his horse only feet from the leader. "Fools! You are attacking his stepdaughter!"

At this, the leader, a rough character with scarred face, wearing mail beneath his black tunic, looked toward Mariota and the Lord of the Isles' banner waving near the wagon, the black galley on a saffron field, surrounded by the royal double tressure of the Stewart kings in red.

Holding his horse still, he shouted orders to his caterans to pull back. The clash of swords ceased. Facing Lord Donald, he said, "And who might you be, Bold One?"

With a voice cold as the steel in his hand, he said, "Donald of Islay, chief of the Macdonalds. The lady who travels with me is Lady Mariota of Ross, my betrothed. You tread on us, you tread on the might of the Isles."

The swarthy cateran leader looked Lord Donald over carefully. "So, it was your banner. I wondered. You are the Lord of the Isles, the king's grandson." In resigned voice, he said, "Very well, we will go, but first, we would have the wagon."

"No, you will not, else you leave my betrothed—the stepdaughter of your master, I remind you—nothing to wear."

Something about Lord Donald's manner must have convinced the outlaw further pursuit was not in his interest. With a shouted order, he called his men to him and rode off, leaving behind the bodies of caterans spread across the grass.

Lord Donald's men cheered as he returned to them. Then he rode to where Mariota sat her horse surrounded by her defenders, who made way for him. "Are you all right, my lady?"

"We are well, my lord." She wanted to throw her arms around him, but instead, she thanked God he lived and said, "A fine display of courage by you and your men, my lord. We owe you our thanks and our lives." Then with a smile, "I am duly impressed."

Lord Alexander, his brother, chuckled, shaking his head. "Aye, my lady. He is wont to make a grand show of it. I suspect 'tis all that book learning."

Lord Donald said, "I thought they might be the Wolf's men. I appealed to their leader the only way that would cause him to retreat. He is more afraid of the Wolf of Badenoch than he is of our swords."

"You were covered with our prayers," said Chaplain Bean.

"For which I am grateful," said Lord Donald. He looked back to where his men had dismounted. In a more serious tone, he asked his brother, "Any wounded?"

"Sir Thomas went to check," said Lord Alexander. "I see a few men down but, from here, I cannot tell if they be ours or the caterans."

"John, Bean," said Lord Donald, addressing the two priests, "You'd best come with me should any be in need of your services."

Mariota said, "I am not weak at the sight of blood, my lord. With your leave, I would go as well. It may be I can assist your physician in tending the wounded."

"Very well, you may come." He shot his brother a glance. "Alex, post a guard for the wagon and my lady's handmaiden should the Wolf's men return, and then join me. Gwyn, you can come with me to guard my lady."

AS THEY NEARED the scene where men had fallen, Donald scanned the caterans, some with arrows protruding from their bodies.

"Gwyn," he said to the Welsh bowman, "is this your doing?"

"Aye, must be, my lord. I do not think any other drew a bow."

"Good work. I shall remember to travel with more of my archers in the future." Some of Donald's warriors were bending over three men lying on the ground. Donald recognized them as his own. He asked Fergus, his physician, "How bad?"

"Alan here took a sword in his arm," said the physician, as he wrapped white strips around the wound. "I have stitched him up. He'll live to fight again. The others were grazed by a sword. The mail beneath their tunics spared them a deeper cut."

Lady Mariota dropped from her horse and went to them.

"My lady has offered to assist you."

Fergus looked up from where he knelt beside Alan whose eyes flickered open. The physician offered Lady Mariota a folded cloth. "For the blood. I am almost finished here and will be with you shortly."

Donald cast his gaze around what had become a battlefield. Directing his attention to Sir Thomas, he asked, "Do any of the Wolf's men still live?"

"No," my lord.

"Just as well. I do not wish to take them with us. They could tell us nothing we do not already know." As his physician relieved Lady Mariota, Donald said, "They will soon have our wounded loaded in the wagon. It is best we return to our horses."

ONE MOMENT HE had been felling outlaws and ordering about the Devil's own, and now, in a calm voice, he was bidding her to return to their horses. Mariota sensed no anxiety, no disturbance beneath his unruffled manner.

The remainder of that day and the next were thankfully devoid of outlaws. Abby had finally calmed and now rode quietly behind Mariota. The long hours on the road had provided Mariota with much time to admire the beauty of Wester Ross. And it provided time to consider more carefully the man she was to marry.

Lord Donald and his men showed her and her handmaiden every

courtesy. Important to Mariota, he appeared genuinely interested in her opinions. When she told him both she and her mother would be glad to see Alexander Stewart, Earl of Buchan, gone from their lives, he agreed that was understandable. "He cannot have been much of a husband, and he constantly angers the church for his errant ways. One would have expected more of a king's son."

"Do you think his brothers will be any better?" she asked.

"Doubtful. John, Earl of Carrick, is the senior, next in line to be king, but he is weak. The real power in Scotland is held by his younger brother, Robert, Earl of Fife, who named himself Guardian of Scotland. He is ambitious, and while all are pleased he has promised to take the Wolf in hand, we have yet to see his true mettle."

Lord Donald told her of the lordship and the clans that were a part of it and paid homage to the Macdonalds. To Mariota, it sounded like a whole other Scotland. "However do you manage all the clans?"

"I must care for their interests and those of the people above my own. As long as they believe they have a leader they can trust, they will follow. The Council of the Isles confirms the new chief but the position is largely hereditary. Our son will one day inherit the title, and the responsibility. You will meet the chiefs on Islay. They will be very interested to greet the woman who is to be the next Lady of the Isles."

Mariota liked the title, and she determined from all Lord Donald had told her that the position would not be tedious. "I am looking forward to meeting them."

They arrived at the sea loch where he had left his galleys and men to guard them. Viewed at sunset, Loch Carron took her breath away, a long loch stretching before her with wooded coast on either side. The sun had just set, turning the sky and the water a mellow gold. Even the seals basking on the rocks were cast in a golden light. "Are the Isles as beautiful as this place?" she asked Lord Donald.

"Yes, my lady, even more so. You will not lack for beauty in your life, I promise."

His magnificent smile followed his words, his blue eyes drawing her in. She had the sudden urge to kiss him, she who had never been kissed.

CHAPTER 7

THE NEXT MORNING at first light Donald ordered the crews to load the galleys beached the on the shore of Loch Carron. After the wagon and chests were lifted aboard Donald's ship, the crews began to load the horses, leading them one by one up the gangplanks laid through the opening in the gunwales. The galleys had been adapted for the special cargo by adding wooden stalls, mangers for fodder and slings for the horses' protection on rough seas. It was a process Donald had supervised many times. However, all this made for crowded decks.

Not wishing to lose his bride-to-be over the side, Donald led Mariota to the bow of his ship, flying the Lord of the Isles pennon. He asked John MacAlister to keep an eye on Mariota. To her he said, "Hold on until you are used to the movement. When we reach the Kyle of Lochalsh, we will have to maneuver through some fast-moving waters, and there will be strong winds."

"Lochalsh..." she said, "that means the strait of the foaming loch?" Her face bore a look of trepidation.

"You need have no fear; we have much experience in these waters." He had given her handmaiden into the care of his brother, who along with Donald's chaplain, could attend the frightened lass on the second galley.

He was relieved when Mariota did not become ill as the galley rolled and pitched on the loch. From what he could see from the stern, she appeared to keep up a lively conversation with John, whose tall, powerful form stood at ease with the ship's movement.

Mariota's face was radiant with delight as the crew began to chant while they rowed the galley across the blue waters of the loch.

Leaving the loch for the Inner Sound, they approached the Kyle. The wind picked up. The galley slipped into a trough only to rise again, dousing the deck in cold seawater. The horses began to snort, tossing their heads. Donald ordered the groom to attend them and then went to one particular mare to soothe her.

Expecting Lady Mariota might need his comfort, Donald joined her and John in the prow. He was not prepared for her wide smile and her green-gold eyes sparkling with excitement, despite the seawater clinging to her cloak.

His cousin tossed him a grin. "It seems Lady Mariota was made for the sea."

The wind, blowing strong and fair, swept her hood off her head to reveal her long hair. "This is thrilling," she said to Donald. "Though perhaps it would not be so were I not on your ship."

To hear of her confidence in him was pleasing. "Then you must always sail on my ship, my lady."

Suddenly, out of nowhere, dozens of gannets, white with black wing tips, and great black-backed gulls flew past them, low and very close to the ship. His betrothed stared at them, a look of wonder on her face. "Never have I seen so many birds so close. These are common to the Isles?"

"They are," said Donald. "Gannets and gulls are not deterred by rough waters, rain or wind. They go with the fish."

Sensing they were coming to the end of the Kyle, Donald said, "Once we are past the Kyle of Lochalsh, we will turn south through the narrows of Kyle Rhea. The current there will be swifter still but, thankfully, not against us."

A group of dolphin mothers with their two-foot-long calves, suddenly appeared alongside the bow, splashing, dancing and shimmering in response to the movement of their mothers. "Look!" Mariota cried. "Are those dolphins?"

"Yes, my lady," said Donald. "Very playful ones, too."

After that, he left his lady to be watched over by his cousin and, from the stern, kept a close eye on her while he conferred with his captain. Once they were through the Kyle Rhea and the rough waters smoothed, he returned to the bow. "We will put in first at Ardtornish, my castle on the Sound of Mull, and sail to Islay tomorrow."

"Is Ardtornish to be our home?" she asked him.

Donald could not suppress a smile. "One of them."

MARIOTA THOUGHT THE setting of Lord Donald's castle of Ardtornish was magnificent. Surrounded by water on three sides, the stone keep stood on a point jutting into the Sound of Mull. "All of our castles are located on water, situated to provide a strategic defense," he had told her, "so approaching ships can be seen from afar."

The day's voyage and the day before had left her tired. A servant took her wet cloak and, after a brief meal, she retired to her chamber. There, Abby helped her out of her gown. Her handmaiden, who had never before left Ross, had survived an ambush and travel by galley over rough waters. "You did well, Abby."

"I did not get sick," she proudly declared, her dark curls hanging in disarray. "But I was very afraid."

"In time, we will both think of sailing as the easiest of travel." Mariota hoped it would be true.

Abby dropped her gaze. "'Tis possible, I suppose." Raising her head, she said, "The servants built up the fire and set the warming pan between the sheets."

"I shall look forward to that." Mariota looked with longing at the poster bed with its feathered bedcovering. Not long after, Abby departed for her own bed and Mariota, feeling pleased with her new home, was soon asleep.

She awakened to the song of the thrush and the arrival of dawn.

Hearing the crackle of a fire, she silently thanked the servant who had appeared to light the fire while she slept. Slipping on her robe, Mariota padded over the carpet to the window that looked out on the Sound of Mull. The dawn had turned the sky a golden hue with lavender layers resting above the blue waters. "'Tis magical," she whispered, staring in awe.

Abby opened the door to Mariota's chamber, a smile on her face. Her dark curls had been neatly combed.

"You slept well?" Mariota asked.

"Like the dead, my lady."

Fighting a laugh and mindful that Abby could be dreading the day's sail to Islay, she asked, "What do you think of our new home?" Then recalling Lord Donald's comment, she added, "'Tis one of my lord's castles."

"The great hall is as beautiful as that at Dingwall, though mayhap not as large. You can tell it has had a woman's touch with the tapestries, the carpets, the beeswax candles..."

"Lord Donald told me his mother, Princess Margaret, had much to do with that."

Abby cared more for the comforts to be found inside the castle while Mariota cared even more for what lay beyond. The thrush in the trees outside chose that moment to burst forth in song, reminding her she had best be dressed.

Abby walked to where Mariota's mantle lay over a chair by the fire. "Your cloak has dried, and I have brushed it. I have also laid out a fresh woolen gown, the green one that is so attractive with your eyes." As Mariota went to pick up the gown, Abby added, "On my way to your chamber, I heard the men stirring in the hall."

"All the more reason for haste." Once Mariota was dressed, Abby combed her long hair, braiding it into one plait for their travel. Reaching for her cloak, Mariota said. "Lord Donald told me last night that we will arrive at Islay by midday."

"Do we sail to another castle?"

"Not precisely. There is one on Islay, but he gave it to the brother who rebelled. He has a favorite manor on the west coast of Islay, but we do not go there. Instead, we are to sail to a sea loch on the south side of the isle and, from there, we travel by horse inland to a place called Finlaggan, an island in a loch, the ancient seat of the clan."

"An island in a loch within an island," mumbled Abby. "I cannot imagine," she said following Mariota out of the door.

In the great hall, two deerhounds lay sleeping in front of the fire. Lord Donald was breaking his fast with his companions. He rose as she entered. "Lady Mariota, come sit by me."

She greeted Lord Alexander, the two priests, the physician, Sir Thomas and the others before taking her seat.

"I trust you rested well, my lady," said Lord Donald. He passed a platter of bread, honey, cheese and fruit to her and asked a servant for more trout.

"I did, thank you. I would have been here sooner but I was enjoying the view from my chamber. When dawn came, the sky and the birdsong were captivating."

The fried trout, surrounded by baked apple slices, arrived at the table. "Here, allow me," said Lord Donald, lifting a portion of fish to her plate.

"It smells delicious," she said, taking a bite and finding it sweet.

"The weather today should be fair," said Lord Alexander, "so we expect a smooth sail to Islay. We will take two galleys to accommodate all who are going, including your handmaiden and your chests."

She nodded. "Tell me about Finlaggan."

Lord Donald raised his brow to his cousin, the priest, who sat across from her. "You know the history as well as anyone, John. Why don't you tell her?"

With a nod in her direction, the priest said, "Somerled, the first Lord of the Isles—called the King of the Isles in that day—thought it would make a sheltered place of peace for the clans to gather. Centuries before, a monastic community existed on *Eilean Mor*, the larger of the two islands in the loch, possibly established by St. Findlugan, an Irish monk and a contemporary of St. Columba." At her furrowed brows, he added, "You will understand when you see it. There is no castle there. Rather, there are many buildings, each dedicated to a purpose. They provide a great hall for feasting, housing for the lord, his family and the Council leadership, a stone chapel for worship, a kitchen and workshops. On the loch's shores, there are stables, a smith, a shipwright, guardhouses and kennels. A contingent of Macdonald galloglass lodge in the guardhouses when the Council is in session. The smaller isle in the loch is where the Council meets, to conduct business, to debate matters of importance and to dispense justice."

"It sounds very well organized. Is there room for all?" she asked.

"We manage to accommodate all who come," said Lord Donald. "The Bishop of the Isles and the Abbot of Iona have residences nearby on crannogs in small lochs. If the weather is good, many chiefs and their families will camp on the loch's banks. When business is concluded, the clans celebrate. It will be a chance for you to meet most everyone. Our half-sister, Mary, wife of Lachlan, chief of the Macleans, has offered to be your companion and chaperone while I am with the Council. She is the mother of one of my best generals, Hector, better known as Red Hector, named for his uncle, Hector Maclean of Lochbuie, the chief's brother. Hector's skill with a sword is legendary, and he is still a young man. I expect Mary to arrive soon from Duart Castle to sail with us."

"That was very thoughtful of you to arrange," said Mariota, for she was certain he had arranged it. To have a woman of the clan with her meant much. Not just a chaperone but a guide and, mayhap, a friend.

When they had eaten, Mariota followed Lord Donald and the others outside to await Mary Macdonald. Minutes later a galley approached, flying the pennon of the Macleans, which Lord Donald described as an embattled silver tower on an azure field. As the crew beached the ship, he offered his hand to assist Lady Mary to the sand. Her movements were graceful as if she had climbed down from galleys a thousand times. Elegantly attired in a woad blue woolen gown and fur-lined cloak, her long dark curls extended beneath her hood, falling to her shoulders. Much different than the fair hair of Lord Donald and his brother, but then she remembered that Mary was sister to Lord Donald's half-brother, Ranald.

Mariota walked to meet them.

"Mary," Lord Donald said to his sister, "allow me to introduce you to my betrothed, Lady Mariota Leslie of Ross."

Mariota curtseyed briefly before the older woman. "I am happy to meet the mother of Red Hector, whose skill with a sword Lord Donald praises."

Mary smiled. "Of my five sons, he is the one most likely to get into trouble, owing to those skills you speak of. He thinks he is nigh on invincible."

"Does he sail with Lachlan to Islay?" Lord Donald asked.

"Yes, all our sons sailed with their father before I left to come here. When do we leave?"

"Shortly." Then teasingly, "We were only waiting for you."

"Good. While you and the men ready the ships, I will speak with Mariota."

To Mariota's mind, there were probably few who could speak so to the Macdonald chief. His older half-sister was obviously one. Lord Donald made no objection but nodded. Tossing Mariota a parting smile, he rejoined his brother and cousin.

Mary took Mariota's arm and they began to walk along the shore. "I want you to know I am here for you, Mariota. Ask me anything and I will give you an honest answer."

Two otters feeding among the kelp splashed into the water, their antics causing Mariota to smile. "We don't have otters in Ross where I live."

"Where you will not live for much longer," Mary corrected. "You will see more creatures and many birds as you spend time with us. The Isles are full of them. What has Donald told you of our destination?"

"The priest, John MacAlister, told me the history, describing the place, its purpose and the meeting of the clans that takes place there. I am most anxious to see it."

"Our time at Finlaggan is usually a festive one. The chiefs bring their families and there are games of skill, music and feasting."

They turned to walk back to the galleys where the crews were finished loading the chests. One man led Lord Donald's hounds on board. Abby stood talking with his cousin. "They load hounds but no horses?" Mariota asked. "Mine is here at Ardtornish."

"Donnie will want his hounds on Islay if there is to be a hunt. As for horses, there will be horses on Islay waiting for us when the galleys arrive."

"It all seems so efficient," said Mariota.

"It is, particularly for the Macdonald and his family, of which you will soon be a part. I could tell from the look Donnie gave you that he is happy for you to become his bride. And you, Mariota, are you happy that you are to wed our Donnie?"

Mariota did not have to search her heart for the answer. It was there, just below the surface. "Yes, I am well content."

"That is good. He may be young but, in the few years he has been chief, Donnie has done well. The clans will be pleased to see their lord happily wed. Heirs are always an issue for the lordship."

"As they are for the earls of Ross."

The crews rowed east down the Sound of Mull between Morvern on their left and the Isle of Mull on their right. Soon, the sails were raised and the wind swept them along. Mariota drew her cloak around her, bracing herself against the movement of the galley.

As they rounded the Isle of Mull, Mary pointed to a magnificent castle standing proudly on a green clifftop looking toward the Scottish mainland. "That is my home," she said, smiling. "That is Duart Castle. It guards the sound."

Mariota said, "It stands like a jewel in its setting."

They continued south with Scotland's mainland on their left. Some time on, the galleys sailed between two land masses, or what Mariota thought were land masses. Mary corrected her. "On your left is the Isle of Jura, a wild land frequented by red deer. Donnie intends to give the Macleans the north end."

"Those mountains rise dramatically from the land," observed Mariota.

"Those hills are called the Paps of Jura. You can see them from Finlaggan. Opposite Jura are the smaller Isles of Colonsay and Oronsay, connected to each other by a causeway. Colonsay is home to the Macduffies, the recordkeepers for Clan Donald. The priory on Oronsay was the last project of our father, John of Islay, before he died."

Southwest of Jura, they reached Islay and sailed down its western coast. Mary pointed to a wide bay with a sandy beach. "That is Machir Bay where Donnie's manor is located. 'Tis a beautiful spot. From Islay, the Macdonalds who came before us controlled the eastern reaches of the Atlantic and the seas around Argyll and the Isle of Arran, beyond which lay Carrick and the mainland of Scotland. Though nominally under Scotland, the Macdonald Islesmen ruled as independent kings. Some would tell you they still do."

Mariota was overwhelmed by the size of Donald's kingdom. "I am beginning to realize the Isles stretch over vast areas of sea and land."

"Oh, they do, which is one reason it is good you travel well by galley."

The ship took a southern turn around Islay's coast to enter a large sea loch. Wind whipped her cloak behind her. The air was chilled and sometimes a spray of seawater fell across the galley, but she had grown used to it, and Mary was not bothered at all.

"This is Indaal Bay," said Mary, "the door to Finlaggan."

Mariota saw only blue water in all directions. "It is very large."

"It has to be. Imagine the loch filled with hundreds of galleys as it has been in past times. It is what Somerled saw in his mind when he chose Finlaggan, or so I am told. Very soon, it will be home to thousands of barnacle geese who winter here. They are handsome birds but very noisy. Their cries add to the roars of the rutting red stags."

"We have red deer in Ross."

"Then you will not be surprised at how loudly the males can bellow."

Between the blustering wind in the sail, the creaking of the planks, the waves splashing over the gunwale and the captain's shouted orders to the crew, the voyage was not a silent one. At times, she and Mary had to raise their voices to be heard. Sailing on Lord Donald's galley roused in Mariota an excitement she had not experienced before. This was a land of strong men and strong women who were as at home on the sea as on land. Soon, she would be part of them.

As the galleys neared the shore. Mariota saw more than a dozen other galleys beached there already, their colorful pennons blowing in the wind. "Are those from clans that have already arrived?"

"They are."

The crew took down the sail and shipped the oars.

Mary turned to her. "I don't suppose Donnie told you there is likely to be a hanging while we are at Finlaggan?"

"No." She shook her head. "He mentioned nothing of that."

Mary let out a breath. "Men always leave out details they think will trouble their women. Did you know of the rebellion?"

"Yes...his younger brother."

"Well, the MacKinnon chief and his brother, Finguine, Abbot of Iona, were behind it. Oh, there were others who would throw off the authority of the chief, including greedy Macleods and even some Macleans, an embarrassment to Lachlan. Donnie's brother, John Mor, played his part as their pawn. We think he was lured to their cause by the promise of more land and the charms of the daughter of the abbot's concubine."

"Surely they will not hang the abbot," Mariota said, taken aback.

"No, his abbot's robes will save him. But they will make an example of the MacKinnon chief, as is only right. The Council will decide his fate but doubtless they will condemn him to death. I just wanted you to be aware."

"Thank you," Mariota said. "I have never seen a man hanged. In the king's court, death comes most often by treachery in the dead of night."

Mary chuckled. "Aye, we have observed that."

Lord Donald returned to her as the galley was beached. "Well, has Mary told you all there is to know about us?"

Smiling at her new friend, Mariota said, "Lady Mary has kindly illuminated me about many things, but I am certain I do not know all."

Finlaggan, Isle of Islay, late September 1389

THE PATH DONALD took from the beach at Loch Indaal to

Finlaggan was grass-covered and worn, a familiar path he had traversed many times with his father and his family. Now it was his turn as chief to lead the Council in the business of the lordship. His brow furrowed as he considered how unfortunate it was that his first meeting would be one where he handed out penalties for treason.

"Something worries you," said Lady Mariota, riding beside him.

"You are perceptive, my lady. The truth is not all of the business that lies ahead of me will be pleasant."

"Lady Mary told me. I am sorry."

He turned to see her beautiful eyes full of understanding. "To lead is to carry the responsibility for such decisions. I do not shrink from them; I only regret they are necessary."

"Will your mother and sisters be here?"

"No, except for Mary, whom you have met. My sister Christiana is married to Robert Savage in Ulster. Agnes is married to Sir John Montgomerie and lives in Ardrossan on Scotland's west coast. My youngest siblings are with our mother who, since my father's death, has retired from the meetings of the clans. When she is not with her father, the king, she spends her days in Argyll. At the moment, she is not happy with me for my decision to grant certain lands to my brothers. She complains to her brother, Robert Stewart, Earl of Fife."

Mariota rode beside him through the fertile valley lying between the green hills. She was often silent. He liked that about her. She did not prattle on as some women did. She made meaningful comments, yet she could be content with silence, a rare but desired quality.

Cattle grazed on one heather-covered slope and, occasionally, a few red deer followed a stag out from beneath pine trees. In the distance, he heard a stag bellow. Soon, there would be the clash of antlers. A peregrine falcon swept across the sky that had turned gray.

His betrothed looked up, following the bird's flight. "It is beautiful here, so peaceful. I see why your ancestor selected it at a time when peace was not easily found."

"There have been many times since Somerled drove the Norse pirates from the Isles when peace proved elusive. Always this is the place we retreat to."

An hour later, they arrived at the south end of Loch Finlaggan.

Their shared words and companionable silence led Donald to believe a closeness was growing between them.

"I see now what John meant," she said, looking ahead. "An island in a loch within an island."

"Two islands in the loch, but *Eilean na Comhairle*, the Council Isle, is much smaller. You will be able to see it as we draw closer. Islay has other lochs that provide crannogs on which our abbot and bishop have homes. They are close, as is my manor house of Kilcummin at Machir Bay on Islay's west coast."

Alex rode up beside Donald. "What arrangements for lodging?"

"Lady Mariota and her handmaiden are to be given the lord's chamber. Since your wife will not be joining us this year owing to her being late in her pregnancy, you and I will use the added family quarters along with John. Michael, the new Bishop of the Isles, can have the house on the Council Isle whenever he arrives, but he may want to lodge at Moyberge, his house on Loch Lossit. Chaplain Bean and my physician can lodge where they typically do. Mary will want to join her family at the Maclean cottage. My hounds can sleep in the great hall. The crews will sleep on the bank of the loch or with the guard in the guardhouse along with the galloglass."

"Very well. I will ride ahead and arrange it."

"The Bishop of the Isles attends?" asked Lady Mariota.

"Both he and the Abbot of Iona attend but, this time, the abbot will be here only as a prisoner." In the distance, Donald could see many tents pitched on the banks of the loch. "Apparently some have decided it is warm enough for tents."

"I have yet to meet Lord Alexander's wife," said his betrothed.

"Another Mary, the daughter of the Earl of Lennox. You will like her."

MARIOTA WAS AMAZED at what she saw as they approached the north end of the loch. At first, she thought Finlaggan consisted of a few buildings spread over the large island but, as she came closer, the many thatched-covered stone buildings, workshops, stone chapel and great hall towering over all as well as the structures on the banks of the loch made Finlaggan appear more like a bustling town.

Smiling people moved about on the island and the loch's banks where the tents rose like a field of huge white mushrooms. The atmosphere was that of a harvest fair with conversations and music. Enticing smells of meat roasting on spits filled the air. Children, shouting to each other, ran between groups of people. Young women dressed in colorful gowns with ribbons in their long hair walked together, laughing.

"Is it always like this?" she asked Lord Donald.

"Most often. Except for the unusual circumstances that prevailed at the time, I would have been installed here as chief and a celebration would have followed. As it was, the ceremony occurred on the Isle of Eigg and no families attended. This is our first time together since then."

Mariota gazed toward the island in the loch. "How do we get onto the island?"

"There is a causeway just ahead, and we also use boats."

As they passed through the crowds, the people stopped to greet their lord. From their smiles, it was clear they were pleased to see him.

"This is your new family, Lady Mariota," he said, his blue eyes shining. "These are the clans of the lordship. These are my people and, soon, they will be yours."

Wanting them to think well of their new lady, Mariota smiled at all who looked upon her.

Two boys, about five years old, one with dark red hair and one with a head of brown curls ran up to her horse.

The one with the brown curls reached up to touch her horse's mane. "Are you our new lady?"

The red-haired boy poked his companion in the arm and smiled up at Mariota.

Before she could think how to answer, Lord Donald said to the first boy, "She soon will be, Neil."

"She is very pretty, my lord," the lad said before grabbing the hand of his companion and dashing off behind them.

Mariota felt a blush heat her cheeks. "A charming lad...his companion, too."

"Neil is one of Lachlan Maclean's younger sons, and the one with red hair, confusingly also named Lachlan, is the son of Lachlan's eldest, Hector. I expect Neil is on some errand for his father." Lord Donald turned in his saddle to look behind him. "He is searching for his mother. Mary rides a few horses behind us. Wait until you meet Neil's older brother, Hector. He, too, is quite charming. It must run in the family as Lachlan, chief of the Macleans, charmed my half-sister. Their marriage was a love match and still is."

Mariota wondered if her marriage would be such a union, for she found the Lord of the Isles to be very charming.

AT DAYBREAK the next morning, Donald went first to the chapel to pray. John, his cousin, had arrived before him and was kneeling at the altar, his black robes spread out behind him. Donald knelt beside his friend, bowed his head and asked the Lord for wisdom to guide the Council.

John rose with him. "We will need God's help for what lies ahead."

"That is certain," said Donald.

They returned to the hall to eat and found Lady Mariota and Donald's half-sister, Mary, already there with Alex. "Morning, Donnie," said Alex. "I have been keeping the ladies company while you were, doubtless, in prayer."

"And you are having a good time of it, I see," Donald said, his eyes fixed on Mariota. "Did you ladies sleep well?"

"Very well," said Lady Mariota. Her smile was subtle but it told him she was glad to see him.

Mary said, "With my younger sons and Hector's boy to calm down, sleep was a long time in coming. They are always in an excited state when the clans gather and their playmates arrive in abundance."

When they had finished their meal, the two women and three men went outside to greet the day. "The sky remains gray," said Alex, "but at least we are spared rain. The clans will be happy for that."

Donald turned to Lady Mariota. "The Council meets this morning. I do not know how long I will be, but certainly, we will dine together this evening."

A blast on a horn drew his attention.

Lady Mariota looked up. "What does that mean?"

"The Council is summoned," said Donald. "We must go." He took her hand and bowed over it. "I will see you anon, my lady."

"Come, Mariota," said Mary, taking Lady Mariota's arm. "I have much to show you and you have many people to meet."

Flanked by Alex and John, Donald strode to the causeway that led to the smaller isle where the rectangular stone keep that was the Council's chambers stood.

As they entered the large room, crowded with the leaders of the lordship, all talking at once, Lachlan Maclean approached, his silver hair and gray beard giving him the appearance of an elder, which he was. "The MacKinnon prisoners will be brought in when the Council is ready. Those who conspired with them are being kept apart until and unless you want them."

Donald nodded and went forward to greet the assembled nobles, thanes, and great men of the royal blood of Clan Donald. The nobles included Lachlan, the Maclean chief of Duart, Murdoch, the Maclean chief of Lochbuie, Roderick, the Macleod chief of Lewis and the Macleod chief of Harris. Since the Macleods of Harris had been involved in the rebellion, all eyes were watching Ian Ciar, the black-haired, cruel and dreaded chief of the Harris Macleods.

The four thanes would have included the MacKinnon chief, but as he was the leader of the rebellion, he would attend only as one of the accused. Donald had invited Muirceartach, chief of the MacNeils of Barra, Lachlan, chief of the Mackintoshes, Gillespie, chief of the Macduffies and Donald Dubh, chief of the Camerons.

To these he added the chief of Clanranald, who, after Ranald's death, was his son, Allan, John MacIain MacDonald of Glen Coe and Donald's brother, Alex, Lord of Lochaber.

In addition, the Macdonald's bard, one of the MacMhuirich kindred, was always in attendance as was Donald's hereditary harpist.

While every chief had his chaplain, the Council was always attended by the lordship's spiritual leaders, the Abbot of Iona and the

Bishop of the Isles. Since the Abbot of Iona was one of the accused, for this Council, the church would be represented by Michael, Bishop of the Isles, and John MacAlister. Donald had a mind to make John the new Prior of Iona, but he had not yet spoken of it to his friend. He could not make John the Abbot of Iona as long as Finguine MacKinnon occupied the position.

When everyone was assembled, Donald asked them to remain standing while the bishop prayed.

Clothed in his mitre and vestments of white and crimson, his gold pectoral cross prominently displayed on his chest, the bishop came slowly to the front and bowed his head. "O Lord, you know what is best for us, let your will be done, and give our chief and the Council wisdom in all their deliberations."

The bishop raised his head and nodded to Donald.

Bracing himself for what lay ahead, he stepped to the front of the room. "We have gathered to decide a matter of grave importance wherein these two before you are charged with treason. You confirmed me as your chief; they sought to set me aside. Many of you supported me in bringing them to justice. Now you must decide their fates. I stand with you, for the integrity and honor of the lordship is at stake."

CHAPTER 8

MARIOTA BIT HER lip as she waited with Mary on the large island, looking toward the Council chambers just across the causeway. They had been walking among the people most of the day and she had met many in the clan. It was now late afternoon and the wind had picked up. She drew her cloak tightly around her, shivering and impatient for news. "It's taking a long time…"

"Aye," said Mary. "To try a man for treason when the penalty is death is no easy task. Worse still if he be a chief, one of their own. Then there is the sticky matter of the abbot. Donnie will proceed cautiously even though he knows the truth of it. Once the fate of the two MacKinnons is decided, they must consider what to do with the others who followed them. At least two of the clans had men in the rebellion, and they will have their say."

"And Lord Donald's brother, John Mor?"

"He is not here to face charges or explain his folly. When he is, Donnie will have to deal with him."

Just then, the door of the Council chambers opened and two burly galloglass stepped out, holding between them an older man struggling against their restraint.

"'Tis the MacKinnon chief," said Mary. "By the look of him, he was found guilty."

Mariota agreed. The man's face, twisted with anger, was ashen gray like his hair and beard. In his eyes was a look of terror. Behind these three were two more guards, between them a priest, walking freely with a downcast expression.

"I will be interested to know what the Council decided is to be the fate of the abbot," said Mary. "For his treachery, there is no precedent."

The six men passed them by, the convicted averting their gazes. Mariota wondered aloud, "Where are they taking them?"

"We will soon know. Here comes Alex."

Lord Alexander strode over the causeway and stopped in front of them. Sweeping a stray lock of hair behind his ear, he said to Mariota, "Donnie wanted me to let you know where things stand. He knew you would be concerned as the day grew long."

Even Mary looked impatient. "Well, what did the Council decide?"

"Ewen, the MacKinnon chief, is to be hanged at sunset. The abbot is to be imprisoned for the rest of his life—on Iona—so that he will ponder all he has lost for his treachery."

Mary nodded. "A fitting end to his treason."

"It was Donnie's idea," said Lord Alexander. "All the chiefs approved."

"And the others?" asked Mary.

"The chiefs involved will deal with their own. I suspect the Macleods of Harris who took part in the rebellion will not live long. Ian Ciar, their chief, is a cruel and intolerant man."

"Aye," said Mary, "and his wife is no better, although she is the daughter of an O'Neill chieftain." Looking at Mariota, she said, "When his daughters thought to escape her by taking two MacQueen brothers for their husbands, she had the men flogged to death and their bodies thrown into the sea."

Mariota could not imagine a mother doing something so evil.

Her distaste of the Macleod chief and his wife must have shown on her face as Lord Alexander quickly added, "The Council was clear that those who were merely following orders are to live but will forfeit any lands they possess."

"Lord Donald?" asked Mariota, looking past Lord Alexander toward the open door of the Council chambers.

"He will be along shortly. After the rebellion was dealt with the chiefs asked about the Stewarts, and he stayed behind to speak with them. It is believed King Robert is not long for this life."

"What did Donnie say?" asked Mary.

"He told them the truth, that John, Earl of Carrick, the king's eldest son, will inherit the crown, but the real power behind the throne is his younger brother, Robert, the ambitious Earl of Fife. As regent, he is king in all but name."

Behind Lord Alexander, Mariota glimpsed John MacAlister coming toward them. The priest's stride spoke of confidence, but his expression was placid, disclosing nothing.

Arriving in front of them, he said to her, "You would have been proud of him. Donnie gave a rousing speech, reminding the chiefs of the honor of the lordship. He recounted our history and that of Iona, our spiritual heritage. He encouraged them to protect our legacy against dishonesty and treachery to make clear such will not be tolerated. The debate went on for some time. He is exhausted, but satisfied, I think, with the result."

In the distance, Lord Donald appeared, walking over the causeway, followed by the chiefs. The wind blew his pale hair behind him. As he came closer, Mariota could see the fatigue in his face.

"At least they have tomorrow to look forward to," said Lord Alexander. "Donnie reminded the chiefs it is Michaelmas and there will be a great feast."

"Fitting," said John, "for Michael is the archangel who has victory over the powers of darkness."

Lord Donald came up to her. "It is over, thank God. Justice is done and the lordship can move on."

THE NEXT MORNING dawned cool and full of sun. Donald left the chapel and his morning prayer to walk along the shores of *Eilean Mor*, the larger island in Loch Finlaggan, reflecting on all that had occurred the day before. The galley carrying Ewen MacKinnon's body for burial and the fallen abbot to his prison would have sailed to Iona by now. It could have been otherwise had they remained loyal, had they remained faithful. A sad ending to both lives. Even though the abbot would live, his last years would not be happy ones.

Donald thought of his brother, John Mor. Reports from his scouts in Ireland said they were closing in on him in the Glens of Antrim. Donald could not put the rebellion behind him until John Mor's betrayal was dealt with, but he would not think more on that at the moment. He was determined this day would be full of joy. He would spend it with Lady Mariota.

People were waking, going about their morning tasks, greeting him as he passed. He felt closer to them now than he ever had before, now that he had taken action to assure their safety and the lordship's future. He thanked God for helping him to lead so great a people.

Returning to his lodging, he encountered Mary. "Thank you for escorting Mariota yesterday. How did it go?"

"I know what you are asking, Donnie. You will be pleased to know all responded well to her. In turn, she was gracious. She is an intelligent, capable woman, and will do well as your lady wife. Her role as the Lady of the Isles will keep her mind occupied."

"I am relieved. I was worried about the chaos that sometimes reigns at Finlaggan. She is not used to it."

"No, but I believe she will thrive on it." Then, as if recalling something humorous, Mary smiled. "She laughed at the children running around and tried to learn their names, which, as you know, is a daunting task with so many having the same given name."

Pleased that his betrothed was doing so well among the people, he said, "I plan to spend the day with her and join in the feast."

"That will please her. In which case, I will be off to my husband and my younger sons. We will see you later."

Encouraged, Donald knocked on the door of the lord's quarters where his betrothed was staying.

Her handmaiden opened the door. "My lord, Lady Mariota is

ready." She stepped back and Mariota came out to join him. She wore a gown of crimson wool, the sleeves and bodice embroidered with silver thread. Her hair was drawn back at the sides, leaving her long, golden locks hanging down her back. On her ears were jewels that looked like garnets.

"You are a feast for my eyes."

"I am glad you think so," she said. "I was not sure what to wear. We are in the seat of your lordship, among your people, but we are not in a castle where you hold court. Yet I would have you proud of me as we join in the Michaelmas celebration."

"You chose well. Come," he said offering his arm, "let us have a bite to eat and then see what delights the day holds for us."

In the great hall, Donald found his brother and cousin eating with Lachlan Maclean and his son, Red Hector, the two Macleans rising at Lady Mariota's entrance. Hector was taller than his father, as tall as Donald, but with a galloglass' powerful body. His features were well-formed, and his shock of dark red hair the same color as his beard. On each side of his head, he had plaited part of his hair away from his face.

"Lady Mariota," said Donald, "allow me to introduce you to Lachlan, chief of the Macleans, and his eldest, my nephew, Hector Roy Maclean, a renowned swordsman."

The two Macleans greeted his betrothed and she them.

"Rising late?" Donald asked the group of men, as he and Lady Mariota took their seats.

"Hector and I have been up for hours," said Lachlan, "tending to errands my wife and Hector's set for us. I suppose the MacKinnons have departed?"

"They have," said Donald.

His steady gaze still on Donald, Lachlan said, "You did very well with the chiefs yesterday. They can be an unruly bunch."

"Thank you," said Donald. "I am glad it is behind us."

Alex said, "John and I are not late either, Brother. I went to inquire of the guards and the crews and have only just returned."

"And I went to inquire of the family of the MacKinnon chief," said John.

"How are they?" asked Donald, concerned. "Should I have called upon them this morning?"

"Your meeting with them last night was sufficient, I think," said John. "His wife told me she was not surprised by the verdict. She has accepted the will of the Council, believing it to be the will of God. In our conversation, she told me she had a bad feeling the first time Ewen invited John Mor to their castle."

Glancing at Lady Mariota, Donald said, "Would that the MacKinnon chief had listened to his wife."

MARIOTA HAD NOT missed Lord Donald's eyes upon her. She would be his right arm if she could, speaking her mind to give him advice and encouragement when there was opportunity, for the burden he carried was great.

Turning his eyes from her, he asked his brother, "Is the feast well in hand?"

"Aye, the hunt yesterday brought some large bucks. This morning, the men will fish and tonight…well, there is hope for the geese."

"The barnacle geese?" asked Mariota.

"The very ones," said Lord Alexander. "Their arrival is a sight that astounds no matter how many times you witness it."

When they had finished eating, Lord Donald offered her his hand. She took it, relishing the warmth of his skin against hers. His hand was strong and browned from the sun, a hand she thought to hold for the rest of her life.

He announced to the others, "I am taking my betrothed on a tour of the festivities."

"Alone?" asked Lord Alexander with feigned incredulity.

"Alone!" said Lord Donald.

"The chief demands his way," said Lachlan Maclean with a smirk as he nudged his son, Hector.

"Enough!" said Lord Donald. "We will see you at the feast."

"Will you be engaging in any of the games of skill?" asked John. "I might want to watch."

"We will see," said Lord Donald as he guided her to the door.

"He is very good at archery!" shouted Lord Alexander when they were nearly there. "But not as good as me!"

Laughter sounded behind them as they left the great hall.

"Would you allow me to call you Mariota?"

She met his blue-eyed gaze. "Yes, and will you be just 'Donald' then to me?"

"I would like that, and you may call me Donnie, if you like. Many in my family do."

With that, he swept her away to a halcyon day she would always remember.

They strolled along the shore of the large island, greeting everyone they met with smiles that spoke of their contentment in their own company. He greeted the people by name, receiving in turn their many greetings.

"Will you always hold my hand like this?" she asked.

"Always," he said, squeezing her hand.

Minstrels played their instruments of lute, harp, pipe and tabor, the music wafting through the air. In one corner, a bard recited verses, drawing a crowd. One clever clansman was telling a group of children a story using a poppin-show, the cloth figures with funny faces and odd-fitting clothing making the children laugh. She thought of the children she and Donald would one day have, imagining them sitting here before the storyteller.

Farther on, they crossed over the causeway to the banks of the loch, past the tents, kennels, stables and guardhouse to where three large archery targets had been set up in a row. "We will return here to see Alex display his skills."

"And you?"

"Perhaps. Then, too, your Welshman, Gwyn, might compete."

She had not mentioned the two men from Ross she had sent earlier to learn of him. Now it seemed right to do so. "You did not mind that I dispatched two of my own to the Isles to observe my betrothed?"

His mouth quirked up on one side. "I thought you very clever to do so. Did they give a good report?"

"A very good report. I told my mother that she had lost them to your service, so enthralled were they with the new Lord of the Isles."

"If you and Sir Thomas agree," he said, "I would make him the head of your guard. As the Lady of the Isles, you will need one. With your permission, I would keep Gwyn in my service as his bow has proved needful."

"I have no objection. It would give me comfort to know Gwyn is one of those who protects my lord."

The sounds of the celebration faded behind them as Mariota and Donald walked farther along the banks of the loch. In the distance, she could see the Paps rising on the Isle of Jura. The only sound was the wind blowing through the long grass and the occasional birdsong. When they came to an end of words, they found themselves alone amidst a field of heather.

He turned to her, taking both of her hands. "We have been betrothed since we were children, but I would ask, 'Would you, of your own free will, marry me, Mariota Leslie'?"

In a playful mood, she answered, "What would you say if I said, 'No'?"

He raised a brow as a wry smile spread across his face. "I would kiss you and then ask you again."

Slowly, she said, "All right."

Placing his warm hand on the back of her neck beneath her hair, he brought her to him, his mouth descending on hers. His lips were warm and inviting. She met them with eager anticipation, her hands slipping up his arms to his shoulders. The scent of him wrapped around her, the scent of the sea mingled with the scent of heather. His kiss was deep and, for long moments, she could not have said where she was.

Raising his head, his blue eyes intense, he said, "Well?"

"Yes. I will marry you, Donald, for if that was a sample, I do not think I could live without your kisses."

He laughed, lifted her up and swung her around. Setting her on her feet, he asked, "Shall we marry when I return you to Dingwall, or would you rather the wedding take place after winter?"

She was tempted to choose the earlier date just to be with him sooner, but to prepare for a grand wedding that would please her mother and her relations, she would need the winter, and they couldn't marry during Lent. "Next spring, just after Easter."

"Very well. It shall be April, though it seems a very long time from now."

Overhead, she heard the honking of geese; it sounded like they were barking. Looking up, she saw many formations of the birds making their way across the sky. "Donald! It's the geese!"

"So it is."

Their numbers continued to grow until the sky above was nearly black with them, the sound deafening. "There are thousands of them!" she said, amazed at the sight. They began to land on the waters of the loch in great numbers. "So many!"

Still more arrived, joining the others. Some settled on the shores of the loch, their distinctive black and white plumage stark against the green grass. Their faces were white, their heads, necks and breasts black. Their wings and backs were silver, their underbellies white. "Mary was right. They are very handsome," said Mariota. "Noisy, too."

"And good to eat," said Donald. "Alex is doubtless nocking an arrow at this very moment."

Hand in hand, they walked back to the festival, the din of the geese all around them. Beside Donald, Mariota felt more at ease with the world than she could ever recall. It was the man next to her who caused her to grin with happiness. He wore the same grin. Others soon noticed.

"Where have you two been?" asked Mary Macdonald, looking between them and then dropping her gaze to their clasped hands. "Wherever it was must have been pleasant."

"We took a walk and decided to wed next April," said Donald. "You and your brood will be invited to Ross with any others who would come."

"Aye, well, I'll speak of it with Lachlan. Meanwhile, your men are looking for you, Donnie. They would ask you to join them on the hunt for the geese."

"One hardly needs to hunt for them," said Donald. "They are landing on the shores like pebbles tossed on a beach. But I will gather my arrows and join them. Will you attend my lady while I do? And then I may take a hand at the archery contest."

Mariota enjoyed walking around the festival with Lady Mary as her guide. There was much to see. The people appeared happy, the events of the prior day behind them. They might have their differences but here, at least, they were one family. She had been to harvest fairs in Ross, but none were quite as intimate as this one.

She noticed young women and men eyeing each other and remarked to Mary, "Finlaggan must be a place where marriages are made."

"Sometimes, but often, the chiefs have in mind a mate when their children are young, like you and Donnie. In others, the chiefs can be swayed by the desire of their children. My father, allowed Lachlan Maclean and I to follow our hearts, and the Macleans were pleased to see their son wed the lord's daughter."

Sometime later, Donald and Alex found them. Their bows were slung over one shoulder. In each hand, they carried a brace of large geese. "Our contribution to the feast," Donald said, handing them to those supervising the cooking. "Time for the archery contest."

"We will follow you," said Mary.

Donald dipped his head to Mariota and strode off with his brother to the archery field. She and Mary followed, taking a position to one side where they could observe all. The archery butts were set up on one end of the large area, each mound of dirt bearing a white circle the archers would aim for.

A score of men came forward, their quivers with sheaves of arrows secured at their waists. Donald and his brother joined them. She glimpsed Gwyn's dark hair in the group and silently wished him luck. He was shorter than the others, as were many Welshmen when compared to the tall Islesmen, but in this contest, height would be no advantage. Like the others, Gwyn wore only a short tunic and a sleeveless leather gambeson.

"The closest bolt to the center will go forward to the next round," said the presiding Isleman who acted as judge.

Four rounds were completed before the remaining archers had been reduced to a half-dozen. Donald, Alex and Gwyn were among them. Mariota was biting her thumb, anxious to see who would win.

The archers were moved back twenty paces to increase the shooting distance.

In the next round all save Donald, Alex and Gwyn were eliminated. "There would be more archers competing had Donald brought his bowmen," said Mary, "but typically he allows them to remain at home when he is at Finlaggan. My sons prefer the sword, though that could be due to Hector's great success with the weapon."

All three men shot at the same time, their arrows hissing through the air to hit the butt with a "thwack". From where Mariota stood, it looked like each arrow hit the center but, when carefully examined, the official pronounced Gwyn had won.

Loud shouts erupted in praise of his shooting.

Donald and Alex each took a turn slapping the back of the Welshman, congratulating him. Donald turned to the crowd and announced, "Meet Gwyn Kimball, my newest bowman!"

Shouts of approval followed.

Donald strode toward Mariota and his half-sister, who were standing to one side. "It was good Gwyn won as the prize is a finely tooled leather quiver. It will serve him well."

"Gwyn was the best archer in Dingwall," said Mariota.

Donald smiled, shaking his head. "I should have known. 'Tis not surprising given what I have observed."

Mary said, "I had better find my younger sons. I left them in Hector's care, which is always a dubious arrangement."

"We will join you," said Donald.

Mariota and Donald walked with Mary to where the food was being prepared. The smells of roasting geese blended with sides of beef turning on spits over open fires. Added to that was the smell of fresh fish frying in pans set on coals.

Cups of ale were being handed out from large barrels.

"If I know my son, Hector will be here," said Mary.

And so he was. A dark-haired beauty, shorter than Mariota, was by his side. Several boys stood with them.

Red Hector handed his tankard to the young woman and said to Mariota, "Allow me to introduce you to my wife, Anne Douglas."

Mariota and Anne exchanged greetings.

"I don't know about all of you," said Alex coming up to them with John in tow, "but we are hungry!"

"Aye," said Hector. "The aroma of roasting meat draws me." The boys with him, who must have been his younger brothers, ran to their mother. "Can we eat now?"

"Soon, my sons," said Mary.

"Where's Chaplain Bean?" asked Donald, looking around. "You could bless the feast, John, but, typically, it is Bean's duty to thank God for the harvest and pray for our feast."

Bean was soon found and asked to pray. The people must have been used to their lord's priorities, for Mariota observed everyone bowed their heads, even the children.

When the prayer ended, Donald shouted, "Let the feasting begin!"

The feast that followed was the best meal Mariota could recall. Not so much for the food, which was delicious, but for the company, the people and their laughter. She enjoyed Hector and his wife and the bantering that he engaged in with his brothers, who clearly admired him.

When all had eaten, lively music began. Donald took her hand and pulled her up from where she sat. "A dance with my bride-to-be is in order!"

Mariota felt the eyes of the people upon her as she danced with their lord by the light of the fires set around the tents. Often, her gaze locked with his and she could not look away.

By the time they left the gathering hours later, the sun had set and the sky had turned a pale blue lavender. Donald walked with her over the causeway to the large island and the lord's lodging, the sound of roosting geese in the background. Arriving at her door, he raised her hands to his lips and placed a kiss on her knuckles. "Until tomorrow."

THE NEXT DAY saw many families departing. As Donald had business with some of the chiefs, he stayed at Finlaggan for another day. Once his business was done, he and all in his retinue sailed.

When they arrived at Ardtornish, Donald made sure Mariota was settled with her handmaiden and then he took John aside. "When I depart for Dingwall, I would ask you to take a galley to Iona with a contingent of guards to assess matters there. As I recall, the MacKinnon abbot's son was the prior at Iona. If that is the case, and he is as bad as his father, I will replace him."

John nodded, his expression thoughtful. "I am happy to do it and more than a little curious to learn what has transpired with the abbot's imprisonment. I will speak to the abbey chapter and some monks to see what can be learned and to assure them of your support."

"A good thought. I should be back at Ardtornish in two weeks' time and will ask your views then. I am hoping to spend Christmastide at my manor on Islay. I have invited the Macleans. Will you join us?"

"Happily."

Donald left Alex behind to tend the business of the lordship as he made the return journey to Dingwall with Mariota and a host of galloglass. Given their experience on the first trip across Ross, he wanted no surprises. As it turned out, they had no more sightings of the Earl of Buchan's caterans. Though the trip was uneventful, it rained often now that they were into October, and it was sad for he and Mariota as they would soon be parted.

The countess welcomed them on their arrival, pleased to find her daughter in good health. "You look well, my daughter; you, too, my lord." She ordered servants to set refreshments before them and bid them sit by the fire in the great hall. "I trust the visit to the Isles and Finlaggan was a good one."

Mariota glanced at him before replying. "It was wonderful, Mother. The people, the Isles, the celebration of Michaelmas."

The countess gave her daughter a fond look. "Your new home pleases you."

"Oh, yes." She glanced again at Donald. "Very much."

"With your permission, Countess," he said, "we would marry here in Ross next April, after Easter."

"That would suit me," said Countess Euphemia. "I would have

my daughter for Christmastide and months to plan what will be a large wedding. If he is well enough, the king may attend."

"I expect I would bring some of the chiefs from the Isles and their families to join in the celebration," said Donald. "Could you accommodate them?"

"We have many rooms in this castle," said the countess, "and connected to us by a tunnel, is nearby Tulloch Castle, smaller but able to lodge many. It is a favorite of mine as Mariota was born there."

That evening, Donald dined with Mariota, the countess, and her son, the teenaged Alexander. Afterward, he and Mariota went for a long walk. The sun had set but there was still light and they had their cloaks against the chill.

"Our time in the Isles was well spent," he said. "We know each other better and you are now familiar with your future home."

"I had not realized the beauty of the Isles before these last weeks. It was clever of you to take me there before we wed."

"I had not realized all that is Ross before we crossed it together. Our future and that of our children is tied to the land." Satisfied that all would be well, Donald lifted his betrothed's hand to his lips and pressed a kiss to the delicate skin. "Tomorrow at first light, I will leave. The months ahead will seem endless until we are together."

"For me as well." In her beautiful eyes, he saw the welling of tears.

CHAPTER 9

Red Bay Castle, the Glens of Antrim, Ulster, November 1389

FROM WHERE HE stood on the castle parapet, gazing across the blue water, John Mor could see Kintyre, a mere twelve miles away. How ironic that he was looking upon the very lands Donald had given him along with Dunyvaig Castle on Islay. Were they still his? Only that morning, his scouts had brought word Donald's forces were closing in on the Glens where John and his men had taken refuge.

Isolated from the rest of Ulster by the rocks of the Antrim Plateau in the west and a high promontory in Glenarm to the south, the Glens were thought safe from inland invasion, but they were vulnerable to galleys that could land on the many beaches of the Glens' long coast.

Word of the MacKinnon chief's fate had reached John in Antrim, causing his men to be fearful of meeting the same end. "Unless the Macdonald pardons you and spares us for your sake, we will be lost," said his friend, Archibald Boyd.

Seeing the plea in Archie's eyes, and knowing he spoke truth, John asked, "What do we know of Donald's whereabouts?"

Archie ran his hand over his dark beard. "The last we heard, the

Macdonald was on Islay at his manor at Kilcummin. It is from there his galleys have set forth in search of you."

In seeking a refuge, John had made contact with the Bissett family, allies of Clan Donald, who were long in possession of the Glens, in part owing to his father, John of Islay. They had welcomed him and put Red Bay Castle at his disposal. The castle overlooked the Irish Sea. To the north was Kintyre; to the east lay Galloway on Scotland's west coast. Since his trip to London with Donald to visit King Richard, he knew that England had interests in Ulster, and there was work for him in service to England's king should he want it—work he could have done for his brother from Dunyvaig.

Overwhelmed by regret, he wished he had never been persuaded to rebel. Donnie had always looked out for him. "My rebellion must have torn my brother apart." Realizing he had no other choice, with a last look toward Kintyre, he said, "No matter my fate, Archie, I will go."

Kilcummin, west coast of Islay, December 1389

FROM ARDTORNISH, Donald had sailed south with John MacAlister to Machir Bay and his manor on the west coast of Islay, a most beautiful place with a long white sand beach where he planned to spend the winter, receiving all who would come. Accompanying him was his physician, his chaplain and his bard.

His cousin had assured him things were stable at Iona, although they still had to contend with the abbot's two sons, and there was much to be done to restore the abbey. This they planned to discuss at some length. Winter was a time to plan.

Among those summoned to meet with Donald at Kilcummin were his captains monitoring the herring fishery in the northern Irish Sea off Ulster's coast. The fishery was thriving this year and there were profits to be made. He also wanted to meet with those engaged in the Isles' trade in smoked salmon, a lucrative business that brought them the finest claret wine from France.

For Christmas, he had invited some of the chiefs and their families. The Macduffies, the recordkeepers for the lordship, would come from Colonsay and the Macleans from Mull. His brother, Alex, had decided to spend the winter in Lochaber with his wife and newborn child and to assure the defense of his lands against the Wolf of Badenoch's caterans.

As Donald and John were lingering over a glass of claret, a letter arrived from Lachlan Maclean. Donald perused it. Cheered, he handed it to his cousin.

From Lachlan, chief of the Macleans, to Donald of Islay, Lord of the Isles,

> *I understand John MacAlister is with you on Islay. Thus, I write to you both at Kilcummin. On your behalf, John asked about the character of the two sons of the imprisoned MacKinnon abbot. The one who is prior sought to be abbot in his father's place and the other would be prior. I told John that these two walk about Iona garbed as priests but their actions are far from priestly. Now, there is proof.*
>
> *In their wickedness, they killed a son of the new MacKinnon chief who was fostering with Donald Ferguson, the grandchild of Baron Ferguson. With the help of MacKinnon, the Fergusons killed the abbot's two sons. It seems the entire family was rotten to the core.*
>
> *We stand ready to assist you and John in any way we can and look forward to being with you at Christmas.*

John raised his eyes from the parchment, his countenance paling at the news. "A sad ending to two so young."

"That may be, but their end does make our task easier," said Donald. "We will need a new abbot and a new prior. The positions are not hereditary though the MacKinnons might think so. As patron of the abbey, it is my duty to nominate who I would see in both positions. Unless we seek approval from the pope for his removal, as long as Finguine lives, though imprisoned, he remains the titular abbot. Thus, I will appoint a prior who will act as abbot." He paused to study the face of his loyal friend who took seriously his duty to God. "I can think of only one person I would have be guardian of Iona and the lordship's spiritual heritage—you."

John heaved a sigh. "I am humbled by your confidence in me. It is a trust I would never violate, but the MacKinnons will not easily give up what they have held for so long. The new MacKinnon chief will surely complain to the pope."

"Mayhap he will but without success, not after their mutinous rebellion against their lord. Now that there are two popes, one ruling from Avignon and one from Rome, they may well find sympathy from one of them, but it will not stand. I will put you forward as prior with full authority to take whatever action is required to restore the monastic revenues and buildings of Iona's abbey and worship of God in its church. I am confident the Bishop of the Isles will confirm you."

"My assessment of the abbey's books and listing of the abbey's endowed properties continues with a view toward bringing the incomes due the abbey into its coffers. If I am to be your agent in acting as the abbot, there are scores of monasteries to oversee."

"You should continue that work," said Donald. "Meantime, I will write the bishops of Glasgow and Dunkeld to make known all that has transpired and my support for you. It might be wise for me to visit Iona with you to make clear to the monks what is happening. Whenever you need me beside you, I will go." With a glance at John's plain black robe, Donald said, "As long as you are being elevated, you might add to your simple black frock."

John's brows furrowed and Donald sensed an impending storm. "I would not dress like a pope as Abbot Finguine did!"

"No, and I would not suggest it. But since Iona's abbot has been authorized to dress above other abbots, perhaps we can compromise on something in between. A sash of color, a pectoral cross?" Hearing no objection, Donald said, "The cross at least. When I am at Iona, I will have one designed that is suitably understated."

"If you insist," said his cousin, his expression telling Donald his friend was resigned to dressing in accord with his new status.

"While I am there, I must ask Iona's artisans to fashion a ring for my bride."

CHRISTMAS WAS MERE days away when Donald's guests began to arrive. Lachlan Maclean and his wife, Mary, came with their four younger sons. Their eldest son, Hector, and his wife, Anne, and their young redheaded son, Lachlan, arrived a day later from Galloway where they had been visiting Hector's father-in-law, Sir Archibald Douglas. Finally the Macduffies came on a rainy afternoon, led by their chief, Gillespie.

It was a merry group that dined together that night, warmed by the blazing fire and a good meal and entertained by Donald's talented MacMhuirich bard.

John MacAlister was congratulated by all on his new position as Iona's prior with authority to act as abbot. "At last, a worthy clergyman guarding our spiritual heritage," said Lachlan Maclean. A vigorous man, Lachlan's dark hair had gained more gray in the time since the MacKinnons' treachery, but his stance was that of a man in his youth. With his castle on Mull, where many MacKinnons lived, he had to be worried about future skirmishes.

The next day was unusually fair, the sun shining from a cloudless blue sky, though it was windy and cold. They gathered in what sufficed for a great hall, the adults sipping hot spiced wine as they shared news. Outside, wrapped in their cloaks, the children were at play when the door opened and two of Donald's guards stepped in, flanking a man Donald instantly recognized.

The room fell silent.

John Mor's face had the haggard look of the hunted, and his fair hair had grown long in the time that had passed since they were last together.

Rising from his chair, Donald waved the guards off and waited for his brother to approach. Their gazes locked as John Mor walked slowly forward. When he was close, he dropped to the floor and lay prostrate. "I beg your mercy, Brother, for my rebellion. I was wrong. Though I am undeserving, I ask for your forgiveness. Pardon me and I vow before God that I will serve you faithfully all of my days."

Donald's heart melted at the sight of his younger brother, who had been his companion in their youth, his friend before the MacKinnons led him astray. But could he trust him now? The words of John

Wycliffe came to him. *Our Lord forgives all who come to Him in faith with a repentant heart.*

He walked forward and lifted his brother from the floor. "How can I not forgive you when God has forgiven me?" He embraced his brother. "Welcome home."

Behind him, Donald heard John MacAlister say, "Blessed are the merciful...."

Tears welled in John Mor's eyes. "Thank you. I meant what I said. I will serve you all of my life and fight by your side whenever you have need of my sword." He paused and then said, "Will you spare those with me?"

Seeing his brother was anxious for his men but unable to resist a smile, Donald said, "Yes, I will spare them, but you had best bring them inside so I can have a look at the men to whom I am granting mercy."

John Mor led a score of men inside. Their deep bows and humble manner told Donald they knew the fate he was saving them from. There were a few Macleans among them. Lachlan, their chief, his brow furrowed, took them aside for stern counsel.

The others were men of an age with John Mor who had known him all their lives. "Your men can lodge with my galley crews," Donald told his brother, "though I may first have to explain the circumstances else my men kill them in the night."

Donald knew not all in the lordship would be as quick to forgive John Mor as he had. But since Mary was half-sister to them both, he was not surprised when she came forward. "'Tis past time you saw the light," she said to John Mor before taking him into her arms.

Lachlan was slower to agree, and likely felt guilty for having some of his clan in the rebellion. In the end, he said to John Mor, "We will hold you to your promise made to the Macdonald."

Hector, too, came forward to welcome the prodigal home, followed by the Macduffies who also forgave John Mor.

Their cousin, John MacAlister came up to Donald and whispered, "Only time will tell if he stays true but forgiving him is a beginning."

That afternoon, as it grew colder, the children were brought inside and gathered around the fireplace to hear a story from Donald's bard. On the other side of the great room, hot spiced wine was passed around to the adults who had gathered to hear John Mor speak of matters in Ulster.

"With the death of Hugh Bissett, Lord of the Glens," John Mor said, "King Richard gave Edmund Savage, who lives south of the Glens, the wardship of Bissett's two daughters. Their mother was an O'Neill princess. With the wardship came permission for Savage to marry them to any of the king's loyal lieges. The dowry for the eldest, Margery, will be the Glens and Rathlin Island."

"I see," said Donald, and he did. In the eyes of the others, too, there was understanding. His brother thought to gain the Glens through marriage and to serve King Richard in the process, as he had once asked of them. But not from the Isles. Now, it would be from the Glens in Ulster. "Would you still call Dunyvaig home?"

"With your permission, I would keep Dunyvaig, but I would also hope to keep Red Bay Castle in the Glens that the Bissetts have given me. There is a fine castle on Rathlin as well."

Donald nodded. He would allow his brother to follow this path while keeping an eye on him to see if he proved loyal. "'Tis a good strategy and will keep us involved in Ulster, which will please King Richard. You can serve as my agent with the English king."

"I would be happy to do so," said John Mor.

"In April," said Donald, "I would ask you to attend my wedding to Lady Mariota of Ross." A smile on his lips, Donald added, "Then perhaps my bride and I might attend your wedding, that is if you can accomplish so much in a matter of months."

John Mor smiled, the first since his repentance. "I will certainly try."

THE DAYS SINCE Mariota's return to Dingwall seemed to flee before her. Her mother had done much to prepare for the wedding, for which Mariota was most grateful. Together they assigned lodging for the expected guests and prepared menus. Now that Christmas was past and there were signs of early spring on the hillsides, they worked to refine the guest list.

"One cannot fail to invite the king," said her mother. "Though 'tis said he is ailing and is not likely to attend."

Nodding, Mariota said, "And we must invite the rest of the Stewarts, even my stepfather, the Earl of Buchan."

"We can hardly leave him out since he has formally acquiesced in the decision of the Bishops of Moray and Ross responding to my plea and restoring my rights and status as his wife and compelling him to send away his mistress. Between us, I doubt Alexander will suddenly change his behavior. I still sleep alone."

"But he gave as his sureties Alexander Moray of Culbin, the Earl of Sutherland, and Thomas Chisholm, Constable of Urquhart Castle."

"He did," said her mother. "And they must each pay the bishops two hundred pounds whenever Buchan contravenes the terms of the judgment."

"I can hear the Wolf grinding his teeth at the prospect," said Mariota. "But, as you say, we must invite him…as well as the bishops. Is the Bishop of Ross to officiate?"

"I owe the Bishop of Moray much, but this is Ross' territory."

Mariota studied the list. "There is someone who is missing, a Stewart."

"Who?"

"Donald's mother, Princess Margaret." When her mother didn't immediately respond, Mariota added, "The king's daughter?"

"Oh, yes. Margaret must be added."

Mariota added Lady Margaret Stewart to the list and marked it for a question. "She may not attend. Donald told me she is not pleased with the lands he has given his brothers. In any event, we will have hundreds coming, and she would not be the only guest who has complaints against another." Then, with a chuckle, "Should I ask Donald to bring his galloglass warriors?"

"I wager he will do that in any case," said her mother. "The Stewarts might be his kin but he is no fool to think they would welcome one so powerful as the Lord of the Isles to wed the daughter of the Earl of Ross. Buchan may have gained the lands through marriage to me, but he never gained the title."

"Since we promised Donald that we would house his Islesmen,

we must tell those we cannot accommodate they have to find lodging elsewhere."

"Doubtless they will know to do so. The more I think on it, giving Donald's guests Tulloch Castle might appeal to them."

Mariota made a note of it.

"How is your wedding gown coming?" her mother asked.

"When we finish here, you must see it," said Mariota, looking up from her list and recalling the nearly finished gown she had tried on that morning. "The ultramarine silk is so beautiful it shines with an inner light. And the trim Donald gave me fits perfectly the bodice, sleeves and hem. I do hope he likes it."

"If you are wearing it, he will like it. I think my sapphire necklace would complement the gown, but you must be the one to decide."

A week later, Mariota received a letter from Donald. She read a portion to her mother.

> There will be one more guest, a man you have yet to meet—my brother, John Mor. He came to me on Islay, prostrated himself and begged my forgiveness. Seeing he was truly repentant, I gave it. If all goes well, he will retain interests in Ulster on our behalf, for he hopes to marry the heiress of the Glens. If he does, that is a wedding you and I will attend.
>
> You will remember my cousin, John MacAlister, the priest who was with us for much of your stay in the Isles. I have made him Prior of Iona. He is a man worthy of being charged with keeping our spiritual heritage. In time, I would see him made Abbot of Iona, but that will await the death of the imprisoned MacKinnon abbot.
>
> I look forward to meeting your kinsmen in April, just after Easter.

She did not read the next part that spoke of his affection and eagerness for their marriage. His words warmed her heart. Looking up from the letter, she said, "I will have to write Donald to explain what he may face in our wedding guests. With both the bishops and my stepfather invited, not to mention the other unruly Stewart brothers, there may be an anxious crowd. I will suggest he bring his galloglass."

"*Praemonitus, praemunitus*," said her mother. "Since Lord Donald speaks Latin, he will know the expression. Being forewarned, he will doubtless be forearmed."

Dingwall Castle, Ross, mid-April 1390

DONALD GUIDED HIS horse across the wide green field dotted with yellow wildflowers toward the castle in the distance. He had been here before to greet his betrothed, but that had been in autumn. Now the countryside was alive with spring's new growth in a myriad of colors.

Above him, white clouds billowed in a blue sky, and a white-tailed eagle shrieked, calling for its mate. The air was cold but not unpleasant if one was clothed in wool and a fur-lined cloak as Donald was.

Behind him stretched a train of his people, some mounted on horseback, with several carts carrying baggage. Many had come. Whether out of curiosity or loyalty, or because they were fond of celebrations, he could not say, but he was grateful they were here. Mariota's kinsmen and the Stewarts should have a glimpse of the Islesmen, should be reminded of the proud independence of the Isles. Among them were his brothers John Mor and Alex, the latter coming with his wife, Mary Lennox, and John MacAlister, now Prior of Iona, and those chiefs and their wives closest to Donald. Also at hand were his guard, expanded for the occasion, and his chaplain and physician.

Mariota must have asked to be told when they were in sight, for she was waiting in the bailey as he entered. Dismounting, he handed the reins to a groom and stepped to her. "How are you?"

Her green-gold eyes sparkled. "Now that you are here, I am well, my lord."

Were she willing, he would have taken her into his arms and kissed her, no matter that hundreds looked on, but wanting to honor her, he took her hands in his, lifted them to his lips and kissed her knuckles. "The wedding will be soon?"

"Tomorrow. Already the guests have arrived; so many my servants have had to ward off those who would have your chambers. Thinking yours would be a large retinue, my mother has given you

Tulloch Castle. But if you like, we can accommodate you and your closest companions in Dingwall. The king, though invited, will not attend. He lies ill at Dundonald Castle, in the west. We are told he may be on his deathbed. Because of that, many of the Stewarts will leave the day after tomorrow."

"I am sorry to hear of the king's ill health. I have not seen him in recent years, but I know my grandfather was raised in that area and enlarged the castle when he took the throne. I am not surprised he would choose to end his days there."

"Your mother was invited but, since she is not here now, she may have gone straight to Dundonald hoping to see her father before he passes."

"You invited my mother?"

"I thought it best since she will soon be my mother-in-law. Besides, she has known my mother since they were girls, being nearly the same age."

Donald nodded. "A wise decision." Then offering her his arm, he said, "Come, I will introduce you to my brother, John Mor. The rest you know."

His brothers, having already dismounted, bowed to her.

"As you can see," Donald said, "we are three of a kind."

"I do see," she said. "Tall, blond and blue-eyed, and bristling with weapons."

Alex laughed.

"Our father did well to bring you so beautiful a bride," said John Mor.

ALL THREE BROTHERS had the fair looks of their mother, Princess Margaret. Mariota knew Alex to be a bold warrior, who spoke his mind. John Mor was like them but, to her eyes, lesser than Donald. Perhaps it was the mature presence of the one who carried the burden of the lordship, or the wisdom she knew he possessed, or her growing love for him. In any event, she was glad the two brothers had reconciled, though only time would tell if John Mor would be loyal.

"I am relieved you have safely arrived," she said to them.

John MacAlister, Chaplain Bean and Donald's physician, Fergus Beaton, approached with Lachlan, the Maclean chief, and his wife, Mary Macdonald, and their younger sons. Hector and his wife, Anne Douglas, were just behind them. "Welcome to Dingwall," she said to all. Looking behind them, she was puzzled. "I see the other chiefs and their wives," she said to Donald, "but where are your galloglass? After my letter, I thought you would bring many."

He raised a brow. "Do you not see them?" He turned, gesturing to a group of tall men standing to one side. "I thought it best to bring my galloglass in disguise, wearing fine tunics and carrying only swords and dirks. They left their sparth axes in the Isles."

"Clever man," she said. "Now that I look closely, I see the powerful shoulders and arms that wield those axes." Then turning to the guests he had brought, who had dismounted in the bailey, she said, "Your journey has been long. Come into the great hall where my mother, the countess, awaits with refreshments."

She did not mention that her stepfather was also in residence, albeit in a different chamber than her mother. At the moment, he was away from the castle, hunting with some of his men.

Donald escorted her toward the castle. She was happy to have him as her anchor. Followed by his companions and the Macleans, they walked past the inner gateway to Dingwall's entrance. "So, how many Stewarts are here?" he asked.

She gave him a teasing grin. "Including you and your brothers?"

He laughed. "We don't see ourselves as Stewarts as much as Islesmen. So, how many?"

"At least a dozen and their spouses, all of King Robert's legitimate sons and daughters, though some, including my stepfather, will leave soon after the wedding to attend the bedside of the king. The bishops are here, too, as well as my kinsmen and friends. Ours will be a large wedding."

THE NEXT DAY, Donald stood at the door of the chapel, watching his bride approach on the arm of her stepfather. The Wolf was a fierce-looking man with black hair and beard, and on this occasion, he was dressed like the king's son he was in rich finery. Mariota walked with grace, her head held high, the folds of her ultramarine gown shimmering in the sunlight. Silently, he thanked his father for choosing her as his life's mate, the woman who would bear his sons. John of Islay had befriended King Robert the Second before he took the throne and, setting Ranald's mother aside, married the king's daughter, Margaret. Years later, with the king's approval, John of Islay claimed Mariota as a great prize for the lordship, a great prize for his heir.

Not all of the wedding guests were smiling as he offered Mariota his hand and they turned to face Alexander de Kylwos, the Bishop of Ross who would marry them.

Though Mariota was the eldest, her brother, Alexander, would one day be Earl of Ross, following the passing of their mother, Euphemia. But if anything happened to the young Alexander, Mariota would become the Countess of Ross. Donald was certain that was the thought running through the mind of his uncle, Robert Stewart, the Earl of Fife, who stood looking on, his mien unduly serious for such an occasion.

The bishop began by speaking of the church's high regard for marriage and the sacred bond between a man and his wife, its purpose being procreation and the glory of God. Donald noted the bishop's gaze diverted once to where Alexander Stewart, Earl of Buchan, stood, making Donald think the bishop was speaking as much to Countess Euphemia's husband as he was to the couple before him.

The vows were simple and ageless. Donald promised to have and to hold Mariota and, forsaking all others, to be faithful to her until death parted them, according to God's holy ordinance. Mariota's vows were like his, but she also promised to obey.

Following the vows, the bishop called for the rings. Holding the ring he had designed with the artisans at Iona over her hand, Donald said, "In the name of the Father, and of the Son, and of the Holy Ghost, with this ring I, Donald of Islay, thee wed." He slid the ring onto the third finger of her right hand. The sapphire glistened from its gold band. He looked from the ring to her beautiful eyes.

In turn, she placed a plain golden band on the third finger of his right hand.

The Bishop of Ross then joined their right hands together. "Those whom God hath joined together let no man put asunder. For as much as Donald and Mariota have consented together in holy wedlock, have witnessed the same before God and this company, have pledged their troth each to the other, and have declared the same by giving and receiving of a ring, I pronounce they are man and wife in the name of God and our king, the protector of our people. Amen."

All were then invited into the chapel to celebrate Mass.

When that was concluded, the bishop pronounced a blessing over their union. "May God bless, preserve, and keep you; may the Lord mercifully show His favor while looking upon you, and so fill you with all spiritual benediction and grace, that you may so live together in this life, that in the world to come you may have life everlasting. Amen." To Donald he said, "You may bestow a kiss upon your bride."

It was not the kiss they had shared in the meadow. Though it was less passionate, it was all the sweeter for sealing a more permanent union.

And so it was that he and Mariota were joined for the rest of their lives. As they left the chapel, hand in hand, minstrels began to play and many guests showered them with expressions of goodwill.

CHAPTER 10

Dingwall Castle, Ross

THE WEDDING FEAST was held in Dingwall's great hall, which had been decorated with flowers, silver candlesticks, and bowls piled high with fruit set on linen tablecloths. Mariota delighted in the beauty of the scene, the glow of the candles, the smell of the flowers and the shining garments of silk and brocade worn by the guests.

Flanking the fireplace, high on the wall, hung the red and yellow banners bearing the coats of arms of the Earl of Ross and the Macdonald, Lord of the Isles, reminding all of the two great families being joined.

From the wooden gallery elevated above the chamber, minstrels played, their music lilting and lively, but not loud enough to dampen the conversations.

At the head table, Mariota sat on Donald's right with his brothers. On Donald's left were Mariota's mother and her dark, brooding husband, Alexander Stewart, the Wolf of Badenoch. Beside him was Mariota's younger brother, Alexander.

Mariota had never been happier. She had wed a man she respected, a warrior king, yes, but one who could be gentle, a man with the rare gift of knowing how to lead other men. The seeds of love had been sown, and she believed they would bloom, the love between them deepening in the years to come.

She tasted the mead wine that flowed freely, its floral scent mingling with the honey taste. For those who preferred red wine, pitchers of claret were set on every table.

One course after another was carried in on large platters by servants kept busy with so many guests. Roast beef, dressed roast fowl, trout wrapped in bacon, and savory pies were among the dishes. Between courses, a thick soup of barley and venison was served along with spiced squash, buttered carrots, and salads of spring greens, spinach, dried plums and crushed nuts. Warm bread from the ovens appeared in abundance.

"No one will leave hungry," said Donald, leaning into her. "You and the countess must have planned all winter. I congratulate you on a great success."

"It took some of winter and early spring," said Mariota. "But we enjoyed ourselves, examining all the recipes and judging them according to their merits. Of course, we had to taste what the cooks did with them." Gazing out at the guests, she said, "Everyone seems to be pleased with the smoked salmon you brought. That was very thoughtful of you." Donald had brought enough to feed everyone. It was a delicacy the Isles were known for, one that Mariota loved.

"I thought they might. It is very popular in France."

At one of the two tables set perpendicular to the head table, Donald's cousin, John MacAlister, sat between the Bishop of Moray and the Bishop of Ross. The prior and the two bishops were engaged in what looked to Mariota like a deep conversation. "The bishops seem at ease with your cousin."

"It is not difficult to be at ease with John, and I expect the bishops are eager for news of Iona."

"John MacAlister always reminds me of one of your galloglass but costumed as a priest."

Donald chuckled. "He has the body of one. Many of his relations are well-known galloglass commanders in Ireland, but he chose a different path, much to the gain of the lordship. His life's work is to keep safe our spiritual heritage."

"'Tis a worthy calling," said Mariota. Scanning the other guests, she was glad to see Hector Maclean laughing with Thomas Dunbar, the son of the Earl of Moray.

Her gaze drifted across Donald and her mother to observe her stepfather, who she had been watching off and on. He had downed several goblets of wine but, otherwise, appeared to be on his best behavior, conversing with her mother and Alexander. Often, however, the Wolf's gaze strayed to his older brother, Robert, Earl of Fife, who had taken seriously his promise to rein in his younger brother, removed him from the positions of Justiciar of the North and the Sheriff of Inverness. She wondered aloud to Donald, "Is this the calm before the storm, or is there a truce among the Stewarts?"

"A truce, if it is, will be a short one," said Donald. "Distrust hangs in the air, for Fife would gain at the expense of his brothers. It was wise of you not to seat them together. Aside from the mistrust between the king's sons, Buchan stares often at the Bishop of Moray and the Earl of Moray. One can only wonder what is in his mind."

Mariota was puzzled. "Yet he agreed to the bishop's demands as concerns my mother."

"Perhaps he did," said Donald, "but the looks he is giving the bishop tell me all is not well."

"Should we worry about him while he is here?"

"Buchan will risk nothing here. My galloglass may be in disguise but he has realized who they are. Even should he want to do something, his caterans are not here. As long as there is peace, let us enjoy it." He covered her hand with his. "We will soon leave for the Isles."

Mariota smiled at her new husband, deciding at that moment that she would not question the peace. Besides, tomorrow, most of the Stewarts would depart for Dundonald Castle.

The sweet course arrived, strawberry tarts spiced with cinnamon and ginger, sending a wonderful aroma around the hall. By the time they were licking their fingers, the guests were rising to toast the bride and groom.

Her stepfather was first to rise from his chair and lift his goblet high. If he wobbled a bit no one commented on it. "Here's to the husband and here's to the wife; may they remain lovers for life; their descendants numerous as the stars."

Mariota glanced at her mother who managed to keep her head high despite what she must have seen as veiled criticism for she had never given the Earl of Buchan an heir.

Donald's brother, Alex, stood next, raising his goblet to say, "May their joys be as deep as the ocean and their misfortunes as light as the foam. All the best for a happy life, Brother and Sister-in-law."

John Mor stood to loudly proclaim, "Hear, hear!"

More toasts followed, including many from the Isle chieftains. Mariota was thankful they did not focus on her fertility but on wishes for a good life together. Donald held her hand under the table for the whole of it.

When the toasts ended, the guests washed their hands in bowls of perfumed water, and the trestle tables were cleared and set against the walls to allow room for dancing. She and Donald had danced before at Finlaggan, so they went to each other smiling like a couple long used to each other's ways. "You are mine," he whispered in her ear.

"And you are mine," she echoed, smiling.

While the celebration was still going on, one dance ended and Donald took her hand. "Come, my love, let us sneak away while our guests are occupied."

The chamber prepared for them was bathed in candlelight, the crimson bedcovering turned down and covered with white flower petals. "Shall I call my handmaiden?" she asked.

"No," he said, looking long into her eyes. "Tonight, I will attend you and you me."

Mariota did not fear the consummation. Her mother had told her a little. The rest she had gleaned from servants or imagined. And that last glass of mead helped to soothe whatever nerves she might have had. Knowing something of Donald, she knew it would not be a rough wooing. When he quickly removed her gown, she asked, "Is that a skill you recently acquired?"

He laughed. "No and I'll say no more. Yours is the only lady's gown I shall ever loose again."

It took her a little time to reduce him to his natural state. She had only seen one dirk at his waist but she found two smaller ones hidden on his person. He drew her into his arms and kissed her. His chest was warm against her breasts, yet the touch made her shiver.

"This is only the beginning," he said. With the fire blazing in the hearth, he removed the warming pan, blew out all the candles save one, and led her to the bed.

Hours later, the fire had dwindled to glowing coals and the bedside candle burned low. Mariota ran her hand over Donald's sculpted chest. "I did not imagine your chest hair was dark red like your beard."

He picked up a stray lock of her long hair. "Nor did I imagine how glorious you would look clothed only in your golden hair."

Resting her chin on her hand that was flat against his chest, she whispered, "Thank you for your gentleness." Their coupling had been slow and sweet. He took his time, bringing them to completion together.

"I could not do otherwise with the gift God has given me."

DONALD DECIDED TO stay a few days more at Dingwall, which allowed him time with his bride before their travel. They rose late and retired early and took some meals in their chamber, for which his brothers and the Macleans, who also stayed, teased him mercilessly.

The day after the wedding, his cousin, John MacAlister, gave them his blessing and left with some of the chiefs, promising to see Donald at Ardtornish.

Donald had brought a gift for his bride, one they could enjoy together, another of Chaucer's *Canterbury Tales*, this one told by the Wife of Bath. "You will enjoy this, my love, for in it we learn what women want most."

"Being a woman, I should think I would know that," she said.

"At the end of it, you can tell me if you agree with Chaucer."

Sitting before the fire, they took turns reading to each other. Donald was not surprised when Mariota quickly became absorbed in the story. It told of a knight who defiled a maiden and escaped a judgment of death by agreeing to complete a task the queen assigned him: to discover the truth of what women really want. Having questioned many women, all with different answers, and nearly out of time, he encountered an old hag in the woods who seemed to be wise. She told him that what women want is sovereignty over their husbands. When the knight reported this back to the queen, his answer was accepted. There was more to the story, but Donald paused here in his reading to see his bride's reaction. "So? What do you think?"

She pursed her lips as if considering. "Perhaps that is true. Was that not part of the curse the Lord pronounced on Eve in the garden? Because she usurped Adam's authority by eating the fruit, she was cursed with the desire to dominate him, but he was given lordship over her."

"And yet," said Donald, "both had to learn to love each other in the roles God had given them. In other words, I must listen to you even though the final responsibility for the decision is mine."

"That seems a fair arrangement. So what happened to the knight?"

"He had made an agreement with the old hag to do as she requested if he was saved. When his answer was accepted, she asked him to marry her."

"And did he?"

"He did. The hag convinced him he had made a good bargain. Better an ugly hag who is true than a beautiful wife who is not was her reasoning." At his bride's frown, he said, "And being a witch, she then turned herself into a great beauty."

"Ha!" exclaimed Mariota. "A man writes a tale where the rogue's only punishment is to wed a beautiful woman."

Whereupon Donald picked her up and tumbled her onto the bed. "No more reading tonight."

The next afternoon, Mariota asked him for time with her ladies since she would not see them again for some while. Happy to please her, Donald went hunting for red deer with his brothers, and Hector and Callum Beg Mackintosh, Hector's good friend.

It had rained that morning, but now the sky was blue with only a few drifting clouds. They chose a likely forest in which to hunt. Red deer in Ross were numerous. Donald had brought his scent hounds with just such an activity in mind.

It was as if time had turned back to his youth when he and his brothers were free of life's burdens and had made few mistakes. Delighting in each other's company, they rode through the forest, all the while watching for deer and listening for the hounds.

Some distance on, Donald heard his hounds baying and spotted a hart dashing before them through the brush. He pursued the stag deeper into the woods.

Weaving through the trees, Donald glimpsed the stag running some distance ahead. Guiding his horse with only his knees, he lifted his bow, nocked and loosed his arrow. The hart went down in a clump of bushes. He rode over to look and was joined by the others. "Whose are the other arrows?" he asked, for three arrows were in the stag's side.

"Mine," said Alex.

"And mine," said John Mor.

"I could see it was getting crowded, or I would have loosed my own arrow," said Hector with a grin.

Callum laughed. "No matter who brought the deer down, I'll be eating my share."

THE NEXT MORNING, Mariota said a teary goodbye to her mother and the servants she had known all her life and departed for the Isles. Accompanying her was Abby, her handmaiden, who had agreed to make a new life there, and Sir Thomas, now head of her guard. Ross had been home, and she would return, but excitement filled her as she looked west to the land of her new life.

Days later, in the late afternoon, Donald's three galleys put in at Ardtornish. Mariota and Abby watched from the prow of the ship. Both women had become comfortable sailing.

Alex and his Lennox wife had returned directly to Lochaber, and the Macleans' galley had veered off at Duart Castle while Donald's galleys continued down the Sound of Mull to Ardtornish.

Anxious to get back to Margery Bissett, who he was courting, John Mor informed them he would depart for the Glens tomorrow. "With your permission," he said to Donald, "I will stop at Dunyvaig."

"Do not dally," Donald chided him, "we are anxious to meet your lady."

John MacAlister met them at the castle door. "My lady," he said bowing. And then to Donald, "You look no worse for the miles you have traveled."

"We are tired but content," said Donald, glancing at Mariota. "How are things at Iona?"

"Settling down, I am glad to say. The monks are pleased with the change. But rumor has it the MacKinnons will stir the pot on behalf of their imprisoned abbot. I can tell you more later. Cook told me supper will be ready soon."

That night as they dined together, John MacAlister, with a somber expression, said, "There is news from Dundonald I have withheld until now."

Mariota feared the words he would next say.

"King Robert has died at Dundonald Castle. His eldest son, John, Earl of Carrick, has ascended to the throne, but not as 'John' for the name, as you know, raises bad memories for Scots since it was the name of King John Balliol, the discredited choice of Edward I. To be better remembered, John took the name Robert III."

"I imagine his younger brother, Robert, Earl of Fife, did not approve, given his ambitions," said Donald.

"I do not doubt he thought to reserve that title for himself," said John MacAlister, "though he is not in the direct line of succession. That would go to the king's young son, David."

The death of the king and his eldest son's ascension to the throne, though expected, made for a subdued evening. "What will it mean for the relationship between the Stewart brothers?" she asked.

"Only time will tell," said Donald, "though a weak king is no match for the Earl of Fife. I must ask Alex how things fare in Lochaber."

The next day, with a smile on his face and amid shouts of "Godspeed", John Mor sailed for Dunyvaig and the Glens of Antrim.

The month of May, now upon them, brought warmer, sunnier days. Mariota went riding each morning with Sir Thomas and sometimes, when his business allowed, with Donald.

"I want to visit Iona with John," he told her one morning. "You are welcome to come."

"If you agree," she said, "I might stay at Ardtornish this time to become familiar with the castle and the people."

"If it pleases you, my love, stay. I will only be gone a few days."

UPON HIS RETURN to Ardtornish, Donald found Alex waiting for him, having arrived only that morning from Lochaber. "You wear a solemn expression, Brother," he said to Alex. "Come inside where I would hear your news."

As they walked up the promontory to the castle, Alex asked, "Where is our new prior?"

"He wanted to stay at Iona for a brief while. I have put a galley at his disposal since he has many churches to see to in the lordship."

At the door, Donald was greeted by his wife with a kiss on his cheek. "I missed you, my lord."

"And I you," he said. "Alex has news we'd best hear. By the look of him, it is not good."

Inside, refreshed with a tankard of ale, Donald prepared himself for what Alex had to say.

"It seems Buchan's acquiescence was a mere pretense, and neither the bishops' decree nor the risk of pecuniary loss to his friends gave him any concern." With a glance toward Mariota, Alex said, "He not only failed to dismiss his mistress and act honorably toward your mother, Countess Euphemia, but when the Earl of Moray rode south for a tournament, in a spirit of revenge against Alexander Bur, Bishop of Moray, the Wolf descended on Moray with his caterans. He sacked the town of Forres and then headed east to Pluscarden Abbey, where he set the abbey ablaze."

Donald shook his head. "And his brother, Robert III, is not even crowned."

Mariota stopped eating and furrowed her brow. "I hope my mother is not in danger."

"No," Alex assured her, "he seeks vengeance against the church, not your mother. And some of this might be a rebellion against his brother, the Earl of Fife, who took from Buchan positions that brought him status. After all, Moray was once his to defend. Now that his father is dead, he may feel free to pursue his own interests."

"A war on the church cannot be won," said Donald. "That is fool-hardy."

A month later, in late June, a letter arrived from Countess Euphemia, attesting to all that Alex had told Donald earlier. By this time, Alex was on the lordship's business in Lochaber and John MacAlister had joined Donald at Ardtornish.

Mariota read the letter in their presence. She raised her head from the parchment and looked at Donald. "I now realize why Buchan was glaring at the Bishop of Moray at our wedding. Aside from the humiliation at being called to account for his treatment of my mother, when his brother, the Earl of Fife, removed him from his position as Sheriff of Inverness, the bishop entered into an agreement with John Dunbar, Earl of Moray, to defend the bishop's possessions. Buchan was not having either that or the bishop's judgment in favor of my mother."

Again reading, she said, "After he destroyed Pluscarden Abbey, he rode east with his sons and his caterans to Elgin where they burned much of the town, including the monastery of the Greyfriars, St. Giles parish church and the Hospital of Maison Dieu." Raising her gaze from the letter, she said, "As if that were not enough, he destroyed Elgin Cathedral."

"Elgin!" said Donald, shocked. "I cannot imagine such a great loss for Christendom."

John appeared as stunned as Donald. "Elgin's cathedral, the Lantern of the North, was the most beautiful in the kingdom, a place where God was properly worshipped, not to mention its high bell towers, its venerable furnishings and uncountable jewels."

From Mariota's expression, Donald anticipated what she would say next. "My mother says the Bishop of Moray has pronounced the sentence of excommunication against Buchan."

"The ultimate punishment," said John, "for it reaches beyond the grave. Unless it is lifted, Buchan will die in his sins."

Mariota read more from the letter. "'Tis said the monk who came to Lochindorb Castle to inform Buchan of his excommunication was thrown into the castle's water pit vault."

"You see," said John, "he has no respect for the church."

Mariota continued, "The bishop has said he will only lift the edict on excommunication if Buchan seeks absolution in front of the high altar in Perth in the presence of the king and the Earl of Fife and the council-general, and pays for all the damage he has caused in Moray. The bishop has also written the king, asking for help redressing his brother's evil deeds. In turn, the king has called upon Buchan to do penance and pay significant amounts. Only then will he pardon his brother."

"The Wolf of Badenoch will pay for more than the damage he has caused," said John. "He will pay the price of public humiliation, for all of Christendom will know of his perfidy, since the pope must agree to lift the edict."

"Should we pity him?" asked Mariota, setting down the letter. "After all, he could not marry his mistress, the one woman he may have loved. All his children are bastards. Mayhap he only married my mother because his father, the king, demanded it. He was treated badly by his older brother, and has lost the father who favored him. If, as I suspect, my mother will press her case with the pope to end their marriage, he will also lose Ross."

Donald smiled at his tenderhearted wife. "He is undeserving of your pity, my love. He has squandered his royal lineage. Many of his losses are the result of his bad choices and ruthless acts of vengeance. His raid on Elgin was a grave mistake. Moreover, he allowed his marriage to your mother to collapse and, for that, as you point out, he will doubtless lose the largest earldom in Scotland."

"I suppose you are right," said Mariota. "That is the sad truth of it."

Donald was not so concerned about Buchan. The church would deal with him. But there was Ross to consider. If Buchan lost the earldom, Mariota's brother, Alexander, was of key importance. "With a weak King Robert III and an ambitious Earl of Fife, who is really the one ruling Scotland, we must keep our eyes on your brother and Ross."

Mariota sighed, nodding.

"Have you considered," said John, addressing Mariota, "your father's willingness to contract with John of Islay for your marriage to Donald may reflect Ross' opposition to your stepfather, the Earl of Buchan? After all, he has no kinship within the earldom and he was no great lord there."

"That may be," said Mariota. "Even before my marriage to Donald, the ties to the Macdonalds of the Isles were strong in Ross. And it is the Ross kindred with whom my family identifies in our names. My brother is called Alexander Ross, not often Alexander Leslie, and I am Mariota of Ross, Lady of the Isles."

Donald was pleased to be reminded of his family's ties to Ross that the Earl of Buchan and his Stewart brothers lacked.

John said, "Now that Buchan's position is weakened, Dunbar will be looking for help in protecting Moray. What about Alex? It would put him on Ross' eastern boundary."

"Such a role would appeal to him," said Donald. "When Buchan gained lands at the head of Loch Ness from John Dunbar, the Earl of Moray, we were concerned the Wolf threatened the Great Glen. This would allow Alex to keep his eyes well beyond the shores of Loch Ness. I will encourage him to pursue it."

IT WAS HIGH summer when Donald received an invitation to John Mor's wedding that would take place in the Glens. With the approval of Edmund Savage, pursuant to the prior permission of King Richard of England, Margery Bissett would become John Mor's bride. Donald considered it a good match for both.

"The Macdonalds will gain a stronger hold on lands in Ireland," he told Mariota, "and John Mor will eventually gain the title Lord of the Glens. Too, Margery and the Savages will find greater security in an alliance with the family of the Lord of the Isles."

"The marriage should please King Richard," said Mariota, as they discussed it over dinner.

"It will, as he hopes to secure his personal rule in Ulster and re-build English power in the area. Richard is well aware of the military might of the Isles, which he may need to secure his hold. We already safeguard trade routes and check Scottish expansion in the northern Irish Sea."

"Have you met with King Richard since you were last in London?" she asked.

"No, but my half-brother, Godfrey of Uist, and I are in negotiations with King Richard through the Bishop of Sodor."

"Your reach is far," said Mariota.

"It needs to be with the Stewarts at our backs. They are allied with the O'Donnells in western Ulster against the English. This marriage will allow us to strengthen our ties with King Richard, and with the O'Neills of Tyrone against the O'Donnells. Thus, I hope to maintain some balance at least."

"It always amuses me that you do not think of yourself as a Stewart."

"Can you think why I should want to separate myself and my clan from that family?"

"Well, yes, I can."

Changing the subject, he asked, "Are you looking forward to John Mor's wedding?"

"I am," she said with a sparkle in her eyes. "I have never been to Ireland. Have you?"

"Several times with my father. It is beautiful, particularly the Glens where we will be. Since it is summer, we should have some glorious days. We will stop for a few days at Kilcummin on Islay, my manor you have yet to see, and then go on to Red Bay Castle on the east coast of the Glens. Does that appeal?"

"It does," she said with enthusiasm.

"My brother, Alex, and Prior John will go with us, and before we leave Ardtornish, the Macleans will be crossing the sound to visit. I have been considering making Lachlan Maclean the steward of our household. What do you think?"

"From all I have seen, the Maclean chief is a good administrator. To name him your steward would please him, I think."

"Good. We are of one mind."

CHAPTER 11

BY THE TIME they sailed for Ireland, Mariota was almost certain she was with child. Though she wanted to share her joy with Donald, she delayed telling him after Alex arrived at Ardtornish and explained that his wife, Mary Lennox, would not be coming with them because she was pregnant. Mariota's only symptom was a queasy stomach in the afternoon, which she had solved by nibbling on bread. Still, she was glad Donald's physician always sailed with them. Abby knew Mariota's secret and had sworn to say nothing.

At Machir Bay on Islay's west coast, they spent a few days at Donald's manor at Kilcummin. Those days were among Mariota's happiest. Unfettered from the lordship's business for most of the time, Donald was free to enjoy her own company and that of Alex and John. Even Abby was glad they had come despite a brief period of rough water as they sailed south.

The fair weather held, allowing Mariota and Donald to spend much time outside, walking on the white sand beach at Machir Bay and admiring the waves rushing to shore, not present on the Isles' eastern shores. Often, Alex and Prior John were with them.

With the cool breeze off the sea, they were seldom plagued by midges. In the evenings, they watched the sun making its glorious descent into the sea, leaving a golden sky that lingered with the long days. Only then would she don a wool cloak for warmth.

As they dined that first day, they discussed the news. Alex said, "Buchan prostrated himself before the altar in Perth, seeking forgiveness and has been pardoned. With the infusion of Stewart money, Bishop Alexander Bur has begun rebuilding Elgin Cathedral."

"So, the Wolf has mended his ways?" asked John.

"He has ended his violent raids," said Alex, "but his sons have not. His eldest, also named Alexander Stewart, who rode with him to destroy Elgin Cathedral, is as bad as his father and continues to raid with the caterans."

"Now that Buchan is no longer the Sheriff of Inverness," said Donald, "the Earl of Moray will be wanting help with the defense of his lands. You might consider making him an offer."

Nodding, Alex said, "A good thought. 'Twould keep my men busy and for coin. I will call upon him when I return to Lochaber."

Curious about who she might meet in Ireland, Mariota asked, "Who might attend John Mor's wedding to the Bissett heiress?"

"Some of my kin," said John. "The Clan Alexander galloglasses who serve Niall Mor O'Neill, King of Tirowen."

"Yes, the O'Neills will be there," put in Donald. "Niall, King of Tirowen, and Murtagh O'Neill, King of Clandeboye in Antrim, are closely allied with each other and with King Richard. Their eldest sons may be with them. Then there is my sister, Christiana, who married Robert Savage of Ardkeen, nephew of Edmund Savage, Seneschal of Ulster and Margery's guardian."

"The Savages are strong supporters of England's king," said Alex.

"And here I thought we were just attending a family wedding," said Mariota, amused. "I can see it is to be far more."

"Surely by now you realize," said Alex, "Donnie always has more than one reason for what he does." Shooting a glance at Donald, he added, "I would not be surprised to learn he had a hand in our sister Christiana's marriage to Robert Savage."

Mariota knew her husband of mere months was a man who

thought deeply. In reply to Alex, he said only, "It is important we strengthen our ties to the Ulster lords and to King Richard. With John Mor's marriage, as well as Christiana's, we will confirm significant alliances, especially since it is known the Macdonalds are allies of England's king. In choosing Margery Bissett as his bride, our brother has made a wise decision. She is of noble and ancient stock; her family came to England with the Conqueror. Later, they removed to Scotland, and from there to the Glens. Her mother, Sabia, was the revered daughter of Hugh O'Neill, and married the MacEoin Bissett, Lord of the Glens."

"Sabia O'Neill was said to be a woman of great beauty," offered Alex.

"Ah," said Mariota. "A beauty who brings to her marriage both lands and a title. No wonder John Mor set his sights on her."

The next day, they went together to the stone church at Kilcummin to worship. A beautiful carved stone cross depicting Jesus on the cross circled by angels stood outside the church. She had only observed it from afar until now. "It reminds me of those at Iona," she said.

"It is the same workmanship," said Prior John. "Iona is home to worthy artisans. Donald had one of them make your wedding ring."

Mariota glanced first at Donald and then considered the blue sapphire on the golden band circling her finger. It was one of the most beautiful rings she had ever seen. "My husband has excellent taste."

"The ring was destined for a worthy bride," said Donald. Then, turning to the cross, he said, "The Macdonald chiefs who came before me installed the cross as they built the church. Angus Mor, my great-grandfather, who was Lord of the Isles, loved this place."

Mariota loved Kilcummin, too, and considered the manor house more livable in some ways than Ardtornish Castle. For one thing, it had fewer levels and, thus, fewer stairs. The chambers were designed for entertaining on a smaller scale. The ocean was at their door and a beautiful church nearby. But, mostly, it was the place itself, as God made it. "I can see why you love it here, the smell of the sea, the sound of the waves and its isolated location."

"Then we will come often," said Donald, taking her hand.

Their last morning at Kilcummin, walking on the beach with Abby, Mariota placed her hand on her still flat belly and said, "I can see my children playing on this beach."

"I will pray your firstborn is a son," said her handmaiden. "That would make your lord happy."

Mariota's attention was diverted just then to a peregrine falcon soaring overhead as he hunted for prey. She watched it arc through the sky until it was out of sight. Birds of all kinds frequented the dunes and shore, among them gannets, black choughs, and guillemots with their young. But Mariota's favorites were the peregrines. "The peregrines remind me of Ross," she told Abby.

"Do you miss home?" Abby asked, giving her a probing glance.

"Sometimes. More, I miss my mother, especially now that I am with child."

Shortly thereafter, they left Kilcummin and sailed southeast to the Glens of Antrim on Ulster's east coast to arrive at Red Bay Castle in Glenariff.

When the galley was beached, Donald helped Mariota and Abby to the sand.

Looking up at the green tree-covered cliffs, Prior John said, "Many consider Glenariff to be the most splendid of all the seven glens."

Mariota had watched closely the coast as they sailed south along the Glens and had seen the stone castle that was Red Bay rising from the peak overlooking the Irish Sea. "What I have seen is lush and green."

"You have yet to see the waterfalls," said Prior John. "Some are magnificent."

John Mor warmly greeted them as they climbed to the castle door.

Mariota asked him, "Is this where you will live with your new bride?"

"Part of the time, yes," he said, "when my business in Ireland requires. The Bissetts have been generous. But often, we will be at Dunyvaig on Islay or one of the castles on Kintyre, where I can better serve Donald and the lordship."

It pleased Mariota to see the brothers were truly reconciled, their manner with each other amenable, as though the rebellion had never occurred. That night, as she and Donald lay in bed, Mariota asked Donald about the reconciliation.

"John Mor has learned his lesson," he said. "Besides, with Margery, he will have the kingdom he wanted, both his inheritance in the Isles and, eventually, a lordship in the Glens. It will be the beginning of a new dynasty."

As it turned out, Mariota did not get to see the waterfalls, for they spent only one night at Red Bay Castle. John Mor was anxious to sail south to County Down and the Ards peninsula where his bride was waiting.

"Ardkeen Castle is the seat of the Savages," John Mor explained as they broke their fast the next morning. "A day's sail will bring us to the peninsula jutting into Strangford Lough in the Ards. That is the location of Castle Hill, our destination, which is protected on three sides by the sea."

What surprised Mariota when they arrived was not the well-fortified camp or the stone tower house rising from Castle Hill where the Savages resided, or even the stone church standing a small distance away. Rather, it was the beautiful vistas she could see all around them and the extensive pastures behind the castle where the Savages kept their cattle.

"It is all very convenient," she remarked to Donald, as he took her hand and led her toward the castle.

"And very secure," he replied.

"'TIS THE MACDONALD with his new bride!" shouted Niall Mor. Donald recognized his friend, the aging ginger-haired King of Tirowen, and waved.

"Later, O'Neill!" Donald shouted, as he and his party continued striding toward the castle. With every step, his spirit settled within him, for he was among friends, which made this reunion of sorts a joyous occasion. It was not just because they were here to celebrate his brother's wedding. The Macdonald ties to Ulster and the Irish people went back generations. His ancestor, Somerled, who was truly the first Lord of the Isles, had roots in Antrim; his grandfather, Angus Og had fought with Irish lords and married an Irish princess; and Donald's father, John of Islay, had been deeply involved in Ulster matters. Donald turned to Mariota, walking by his side. "I promise to introduce you to everyone I know, but first, we must greet our host."

The beaches that graced the peninsula's shores were lined with galleys flying pennons Donald recognized. On the shores and around the castle, tents rose from the grass. The tents would accommodate the guests and their retainers that would not be housed in the castle. Temporary stables had been set up for the horses belonging to those who had ridden here, for it was possible to do so. Above all, the sun poured its light on the gathered crowds. Everywhere, the Irish smiled at them and waved before turning back to their conversations.

Already, music filled the air, the lilting sound of harp, whistle and stringed timpan.

Walking on the other side of Mariota, John Mor said to her, "Each Irish chieftain as well as the Anglo-Irish lords will have brought their bards, minstrels and timpanists with many instruments." Pointing to one bard, he said, "The chief bards wear the blue caps with the golden crescent and tunics of bright colors. Carrol Mor O'Daly from Meath, the chief composer of Ireland, is an invited guest."

Donald could see his bride was delighted. "This place," she said, "the happy faces and the gaiety remind me of Finlaggan."

Donald nodded his agreement. "The atmosphere is much like what you experienced there, though the Irish might dress a bit differently and speak with a regional tongue, they are close to us, often kin." As they neared the castle door, he said, "I imagine we will dine in the hall with most of the guests, but there will be cookfires outside for guards, retainers, galley crews and servants. The evening fires will encourage storytelling and dancing. The celebration is likely to continue for days." Donald did not see young children among those standing around but there were wives and older sons and daughters.

John Mor led the way to the castle entrance where Edmund Savage in dark blue flowing velvet greeted them with great fanfare. "Hail! The bridegroom comes with his illustrious brother!"

"Greetings," said Donald, removing his bycocket hat and shaking Lord Savage's offered hand. Introducing their host to his bride, he presented her as "Mariota of Ross, who since April is my wife and the Lady of the Isles."

The aging, gray-haired Edmund Savage, who held the important position of Seneschal of Ulster and, formerly, the Constable of Carrickfergus Castle, was a gentleman of great prominence. He bowed over her hand. "My lady, we are pleased to receive you at Ardkeen." Then with a smile, he added, "And glad to see the Macdonald has finally taken a bride!"

John Mor greeted their host with the enthusiasm of one soon to be his son-in-law, and then introduced their brother. "Alex is Lord of Lochaber, our younger brother."

The designation "younger" brought a smile to Alex's face at the teasing tone of John Mor's words.

"Anyone can see that Lord Alexander is a Macdonald," said Lord Savage. "The same blue eyes, the same fair hair, though yours, Lord Alexander, is nearly white." It was true; Alex had always been the fairest among them, a striking contrast with his skin bronzed from the sun.

Donald then introduced his cousin. "Allow me to present John MacAlister of Clan Alexander, my cousin, my good friend and the Prior of Iona. At my request, he has undertaken the duties of abbot, though I imagine you know of him and his galloglass kin."

"Indeed, I do. You are most welcome, Prior John. We in the Ards have heard about Iona's respected new churchman. There are many of your kin here." With a smile, he added, "They are the large, well-armed ones who came with the O'Neills."

John chuckled in his good-natured way. Gesturing to his black robe, he said, "As you have recognized, I wear a different garb."

At Donald's instruction, his own guard of galloglass warriors stood a ways off, watching. With them was Sir Thomas. They would join him and Mariota later.

"Wine and food, should you have a thirst or hunger," said Lord Savage, "are set out on tables in the hall for any who want them. My nephew, Robert, and his wife Christiana, are in the great hall. Should you desire rest, my servants can show you to your chambers." To John Mor, he said, "Margery is with her sister, Elizabeth, and her ladies, preparing for the wedding tomorrow, but she will join us for supper."

MARIOTA PAUSED, ALLOWING her eyes to adjust to the dim light inside the castle where all was decorated for the festivities. Flowers in abundance graced the tables, the mantel and the side tables. A garland of yellow and white blossoms wound its way up the stairs. The flowers' scent changed what might have been a musty hall into a fragrant garden-like atmosphere.

A servant brought them wine. Mariota's throat was dry so she gladly accepted the goblet of claret and reached for a crust of bread. A woman with hair fairer than Mariota's waved to Donald and crossed the hall to them. "Brother! It has been overlong."

Donald kissed her cheek. "It has. Meet my lady wife, Mariota of Ross."

Christiana had the happy expression of a young woman who was well-loved. "It is good to meet you, Lady Mariota. My new sister!"

Mariota took an instant like to Donald's younger sibling.

"How are you faring in Ulster?" Donald asked her.

"I am well," she said, "happy that the women here do not wear wimples, well, except for rare occasions. And pleased to tell you I am with child. Robert is delighted."

Donald looked behind her. "I imagine he is. Where is that husband of yours?"

Christiana turned to look over her shoulder. "In front of the fireplace, talking to the young Sir Roger." To Mariota, Christiana said, "Sir Roger Mortimer, Earl of March and Ulster, is King Richard's heir presumptive, recently knighted. He is the closest noble to King Richard of those here. The Savages are honored he made time to attend."

Not long after, they were shown to their chamber which was well-appointed and warm with a fire recently tended. Donald traveled with a manservant, but he dismissed him at the door. Miraculously, their baggage was waiting for them at the end of the bed, a four-poster with heavy velvet curtains. "Abby has been here," said Mariota, noticing the bedcover turned down and her things set out.

"Shall I help you undress?" Donald asked, his smile wry, his blue gaze intense.

"You are getting very good at it."

When she was down to her chemise, he placed his hands on her shoulders and looked long into her eyes. "My beautiful wife, when were you planning to tell me you are expecting our first child?"

Mariota felt her cheeks heat. Her eyes downcast, she said, "I was afraid you would make me stay home, and I so wanted to come."

He raised her chin with his finger. "I might have done so were you ready to give birth, but these are early days and it is summer. Your body has begun to change and, knowing my wife, I did not miss the signs."

"Then it is all right I came along?"

"I would not have left you behind."

"And you are happy at my news?"

His smile was wide. "Very happy."

An hour passed before they washed and donned fresh clothing. Mariota decided on an emerald silk gown with seed pearl trim that Donald favored because he said it brought out the green in her eyes. For his part, Donald wore a fine woolen tunic of deep crimson. His gilded belt and the gold brooch that secured his cloak at his shoulder made him look every bit the lord he was.

BY THE TIME they entered the great hall, the crowd had moved inside, attired for the evening. Seeing John Mor speaking with Alex and two young women, Donald led Mariota to them. He was certain the women were the Bissett sisters.

"Finally, Brother, you have come from your chamber!" exclaimed John Mor. "Margery was beginning to doubt your existence."

"We must apologize for being late."

"With so beautiful a lady wife," said the one Donald assumed was Margery, "one cannot question your wanting to be alone."

John Mor said, "Allow me to introduce you and Lady Mariota to my betrothed, Margery, and her sister, Elizabeth."

Both girls smiled. Donald inclined his head to them. They were attractive young women, their smiles sincere and their manner utterly charming. It seemed John Mor was gaining more than land and a title. For those, his brother would have taken any young woman to wife but here was a jewel.

Margery said, "I have heard much about you from John, my lord. I would have recognized you and Lord Alexander, whom I just met, as his brothers anywhere."

Margery was full of news for the ceremony the next day. "John Ross, the Bishop of Down will officiate," she told them, "and Ireland's famous bard, O'Daly, will entertain at the feast."

Donald's sister, Christiana, joined them. She wanted to hear more about Carrol Mor O'Daly. "Has he written something just for your marriage?" she asked Margery.

"I am told so," said the young woman.

After some talk of the coming ceremony, Donald left Mariota with his sister Christiana, who wanted to introduce her to the other women, while he and Alex went to speak to Donald's guard and the captain of his crew. That done, he invited Sir Thomas to stay close as the evening wore on. "I do not worry for our safety, as we are among friends, but you are an English knight and your place is here in the hall."

Alex said to Sir Thomas, "King Richard has many friends in this gathering, and they will be glad to see an English knight serving the Lord of the Isles."

Donald had much to discuss with the Irish nobles who had come to Ardkeen. And so, taking Alex with him, he ventured into the crowd. Among the issues he wanted to discuss was the herring fishery in the northern Irish Sea, which had done very well this last year. Also of importance was his monitoring of the waters between Scotland and Ireland at King Richard's request to keep the area free for trade. The Stewarts' alliance with the O'Donnells that could interfere with that and many other things was a concern, especially to the O'Neills of Tirowen. The O'Donnells, it seemed, were building a strong alliance of their own in western Ulster. Donald assured the nobles that the Macdonald lordship was strong and its fleet of ships could be counted upon in times of war.

Later, he reclaimed his wife who was still with Christiana. "By the by," he asked his sister, "is Mother still angry with me at my distribution of lands to my brothers?"

"You won't like my answer, Donnie. Mother is still upset, particularly about the Kintyre lands you gave to John Mor. The last time I spoke with her, she had complained to the king and he has ordered our uncle, the Earl of Fife, to take her under his protection."

Donald shared a frown with Alex. "The last person I would want involved in my affairs."

"What will you do if he comes after you on Mother's behalf?"

"Ignore him, I expect. Our mother has no room to complain. She is well taken care of and she knows the lands are mine to dispense to my brothers as the Macdonald chief."

"We have our own squabbles in Ulster," said his sister, "but at the moment, they are not as threatening as those you face in Scotland."

"At least we have King Richard's favor, as he is eager for our friendship to protect his Earldom of Ulster," he reminded her.

"Another reason the closer alliance with the Savages is important," said Alex, who Donald observed had been listening closely.

"Which is doubtless why Lord Savage arranged my marriage," said Christiana.

Donald explained, "Following the ratification of your marriage to Robert by the council at Westminster, John, Bishop of Sodor, was dispatched to the Isles to negotiate an alliance with me and our half-brother, Godfrey of Uist."

"I did not realize that," said Christiana.

A half-smile played about Donald's lips. "It is all part of a grand plan in which we each play our part."

MARIOTA WAS introduced to many of the Irish noblewomen, as well as a few of their husbands. All had been gracious to welcome her. Christiana appeared to be much loved, but the names, new to

Mariota, were now a blur and weariness was setting in.

"They will soon set up the tables for supper," said Donald. "Would you like to take a walk outside?"

"I would like that very much," she said, the thought of fresh air appealing.

"Perhaps I might find my husband." said the fair Christiana, looking around them, "and pry him from his business long enough to do the same." She walked off toward a group of men.

"I will see you at the evening meal," Alex told them and headed to where Prior John was speaking with a group of men who looked to be galloglass by their powerful bodies and warrior-like dress. But for his black robes, John could have been one of them.

Taking Donald's arm, Mariota strolled outside. The breeze had increased, and the late afternoon light had mellowed. Mariota briefly studied her husband's face. Today, it was clear of any cloud of worry. "You are happy here."

Donald took a deep breath and let it out, staring beyond Castle Hill to the waters that circled the peninsula. "I suppose I am. It feels like coming home after a long absence. Not home really, but something much deeper. It pleases me we are well received and the lordship desired as an ally and a friend. There may come a time when we will need their support and they will need ours. Lacking strong ties to the Stewarts, notwithstanding his marriage to Princess Margaret, my father bound us to England. I have followed in his footsteps with no regret, believing it is our best course."

"And England's king has welcomed you as a brother."

"I am not so naïve as to think he does so out of his generosity. He sees the English fleeing the Earldom of Ulster in the face of the bold Irish lords, and he wants to secure his lordship. Together with the O'Neills and the Savages, we are his security."

Sir Thomas came to get them. "My lord, they are sitting down to eat."

"Very well," said Donald. Then offering her his arm, he smiled. "You must be tired of nibbling on bread."

THE NEXT MORNING, the wedding took place before John Ross, the Bishop of Down, at the door of St. Mary's Church near the castle. Mariota had learned from Donald it was to be a very Irish affair that was not unlike their own wedding with solemn vows, followed by a celebration of Mass, feasting, music and dancing but with the addition of Irish music and an Irish bard.

She and Donald gathered with the other guests around St. Mary's to welcome the newly wedded couple. The Irish had dressed in their silks, satins and fine woolens in bright colors of emerald, deep blue, madder, gold and russet trimmed in Celtic braid.

The bride wore an azure blue silk gown with a golden braid trim. On her head was a circlet of gold carved with vines from which a transparent veil flowed down her back like a waterfall over her long blonde hair.

Mariota thought the occasion worthy of wearing her gown of ultramarine blue silk which she loved. With it, she wore the sapphire necklace her mother had given her on her own wedding day. She received many compliments on both.

The first things that drew Mariota's attention as they entered the hall were the large sugar sculptures of galleys with furled sails, called subtleties, set in the center of each table in honor—so said their host Edmund Savage—of the groom and his family of Macdonalds.

At the feast, they were seated with Robert Savage and his wife, Christiana, Prior John and Donald's brother, Alex. The O'Neill kings and their wives sat across from them, jovial and obviously pleased at the Macdonald's presence. Mariota observed these aging ginger-haired O'Neills were proud men with a strength derived, she supposed, from their heritage where only the strongest survived, for they were constantly at war.

Servants filed in carrying platters laden with roast beef, fish cooked in herbed sauce and roast duck in honeyed wine sauce. Savories, vegetables and rounded custard cream tarts, yellow with saffron, accompanied them.

Minstrels played the harp and lute while the eating went on. At the end of the meal, Ireland's renowned bard, Carrol O'Daly, came forward to sit on a stool and read verses he had written for the occasion.

His voice, accompanied by a harpist, was soothing, even mesmerizing, as he told the tale of a lass named Eileen Aroon in rhyming verses. Mariota was enthralled as he spoke of a young woman who was "the fairest gem", dearest, not for her beauty or sweet charms, which she possessed in abundance, but for her constancy. The poem ended with a refrain Mariota would not soon forget.

Youth will in time decay.
Beauty must fade away.
Castles are sacked in war, chieftains are scattered far.
Truth is a fixed star, Eileen Aroon.

When the bard read the last line, silence hung in the air for a moment and then loud applause erupted. O'Daly rolled up the parchment he had been reading from and, tying it with a ribbon, he rose to bow before the bride and groom, presenting the small scroll to Margery Bissett, now John Mor's wife.

A day later, Mariota and Donald returned to Islay and Kilcummin where the newly married couple would, after some time, join them.

CHAPTER 12

Dingwall Castle, Ross, January 1391

MARIOTA'S FIRST CHILD, a boy she and Donald named Alexander, was born at Dingwall Castle as the year turned. Destined to be his father's heir, "Sandy", as they called him, was the joy of his parents and both his uncles for whom he was named. His head was covered in a pale blond down and his eyes were blue, but then most newborn babies' eyes were.

With Donald so frequently away attending to the business of the Isles, Mariota had wanted to be at Dingwall for the birth in order to have her mother at her side. Donald consented, so they went to Ross before Martinmas and stayed through Christmastide. Just after the babe's birth on Twelfth Night, Donald's brother, Alex, traveled from Lochaber to join them.

Snow blanketed the hills and a sharp wind, whistling around the castle's stone walls, could be heard though the windows. But inside, fires and braziers kept away the chill. Candles and torches set in sconces illuminated the tapestries and the seasonal evergreens that still decorated the hall. Mariota wore her heaviest gowns and often her fur-lined cloak.

"What are Lord Donald and his brother up to in Moray?" asked her mother the morning the two men rode out with Donald's guard. The two women were sitting before the fire in the great hall, an open book in her mother's lap.

At Mariota's feet, she rocked the cradle in which her newborn son slept. "They have business with John Dunbar, the Earl of Moray, and his son Thomas. Now that the Bishop of Moray and the Dunbars must look elsewhere for protection, Buchan being deprived of that role, Alex will offer his services."

"To protect Moray from Buchan's caterans?"

"As I understand it, the caterans are now led by Buchan's eldest natural son, also named Alexander Stewart. It seems he has inherited the vices of his father, raiding and murdering indiscriminately."

"The Earl of Moray must consider Buchan and his sons to be outlaws. Which reminds me, Buchan's brother, Robert Stewart, Earl of Fife, has encouraged me to pursue a divorce."

"About time," said Mariota. "Having ignored his vows to the bishop, what alternative are you left with?"

"None, really. Besides, it is in the interest of your brother that the earldom be free of that man. With Fife's help, I have appealed to the papal court at Avignon, stating my case that Buchan has caused wars, plundering, arson and murders, not to mention his infidelity. Though I thought of a divorce, since our union has produced no offspring, it is possible the pope will grant an annulment."

"Fife may be helping you now," said Mariota, "and doubtless Buchan deserves what he gets, but Donald is wary of Fife. He may be the king's brother but he is willing, if not eager, to gain greater authority at others' expense, including that of his own family."

"Some members of the Leslie family in the earldom are also wary of Fife," said the countess, "in particular William, Lord of Balnagowan, and my cousin, Hugh Munro, Baron of Foulis, a man of formidable power. They prefer to be allied with the Lord of the Isles. And while I must strengthen our local ties for the sake of your brother's one day claiming the title Earl of Ross, it would be unwise to turn away Fife's help in procuring my freedom from his brother."

Mariota lifted the cloth that hung over the cradle handle to confirm her infant son still slept. His face, aglow from the firelight, was that of a cherub, his tiny fist under his chin. Already, he had the look of his father. Restoring the cloth, she said, "I am beginning to understand how precarious is the position of Ross. You are wedged between Clan Donald in the west, the Earl of Buchan in the east and the Stewart lords, headed by King Robert and his brother the Earl of Fife, in the middle. It is a complicated game, and you play it well." Indeed, Mariota admired her mother's astute dealings with their family as well as the Stewarts, few of whom could be trusted.

"Did Lord Donald say when he would return?" asked her mother.

"A week perhaps, depending on the weather. They planned to overnight in Inverness before riding on to Darnaway Castle in Forres."

Mariota's mother sat back, staring into the fire. "John Dunbar has had the earldom since the year after he married Marjorie, daughter of King Robert the Second, sister to Donald's mother. The king confirmed the earldom by charter and Darnaway has been the seat of the Moray earls ever since."

THE SMELL OF ALE, long-soaked into the wooden floor, assaulted Donald's nostrils as he and Alex stepped from the cold into the heated common room of the inn at Inverness, followed by Donald's guard of five galloglass.

Boisterous laughter rose from the tables where men sat eating and drinking, the air redolent of stew and wood smoke. The inn was one frequented by shipbuilders and merchants. Inverness was a busy port on the River Ness, exporting wool, fur and hides. Many fishermen also operated out of the town. The Earl of Moray was Sheriff of Inverness since the Wolf of Badenoch's removal.

The noise died suddenly as their group of seven strode inside. Alex headed for a corner table where they could keep their backs to the wall. After gaining the innkeeper's attention, Donald gestured his men to a nearby table and joined Alex.

"What are you serving?" Alex asked the burly innkeeper who

arrived at their table. The man might have once been a fisherman or one who worked on ships, for his face was leathery and his body well-muscled.

"Mutton stew, sausage, cheese and bread. Ale is plentiful. If you prefer wine, we have it plain or spiced and hot."

Still trying to get warm, Donald took off his gloves and rubbed his hands together. "Hot spiced wine and the stew, bread and cheese will be fine for me."

Alex nodded. "For me as well."

Their dress would have told the innkeeper they were not paupers though Donald was careful when on the road not to dress in accordance with his rank so as to avoid brigands. However, his guard's appearance told everyone who cared to notice that they were persons who could afford—and might need—protection. Their blond hair, especially Alex's that was very fair, and their blue eyes would label them as from the west, even the Isles.

The wine arrived and Donald wrapped his hands around the warm mug. "Will the Earl of Moray be expecting us?"

"Aye. I sent word ahead at Christmas."

"Do you think he will be receptive to your offer?"

"He has few options," said Alex. "And we are there at his western flank whether in Argyll or Ross."

"What will you ask in return?"

"I have given it some thought. It seems prudent to ask for lands in the Great Glen, the same lands the Earl of Moray once gave to the Wolf of Badenoch when Buchan was the sheriff here. The rents from those will allow me to pay the added men I will need. I would begin by asking for Bona at the north end of Loch Ness, south of here. That, too, is controlled by Moray."

"I agree it would be in our interest to hold those lands. That way the Stewarts could not block our access to Glen. Though it might take some negotiating, the earl should agree and the bishop, whose church lands must be protected, should see the wisdom of it."

The stew, steaming and hot, arrived at their table along with the cheese and fresh baked bread. Donald and Alex left off their talk of Moray to eat and speak of their young sons. "Will you stand as godfather to my son?" Donald asked. "Mariota's brother will be godfather, too."

"I will and gladly," said Alex, smiling broadly. "I thought you'd never ask. And, in turn, I would ask you to be godfather to my child, whose birth is expected shortly."

Donald returned his brother a look of amusement. "It pays to plan ahead. Upon our return to Dingwall, while we await the birth of your son or daughter, we can attend to Sandy's christening. The countess has invited half the province and many luminaries."

The next morning, Donald and Alex left the inn for the stables, the snow making a crunching sound as it was compressed beneath their boots. Donald was glad to see the sun shining and the sky a clear blue, boding well for their travel. "I am hoping for supper at the Earl of Moray's table," he told Alex.

"We should make it," came his brother's encouraging reply.

At the stables, Donald's guard was waiting for them, the horses saddled and ready. "We ride hard, men," said Donald, "for supper and a warm bed at Darnaway!"

A FULL DAY'S ride brought them to a forest of snow-covered trees— the royal hunting reserve—a few miles south of Forres, not far from the River Findhorn. Darnaway Castle stood on a low ridge in the midst of the forest, its roof still blanketed with snow. With the shorter winter days, it was nearly twilight and, with the wind picking up, growing colder by the moment.

What Donald could see of the castle told him it was a considerable edifice with a stone tower and a large great hall. The tower rose three stories into the air with many chambers. Light from candles or braziers escaped through the window coverings.

They were obviously expected, greeted as they were by servants hurrying from the castle to take their horses and those of Donald's guard. They dismounted and, handing over the reins, strode across the bridge over the moat toward the entrance, anxious to be in from the wind that made the cold worse.

Thomas Dunbar, the eldest of the earl's three sons, met them just inside the door a guard opened for them. In his twenties, the dark-haired young man with fair skin and a short beard displayed an air of confidence—as one might expect of the heir. "Come in, my lords, and be warm!"

Servants stood waiting to take their heavy cloaks and hats. Another offered them goblets of hot spiced wine. Donald gazed up at the roof timbers far above him. They appeared new. "That's a great deal of timber," he said.

"Yes, and just finished before the snow, thank God," said Thomas Dunbar. He gestured them into the great hall. "There is a blazing fire just ahead."

"We are most grateful," said Donald, stepping into the hall that could have seated many hundreds. He removed his gloves, tucking them into his belt, and reached his hands toward the fire. A heavy log burned brightly in the fireplace that was so large a man could walk into it. "You know my brother, Alexander, Lord of Lochaber. The others with us comprise my guard."

Thomas Dunbar glanced at the weapons Donald's galloglass carried, which never failed to impress. "We were not certain when you might arrive, so I have had men keeping watch. I am relieved you did not find yourselves lost in blinding snow."

The earl's son, but not the earl or his countess, had been a guest at Donald's wedding. The Dunbars were friends of the Bishop of Moray and known to the Countess of Ross. At the time, they were told the earl was still recovering from wounds he received in a tournament in England. As Sheriff of Inverness, John Dunbar had military as well as legal responsibilities that had once been the purview of the Earl of Buchan. It was those military duties that had brought Donald and Alex to Moray.

"Is your father about?" asked Alex.

"He is resting but will join us for supper, along with my mother, the countess. My siblings are elsewhere."

"Is our visit inconvenient?" asked Donald. He wondered if the earl's health allowed for entertaining.

"To the contrary, we are happy to have you. But since his injuries received from Sir Thomas Mowbray in that tournament, he tries to rest in the afternoons. Though I do wonder why you didn't wait for spring when birdsong is in the air and flowers are in bloom."

Donald took another drink of the spiced wine; it warmed him considerably. "Our visit in winter resulted from a decision of my wife. She wanted to give birth to our first child in Dingwall so her mother could be with her, which I acknowledged as quite reasonable; and the babe chose this month to be born."

Thomas Dunbar smiled. "Well, then congratulations are in order." When they had finished their wine, he waved to his steward and said to Donald, "My servants can show you and your guard to your chambers. Your satchels will have been brought in and placed there for you. Supper will be served in an hour. We assume you will spend the night. To do otherwise would not be prudent."

"That is most kind of you," said Donald.

"Aye," said Alex. "We are grateful for your hospitality."

AN HOUR LATER, rested and refreshed, Donald and Alex returned to the hall to find John Dunbar, Earl of Moray, waiting there with his wife, Marjorie, and their eldest son. Years younger than her husband, Marjorie Stewart reminded Donald of his mother, the two sisters only a few years apart. Her face, lined with few wrinkles, was framed by white silk, but her dark brows told him her hair, unlike his mother's, was dark. The earl, though not yet fifty, looked older. His hair and beard were liberally threaded with silver. His skin was sallow for a man who spent time at tourneys.

"Welcome to Darnaway," said the earl, reaching out his hand to Donald. "Thomas tells me congratulations are in order."

"Yes, thank you," said Donald. "A son, my first."

"Another nephew for me," said the countess. "What did you name him?"

"Alexander," said Donald, "after my brother and Mariota's."

The countess smiled. "May there be many more. I imagine the Countess of Ross is pleased with her first grandchild."

"She is a doting grandmother," acknowledged Donald.

When the countess suggested they take their seats as the meal would soon be served, Donald noticed a slight grimace distort their host's face and guessed it pained the earl to stand. They walked to the chairs set around a table, dwarfed by the huge great hall. "I trust you are well, my lord," Donald said. "When you were unable to attend my wedding because of your injuries received in England, we were worried."

He brushed off the inquiry. "I am recovered, thank you. In fact, I am planning another trip to England this summer."

"We are happy to hear it," said Donald.

Donald would always remember that evening as it was the beginning of many things. The chance to control the Great Glen and push farther into Ross was too good an opportunity to miss and might not come again. But he did not doubt there would be consequences from such advancement under the greedy eyes of Robert Stewart, Earl of Fife, who more than his brother the king, governed Scotland.

After they were seated, platters of honeyed chicken in a sauce of dried currants, cherries and raisins arrived at the table, along with turnips in cheese sauce and buttered carrots. The aromas stirred Donald's appetite. He was vaguely aware of music coming from the other end of the hall, obviously not meant to intrude on a meeting of business, which suited him well.

Thomas Dunbar said, "We assume you have come about Buchan's loss of position and the need for protection for the regality of Moray and the province's church lands."

Alex nodded. "We have." He began to eat the chicken, which Donald thought very tasty. "It would seem that given the current state of affairs, what Moray needs the Macdonalds can provide. As Lord of Lochaber, I would be the one to do it."

"And such an arrangement would serve the Macdonalds' interests as well?" asked the earl, his inquiry directed to Donald.

Donald met the earl's steady gaze. The older man was more astute than his son. Wisdom was not far from his question. "That is certainly our hope. For some years, we have been concerned about the Wolf of Badenoch's activities in the Great Glen." Donald had intentionally used the alias for Alexander Stewart, Earl of Buchan, to emphasize his misdeeds, which had brought them to this meeting.

"The Glen is an important waterway plied by our galleys. We would see it remain open and free. To protect Moray's lands and those of the church would include protecting access to the Glen. Thus, an arrangement between us would be of mutual benefit."

"That is good," said the earl, his expression thoughtful. "Any agreement would be stronger for it. And what would you ask in return?"

"I would ask for the lands you once gave Buchan along the Great Glen," said Alex, "starting with Bona that commands the passage to Loch Ness."

The earl nodded in a manner that told Donald the town of Bona would be Alex's. The terms of the agreement were not discussed in detail that night but Donald was satisfied their long ride through the snow had been justified. Knowing the earl and his son were willing to move forward meant that no other offer would be entertained.

Donald went to sleep that night content that the Earl of Fife would not be stealing their advantage. Control of the Great Glen would be theirs.

The next morning, they rode out as a light snow was falling. "If we are fortunate," said Alex, "it will grow no worse and we will arrive unscathed at Inverness."

Some hours on, they stopped in a small glade to rest the horses. Donald had just taken a drink from his water flask when, wiping his mouth, he noticed dark forms moving through the trees some distance away. A dozen men on horseback. Signaling to Alex and his guard, they led their horses behind a stand of trees.

"Who might they be?" Alex asked in a low voice.

Donald peered through the falling snow. The first rider wore a fur-lined cloak and a feathered hat; the others a mixture of clothing with fur pelts over their shoulders. "I'm guessing 'tis my first cousin, Alexander Stewart, Buchan's eldest bastard, and his caterans come from Inverness. They raid with impunity."

"Let's hope they have no ill designs on Darnaway."

"I do not think he would risk that," said Donald, "not after his father's falling. Still, our visit may have been timely. Having agreed in principle to our protection, the Earl of Moray could hardly encourage

Alexander Stewart."

When the dozen riders passed, Donald and his brother continued on, making Inverness before nightfall, brushing the loose snow from their cloaks before settling into the inn.

The next day would see them to Dingwall.

MARIOTA WELCOMED HER husband with a kiss. "You must be tired after so long a ride in the cold." She helped him remove his cloak and sent him and his brother to the fireplace where hot wine awaited. "Dinner is not far off. Do you want food now?"

"We can wait," said Donald. "Where is that young son of mine?"

"In the nursery, napping. Shall I have his nurse fetch him?"

"When he wakes," said Donald. "My brother has agreed to stand godfather for Sandy along with your brother, so we can proceed with the christening."

"Wonderful," she said, smiling at Alex.

"Donnie will stand godfather for my new lad or lass," said Alex. "Has my Mary sent news?"

"No," said Mariota. "I assume there is still time for you to be there for the birth."

In the next few days, before a large crowd of Ross kindreds, Sandy was christened. Thereafter, with several days of sun, they set off for the coast, parting with Alex as he separated from them for Lochaber.

From Loch Carron on Ross' coast, they sailed to Ardtornish in Morvern. Sandy slept for most of the travel in Mariota's arms, wrapped in furs that kept him warm. Abby was very fond of the child and doted on him, relieving Mariota from time to time, though at Ardtornish, he would have a proper nurse.

The day after they arrived at Ardtornish, Hector Maclean appeared, full of news and eager to see his new cousin. When Donald asked how he knew they had returned, the red-haired giant said, "I had a man watching for your galley from Dounarwyse." Mariota had spent one glorious afternoon at Dounarwyse Castle with Donald. The Macdonalds used the fortified hill fort on the south side of the Sound of Mull on occasion. From there, Hector's man could easily observe the galleys passing by.

Hector made a fuss over the babe. "Is there a chance he might have red hair?"

"Not likely," said Donald, "given the down that grows on his head, which is how we came by his nickname."

"Ah, well, maybe the next one," said Hector, taking a seat by the fire.

Donald took a seat next to him and accepted the sleeping babe from Mariota. Without removing his gaze from the babe, Donald said, "So, tell us the news."

Hector settled back in his chair. "Well, to begin, there is news from Ireland where I was for a time, visiting Uncle John and Margery at Red Bay Castle. King Richard has ordered all the English settlers who fled to England back to Ulster, and he has begun amassing a fleet of hundreds of ships for an expedition."

"That is unusual," said Donald, handing his sleeping son back to Mariota.

"The king apparently considers the effort to be one of importance," said Hector. "He has put his cousin, Sir Edward of Norwich, who he made Earl of Rutland last year, in charge."

Donald furrowed his brow. "Richard means to lead thousands of men-at-arms to Ireland?"

"Aye," said Hector. "And thousands of archers. He wants the Irish lords, particularly MacMurrough and the Leinster Irish, to swear obeisance to him. I was told the Earl of Ulster will supply a large contingent of men. John Mor wonders if we should volunteer some of the lordship's galleys since the king is desperate for ships."

Donald paused before answering. Mariota could see from his furrowed brow he had reservations. "We must ask what our allies would think, specifically the O'Neill. He might be loyal to King Richard and would be quick to swear obeisance, but he might not want to see us bringing the English soldiers to his shores. Did John Mor consider that? Assuming our Irish allies agree, we could offer Richard transport," said Donald. "Otherwise, and in light of the fact King Richard has asked no help from us, we will keep our galleys home." Then with a smile, he added, "No matter how much you would like to match swords with Leinster's lords. You will just have to content yourself with matching mine in the practice field."

Hector gave a resigned shrug. "Very well. Meantime, why do you think King Richard is doing this?"

Donald stroked his short red beard and stared into the fire. Mariota had seen him do this before when concentrating on a problem. "We know the king is concerned about holding on to his lordship in Ulster. It might be he sees no other way but to lead an army to Ireland in a show of strength. His English lieges seem powerless and look to him as the situation grows worse."

Mariota handed her sleeping child to his new nurse. "Why not send for your cousin John MacAlister to see if he has been in contact with Clan Alexander?" she suggested. "He might be able to tell us what the O'Neill thinks of this."

"A very good thought," replied Donald. "While he is here, he can report on how things are going at Iona."

Two days later, John MacAlister beached his galley at Ardtornish. Iona wasn't far and the messenger had reached him there. Over dinner, John first gave them news of Iona's abbey. "I am kept busy at the abbey sorting out the monks and staff with the aim of gaining their trust and obedience and weeding out MacKinnon sympathizers and spies. I am also going through all the abbey books and sailing to the endowed properties with a view to bringing back all the incomes to the abbey coffers. There is also urgent repair work that must be done to assure walls do not collapse. Beyond that, I must sort out the 'women folk' who remain there. One of the illegitimate children is John Mor's bastard son by MacKinnon's daughter."

"My brother will have to sort that out himself," said Donald. "It is his to make provision for the lad. I will send him a message to let him know, though I imagine he has not forgotten."

The prior went on to relate what he knew of King Richard's plans. "The O'Neill believes the king's main target is MacMurrough in Leinster, but he worries that some of the king's actions will affect the whole country. For example, if the king puts in place a sea blockade with his hundreds of ships, all of Ireland will be affected. I fear Richard will not be interested in diplomacy. My advice is to stay out of it for now."

CHAPTER 13

Duart Castle, Isle of Mull

DURING THE THREE years following Donald's visit to the Earl of Moray, Mariota's time was dominated by her young children. One arrived nearly every year with the coming of spring or early summer, owing to Donald's virility and his enthusiasm for the task. He was a considerate lover who never left her in doubt about his passion for her or his love for their growing brood.

Mariota's next child after Sandy was a girl. At Donald's insistence, they named her Mariota, but she was called Mari. Hector finally got his wish, as the lass was born with her head sprouting small tufts of red hair.

Donald and Mariota were not the only Macdonalds raising a family. John Mor and Margery already had one son, Donald. His name, in Mariota's eyes, was a seal on John Mor's bond to his eldest brother. Alex and Mary Lennox had one son, Angus, a child of fair countenance, for whom Donald acted as godfather.

Mariota looked forward to the summer meetings at Finlaggan where there would be a passel of children gathered around the fire eager to hear stories. She and Donald had already made a summer pilgrimage to Kilcummin where their two young ones did, indeed, play on the beach at Machir Bay.

The same year little Mari was born, 1392, Mariota's mother, Euphemia, Countess of Ross, was given an annulment by the Avignon Pope, Clement VII. By this, Alexander Stewart, Earl of Buchan, lost all claim to the lands held by Mariota's mother, which were returned to her and would, upon her death, come to Mariota's brother, Alexander, along with the title Earl of Ross.

About this time, Donald made Lachlan Maclean steward of his household and bailee of Tiree. The Maclean chief was often with them on Islay or at Ardtornish. His son, Hector, and his wife, Anne Douglas, lived at Duart Castle, bringing the Macdonalds and the Macleans frequently together. Lachlan had agreed, when John Mor's son, Donald, was of age, to foster the lad at Duart.

In the summer of 1393, Mariota gave birth to a second daughter, Anna, a pretty child, who had hazel eyes like her mother and light brown curls.

In the next year, Donald finally delivered on his promise to his nephew, Hector, to match swords in lieu of Hector's fighting in Ireland. The weather on Mull in early July was glorious. A crowd had gathered to watch the Macdonald face his famous nephew on the practice field next to Duart Castle.

Mariota stood watching with Mary Macdonald, wife of the Maclean chief and Hector's mother. Next to her stood Hector's wife, Anne, the dark-haired daughter of Archibald the Grim. As the match began, Alex and his wife, Mary Lennox, joined them.

Donald and his nephew had tied back their long hair as they would for battle. Now in his early thirties, her husband's face had matured. His air of confidence, bone structure and striking coloring rendered him a handsome man. Mariota had come to love him deeply. Thus, she had misgivings about this fight, but she would not seek to deprive him of a diversion he relished that took him from his ledgers.

His blue eyes sparkled with delight as the two men circled each other like two boys with wooden swords, only their blades were steel, the sun reflecting off the metal.

Donald and his nephew had declined to wear mail or helmets. "It's only for first blood," he had told her.

His words had given Mariota no comfort. First blood, she reminded him, could be a slice across the neck. Given Hector's reputation as the greatest swordsman in the Isles, she had not encouraged the bout. While the two were of a similar height, Donald had less bulk behind his sword, and had trained less, as the business of the Isles often kept him away from the practice field. But he was determined to do this and did not wish to disappoint his nephew.

Hector's mother feared for them both. "The fools," she said. "They will have blood all over the grass." Her words, said in a mocking manner, belied the deep concern that showed on her face. Mariota had learned to count upon Mary Macdonald's sharp realism.

Hector's wife said nothing, though her intense gaze said much about her worries for her husband. Perhaps she was resigned to the bargain she had made when she fell for a man whose reputation was that of a fierce swordsman.

With the stone walls of the castle behind them, the two circled each other, throwing out taunts and shouts of bravado. The thronging crowd of men, who had waited long for this day, cheered the feigned rivalry.

"Your sword looks a little short, Nephew, if you gather my meaning," said Donald. The crowd broke into loud guffaws and added a few taunts of their own.

His manhood attacked, Hector's temper was roused. His sword clashed with Donald's in a bone-jarring sound of metal on metal. Mariota held her breath.

Hector brought his sword around, the blade flying through the air in a terrible arc, slashing from his full reach.

"Will you look at that!" shouted Alex, as Donald skillfully avoided Hector's blade. It missed Donald's shoulder by inches. Mariota bit her knuckle. She had asked Donald's new chaplain, Father David MacMurchie, a handsome cleric of middle years, to pray for her husband and Hector. It was to God she now looked for their protection.

Thus far, Donald's moves had mostly been defensive. She wondered how long he would hold back.

"Seems to me," said Hector with a sly grin, "I've had sheep that put up more fight than you, Uncle. Where did you learn to wield a sword—Oxford?" A wave of laughter flowed across the crowd, shifting with every move of the combatants.

Donald stood back a few feet as if critically judging his opponent. "You fight well, Nephew. Perhaps I shall name my next daughter after you. Hectorina...I like the sound of it." The crowd, enjoying the jibe, broke into laughter, shouting "Hectorina! Hectorina!"

Hector, laughing himself, took a swipe at Donald, but the Lord of the Isles successfully fended off the attack.

Their swords clashed again and again until the smiles of the two men faded and the teasing ceased. The crowd stared, barely breathing.

Hector's jaw was set; Donald's eyes were fixed on his nephew's every move. Their demeanor turned serious. Clearly, neither wanted to lose.

Mariota had never seen Donald fight like this. Always in the practice yard, he had been measured in his actions, as if in no hurry. But now he moved so fast at times his steps were blurred. Though not as powerfully built as his nephew, he was quick and clever, striking hard only to adroitly move out of range. She remembered the day he had faced the Wolf's caterans, cutting down two in quick succession. He'd been fast then, too.

"Stop moving!" shouted Hector, his face reddening. "You are making me dizzy."

"That is my plan," said Donald. Then, with a smile, "Is it working?" With one quick move, Donald's sword flashed as he sent the flat of his blade down hard on Hector's arm, knocking his sword to the ground. A second swing and Donald made a cut on Hector's wrist. "First blood is mine!"

Hector, stunned, stood staring at his sword lying on the ground. He rubbed his arm. "I'll have to remember that move." Wiping the blood from his wrist, he offered his hand to Donald. "Your win, Uncle." Then with a chuckle, "Enjoy it, for it will not be repeated."

Donald shook his nephew's hand. "You only say that because you would not want to lose twice."

The smiling crowd applauded.

Mariota breathed a sigh of relief. At her side, Mary said, "Donnie has taught the pup a lesson. I approve."

Hector's wife, Anne, said nothing, but Mariota detected a deep sigh emanated from the pretty dark-haired lass.

Beside them, Alex said, "I thought he might have something like that in mind. He was not going to hurt Hector."

Before long, a side of beef was roasting on a spit over an open fire and the men were sitting around, drinking ale, discussing the bout and recalling Hector's exploits of which there were many. Donald was in the middle of the crowd, joking with the men as one of them.

Mariota and the other women stood off a little distance away, talking.

"Donnie never lets his role as their chief get in the way of their camaraderie," said Mary. "They respect him as their leader and would follow his orders without question but they also like him."

Seeing her husband lift his tankard in toast to Hector, Mariota recalled Sir Thomas' original assessment as she observed, "He drinks with them, yet he never comes home drunk."

"No, he would be careful of that," said Mary. "Our father would have counseled him against such behavior by the chief."

The children, barred from the scene until now, were set free to run about. Hector's redheaded son, Lachlan, was one of the older boys. The youngest ones were brought forth by their nurses. Freed, Sandy ran to his father, his little legs pumping, his blond curls flying, and was scooped up into his arms to be held above him. Sandy squealed. Mariota smiled seeing them together. Her son was a happy child who idolized his father.

Abby came to stand with the women, bringing little Mari by the hand. "Mari has just awakened from her nap," said the handmaiden. "Anna is still sleeping. I hear Lord Donald has won the match."

"Aye," said Mary Macdonald. "Which is as it should be."

HIS THROAT DRY from the match, Donald downed a swig of ale and slapped Hector on the back. "No hard feelings, Nephew?"

"No. After all, I let you win," came the retort with a bellowed laugh. "Had to do it for the sake of the lordship."

At this jest, the men began to tease Hector. It was all in good fun. They respected his skills and were not often able to jest about them.

Sitting on Donald's knee, Sandy turned his face to Hector and frowned. "Father won. Sir Thomas said so."

"Exactly," said Alex. "My godson speaks truth."

Hector's son, Lachlan said, "My father is the best swordsman in the Isles."

"Young Lachlan is right about that," said Donald. "I was lucky today."

Angus, Alex's son, came to stand by his father, who put his arm around the boy. "Did *you* see it, Father?"

"I did. Your Uncle Donald disarmed the great Red Hector. It was cleverly done, luck or not." Whereupon young Angus and Sandy, seemingly content, ran off, following Lachlan and the other boys who were going to look for otters.

"They are good lads," said Donald.

"Aye," said Hector, watching the boys run down to the water's edge. "The lot of them."

Donald and Alex rose and walked a short distance away. "Where are you bound from here?" Donald asked his brother now that they were alone.

"To Moray. As you know, since John Dunbar died, his son has been slow to turn his attention to our agreement. It is past time to reduce our understanding to writing."

One of Donald's guards approached. "My lord, a messenger has arrived from the Countess of Ross."

His brow furrowed. "For me?"

"Yes, my lord. He asked for you."

"Show him to me and ask my lady to come as well." To Alex he said, "It is unusual for Lady Euphemia to send me a message. Her letters typically come to Mariota."

The messenger, who Donald recognized from his visits to

Dingwall, wore the red and white livery of Ross. He bowed. "My lord, the countess asked me to bring you this message. She said it was important." He thrust a sealed parchment toward Donald.

The message was contained on a single page:

Euphemia, Countess of Ross to Donald of Islay, Lord of the Isles:

> *Alexander Stewart, Earl of Buchan, my former husband, is dead. 'Tis said he died at his castle at Ruthven where, the night before, he was visited by a mysterious tall stranger clothed all in black. The two were said to play chess. After two hours, the stranger called "check" and then "checkmate", whereupon a great storm ensued that raged through the night. In the morning, Buchan's caterans were found dead outside the castle, their bodies scorched as if by lightning, and the earl was dead in the great hall. There were no marks on his body, but the nails in his boots had all been ripped out. Of course, I do not believe this tale, but the fact remains he is dead, whether by mysterious means or not.*
>
> *His natural sons, Alexander and Duncan, have already seized some of his lands, their caterans sending terror through the Highlands and Lowlands. Now is the time for you to move on the Great Glen and make your presence known in Ross.*

Donald looked up from the message and handed it to his brother. "This changes your timing but not, I suspect, your goal."

Alex read the letter. "God's bones!"

Mariota arrived at Donald's side and she, too, read the message. When she finished, she gazed at him with a look of inquiry. "He played chess with the devil?"

"That is what is implied," said Donald. "One is inclined to believe it, knowing the Wolf of Badenoch."

Mariota looked again at the message. "The rest of it...will you go?"

Her beautiful eyes were full of concern, but there was no help for it. "I must. With the Stewarts dividing up Scotland like a butcher carving up a side of beef, and Ross a sweet temptation, I must act to preserve the future of the lordship. It is my duty as chief."

"We go together," Alex said, as if to reassure her. Then to Donald,

"We could send for John Mor…"

"Eventually, perhaps," said Donald, "but for now, our combined forces should be sufficient." He looked again at his wife and reached out to touch her arm. "It will be all right, my love."

"I suppose I should have known it would happen one day," said Mariota. "You will take your chaplain and your physician?"

"If their presence will give you comfort, I will." Glancing at Hector Maclean standing some distance away, he said. "Meantime, I will also take my general."

"Hector will doubtless insist," said Alex.

Donald had urged quick action and his brother responded, moving into the Glen over the next few weeks with Hector and a large contingent of men from the Isles and Lochaber, while Donald made his presence known in Ross.

Alex's vigorous action alarmed Thomas, Earl of Moray, who wisely bowed to the Lord of Lochaber's might. By formal agreement toward the end of September, 1394, the earl placed the lands and possessions of the Regality of Moray, and the church lands within the province, under Alex's protection for a period of seventeen years.

Donald had suggested the agreement be signed at Cawdor in Nairn, halfway between Inverness and Darnaway Castle. To which Alex replied, "An interesting suggestion. Might it have anything to do with the fact that the thane of Cawdor is a tenant of the Countess of Ross?"

Donald had allowed himself a small smile. "It might." When the agreement was signed, he returned to Ardtornish, satisfied with the results.

A few months later, he learned that after years of doing nothing about their mother's complaints, King Robert decided to take action and ordered the Earl of Fife to move forward.

"Why now after all this time?" Mariota asked him.

"It is not difficult to surmise," said Donald. "This is Fife's doing, not the king's. Alex occupies the Great Glen and has free rein in Moray and, by design, I have often been seen in Ross. That the king should choose this time to act on an old complaint is not unrelated. Fife looks for an excuse to seize land, if not control. The Stewarts would have Kintyre and more. We cannot allow this to go un-addressed."

Mariota said, "I wonder if the king is afraid of his brother."

"A distinct possibility."

Incensed at the charge they were neglecting their mother and worse, that Fife had been put in charge of the matter and given authority to pursue a military expedition, as winter approached, Donald and his brothers—for both Alex and John Mor were with him—rode into Ross. With a small army of men-at-arms and galloglass, they attacked the wealthy lands of Moray, breaking the agreement Alex signed just months before.

By the end of the year, Alex controlled the Great Glen and, with the help of Donald and John Mor, had taken Urquhart Castle on Loch Ness, which was a part of the Earldom of Ross.

Nothing had come of Fife's proposed military expedition.

In the following spring, to no surprise, the king charged Donald and his brothers with treason. "Treason seems a bit harsh when you consider all Buchan did," Donald told them. "Still, it was to be expected the king would take issue with our actions, else he would lose face."

Between the three of them, they decided how they would respond. "Allow me to take the blame," said Alex. "I was the one to break the agreement, and I am the one who has taken Urquhart."

Donald and John Mor agreed. Submitting to the crown, they were pardoned, while the blame for the insurrection, as they intended, was conveniently taken by the Lord of Lochaber, who was declared an unruly element and assigned into Donald's care. Alex was officially "imprisoned" by the Lord of the Isles at Ardtornish, which appeased the crown. The confinement lasted only a year, after which Donald released his brother. But he still had to appear before parliament to explain.

Alex, not at all displeased with his year of "imprisonment", celebrated his new kingdom and gave to his faithful follower, Charles Maclean—son of Hector Maclean of Lochbuie, brother of the Maclean chief—the keeping of Urquhart Castle. During his year of confinement, Alex managed to sire a new son, named Alexander.

Alex and his family took up residence in Keppoch Castle in Loch-aber where he was known as Alexander Macdonald, the first of Keppoch. His reputation was that of a bold and fearless man, as much Viking in appearance as Scot. Donald was proud of his younger brother.

Despite the cost of the crown's anger and demands that the Lord of Lochaber surrender Urquhart Castle, both the castle and the Valley of the River Ness remained in Macdonald hands, effectively supplanting the Stewart lordship in the region.

Donald had made his point. The Lord of the Isles was not to be trifled with.

While all this was going on, and without the use of Donald's galleys, King Richard had led an army of eight thousand men to Ireland and, in a matter of months, obtained the submission of over eighty Irish nobles, including John Macdonnell, cousin to John MacAlister, a grandson of Alexander Macdonald, the third chief of Clan Donald, and the O'Neill. Having already forged an alliance with the Macdonald lordship, King Richard's success in Ireland gained him a permanent settlement that could check Scottish expansion in the Irish Sea. Since any expansion of the Stewarts would have come at a cost to the lordship, Donald was content in his bond with England. Aside from that, the wealth of the herring fisheries he guarded allowed him to build strong trading relationships with England and Europe where smoked salmon remained a delicacy.

"I am pleased we did not have a part in King Richard's invasion," Donald told Mariota. "We were busy enough elsewhere. Meantime, his success only strengthens the lordship."

Before Christmas, Mariota's mother, the Countess of Ross, fell ill. They left immediately with their family for Dingwall. The countess died soon after they arrived, leaving them heartbroken, for she had been a wonderful mother and a gracious friend to the lordship. At her passing, Lady Euphemia was surrounded by her children and grandchildren and, having received last rites, died with a smile on her lips.

With the countess' death, Mariota's brother, Alexander, became the Earl of Ross. All seemed well until, needing an heir, the young earl announced he would marry Isabel Stewart, the daughter of the Earl of Fife.

"Fife must have pressed his daughter on my brother," said Mariota. "Perhaps Alexander felt he owed the earl for having freed our mother from Buchan."

Donald took all this to heart, knowing Fife had a plan. "We will have to watch Ross closely."

Donald's actions in comforting his wife for the loss of her mother led to another child, who turned their sorrow to joy. Born in the spring of 1395, they named him Angus after Donald's grandfather, Angus Og, the friend of Robert the Bruce, who by some accounts, was responsible in large part for the king's victory at Bannockburn. One of Donald's younger brothers, who resided with his mother, was also named Angus. "If you agree," he told Mariota, "and if the lad is suited to the profession, I would give our Angus to the church. One day, should my prayers be answered, I would see him Bishop of the Isles."

Mariota agreed enthusiastically. "It is a noble thought and worthy of the lordship. For all God has done for us, how could we do less? My only request is one you have already touched upon. Angus must be willing to dedicate his life to this calling."

Donald agreed. He asked his cousin, John MacAlister, to attend the christening, which he did, and to stand as godfather for the babe, who would, hopefully, one day follow him into holy orders.

At the christening, John held little Angus in his arms. The babe's wispy brown curls decorated his nearly bald head. John's own tonsured head was browned from the sun, his face, too.

Having noticed, Donald observed, "You have been traveling."

John sighed and fixed his dark eyes on Donald. "I am weary from galley travel, but this trip was welcomed." John looked again to the child whose pale blue eyes stared up at him. "It will be my honor to take your little one under my wing. Before God, I vow to teach him His truth."

Donald could not ask for more from his dear friend. Mariota, standing at Donald's side, appeared pleased.

After the christening, they spoke of other things. One in particular had been on Donald's mind. "I assume you know," he told John, "that in response to a plea from the new MacKinnon chief, the Avignon Pope has reconfirmed Finguine MacKinnon as Abbot of Iona."

"I am aware, yes," said John.

Suppressing his anger, Donald said, "I view this as a futile attempt to undo the imprisonment imposed by the lordship, and intend to ignore it. Finguine will remain confined at Iona. But in light of the MacKinnon chief's action to try and reinstate the erstwhile abbot, I think it best you petition the Bishop of the Isles for a commission to consider the removal of Finguine from his post. Surely once the facts are laid out, the bishops will recommend removal to the pope. I do not want to wait until Finguine's death for you to be abbot."

"I agree it is time," said John. "I will see it done."

Thinking they would have peace, at least for a time, Donald was set back with news in April of 1398 that the king made his brother, Robert Stewart, Earl of Fife, the Duke of Albany. He was fifty-eight. At the same time, his nephew, David Stewart, Earl of Carrick, the king's eldest son and heir, was created Duke of Rothesay, and replaced Albany as the Governor of Scotland. They were the first dukedoms created in Scotland. To Donald's mind, the titles were suggestive of ties to the Highlands and the Isles the two did not possess. The name Albany referred to the territory north of the River Forth, and Rothesay was the name of a castle on the Isle of Bute.

As the young prince's power rose with the queen's influence and his father's blessing, Albany's waned. Donald was keenly aware that, given the latter's ambitions, the two would not long be friends.

CHAPTER 14

Ardtornish Castle, Morvern, January 1400

WHILE DONALD WAS dealing with matters in Scotland, John Mor had sent word that the leading Irish nobles had renounced their prior submissions to King Richard, claiming England had not fulfilled her part of the bargain. In the uprisings that followed, young Roger Mortimer, the king's heir, who Donald had met at John Mor's wedding, was killed.

Angry and seeking revenge, King Richard returned to Ireland, but this time, he was not successful. Worse, upon his return to England, he was deposed by his cousin, Henry of Bolingbroke, Duke of Hereford, eldest son of the Duke of Lancaster. Taking the throne as Henry the Fourth, he promptly imprisoned Richard in Pontefract Castle, the former residence of Henry's father nearly two hundred miles north of London.

Donald reflected on the irony of Richard's untimely death that followed. A king of only thirty-three, who so loved food, was said to be starved to death by his cousin.

Meantime in Scotland, Mariota's brother, the young Earl of Ross, made no protest as Donald and his brother, the Lord of Lochaber, pursued their interests in the Great Glen, Ross and Moray. "Alexander, Earl of Ross, will not oppose us," Donald told Alex, having come from Ross to visit Alex at Keppoch in Lochaber. "In truth, with the kingdom in a state of disorder due to Albany's poor management, I believe Alexander welcomes our presence. The people love Prince David, Duke of Rothesay, for his beauty and his poetry, but the nobles, stirred by Albany, are suspicious. With King Richard gone, I think John Mor and I should make another visit to England. We need to know the new English king is with us."

Alex said, "I'd like to be there when your retainers ride into London wearing the new Macdonald livery."

"I would take you, but given all that is going on, I need you and Lachlan Maclean to watch over the lordship while I am gone."

"Very well," said Alex with a sigh of resignation, "we will make certain it is here when you return."

And so, after exchanging messages with England, Donald and his brother, John Mor, arrived in London at the end of February with a large retinue and, with the king's permission, an escort of eighty horse. Donald's guard wore the new livery, displaying the black galley of the Isles on a field of saffron. But this time, the galley was surmounted on a rising red eagle.

"*You* are the Hebridean Eagle," Hector told him. "It is now the symbol of our chief."

The entire banner was bordered by the royal double tressure of the Stewart kings in red. It proclaimed to all in London that the Lord of the Isles, chief of Clan Donald, was a lord of royal blood and here to see the King of England.

The crowd that lined the streets, watching them open-mouthed, parted to let them pass.

As they moved deeper into the city, Donald remembered the stench of the town from his last visit. It had not changed. At times, his gaze was drawn overhead to the tall spires, only to be brought low to the sounds and smells of the crowded streets where merchants hawked their wares and taverns spilled forth drunken men.

Donald had brought Hector, who made for an impressive sight

with his dark red hair and beard, his powerful shoulders, his great sword and his Maclean livery boldly displaying a silver tower on a field of blue. If ever there was a strong tower in the Isles, it was Hector Maclean.

Hector was flanked by Donald's chaplain and secretary, David MacMurchie, in his black robes, and Fergus Beaton, Donald's physician, whose dark beard was threaded with gray, giving him the appearance of a distinguished scholar, which, when it came to all things medical, he was.

The sky drizzled rain as they rode through London's streets, making Donald glad for the beaver-lined cloak that draped his shoulders and flared over his horse's hindquarters. On his head he wore his favorite bycocket hat, black in contrast to his blond hair.

"We must make quite a sight," said John Mor, "with our fair hair and long limbs, not to mention our guard of galloglass and the Macdonald livery."

Donald studied the faces of the people and knew John Mor had judged correctly. "Doubtless they do not see Islesmen or Highlanders often. We are to meet with King Henry tomorrow, which leaves time for a meeting that might prove to be of some importance."

John Mor cast Donald a side glance. "Do you still have a spy in London?"

"Not a spy exactly," replied Donald. "Willie Thorpe is a friend who was at Oxford with me, another student of Master John Wycliffe. Willie keeps abreast of royal happenings and will have knowledge of the new king. I have invited him to join us for supper."

Their escort, wearing the king's white and blue livery, led them to Westminster Palace where they would lodge while in London. A few hours later, Donald's friend found them in the great hall where a blazing fire and candles illuminated the stone walls, casting shadows on the tapestries. They were just about to sit down to dine when Willie approached.

Donald grasped his friend's forearm. "It has been too long, my friend."

Willie, a man of slender proportions, was not tall either, such that no one would notice him even attired as he was in a splendid tunic of fine dark brown wool. His thin face broke into a grin that took years from his countenance. "I have missed you, Donnie. Judging by your appearance, I can see that your Isles suit you."

"That and a loving wife and growing family," said Donald. "I have missed seeing you, too, my friend, though I do read your few letters."

With a sheepish look, Willie said, "I write when I can."

Donald smiled for he had teased Willie in the past and the man always took it with good grace. "And what of your family?"

A hint of a smile crossed Willie's face. "Three girls, who are my constant delight."

"Two sons and two daughters for me," said Donald, "though I trust God is not done blessing us."

Donald introduced Willie to his brother, "The Lord of Dunyvaig and the Glens of Antrim. The impressive warrior next to John is my nephew, Hector Maclean, the Maclean's eldest son and the Lieutenant General of the Isles."

Then Donald gestured to his chaplain and physician. Once all were introduced, they moved to the far end of the table that was empty of others, allowing them to be private.

Willie addressed John Mor. "Ireland will be of interest to the king, particularly with its proclivity to rebel against English rule."

Servants brought platters of roast beef and fowl along with flasks of wine. Once they were alone again, Willie said, "Word of you has reached London, although the king has been preoccupied with many things. His advisors will doubtless have informed him by the time you meet tomorrow."

"And what is it he will know of us?" asked Donald.

"He will know you rule the Isles like an independent king though you are under the Stewarts. He is aware you were allied with King Richard and served England in many respects, particularly in Ireland where you are allied with the O'Neill. He will also know you are willing to take military action to pursue your objectives and have the might to be successful. Lastly, he will know that you and the Stewarts are not often in agreement."

"Well, that is correct," said John Mor.

Willie returned John Mor a small smile. "Such knowledge will please the king."

Donald was interested in what could be known about the king as well as themselves. "Tell me, what is the king like and what occupies his mind?"

"Henry came to the throne as a usurper and his enemies will not let him forget it. He faces rebellion from many quarters. Just last month, he had to put down a rebellion by King Richard's noble followers." With a somber expression, he added, "They were executed without trial. Moreover," he continued, "King Charles of France refuses to acknowledge Henry as king. He even turned away Henry's ambassadors. There is a fragile truce between the two countries initiated by Richard, but battles are still fought within it."

"And other countries?" asked John Mor.

"Ireland is less stable now than under Richard," said Willie. "Wales, too, is a threat. Owain Glyndwr, a descendant of the princes of Powys, has named himself Prince of Wales and seems determined to throw off English rule. He is a man of some bearing and intelligence, having studied law in London and served in battle with Henry before he was king. When Glyndwr returned to Wales, he was outraged by the effect of England's rule on his people." Willie paused to eat, and then, with a flourish of his eating knife, said, "Of course, you must know about the raids by the Scots on the northern border."

"We have heard of them," said Donald, intentionally understating what he knew.

"There are financial worries, too," said Willie. "Henry is constantly forced to borrow and is less conscientious than Richard in repaying his creditors." Willie grew quiet and then leaned in to whisper. "There are rumors spoken only in hushed conversations in dark taverns…" He paused. "Rumors that the man whose body was carried to St. Paul's and displayed as that of King Richard was not Richard at all but his chaplain, a priest named Maudelain, who greatly resembled him."

Donald's mouth dropped open and a sudden coldness swept over him. "Surely there can be no truth in it. We understood King Richard was starved to death at Pontefract."

"He was said to have despaired so at the murder of his royal supporters that for a time he did not eat, but Richard and food are not long parted."

"You are serious!" exclaimed Donald.

"I spoke of rumors," said Willie in a subdued manner. "If Richard lives and has escaped, I have not seen him, but I thought you should be aware. Henry knows the truth, of course, but he says nothing, as you would expect. Still, I find it curious that the head of the man whose corpse was shown to all in London was concealed, but for the lower part of the face. Richard's yellow hair would have enabled the people to identify their late monarch. Also, the body was not buried in Richard's tomb in Westminster Abbey, but removed to Langley where it was buried in secret."

Donald had been listening carefully. "If I understand all you have told us, King Henry is mired in matters of concern and unstable alliances. Moreover, he is watching his back for a returning Richard. Thus, he will want to make sure he will not face my Islesmen or my brother's Irishmen on the field of battle. For one thing, he cannot afford it."

"Certainly that," said Willie, "though if there is one thing that can be said for Henry it is his prowess on the battlefield." Pausing as if to consider, Willie said, "Like Richard before him, he would have you and your brothers hold the Stewarts at bay in the west. He can hardly face them on two fronts."

"Lord Donald has already seen to some of that," put in Hector.

"Even at the risk of King Robert's displeasure, as I hear tell," said Willie.

"Aye," said Hector, nodding. "It was a splendid rout."

Donald explained, "That was necessary so that the Isles were not overrun by King Robert's brother, the Duke of Albany."

Willie stared into his wine, the flickering candlelight casting shadows on his face. "There is something else I would tell you but, like the rumors about King Richard, you may not breathe a word of it. Not even his council is aware."

With raised brows, Donald waited.

"Despite all I have told you, the king has reason to be in a good mood. He has just received a letter from Joan of Navarre, the Duchess of Brittany, who is an important member of the French royal family. I am told it has warmed the king's heart. They met when he was sojourning in France. She and Henry share their widowed status, their enthusiasm for the Trinity and orthodoxy, and an apparent fondness for each other. But, due to the fragility of the truce between the two countries, the presence of the Navarrese ambassadors at court has been explained by Henry in vague terms without reference to a possible royal wedding."

"How do you know this?" asked Donald.

Willie shrugged. "It is best that I do not tell you. Suffice it to say not all of those the king counts as his friends are true to him. There are few secrets as concerns Henry."

"I am glad you told us all that you have," said Donald. "You need have no worry that we should mention this or you to others, for we have no reason to do so." When all had finished their meal, Donald took a last drink of his wine and rose, offering his hand to his friend. "Willie, you have informed us beyond my expectations and given us leverage with which to make an alliance. I thank you."

"My pleasure, Donnie, for I count you a friend."

THE NEXT MORNING, Donald was summoned for his audience with the king. Willie had told him the king favored fine raiment. Wanting to show the Isles in the best light, Donald wore a tunic of crimson wool edged in scrolling golden thread. Over it, he wore an open robe of dark blue silk with a draping beaver collar. His gilded belt spoke of his lordship, his sword of his willingness to wield his authority. His dark red beard was trimmed close to his face but his fair hair hung to his shoulders.

John Mor was attired in a green silk tunic edged with a Celtic design, proclaiming his ties to Ireland. His hose were madder red.

Hector could not have hidden his bulk had he tried, but his dress this day in gray and black was understated unless you considered the red squirrel pelts that formed a small cape over his shoulders. Behind the three of them walked Donald's impressive galloglass guard, wearing the livery of the Lord of the Isles, for Donald wanted this new king to be aware of the standing of those with whom he was to meet.

His chaplain was to attend as well since he was Donald's secretary. Attired in his black robes, his role would be clear to all.

They entered the hall where the king sat his throne on a raised dais, flanked by men in noble dress. Whether advisors or friends, Donald could not say. While they studied Donald and his Islesmen, he compared this king to the one he had overthrown.

Richard's face, in his twenties when he and Donald met, had been round and rosy-cheeked, his red beard scant. He was a lover of food and Chaucer's tales, whose hatred of Henry had led to his demise. Henry, though in his early thirties, appeared older, his face lined from his many battles, his jousts, his travels to the sun-filled Holy Land, and his current worries. He sat erect, his golden crown shining in the candlelight, his mustache and forked beard were dark and his midnight eyes assessing. His robes were many and ornate, and around his shoulders was the distinctive Lancastrian livery collar composed of silver links, each a letter "s".

They were announced as "Donald of Islay, Lord of the Isles, and his brother, John Mor, Lord of Dunyvaig and the Glens, accompanied by Hector Maclean of Duart, Lieutenant General of the Isles and David MacMurchie, chaplain and secretary to the Lord of the Isles."

"Your Majesty," said Donald, bowing with his companions before England's monarch. Richard had wanted to be addressed in that manner and Donald could not imagine Henry would demand less. Rising, three sets of blue eyes, if you didn't count Donald's guard, gazed at the king, waiting to be acknowledged.

"We are glad you have come," said King Henry. "For some time, we have desired to meet with you. Was your travel to your liking?"

"We sail in all weather," said Donald.

"Ah, yes," said the king. "I am told you have ships…many ships."

Donald acknowledged the truth of it by inclining his head.

"Let us retire to a more private space to discuss our alliance," said the king. He rose and, stepping down from the dais, walked ahead, flanked by two men, toward a corridor. Donald waved his guard to the side where they would wait for him. Then, with John Mor,

Hector and Father MacMurchie, he followed King Henry.

The king must have had a private meeting in mind, for they stepped into a smaller hall where he directed them to chairs circling a table where a platter of cheese, bread and apples was set. A servant arrived to pour wine. Donald did not drink. Neither did the king.

Once seated, King Henry introduced the two men with him as his secretary and his friend and steward, Sir Peter Bucton. "We understand you were educated at Oxford," said the king.

"I was," said Donald. "And, of course, I returned to London a few years ago to meet with your predecessor." He spoke English as Willie had told him it was now the language of the court, owing to the bad relations with France, though both King Henry and Donald could speak French.

"We are aware of the alliance between the Isles and England," said the king. "We would continue it, even enhance it, should you be willing."

"We are not allied with any of your enemies," Donald assured the king, thinking of not only Scotland, but France and Wales. "And we are willing to continue the alliance. In truth, it was the lack of constancy of the Stewart king who was my grandfather, that caused my father to join arms with England. We have long been in Ireland. But in recent years, our presence in Ulster has grown. This has worked to both England's advantage and ours."

The king turned to John Mor. "We believe you are married to Margery Bissett of Antrim."

"I am," said John. "When we are not in the Isles, we are at our castle in the Glens of Antrim where we have many friends."

"Should you be amenable," the king said to John, "I would have you hold the Glens as my vassal."

"In exchange?" Donald interjected.

"In exchange for England's friendship and support for the Macdonalds in both Ireland and Scotland."

It was the support of England's king as to Scotland Donald most wanted, but it made sense not to accept too quickly. "You will give us time to consider?"

"Yes, of course," said King Henry. "Return to me in June with your answer. I will see you have a safe conduct. Until then, the current alliance will, with your agreement, remain in effect."

Satisfied, Donald inclined his head. "I thank you, Your Majesty."

"You and your company are invited to dine with me this evening," said the king.

"It would be our pleasure to accept," said Donald. "I have others with me, including my physician, who would greatly look forward to that."

Back in their lodgings, John Mor and Hector pelted Donald with questions. "Why didn't you just agree?" asked John Mor. "I don't mind being his vassal if it means the might of England secures me."

"And won't he have our backs against the Stewarts?" said Hector. "It seems what we want."

Donald allowed his voice to be firm. "I do not want the English king to think we are at his beck and call. Nor that we are weak and desperate for aid," he said. "From what Willie told us, the king may be in greater need of us than we are of him. There is time to consider and June is a good month for travel. Besides that, John, you should consider what being a vassal of the English king would mean. He may, and likely will, require things of you. And there is another reason to delay our answer. Should the spies of the Duke of Albany report of yet another meeting of the Lord of the Isles with England's king, it will stand us in good stead."

That night, they supped with the king, his friends and councilors. They were joined by the king's eldest son, Henry, Prince of Wales. He was fourteen and proud of the fact he had been in Ireland with King Richard the year before. The widowed king had other, younger sons and two daughters, Blanche and Philippa, who were too young to join them.

Seated between the king and his son, Donald spoke often to the king, but he also struck up a conversation with the prince about his years at Oxford, as young Henry had been educated there, too.

"I not only learned to read and write there," said the prince. "I learned to love music."

"I found much good in those years as well," replied Donald. He did not mention his master, John Wycliffe, who had influenced his thinking of clerics. Willie had told him that while King Henry's father, John of Gaunt, was a friend to the scholar, his son, King Henry, considered Wycliffe's followers to be heretics.

The food served that evening was excellent, but it was not a dinner King Richard would have applauded. The beef was tender, the tarts freshly baked, the vegetables well-cooked, but the menu lacked the panache of the prior king, and the memory of his meeting with Richard made Donald feel sad for a royal life cut short.

The next day, Donald rose early and broke his fast with his companions. "We will stay one day longer in London," he said.

"And what will you do?" asked his brother.

"I want to call on a poet and then buy gifts for my lady and my children."

"Shaming us all," said Hector with a glance at John Mor. "Very well, I will join you to purchase gifts and might as well come along for the other, too. I dare not return empty-handed to my wife."

Ardtornish Castle, Morvern, early March 1400

MARIOTA HAD COME to the front of the castle to gaze out on the Sound of Mull as she often did to watch for Donald's return. Today, the waters flowing between the Isle of Mull and Morvern were the color of slate, matching her mood. He had only been gone for a matter of weeks but she missed him.

Wrapped in her warmest cloak, for the morning was cold and windy, her gaze was drawn to a pair of sea eagles fishing in the sound's waters. As she looked toward the west, she spotted a sail. She knew it could not be Donald's galley, since he would be coming from Duart to the east.

As the galley drew closer, she recognized the outline of Iona Abbey on the pennon that told her it was John MacAlister's ship. Once the crew beached the galley on the sand, she waved to John, who stood out in his black robes, and walked down to the shore. She welcomed him to Ardtornish with great joy, for she had not seen the prior for some while. Gesturing to the bounty of wildflowers growing on the slope leading to the castle, she said, "You have brought us an early spring!"

John looked around as if just noticing the flowers. "God is good," he said. "I am ready to put winter behind me."

They walked up the hill together toward the castle where Sir Thomas stood guard like a brooding dark angel.

"Young Angus has been asking for you," Mariota said to John. "Since he turned five, he has become aware that his father and I would see him follow in your steps, which makes you of special interest. Sandy is appalled, of course, for he assumed his brother would be at his side, taking *his* orders, not God's."

John laughed. "My brothers assumed the same thing about me. Sandy will find others to order about. He will make a strong chief." As they approached the castle door, John greeted Sir Thomas and asked her, "Where are the children this morning?"

"Mari and Anna are learning embroidery in the solar, and the boys are attempting to play chess in the great hall. Sandy is impatient but Angus, who is sometimes more clever at the game though he is younger, is tolerant."

The door was opened and Mariota and the prior strolled into the hall, followed by Sir Thomas. The boys left their game to run to them. "Father John!" said Angus.

John stooped to give them each a hug. "You two have grown!"

"What did you expect?" asked Sandy. "Father says we must grow to be as tall as him!"

John patted Mariota's eldest on the shoulder. "And you surely will!"

Angus took the prior's hand, giving him a fond look, for he admired his mentor and godfather.

Mariota called for refreshments and Sir Thomas invited the boys outside for sword practice with their wooden swords.

"I will see you later," John told them when they were reluctant to leave him.

Mariota poured John a goblet of wine and suggested they move to the fireplace, the warmest place in the castle. Once they were seated, she asked, "Do you have news for us?"

"I have a report about the situation with Abbot Finguine MacKinnon. Is Donnie here?"

"He is expected any day, along with Alex who will be coming from Lochaber. Donald was in London to see the new English king. He had a good relationship with King Richard, and is hoping for the same with King Henry."

The prior took a sip of his wine and leaned back in his chair, staring into the flames. "I will be interested to hear what Donnie has to say about Henry."

John's face had matured since she had last seen him, or, given that his dark beard was still free of gray, perhaps the added lines were from his worry for the spiritual matters of the lordship. "From where have you come?"

"Today, from Iona, but before that from all the parish churches in the lordship."

"Are you pleased with what you have seen?"

"In some cases, very pleased. In others, I would make changes. And then there are some things, I fear, we must bear with patience. I am glad Alex is coming as he may have more information on at least one situation. You are welcome to join us though the internecine squabbles of holy church can be tiring. Still, I know the spiritual needs of the lordship are important to both of you."

STANDING IN THE stern of his galley, Donald felt the brisk sea air on his face as the ship cut through the waves. They had sailed from England, replacing the stench of London with the smell of the sea that was salt, kelp and fish. At Red Bay Castle on Antrim's coast, they left his brother, who was anxious to tell his wife, Margery, of his meeting with King Henry.

Two days later, Donald dropped Hector at Duart Castle and then sailed down the Sound of Mull to Ardtornish Point. His spirits soared as his castle came into view, for he was eager to see Mariota and show her the gifts he had purchased in London. Gifts that would tell her he was thinking of her even as he met with England's king.

His crew beached the ship and Donald's retinue climbed down.

Grabbing his satchel, he jumped to the sand, looking up to the top of the small hill leading to the castle. There stood his brother, Alex, and his friend, John MacAlister, waving.

As he arrived at the top of the hill, Mariota came through the castle door. She beamed at him and came to welcome him home. Her beautiful eyes glistened with tears.

"You missed me?" he asked. Before she could answer, he kissed her. "I missed you as well." His brother and his friend stood smiling.

The door of the castle was flung open to reveal his two sons running toward him. "Father!"

He set down his satchel and swept them into his arms. "Have you been good?"

"Very good," said Sandy.

"Sometimes," said Angus, his more truthful son.

"Well, then," said Donald, "you shall have presents!" Out of his satchel, he drew two spinning tops painted in bright colors and two carved wooden horses. The boys, their faces radiant with joy, accepted their toys and ran into the castle. He rose and said to Mariota, "I have some things for our daughters and for you, too, my love."

Mariota took his arm. "Why don't we all go into the hall where you can be refreshed? Cook will be preparing your favorite dishes for supper, and a bath awaits if you desire. Then I will see the gifts you have brought me."

He gazed into her lovely hazel eyes framed by the golden curls that the wind blew around her face. "Yes, a bath would be welcome. I am sure I smell of fish, though that is an improvement over the streets of London. Can you manage to keep my brother and the prior entertained until I have changed?"

Alex rolled his eyes. "The good prior and I have been entertaining ourselves and your gracious wife for two days, Dear Brother. An hour's wait until we dine will not tire us unduly. But we do want to hear the news from London and John has some news of his own."

Mariota must have ordered the bath when she first spotted his galley. It was waiting for him in their chamber. As he sank into the steaming water, he let out a sigh.

Mariota came through the door. "Here, let me wash your back."

She had done it many times before, but there was something about her care in the task that always made him smile.

"How was London?" she asked.

"Crowded, begrimed and malodorous. But if one is to see the king, one must endure it. After my meeting with Henry, I paid a visit to Mr. Chaucer." She finished scrubbing his back and came around to kneel by the tub. Her eyes lit up. "Chaucer?"

"I thought you would be interested. The poet has taken a lease on a house in the garden of Westminster Abbey, which is quite nice, and he remains in the new king's favor. But he is not well, I am sorry to say. One of your gifts is his newest story, *The Parson's Tale*. I look forward to our reading it together."

"Oh, Donald! How wonderful!" Again, he was reminded that he had a wife who treasured the written word above jewels, though he had given her those, too.

"Dry your hands and look in my satchel. It is there along with two dolls for our daughters."

She did as he asked and carefully lifted the dolls and placed them on the side table. "The girls will treasure them." Then she sat on the bed and took out the manuscript, gazing at it adoringly. "Tonight," she said, "we must begin to read it tonight."

He rose from the bath and wrapped the drying cloth about his waist. Taking the manuscript from her, he carefully set it aside and took her into his arms. "Perhaps, but at this moment, I have something else in mind."

She reached her hands to his shoulders. "A better gift."

CHAPTER 15

IT WAS MORE than an hour later when Mariota and Donald descended the stairs in Ardtornish Castle to the great hall. Prior John and Alex were sitting at the long table, the latter looking at Donald with raised brows. Discerning their thoughts, Mariota felt her cheeks flush. To divert their attention, she asked, "Has Cook said when supper will be served?"

With an exasperated glance at Donald, Alex said, "She has come twice to inquire when the master and his lady might wish to dine."

Mariota turned to a servant and asked that the cook be informed they were ready.

One of Donald's guards approached him with a large package, whispering in his ear.

"Please put it in our chamber," said Donald. Then turning to her, he added, "Your other gift."

"Are we to know what it is?" inquired Alex.

Mariota nodded to Donald. She didn't mind they learned at the same time she did what was hidden behind the wrapping.

"Silk and fine wool for my lady's gowns," said Donald. "You will have to wait to see them until my lady wears them."

Remembering her husband's excellent choice of fabric, Mariota experienced a rush of excitement. "I will look forward to that."

Supper was served soon thereafter. Donald had invited his chaplain, Father MacMurchie, and his physician, Fergus Beaton, to dine with them. They came from their chambers above the hall. "The scent of well-cooked food drew us," said the chaplain. "It being Lent, we eat fewer meals and, by this time, hunger looms."

Mariota was pleased that some of Donald's favorites were acceptable for Lent, which had begun only a week before, including salmon in green sauce and roasted trout with rosemary and thyme. Fresh bread and wine, as well as vegetables, were also allowed. And, for a sweet, apple tarts made with crushed almonds.

Servants carried in platters of food. The men wasted no time in spearing slices of fish with their eating knives.

Donald said, "I brought some wines from the Continent that were being praised in London."

Wiping his mouth, Alex said, "While you were above stairs, two servants carried several small barrels into the kitchens. Perhaps that is what we are drinking now."

"Whatever it is," said John, tasting his wine, "'tis very good."

Donald sipped his wine between bites of fish. "Yes, this is the wine." Then glancing at John, he said, "We are all ears, Cousin. Tell us your news."

John set down his knife. "On the positive side, I have been to see the Bishop of Glasgow, Matthew Glendonwyn, and the Bishop of Dunkeld, Robert de Cardeny, about Finguine MacKinnon. They are the senior, most experienced bishops and most knowledgeable of our local politics. They are also recognized as strong Scottish supporters of the Avignon Pope Benedict. I am convinced that Michael, Bishop of the Isles, who sided with the MacKinnons and enabled Finguine to be reconfirmed as abbot, was misled by the smooth-tongued green abbot."

"And what did they say?" asked Donald.

"They have reviewed the facts and agree the petition should be pursued. Of course, these things take time, Donnie. I believe we will be successful, but this will not happen quickly."

"No, I expect not." Mariota could see her husband was frustrated by the delay, but grateful to John. Donald added, "I am glad you have moved the matter forward. This news you described as positive. Is there negative news?"

John let out a heavy sigh. "There is. I fear the Bishop of Sodor is a royal agent, perhaps he was chosen at the urging of Albany his brother, in order to check your power. I have already suggested why Michael, Bishop of the Isles, is compromised so that we cannot look to him for relief. In addition, your former chaplain, Bean Macgillandris, who is now Bishop of Argyll, holds on to the rectory of Kilmonivaig in Lochaber for the benefice it gains him. However, I am aware that Alex has nominated another to fill that position."

Donald turned to his brother. "Is that so, Alex?"

"Aye. I would have Cristinus Dominici called Macdonnailylech fill the role."

"The position is under the patronage of the Lord of the Isles," said John, "and in this instance the Lord of Lochaber, so it is for you to say, Alex, but Macgillandris will resist."

"Macgillandris would defy his patron?" asked Donald, his expression incredulous.

John shook his head. "Doubtless he is counting on the difficulty of removing an incumbent in possession."

"I will see what I can do," said Donald.

Mariota had listened with interest, all the while watching her husband's face, knowing how much he cared about these developments. The church had great influence and it did not surprise her the Stewarts would try and use it to thwart Donald.

After supper, Mariota and Donald went to see their children, presenting the cloth dolls with embroidered faces to the girls, who were delighted. At seven and eight, such toys appealed but Mariota knew soon they would be wanting silks and satins. They left the girls to their dolls and the boys to watch a game of chess being played by John and Alex.

As they began the climb to their chamber, Donald looked back and said from the stairs, "I have a story to read to my wife. On the morrow, John, you may want to read it. It's Chaucer's new story, *The Parson's Tale.*

"Yes, indeed," said John. "Finally, one I can relate to."

ONCE IN THEIR chamber, Donald unrolled the fabrics he had purchased, a rose-colored patterned silk and a length of fine wool in dark green and laid them on the bed. Both would look lovely with her golden hair and green-gold eyes. Leaning on the bedpost, he watched Mariota's eyes grow large as she fingered the cloth.

"Oh, Donald! These are exquisite."

"I thought you might want to wear the rose silk when we visit your brother at Dingwall, and the green wool will serve you well in the Isles."

"I will have the tailor begin immediately." She left her gift to come to him, reaching her arms around his neck and drawing him close for a kiss. "Thank you, my thoughtful husband."

A fire blazed in the fireplace and candles, set about the room, added a warm glow. Outside the castle walls, the wind howled. He would have been content to spend the evening curled up in her arms, but he had promised her they would read Chaucer's tale together. "Shall we begin *The Parson's Tale?*"

She nodded and they took their seats facing each other in front of the fire. Donald took up the manuscript, opening it to the beginning.

"Here is how he is introduced…"

> *There was also riding with us a good man of religion, the poor parson of a small town. He was poor in wealth, perhaps, but rich in thought and holy works. He was also a learned man, a clerk, who preached Christ's gospel in the most faithful fashion and who taught his parishioners the lessons of devotion. He was gracious, and diligent; in adversity, as he proved many times, he was patient. He had a large parish, with the houses set far apart, but neither rain nor thunder would prevent him from visiting his parishioners in times of grief or dearth. He gave the best possible example to his flock. Perform before you preach. Good deeds are more fruitful than good words. He… protected his flock from the wolves of sin and greed that*

threatened it. He was a true shepherd. He wanted to draw people to God with kind words and good deed. He simply taught, and followed, the law of Christ and the gospel of his apostles.

"It sounds like this parson is your Master Wycliffe," said Mariota.

"He does." Then, scanning the first few pages, Donald said, "The parson refuses to speak in verse but insists on telling his story in prose. He begins by speaking of penitence, that is repentance for sins."

"If Chaucer is nearing the end of his life, it is not surprising he would be concerned with God's view of such things," said Mariota. "I know I would."

"It seems this tale is more serious than the others," Donald said reading ahead. "I will read to you some of what he has written."

Many are the spiritual ways that lead folk to our Lord Jesus Christ and to the reign of glory. Of which ways there is a very noble and a very suitable way, which cannot fail to man nor to woman who through sin has gone astray from the right way to Jerusalem celestial; and this way is called Penitence...

Donald raised his gaze from the page. "I think this is not a tale like the others but a sermon from a virtuous priest, one like Wycliffe."

"Can you tell me what his sermon is concerned with?"

Donald scanned ahead. "He speaks of the seven deadly sins for which Christ suffered and died on our behalf that we might be granted forgiveness upon our repentance. Here is a part of it."

Now is it a suitable thing to tell what are the seven deadly sins, this is to say, chieftains of sins. They all run on one leash, but in diverse manners. Now are they called chieftains, forasmuch as they are chief and origin of all other sins. Of the root of these seven sins, then, is Pride the general root of all harms. For of this root spring certain branches, as Anger, Envy, Accidia or Sloth, Avarice or Covetousness (to common understanding), Gluttony, and Lechery. And every one of these chief sins has his branches and his twigs, as shall be declared in their chapters following.

"A very serious exposition," said Mariota.

"Wycliffe, too, urged us to trust wholly in Christ; to rely altogether on his sufferings; and to beware of seeking to be justified in any other way than by his righteousness."

Mariota nodded. "Wycliffe took his view solely from the Bible. Perhaps we should have John and Father MacMurchie read the tale and then discuss it with us."

Donald hefted the weighty manuscript before him. "That is a good idea, but since Chaucer includes a discussion of marriage toward the end, we might come together on our own to read that part."

She smiled up at him. "John and the chaplain might appreciate that decision."

Donald turned to the end of the manuscript. "At the end he speaks of Heaven that awaits those who strive to please God and turn from sin. He describes the life to come where 'there is neither hunger, thirst, nor cold, but every soul replenished with the sight of the perfect knowing of God.'"

"Yes, I look forward to that," she said. "And perhaps *The Parson's Tale* is a fitting end to all the tales told on the pilgrimage to Canterbury. Is that not the reason one sets out on a pilgrimage?"

Donald set the manuscript aside. "Words spoken by my wise wife."

The next morning, Donald gave the manuscript to John. "Mariota and I entrust this to your care, and to Father MacMurchie, if appropriate, to read and then discuss with us. 'Tis a meaty tome by Mr. Chaucer on the gospel and the seven deadly sins and how we should repent of them. The part about marriage you can leave to us, but we would have your thoughts on the rest."

John accepted the manuscript, handling it with care. "I am honored by your faith in me. I shall try my best."

"The teller of the tale is a virtuous priest," said Donald, "one of Chaucer's pilgrims and not unlike you, my friend."

In May, Donald met with the chiefs at Finlaggan on Islay to discuss the treaty he proposed with King Henry, one of mutual defense. He invited his brothers, John Mor and Alex, Hector Maclean and Prior John MacAlister to hear the debate should there be any. Along with the men came their families as was most often the case at

Finlaggan.

Mariota attended with their four children, now ranging in age from Sandy at nine, to Angus at five, the girls in between them. John Mor brought his wife, Margery, and their young son, Donald. Alex brought his wife, Mary Lennox, and their two children, Angus and Alexander.

As it turned out, the debate on the alliance with England did not last long. The chiefs wholeheartedly affirmed Donald's desire to make a new treaty.

Chief Lachlan Maclean, spoke for the others, in response to Donald's request. "With King Robert weak of body and retired to his lands in the west, and David his son made Lieutenant, but subject to the oversight of his uncle, the ambitious Duke of Albany, there is no strong leader of good conscience in Scotland to whom we can look. Based on all you have said, Lord Donald, I support your intention to continue an alliance with England on whatever terms you deem best. We may need King Henry's resources at some point."

After the meeting, Donald, Mariota, their companions and children retired to his manor at Kilcummin on Islay's west coast. It was his intention to leave from there with John Mor to arrive in England in early June. While he was away, he thought the women and children could spend some blissful days at Machir Bay. The weather had warmed since March and, though it was still cool, it was pleasant enough to suit the children.

They had only been at Kilcummin for a few days when an unexpected visitor—indeed, a shocking one—arrived. The adults were gathered in what served as a great hall, just before the evening meal. Outside, the sky was still blue for the days were lengthening.

The older children were on an excursion with a few of his guards and the younger ones were with their nurses when one of his guards approached. "My lord, there is a man outside, who was brought here by fishermen. He claims to be King Richard the Second."

Taken aback, Donald thought at first it must be a ruse, planned by his brother or his nephew, either of which might play such a trick after what Willie had told them in London. But their faces only mirrored his own shock. "Show him in."

The man who crept hesitatingly into the hall was not dressed like—nor had he the appearance of—a king. He wore the clothes of a fisherman: a brown tunic, stained as if it had seen long wear, rough woolen hose, a rope belt and ill-fitting leather shoes. It was not the clothing of the richly attired monarch who Donald had met six years before in London. On his straggly blond hair, grown longer along with his beard, was a gray fisherman's cap. He looked older than his thirty-three years, and he was thinner, his face less round. But the eyes and the set of the jaw were the same. Donald's memory for faces told him this was, indeed, Richard the Second, England's deposed king. He appeared fearful, unsure of his reception.

"Your Majesty," said Donald, rising from his chair to come toward him. "It is you, isn't it?"

With those words, the man's expression showed great relief. "It is, Lord D-D-Donald."

"Come, sit with us," said Donald "and tell us all that has happened." He called for wine and food. "You must be hungry."

"The fishermen who b-b-brought me here shared their f-f-food, but yes, I am hungry," said Richard. "I seem always to be so these days."

Donald escorted his guest to the table and gave him the center seat. Those who gathered around the table to hear the king's story were the men and women who had come with Donald from Finlaggan, Prior John MacAlister, John Mor and Alex and their wives and Mariota, who came to sit by Donald across from Richard. Donald's chaplain and secretary, Father MacMurchie, and his physician Fergus Beaton, joined them.

They waited until the king had taken some wine and bread, after which he said. "Thank you."

"I remember you from Ireland," said Margery, John Mor's wife. "I was presented to you when you were meeting with the Irish lords."

"How g-good of you to remember," said Richard. It struck Donald then that this man, once the King of England, had been humbled by what had befallen him. His stammering was not as pronounced as before but it was still present when he spoke.

"Lady Margery is married to my brother, John Mor, Lord of

Dunyvaig and the Glens," Donald reminded Richard, gesturing to his brother. "He was with me when we met with you in London, along with Prior John MacAlister and Father MacMurchie."

"I do recall t-t-them quite clearly," said Richard. "I was t-t-told before you arrived in London that you are always in the company of priests."

"So I am," Donald acknowledged with a smile. Seeing the others hanging on Richard's every word, Donald asked, "Everyone thought you dead. However did you escape?"

Richard stared down at the bread in his hands, his brows drawn together. "When my cousin Henry g-gave the order to withhold food from the prisoner, some of those guarding me felt sorry for me. They still considered me their k-k-king, and so plotted a way of escape. They were aided by my noble friends, all of whom, I have been t-t-told, paid with their lives for doing so. The Franciscan friars hid me for some months and helped me make my way west. I knew you to be an honorable lord and, thus, it was always my intention to find r-r-refuge in your Isles. But when I had heard you were in London to meet with Henry, I w-w-worried you might hand me over to him."

"We will not do that," said Donald emphatically. "You are welcome to stay in the Isles, but you are a king and should be treated as one. I would propose to take you to my uncle, King Robert, who will shelter you in one of his castles. He is residing in the west, not far by galley."

Some discussion followed but, in the end, all agreed it was best if Richard could find protection behind King Robert's stone walls. Besides, with the king playing a lesser role in the government, he would have time to spend with Richard and likely would welcome such a royal guest.

After supper, they sent their guest off to bed, for he was greatly fatigued, then the men gathered around the fire to discuss their upcoming trip to England. "We will say nothing of this to King Henry," Donald told his companions. "Else he might demand we give him Richard as a condition of our alliance."

"He would, of course," said John Mor. "It is best Henry only learns of Richard's whereabouts when he is well-ensconced in

Scotland."

"He can stay here until we return and then sail with us," said Donald. "I had planned to take Mariota to visit her brother the Earl of Ross at Dingwall. We can stop at Rothesay Castle on the Isle of Bute where King Robert is residing to see Richard is safe."

"I will go with you," said John MacAlister.

"Your presence is welcome, John, and will likely bring comfort to Richard, as will yours, David," he said to Father MacMurchie. "I will need your services in London, David, but might I ask you, John, to stay with Richard until I return? I will leave some guards and, of course, Mariota will act as hostess. You might share your thoughts with her on Chaucer's tale we left with you."

"It would be my pleasure," said his friend.

It was the first of June when Donald arrived in London with a large escort of horse by permission of King Henry. As before, they dined with Willie Thorpe that evening. No mention was made of the deposed King Richard as Donald did not want to burden his friend with confirmation that the monarch lived, at least not until he was safe.

The next morning they met with King Henry, initially in the throne room. He appeared glad to see them, but Donald looked at the king differently, knowing he had likely ordered Richard's death and then pretended his cousin died though he knew Richard lived. A liar and a would-be murderer, no wonder he had enemies.

"Have you an answer for me, Lord Donald?" asked the king.

"I believe we do. I am prepared to enter into a treaty whereby we have each other's backs, as it were."

"Good. And will the Lord of Dunyvaig and the Glens," he said, shifting his gaze to John Mor, "hold his lands in Antrim as my vassal?"

"Yes, Your Majesty," said Donald's brother. They had talked it through and decided the benefits outweighed any obligations.

"We shall have our secretary draw up the documents to be signed this day," said the king. "They will signify a final peace, alliance and friendship between you and us. We might begin with a period of five years."

"That will be acceptable to us," said Donald. "A good reason to return at the end of that time."

The king smiled his approval and, before the day was ended, the treaty was signed and sealed.

They did not remain in London but departed the next day, for Donald was anxious to get back to Mariota and the children…and to learn how Richard had fared. When they arrived at Kilcummin, the sun was shining. He and his companions climbed down from the galley to the white sand of Machir Bay. Margery met her husband and welcomed him back. Mariota and John MacAlister came with her.

Before his wife could say a word, Donald kissed her on the cheek. "How have things gone here, my love?"

Mariota's demeanor was unruffled. "Judging from your anxious expression, better than you expected. As John will tell you, His Majesty, now attired in clothing more fitting to his station and safely away from those who hunt him in England, has been delighting the children, especially the boys, with stories of his adventures as a young king. That is where he is now. In one of his stories, he told them of his time during the Peasants Revolt when he was only fourteen and, surrounded by rebels, managed to suppress an uprising. Our children were duly impressed by his courage in the face of the mob."

"They were," said Prior John. "I think the deposed king showed them what a young peacemaker can do when determined. Besides, he is a jolly sort and makes the children laugh. And when he is not with the children, he is persuading the cook to try a new recipe."

In truth, Donald had been worried. Now, realizing his decision to leave Richard on Islay while he was away had been a good one, he could smile. "I am glad to hear it." As they turned to go into the manor, he said, "Tomorrow, we will sail north with all but John Mor and Margery who plan to spend some time at Dunyvaig."

Summer was at its zenith when they put in at Rothesay Bay on the east coast of the Isle of Bute. On a rise above the bay stood the round stone fortress that was a Stewart royal castle. Four huge drum towers projected from the round curtain wall to make for a stately edifice. Swans floated unconcerned in the surrounding moat fed by a burn flowing from Loch Fad. Donald had been here in his youth and he wanted his children to see it. "The king is your uncle," he explained to them. "Be on your best behavior."

"That means proper bows," added Mariota, "and polite responses to any questions."

The children gazed at the large fortress and nodded.

The guard at the gatehouse might not recognize Donald, so he announced himself. "Donald of Islay, Lord of the Isles, here to visit my uncle, the king, and to present his nieces and nephews to him." He did not introduce either his chaplain, his physician or Prior John. His retinue would be assumed. Nor did he mention Richard, who wore a hooded cloak. They had decided to wait until they appeared before King Robert to reveal his presence.

They did not have to wait long and were escorted by a liveried guard up a narrow staircase to the great hall where a fire burned in the huge stone hearth. The presence of the children would confirm his stated purpose and quell any alarm raised by a visitor not on the king's schedule.

In the great hall, King Robert did not rise from his chair by the fire, possibly, thought Donald, because he would have needed help to do so. Since a horse had kicked him, he was lame.

Donald and his family and companions walked toward the king. Donald bowed, "Uncle, my lord king, please forgive my uninvited appearance."

"Nonsense," said the king. "It is high time you paid me a visit." His silver hair rested on his shoulders and his long beard, also silver, flowed down his chest. His hooked nose was prominent in his aging, florid face. To Donald's mind, he appeared older than his mid-sixties.

"Allow me to introduce my wife, Mariota of Ross. I believe you knew her mother, the late Countess of Ross."

"I did," said the king, "a grand lady. I see you have her beauty, my lady."

Mariota bowed, "Thank you, Your Majesty."

Donald continued, "And these are our children, Alexander, the eldest called 'Sandy', Mari, our redheaded child, Anna and Angus."

The king beckoned the children to him and they approached, dutifully bowing as they had been taught. "What handsome children!" the king exclaimed.

Then, turning to the clerics with him, Donald introduced them as "my good friend, cousin and the Prior of Iona, John MacAlister, and my chaplain, Father MacMurchie." He then introduced his physician, Fergus Beaton. When this had been accomplished, Donald said, "I had two purposes in coming, Uncle. First, I wanted you to meet my lady wife and our children, and second, I wanted to bring you another unexpected guest, who I hope you will find a boon companion." He turned to the cloaked figure. "King Richard of England."

The deposed king, came forward and slipped the hood from his head to reveal his blond hair well-groomed. Richard was attired in a fine tunic and hose, very different than when he first appeared on Islay. Inclining his head, he said, "King Robert."

The king's mouth fell open. "But you were dead!"

"That is what Henry wanted all to b-b-believe, but with the aid of noble friends, I escaped his death sentence to Lord Donald's Isles."

"Amazing!" King Robert called for his manservant to bring him his staff and, with its aid, he managed to rise. Once standing, he was tall, like Donald. Holding out his hand to Richard, the king said, "I welcome you to Scotland, good sir. We have no love for Henry here." Then looking deeply into Richard's eyes, he said, "I imagine you have been through much."

Richard accepted the hand of friendship. "Indeed, I have."

"I would be happy to keep Richard with me," said Donald, "but as he is of royal birth and now the hunted rightful king, I thought it best to bring him to you for protection."

"Yes, yes, that was wise. Come, let us partake of some wine and food and discuss what is to be done."

There were a dozen of them assembled around the table. The children, always happy to eat, and aware of the royal company they were in, were unusually quiet. John MacAlister sat on one side of them and Mariota on the other.

A platter of cold meats, cheese and bread was served, along with berry tarts and a bowl of summer fruits. There was watered ale and milk for the children and wine for the adults.

Once the servants retreated, the old King of Scots said to King Richard, who was half his age, "It seems we have both been set aside.

Since my accident, I cannot rule as I would wish. My brother, as Earl of Fife, became regent and managed Scotland's affairs, but that changed when, through the good efforts of my wife, Queen Annabella, who has taken on much when I could not, persuaded parliament to appoint my eldest son, David, now Duke of Rothesay, to be Lieutenant of the Kingdom."

"I see," said Richard. "Alas, I had no son to f-f-follow me and my heir was killed."

"Meantime," King Robert said, "Fife, who is now the Duke of Albany, has allied with Sir Archibald Douglas of Galloway. They fail to support my son. In truth, I think Albany dislikes David for the power he has been rightly given. Albany is not liked by the people, as David is. He is ruthlessly ambitious and doubtless jealous. He would prefer, I think, to rule all of Scotland with his son, Murdoch."

"I see the p-parallels," said Richard. "Be careful for your son, King Robert, if Albany is not above murder. But for the g-grace of God, I would have been starved to death at Pontefract."

Donald observed his older children growing restless and young Angus growing sleepy. Sharing a glance with his wife, he said, "Perhaps we should take our leave, my lords, so as not to overstay our visit. My young children have been well behaved up to this point, but I cannot say how long that will continue."

King Robert smiled at the children. "No, that would be unfair to them. But before you go, allow me to call my lady, the queen, to bid you welcome and adieu. She is with her ladies but will want to see you. And, by all means, dear Richard, do remain here as our guest."

"That is most g-g-gracious of you," said Richard.

At King Robert's request, the queen was summoned. She was a slight woman whose brown hair, pulled back from her face, was threaded with gray. But her eyes were alight with interest and intelligence. She wore her crown and elegant raiment so she must have been told who her guests were. By now, she would be in her early fifties. Her last son, young James, had been born six year before. As she entered, all rose from the table, except the king, her husband.

King Robert said, "My dear, I could not let our guests leave until you had the chance to meet them. Here is our nephew, Donald, Lord of the Isles, and his wife, Mariota of Ross and their children."

Donald bowed. "My lady. And with my family are several others." After he introduced John and Father MacMurchie, he said, "and Richard the Second of England."

King Robert added, "…who is to be our houseguest."

The queen stared at Richard but held her composure. "I'm certain my husband, the king, will explain all to me, but allow me to welcome you."

Not long after, Donald began to take his leave, bidding goodbye to his aunt and uncle. As he was parting from King Richard, he whispered, "Keep in touch. Letters can move quickly from here to Ardtornish Castle in Morvern where I am often in residence. If you need anything, please let me know."

"You have done m-m-much for me, Lord Donald. I will write of any news and give thanks to God for you in my prayers."

CHAPTER 16

Dingwall Castle, Ross, late July, 1400

MARIOTA HAD NOT been at Dingwall since her mother's death. Riding in from the west with Donald and their family, seeing it from a distance, the castle looked the same. Her heart warmed, remembering the days of her youth spent here: riding across the hills with her brother, playing in snow in winter and picking flowers to make summer wreaths.

Ross was a large earldom which, at this point, included the Isles of Skye and Lewis and the thanages of Dingwall, Deskford and Glendowachy. The Isle of Lewis only came into the earldom as a part of the marriage settlement of her mother and the Wolf of Badenoch, the crown ignoring the fact it had been in the Lordship of the Isles for over forty years.

Whoever controlled the shire of Ross controlled the majority of the Highlands and, thus, much of Scotland. A tempting domain for those, like Albany, with ambition to rule.

On their mother's death, Mariota's brother Alexander had succeeded to the earldom. He was only in his twenties, but he was capable of leading, and the Leslie family would stand with him. Mariota worried that Alexander might be influenced by Albany, who had helped their mother get free of the Wolf of Badenoch. Making that more certain, Albany had convinced Alexander to marry Isabel, one of his daughters.

A few years ago, Isabel had given birth to a daughter. They named her Euphemia after her grandmother. Mariota had yet to see the babe.

On their way to Dingwall, they had stopped at Ardtornish, and now arrived with a large retinue that included their children, Mariota's handmaiden, Sir Thomas and Donald's chaplain, physician and galloglass guard, as well as others in their service.

"A hearty welcome!" said Alexander, meeting them at the door. He had matured since Mariota had seen him last. A handsome man with golden hair and blue eyes, as she imagined their father might have been. Isabel, a shy thing, stood at his side smiling sweetly, her gaze falling on the Macdonald children gathered around them. Mariota was not surprised to find this daughter of Albany to be biddable. How would she be allowed to be anything else?

Introductions were made, ending with the names of their children: Fair-haired Sandy, redheaded Mari, and Anna and Angus with their light brown curls. Mariota had just discovered she was expecting another child, who would be born in the spring. She had yet to share the good news with Donald.

"We look forward to meeting your new daughter," said Donald.

"Much has happened in the years between your visits," said Alexander.

As they followed their host into the great hall, Donald asked, "We trust all is well here?"

"It is," said Alexander. There was something in his eyes that told Mariota there was more to the story. "I am glad you sent word so we could have your chambers ready." Glancing at the children's eager faces, he said, "Supper is not far off."

The children beamed and Donald said, "You see? I told you your uncle would feed you." And then to Alexander, "They are always hungry these days."

Over the course of their meal that night, Mariota learned that Alexander had been forced to sell some of his land to his kinsman George Leslie of Rothes in order to take control of the earldom from the crown's hands. "It is well you did," said Donald. "We have just been to see the king. It appears he is allowing his son, David, to take the lead in governing Scotland." Neither Mariota nor Donald would speak of Albany's ambitions with his daughter Isabel sitting at the table, but Mariota knew they both had him in mind.

Later, when the children had been sent to bed, supervised by their nurses, the men retired to the fireplace to talk. Mariota asked Isabel if she could see the young child. "She is sleeping now," said Isabel, "but we can visit the nursery to give you a glimpse of her."

Not yet two, the child was asleep, her nurse in attendance, when they went into the nursery. "She is a beautiful child," said Mariota, gazing at the child's rosy cheeks and perfectly shaped head covered with soft brown curls.

Isabel exchanged glances with the nurse. "There is a problem with her spine," said Isabel, looking at her child with a worried expression. "It curves at the top. The physician says it may not grow worse, and we are hoping that is the case. There is nothing he can do." Tears filled Isabel's eyes. Mariota took her hand and held it. "If this persists," said Isabel, "how can Phemie ever marry? How can she ever have a normal life?"

In truth, it might be that the child Euphemia never could, but Mariota wished to give comfort. "Do not worry about that now. Today, she is surrounded by love. That is most important."

"She is an intelligent child," said Isabel, her expression hopeful, as if trying to encourage herself.

"A woman of intelligence is always needed," said Mariota, but she understood well Isabel's questions. Should the child be deformed, she would be unlikely to attract suitors. Indeed, she might not be able to fulfill a woman's most important role, especially being an heiress.

"Your children are bright and active," said Isabel. "I envy you that."

Trying to be encouraging, Mariota said, "You and Alexander are young. God willing, you will have many, too."

That night, Mariota and Donald spoke of little Phemie as they lay in bed. "You were right in what you told her," said Donald. "We can pray that Phemie will have siblings to look after her."

Mariota told Donald her good news. "In the spring, if God wills, we will have another child."

Donald drew her close and kissed her temple. She heard the smile in his voice as he said, "I am pleased."

They kept their stay to a few days, during which time Mariota showed her children around the castle and the lands that had once been her home. One day, while Donald was occupied with her brother, she took her children with Isabel to nearby Tulloch Castle where she had been born. When she told Sandy they had been in Ross since leaving the coast, with wide eyes, he said, "Ross is very big, isn't it?"

"It is," said Mariota. "And your Uncle Alexander governs it all."

"Fortunately," said Isabel, "he does not have to do it alone. He has retainers and family who help us."

Mariota knew the Leslie kindred had done invaluable service to her mother, the countess, and would help Alexander as well. She had to wonder, however, how much Albany was involved. "Is your father here often?" she asked.

"Not often but he keeps his eye on Ross."

"Hardly surprising," remarked Donald when she told him later that day.

Ardtornish Castle, Morvern

AS AUGUST ARRIVED, Donald thought often of his visit to his uncle, King Robert. The deposed King Richard, still at Rothesay Castle, kept Donald informed of what was happening. Offered the opportunity to renew the peace between England and Scotland, King Robert had declined.

In September, Donald received a letter from Richard. It read in part,

King Robert sent a letter to Henry in which he referred to him as

the Duke of Lancaster, his title prior to ascending the throne. Know-
ing Henry as I do, he would have taken great offense to that. Prince
David, Duke of Rothesay, was also reluctant to recognize King Hen-
ry's coup as legitimate. Being aware that I am his father's guest,
such a stance would seem reasonable. However, adding Scotland's
raids across the border, it was not surprising that in August Henry
invaded Scotland. Plagued by bad weather and shortages of food and
supplies, the invasion came to nothing, thank God. Before the end of
the month, King Henry dragged his troops back to England where, I
am told, he had to deal with an uprising from Owain Glyndwr of
Wales.

Donald, watching these events from Ardtornish, was glad King
Robert had not called upon him to send men into the fight. His treaty
with England, made earlier that year, would have precluded such
assistance.

Before the year turned, Donald received word from Willie
Thorpe in London that Geoffrey Chaucer had died. He was saddened
by the news that meant there would be no more stories. But he did
not worry for Chaucer's soul, for his reading of *The Parson's Tale* had
told him the poet was in Heaven.

Mariota was late in her pregnancy and they looked forward with
eager expectation to a new addition to their family. Sandy wanted
another brother, one who would take his orders when he was the
chief. "It's more about serving," Donald told him, "than being
served."

His son, now ten, nodded stoically. "Yes, Father."

Mariota just smiled. "He will learn."

About the same time that Chaucer died, Prince David, Duke of
Rothesay's mother, Queen Anabella, passed from this life. With the
loss of her wise counsel and support, the prince fell prey to his uncle,
the Duke of Albany.

The following year, another letter came from Richard with sor-
rowful news.

Serious differences arose between the prince and his uncle. David
hurt himself by unjustifiably appropriating sums from the burghs on

211

the east coast and confiscating the revenues of the vacant bishopric of St. Andrews. Then he made matters worse by failing to consult his council, as he was required to do. His decisions were seen as threatening to the nobles. He is a young man, exuberant in his enthusiasm for governing, and was bound to make mistakes.

Albany, with the help of the prince's brother-in-law, the Earl of Douglas, had David arrested for his misdeeds (by members of David's own household!). The prince was first imprisoned in St. Andrews Castle. Later, Albany moved him to Falkland Palace, Albany's home in Fife. We heard the prince spent the journey hooded and mounted backward on a mule. King Robert was powerless to interfere.

Albany had to be worried that if King Robert were to die and Prince David made king, he would remember the ill treatment he had received at his uncle's hands. Having experienced such perfidy at my cousin's hands, I knew Albany would somehow bring about David's death. Perhaps Albany borrowed the idea from King Henry, for he confined the prince to Falkland's dungeon without food or drink or light, where he soon died.

The young prince made mistakes, certainly, but none so egregious as to justify death. Albany made it known that the prince had become ill and died in prison. Everyone believes that he was murdered by his uncle, but no one dares to tell this to the poor old king. I watched King Robert weep and mourn greatly for the loss of his son, whom he loved in spite of his weaknesses.

This leaves the king with only one remaining son, the boy James, who is eight years old and too young to rule. King Robert holds the boy close, for he has become afraid of his brother.

When Donald read this to Mariota, she said, "It seems Richard's warning to the king was prescient. Comely David's very existence threatened Albany. The prince was too young to die at Albany's hands."

"And with the help of Douglas, David's brother-in-law," added Donald. "Both will be called to account before parliament, but with Albany's power over the nobles, for which he has paid handsomely, I suspect nothing will come of it."

Mariota nodded. "Another demonstration of what Albany will do to retain power."

THE FOLLOWING SPRING, Mariota gave birth to another girl. She counted herself fortunate to have a husband who did not insist upon sons. In Donald's words, "God has given us another opportunity for an advantageous marriage alliance."

She gazed at Donald, who was holding the babe, as she pondered what they might name her. "Let's see...aside from our redheaded Mari, we have Alexander, Anna, and Angus. What do you think of Agnes for this one? The name means 'lamb' in Latin, and there is your sister, Agnes, who will be delighted."

"True, and there is St. Agnes of Rome to consider. She was said to be a great beauty."

Mariota laughed. "I could hardly argue with that."

And so, despite Sandy's disappointment in not gaining a brother, little Aggie joined the family.

In May, two months after Aggie was born, they received the shocking news that Mariota's brother, Alexander, died of a sudden illness, leaving his widow and, as his heir, his young daughter, Phemie. In a hastily arranged trip, Mariota and Donald traveled to Dingwall to comfort Isabel.

At Dingwall, they sat with the teary-eyed widow, her face red with mourning the loss of her husband. "We had no idea he was so ill," she said. "I should have seen it sooner."

"You must not blame yourself," Mariota told her. "When God calls us home we must go. He was my brother and I loved him but his time had come." Mariota, too, was mourning but for Isabel's sake, she tried not to show it.

"But what will I do? I have only little Phemie."

Mariota would not speak of it now, but Isabel was young and certain to remarry, especially with so powerful a father as Albany. "You have family, Isabel, not just the Stewarts but the Leslies and Donald and me. You are not alone."

"My father is coming," she said, drying her eyes. "He has sent word he intends to make Phemie his ward until she comes of age."

"My fear," Donald told Mariota later that night, "is that Albany will conspire to ensure that the Earldom of Ross, like other Highland earldoms, will be swallowed up by the Stewarts and their allies, and our claim to Ross, which is superior to his, will be ignored. They have created a vast regality for the Stewart heir to the throne, encompassing not only Ayrshire and Carrick, but the Argyll territories of Cowal, Knapdale, Arran and Bute, bordering the Lordship of the Isles. But for Alex and his men who patrol Moray and Lochaber, they would swallow up the Great Glen. I worry, too, about Kintyre."

"Still, there is little we can do about it now," said Mariota. "If Isabel gives her father the wardship and Phemie is her father's heir, we must wait."

"Yes, Donald said with a sigh, "you speak truth."

When Isabel's kin arrived, Mariota welcomed them, relieved others would be in attendance on her brother's widow. Hugh Ross of Rarichies, chief of Clan Ross, and Hugh Munro, Baron of Foulis, Mariota's cousin, came with their wives. The Munros were closely tied to Clan Donald and had fought with King Robert Bruce at Bannockburn. Neither man had much affection for Isabel's father, but they were a great comfort to her.

Knowing Isabel was in good hands, Mariota and Donald returned to Ardtornish where their children rushed to welcome them, all save Sandy, who at eleven was fostering with the Macleans on Mull. Red Hector's son, Lachlan, had fostered with Donald at Ardtornish, which made the bond between them strong.

By the time Sandy went to live with the Macleans, he had already learned Latin and history from Father MacMurchie and their resident bard, and sword fighting from the captain of Donald's guard. At Duart he would gain more experience in hunting the red deer on Mull, and sword fighting from Red Hector and his brothers. Then there was the management of a large estate to consider. Lachlan Maclean, a chief of great age, could teach him much.

Angus, now eight, was being tutored by Father MacMurchie or, when the chaplain was traveling with Donald, by his godfather, John MacAlister. Soon Angus would be fostered with another chief.

Mariota had retained Kenna, the educated wife of their constable, to help her with the older girls, Mari, age ten, and Anna, age nine. It was a busy household most days and Mariota had much to do, for Ardtornish was not their only castle and Donald often entertained the chiefs of the lordship.

IN AUGUST, AFTER dealing with urgent business of the Isles, Donald summoned his brothers and his most trusted chiefs to Ardtornish, along with Hector, his Lieutenant General, and Donald's good friend John MacAlister, to discuss the situation in Ross and the lordship's lands in Argyll threatened by Albany's moves.

Before the men arrived in their galleys, the children had been ushered from the hall and Mariota bid her husband good day.

Donald gave her an inquiring look. "Are you certain you do not wish to stay?"

She shook her head, her eyes full of mirth. "This is one meeting the results of which I would hear from you, Husband."

When his guests arrived, they took their seats around the large table in the great hall. Donald turned to the men whose advice he valued. "I gathered you here to discuss the challenges we face in Ross and our lands that border the ever expanding Stewart realm, including Kintyre."

Donald then began by bringing all up to date with the happenings in Ross. "Upon the unexpected death of my brother-in-law, Alexander Leslie of Ross, Mariota and I visited Alexander's widow, Isabel. She told us that her father, the Duke of Albany, was coming to assume control over her young daughter's affairs."

"Without a word about your wife's claim to Ross should the child fail?" asked Lachlan Maclean, his dark hair laced with gray displaying his age.

"None," said Donald. "And since then, he has seized the child and spirited her away, installing a man known as the Black Captain as guardian of Dingwall Castle. He has also installed his brother-in-law, Alexander Keith, as the Bailie of Kingedward, a part of the Ross patrimony. From his actions, I take it Albany means to control the earldom if not gain the title."

The chiefs frowned with Donald's words.

"What can you tell us about Alexander's young daughter?" asked William, the fair-haired chief of the Macleods.

"The child has a deformity that might prevent her having a normal life, much less leaving an heir to the title Countess of Ross. I expect Albany is counting on this to gain control."

"And the king?" asked Donald Dubh, the black-haired chief of the Camerons. "He is your uncle. Will he do nothing?"

Donald shook his head with regret. "The king has little power now. Albany, his brother, controls all the nobles through marriages and by granting them immunity for their misdeeds. He and his Douglas allies will act to contain any attempt by the king to renew his power. And with his eldest son's murder at Albany's hands, all the king's energies are focused on saving his last remaining son, young James, heir to the throne." With a glance at John MacAlister, he added, "It is not unrealistic to say Albany even controls the church."

"'Tis sad but true," said the Prior of Iona.

"For now," said Malcolm Macduffie of Colonsay, "can we not wait and see what becomes of the child Euphemia?"

"We could," said Hector Maclean, "but by then it may be too late."

"That is so," said Lachlan, chief of the Mackintoshes, whose opinion and battle experience Donald valued. "I would make known to Albany your claim to Ross by right of your wife. It is superior to all save Alexander Leslie's daughter. I would urge you to take action now to send a message to Albany, telling him you will not sit silently by while he takes all."

Donald nodded. "I am inclined to agree." Then, he looked at his brother, John Mor. "We must consider Kintyre, too. I fear Albany has designs on the peninsula, particularly since our mother complained of my giving that to you. It is yours to defend, John."

"I will take steps to see it protected," said his brother, "beginning with increasing the size of my garrisons there."

"Yes, do that," said Donald. "And, should you need help, let us know."

Through all this his other brother had said little. Now, Donald asked him, "What say you, Alex? Lochaber borders Ross."

"I see Albany creeping ever closer to Lochaber and the Isles. Alexander Stewart, the Wolf's bastard, raids with his caterans into Moray. We may have the Great Glen for now but the Stewarts are on our heels. I agree with the Mackintosh. Albany only understands strength and you are the one magnate in Scotland who has it and does not fear him."

The discussion continued but, long before it ended, Donald had made up his mind. Knowing there would be risks in action, but believing it a necessity, when the room grew quiet, he said, "Alex, I have decided to send you and your men from Lochaber across Ross into Moray. You are legitimately there, after all. In effect, you will be reminding Albany of my rightful claim to Ross and sending a signal that he will not take lightly. The borders of Ross extend into the Isles. We cannot wait."

Alex, always ready for a fight, inclined his head. "As you wish, Brother." A slow smile spread across his face. "My men will look forward to such a raid."

Donald scanned the faces of the chiefs before him and that of his other brother. "Are we in agreement?"

Heads nodded and he was satisfied.

Ardtornish Castle, Morvern, late spring 1404

THE FLOWERS WERE in bloom, swaths of yellow and purple blanketing the hills, and mating birds loud with their antics when Donald received a letter from King Richard.

> *According to what King Robert has heard, your brother, the Lord of Lochaber, is using his role as Moray's protector to further his own lordship, even granting episcopal lands to his captains. Worse, in early July, the Lord of Lochaber raided and burned the burgh of Elgin along with the manses of the canons belonging to Elgin Cathedral. They hauled away booty, all they could carry. King Robert says if Lochaber's lord does not reform, he may soon be playing chess with the Devil.*

"Alex may have gone too far in carrying out my orders," he said to Mariota as he handed her the letter. "Burning the clergy's houses does seem to be an act of the Wolf of Badenoch. No wonder the king thinks of that man's end. I can only hope my brother and his army have made our point."

Mariota looked up from reading the message, her hazel eyes full of concern. "Might it be that some of his men have disobeyed orders?"

"Possibly, but Alex leads them. And that does not explain his granting episcopal lands to his followers."

Mariota shook her head. "No, it does not. For this, Bishop de Spynie will certainly excommunicate him. When is Alex due here?"

"Soon. I suspect he knows what must be done. If not, I will remind him."

Word of Alex's raid on Moray had spread across the Isles through the chatter of chaplains and priests, so that even before the message arrived, Donald had some idea of all that had happened.

A week later, Alex stepped through the castle door. His tall stature, nearly white hair and stark blue eyes against his sun-browned skin gave him the look of an angelic being.

"News of your army's raid on Elgin has gone before you," said Donald. "I asked you to go, but what of the burning of the canonry houses in Elgin?"

"Albany's henchmen rode through Moray nipping at our heels. Alexander Stewart, Albany's nephew is one of the worst with his caterans. Tensions rose between us until my men had had enough. I say this not to excuse what happened, only to explain it." Before Donald could reply, Alex said, "Allow me to tell you what has transpired."

"Very well," agreed Donald. "Have some wine and let us sit before the fire."

That accomplished, Alex said, "After the raid on Elgin, Bishop William de Spynie met us at the precinct gate and, in no uncertain terms, reminded my captains and me that the canonry has enjoyed the privileges of a sanctuary ever since its foundation, and that its violation would entail upon us the pains of excommunication. It was a rather long and shaming speech after which we dutifully confessed our fault and earnestly begged to be absolved. The bishop clothed himself in his robes and vestments and proceeded to the great west doorway of the cathedral. There, and afterwards in front of the great altar, he solemnly absolved us."

"Thank God he did," said Donald, relieved. "Still, there will be a price to pay and you must pay it quickly."

A look of resignation crossed Alex' face. "A large sum has already been named. I will pay it and restore what booty I can. The bishop also requires me to construct a cross at the east end of Elgin's High Street as a memorial and to mark where the canonry begins."

"The bishop has always had a flair for the dramatic. You should know that I sent Albany a formal demand to recognize my claim to Ross by right of my wife. He has ignored it and named himself Lord of the Ward of Ross, indicating rather directly his intentions. I wouldn't be at all surprised, given Albany's tendencies, to see my niece Euphemia disappear. Though I still believe the raid was necessary, Albany will use it as an excuse to condemn me before parliament."

Alex grinned. "You are getting rather good at addressing that body with success."

Turning his goblet in his hands, Donald said, "But more of the nobles are in Albany's pocket now."

His eyes downcast, Alex said, "Aye, you speak truth."

"Keep me apprised of what happens in Moray," said Donald. "I will advise the chiefs and John Mor that my claim has been ignored."

Fortunately for Donald, in September, Albany's key ally, Archibald Douglas, became embroiled in a battle with England. Leading ten thousand Scots into Northumberland, he laid waste to the countryside. The English took their revenge at a place called Homildon Hill where Douglas was repeatedly wounded, blinded in one eye, and captured, along with eighty Scottish lords and knights, including Albany's eldest son, Murdoch, and Thomas Dunbar, the Earl of Moray, whom Donald had met years ago. With so many Scots taken prisoner, Albany's military strength was crippled, at least for now.

CHAPTER 17

THE YEAR HAD been prosperous for the Isles. The salmon, cattle and hide business flourished so that the gathering at Finlaggan in August was a time of great celebration, a time of sunshine and children's laughter. A reminder to Donald of the trust he was given, the legacy he held dear and must protect.

Close to the north shore of Loch Finlaggan, on the Council Island, *Eilean na Comhairle*, he presided over the meeting of the chiefs with scarcely a word of dissent being uttered against the Council's decisions.

For the festivities that followed, all his children, save two, were in attendance. The babe they named Marjory that Mariota had given him the prior spring, and Aggie at two remained at Ardtornish with their nurses when Donald and Mariota sailed to Islay. Their other four children, ranging in age from Sandy at thirteen to Angus at nine, came with them. By now, the boys had friends among the children of the chiefs as well as the sons of John Mor, Alex, and Hector.

"I hope they will all be friends as they grow up," said Mariota, as they stood watching the children at play.

"Sandy should find strong allies among the older ones," said Donald. "They will be his future Council."

"They know he is your heir and so does he," said Mariota. "Our only challenge will be to keep him humble."

While still at Finlaggan, John MacAlister came with news concerning Finguine MacKinnon, the imprisoned Abbot of Iona. Donald was standing on the bank of the loch when the prior came toward him, a wide smile on his face. "Finally, we have heard from the pope. He has instructed the Bishops of Glasgow and Dunkeld to summon Finguine to face the charges against him. If the charges be true—which they will, having been well-documented—the bishops are to remove him from his position."

Donald sighed, satisfied the long process would soon be concluded. "And then, at last, as patron, I will submit your name to the pope to be confirmed as Iona's abbot."

"You honor me, Cousin. I would willingly accept the position. There is much yet to do on Iona to enable us to complete our original mission."

Donald nodded to his friend. "And I would be your partner. All the Isles know you for an honorable man, John, and a faithful priest. They will welcome this change."

In late autumn, when Donald and Mariota were back at Ardtornish, word came from Alex in Lochaber that the Duke of Albany, allied with the Earl of Douglas and the Wolf of Badenoch's eldest bastard, Alexander Stewart, was methodically eliminating all of the supporters of the king's late son, Prince David. This came as no surprise to Donald, for it was apparent that the ambitious Robert Stewart, who ruled Scotland, was consolidating his power. Donald deeply regretted the loss of good men he considered friends. How long would Albany's perfidy be allowed to continue?

In December, Donald's brothers and their families and John MacAlister came to Ardtornish for Christmas. Hector Maclean and his wife Anne and their children joined them from Duart Castle on Mull, adding to the number of young ones who would be celebrating Christmastide. Lachlan, the Maclean chief, had been invited but remained behind as he was unwell. "Knowing what it meant to the boys," said Hector, "he insisted we come. Should I be needed, we are not far away."

They were all there when, just before Christmas, news arrived of the ambush and murder of Sir Malcolm Drummond, Lord of Mar, the brother-in-law of the king and husband of Isabel Douglas, Countess of Mar.

Donald knew Sir Malcolm for he had been an important supporter of Rothesay. He was frequently away on royal business being a close advisor of King Robert. Apparently, he was away at one of his castles when he was attacked and killed.

"Ostensibly, the murder was carried out by Alexander Stewart," said Alex, reading from the message, "but so bad is the reputation of the Duke of Albany, it is rumored that he did the killing for his nephew."

"It hardly matters which one perpetrated the crime," said Donald, "since the two of them are in league."

"It gets worse," said Alex. "After the murder, Alexander Stewart forcibly claimed Drummond's wife, Isabel, Countess of Mar, and moved into Kildrummy Castle, her residence."

"A despicable act," said Donald. "To follow murder by defiling the countess is something a vile heathen would do, a man without morals."

"Sadly," observed Hector, "Drummond had no heirs to claim the earldom, though if he had, they, too, might soon be eliminated."

John Mor shrugged. "Something his father, the Wolf, would not have thought beneath him."

Donald had watched Mariota as the news was shared, seeing a look of anger spread across her face. Finally, she spoke. "Poor Isabel to have suffered so from that evil man. She has lost her husband and suffered rape at the hands of the Wolf's son, leaving her a prisoner in her own castle. Given her age, there is little chance of any offspring from this unholy union. I count that a blessing."

Prior John's brow furrowed. "Albany runs the country, so there will be no justice for Isabel or the Drummonds, or any recognition of wrongdoing. At this point, I doubt even the Scottish church would condemn the Albany Stewarts."

Alex said, "The murder of Sir Malcolm and the defiling of the countess will serve Albany's purposes. I am certain Alexander Stewart will force a marriage with the countess to gain the title of earl, and Albany will give his blessing to strengthen the alliance between them."

Alex's wife, Mary Lennox, shook her head. "I cannot imagine being forced to live with such a man."

Hector's wife agreed. Anne was a Douglas like the countess.

Alex looked up from the parchment he held. "This will render my agreement to protect the lands of Moray more difficult, as the agreement requires Thomas Dunbar, the earl, to support my efforts *except* as against the Earl of Mar, who was until now an ally."

"Besides that," said Donald, "Dunbar is still a captive in England, so that Alexander Stewart will be bolder in opposing us. Perhaps this is, in part, aimed at us."

"I would not put it past Albany," said John Mor.

This news made more somber their celebration of the Savior's birth, although Donald encouraged the children to enjoy themselves. Sandy was home from his fostering and ready to join Donald in governing the lordship. "While he has been at Duart, he has become quite a good swordsman," said Hector.

Hearing the compliment, Sandy beamed.

"No doubt due to his instructor," said Donald. He had known Hector was the right man to teach Sandy skill with a sword, and he was proud of his son's accomplishments. Sandy was growing into a confident young man.

"While Sandy was not educated at Oxford, as were you," said John MacAlister, "he has been well-tutored in languages and history and can both read and write, something Albany cannot do, despite he is the king's brother."

Christmas Day fell on a Sunday, and all gathered for Mass, celebrated by Prior John MacAlister and Donald's chaplain. The service included songs that brought worshipful music to Ardtornish. Afterwards, they feasted on roast venison, smoked salmon, roast fowl and pork pies with baked apples. Hot spiced wine was served in the great hall, watered for the children, warming the insides of all. A blazing fire and many candles bathed the large room in a soft glow. The smell of wood smoke and garlands of greenery and holly that Mariota, Abby and their daughters used to decorate the windows and tapestries brought delightful smells of the outdoors into the hall.

Donald's bard, one of the MacMhuirich kindred, accompanied by the minstrels frequently in attendance at Ardtornish, brought them music and poems. In addition, Donald had invited a group of actors to Ardtornish to perform mummers' plays, entertaining both adults and children. In one, St. George and the Dragon fought with wooden swords, depicting good overcoming evil.

Sandy wanted to know why the dragon never won. Donald had to smile when Prior John explained, "Because good always triumphs over evil."

With Albany in mind, Donald added, "Certainly in the next life if not always in this one."

The plays were enjoyed by all, especially the actors. They dressed in brightly colored costumes and funny hats, parading around singing, playing musical instruments and performing feats of skill, including tumbling and juggling.

Their guests stayed through Epiphany, the sixth day of January, and then lingered a few days longer as the weather worsened. Finally, the weather lifted, and all sailed home.

Two weeks later, Hector sent word from Duart that his father, Lachlan, had died.

"He lived to a great age," said Mariota. "I am glad he was with his family at the end."

"We will miss him," said Donald, "for he was a wise chief and a good friend. Hector is now chief of the Macleans. He will do a fine job."

"Yes," said Mariota, "But how sad for his mother, Mary. We must attend the funeral to be with her and the family."

"It will be at Duart. We can leave today."

As the year 1405 proceeded, word reached Donald that Albany was continuing to gobble up land and titles. In one of Donald's petitions to Albany, all of which had been denied or ignored, he had inquired about the barony of Kingedward in Buchan, part of the Ross patrimony. The title had been vacant since the Wolf of Badenoch's death. His hopes were dashed, however, when Albany conferred the Buchan title on his son, John, and illegally ratified the action in his capacity as governor. He then installed his brother-in-law as bailee.

"He governs Scotland solely for the benefit of his family and his allies," said Mariota upon hearing the news. "I have no doubt he believes he is immune from the laws of inheritance. He will have all of Ross if he can."

"I must make certain he does not, which is all the more reason to strengthen our ties with England."

As it turned out, King Henry must have been thinking along the same lines, for in the autumn he sent emissaries to the Isles to treat with Donald and John Mor for a renewed alliance. Donald and his brother entertained the king's men at Dunyvaig Castle on Islay for several days, during which time a treaty was drafted similar to the earlier one.

"His Majesty would request your presence in London, when you are able, for the treaty's signing," said the senior emissary.

"We are happy to come," said Donald.

At the end of their visit, the king's senior emissary had another gift for the two brothers. "His Majesty would show you great favor, Lord Donald, by asking you and your brother to be a part of the negotiations for the ransoms of the noble Scottish prisoners captured at Homildon Hill. As a part of the process, the king has also asked John Dougan, Bishop of Down, and Sir Jenico d'Artois, Admiral of Ireland, to enter into discussions with you."

Scotland's treasury was so impoverished, Donald could not imagine the negotiations would be successful anytime soon, but he wholeheartedly agreed to King Henry's request. A first meeting was to be held at John Mor's castle in Antrim. But before that took place, the English king came to John Mor's aid by acting as mediator between John and certain merchants of Dublin and Drogheda who had caused them much annoyance by raiding in Argyll. John, Bishop of Down, negotiated the peace that ended the raids.

"Good has come from my willingness to be Henry's vassal," said

John Mor.

"A strong man at your side in times of trouble is something to be desired. Following in the steps of our father, we have achieved it." While Donald was pleased that their alliance with King Henry was strong, he often regretted he could not have enjoyed such a friendship with the powers ruling Scotland. He was as much a Stewart as his first cousin, Alexander Stewart, the Wolf's son. More so since Donald was legitimate. But Albany's ambitions did not leave room for a strong Lord of the Isles he considered a threat.

In October, having had their initial meeting with the Bishop of Down and the Admiral of Ireland, at which nothing specific had been decided, Donald and his brother traveled to London. He would have taken Hector but with his father's passing, the new chief of the Macleans had much to do.

The evening before Donald and John Mor were to meet with King Henry, they dined with Donald's friend, Willie Thorpe.

In a private room arranged by Willie in a tavern he frequented, they dined on beef and red wine while discussing the happenings in England. At one point, Willie leaned across the table, the candlelight illuminating his thin face and slight beard. "The king has had to deal with one rebellion after another and at least eight attempts to end his life or his reign since he took the throne. He is now responding with ruthless action, where others might show mercy. Rumors of 'King Richard is alive' persist, but now, added to them is the cry 'Archbishop Scrope is dead'."

Donald stared at his friend aghast. "What?"

"In June," Willie explained, "Henry killed the Archbishop of York, despite Archbishop Arundel's pleas for the clergyman's life."

Donald exploded in shock. "How could this be?"

Willie glanced from Donald to John Mor. Seeing their confusion, he said, "You are not the only ones to react this way. Scrope was apparently used by the Earls of Northumberland and Marshal, who were plotting rebellion. The archbishop had raised the peasants in the north in protest over Henry's taxation of the clergy. But Scrope's objections went further. He felt every class of people was affected, including the merchants and nobles. Scrope wanted reformation, not revolution. Sadly, he was abandoned by Northumberland, who fled to Scotland, and then by the king's man, who assured him of his safety only to deliver him to the king. Henry's summary execution of a well-liked archbishop has stunned all of England, indeed, all of Christendom."

"And doubtless damaged his reputation with the people," said Donald, trying to imagine the horror of it.

"As well it should," added John Mor.

Willie's expression was grave. "The same day as the execution, Henry suffered a sudden illness, a condition affecting his skin—red pustules—which continue to this day although they have faded somewhat. Some say it is God's judgment. I say this to urge you to keep your meeting with the king short. Do not linger before him; do not gaze overlong at his face. He is not in any mood to negotiate."

Donald had no desire to come before an angry king who had killed a high ranking man of the church. "We come only to sign the treaty between us. We are told we will see the king in the Tower of London."

"He is currently lodging there. Meantime, how are things in Scotland?"

"Troublesome," said Donald. "The king is set aside while his brother, the Duke of Albany, wields increasing power. My wife is the heir to Ross, save for her niece, who is hampered by a deformity. The same niece who has been seized and controlled by Albany."

"That does not bode well," said Willie.

"No," said Donald. "A confrontation is coming, I feel it."

After that, Donald thanked Willie and bid him good night. As he and John Mor walked through the nearly deserted streets back to their lodgings, the light was fading though it was not full dark. He had freed his guard for the evening, his lodgings being a short distance from the tavern.

As they walked along, Donald mused aloud on the subject of the English king. "Henry's time on the throne has been fraught with trouble, both financial and military. His country is never at peace."

"That is so," said John Mor. "He is never far from rebellions and battle whether in England, Wales or Ireland. But still, to kill an archbishop. I wonder what the pope will say."

Before Donald could answer, four men darted from the shadows to stand before them, weapons raised. One, a smirk on his broad face, held a sword; the others had long knives raised in a threatening manner. They looked like huge street rats, dirty and grimy. "Drop your swords and hand over your purses and we will allow you to live."

Donald glanced at his brother. The two exchanged smiles. Donald unsheathed his sword, the steel blade sliding free, and pulled his dirk from his hip. Beside him, John did the same. "Well, now, said Donald. "What an interesting welcome. You offer a fight before bed? Splendid!"

John Mor grinned. "I cannot think of anything that would please me more."

They advanced on the four thieves, who stared with shock at the tall, blue-eyed Scots boldly coming toward them.

"Mebbe we should allow them to keep their purses, Chester," said one of the thieves, as he backed away.

Donald brandished his sword, the silver blade catching what light remained. "And deprive us of our evening's entertainment? Surely not!"

"There's only two of them," said the largest of the four thieves.

"Yeah, but they be big," said another, whose gaze was fixed on Donald's sword.

"I think they are losing their appetite for a fight, Brother," said John Mor, his voice heavy with sarcasm.

Donald and his brother advanced until they were within striking distance of the thieves.

The four street rats stared at them for a moment, then turned and ran.

Donald sheathed his sword. "So disappointing, these Londoners. Had Hector come, I can't imagine he would allow them to retreat."

"I agree," said his brother. "Let's not tell him."

Donald laughed. "Agreed. And I will not tell my guard."

"At least the villains spared us from splattering their blood on our tunics," said John Mor.

"Do you remember when Father tested our sword-fighting skills by having us face four of his guards?"

"I do. It was the proudest day of my youth when we fought back-to-back and held our own."

They laughed as they covered the short distance to their lodgings where they rewarded themselves with a goblet of wine. The day of John Mor's betrayal was long past and all but forgotten. They were once again brothers in all.

The next morning, they arrived at the Tower at the appointed time. Donald had his guards remain at the gate and he and his brother were escorted into the king's private audience chamber, smaller than the one at Westminster. Donald had planned to take Willie's advice and say little, keeping the meeting to the signing of the treaty. But King Henry was in a mood to talk.

Resting in a gilded chair on a raised dais, the king leaned back, his assessing eyes taking in the visiting Scots. As before, he was richly attired, but his face bore the scars of his skin disease. "Lord Donald and my loyal Irish subject, Lord John of the Glens, I am delighted to see you. It is good to be among friends. How was your journey?"

"Pleasant, Your Majesty," replied Donald. "We are grateful for your hospitality here in London and for the emissaries you sent to treat with us."

"I also thank you, Your Majesty," said John Mor, "for your help with the merchants of Dublin and Drogheda who were raiding Argyll."

"Ah, yes," said the king. "We were happy to assist in that matter. The Dublin merchants in particular need to be reminded their duty is to us for the revenues promised. My son, Thomas of Lancaster, has returned from Ireland where you may know he served as lieutenant. Knowing our nobles there, he keeps me informed."

"He did many good things while he was there," said John Mor.

The king acknowledged this with a nod. "Have you begun to consider what ransoms might be in order for the Scots we hold prisoner?"

"There has been a first meeting," said Donald, "but we have not yet arrived at ransoms. Given the state of Scotland's treasury, it will take some time to raise whatever ransoms are set."

"Very well. There is time." The king smiled and then stepped down from the dais, walking toward a table where documents were laid out. "If you are ready, we may sign." One of his clerics stood next to the table, gesturing to where the signatures and seals were to be placed.

Donald signed and applied his seal, using the wax provided.

The king signed and stepped back. "It is done. You will return in three years to renew the peace between us?"

Donald inclined his head. "As you wish, Your Majesty."

At the entrance to the palace, Donald rejoined his guard, who were waiting for them with the horses. They rode back to their lodgings and, along the way, John Mor said, "I meant what I told the king. Henry's son, Thomas, did a fine job for his father in Ireland. He only left for lack of funds. It seems the amount his father agreed to pay him did not appear."

"That must have been discouraging for the young man," said Donald.

His brother nodded. "It shows you just how bad are England's finances."

"Like Scotland's own," said Donald.

DONALD RETURNED HIS brother to Dunyvaig, where his wife and son awaited him, and after a few days with them, he sailed on to Morvern, braving the cold seas and rain to arrive in early November.

He recognized John MacAlister's galley, beached at Ardtornish. In the castle, he kissed Mariota, who welcomed him home, hugged his younger children, and looked at his cousin, whose face was beaming.

"Our patience has been rewarded, Donald. The Bishops of Glasgow and Dunkeld have considered the evidence against Finguine MacKinnon and removed him from his post as abbot."

Donald was thrilled. Offering John his hand, he said, "That is very good news! It has been a long road, but we are vindicated. I shall put your name forward immediately to be the next abbot."

Over dinner with Mariota and Donald's older children, they

shared their ideas for expanding and improving Iona Abbey.

"It is my hope," said John, "that Iona can finally undertake its rightful spiritual service."

Donald agreed. "Saving souls and feeding sheep, as Master Wycliffe would have said."

John continued, "To restore these will mean assuring the proper use of the assets endowed by the Macdonalds and seeing that the income is maintained for the monks. In this, you are my liege lord."

"I am your partner, and it is my privilege," said Donald. Turning to Sandy, his eldest, who at fourteen had been invited to the table, he said, "This will be your responsibility one day, my son, for you, too, are an heir of Iona's founder." And then to his younger son, Angus, who was ten, he said, "Hopefully, Iona will be your legacy one day to hold after your cousin, John." Finally, to John, he said, "From now on, you will serve as Lord Spiritual on the Council of the Isles."

"It will be my honor to do so and to see Iona provides all the services needed by the lordship in education, law and medical services, as well as a place of refuge and sanctuary for noblemen and women of your family."

Donald was pleased at John's enthusiasm. They would make good partners in this worthy effort. "You must give me a list of projects you wish to undertake and, together, we will see them done."

His cousin smiled his approval. "The first priority will be to rebuild the choir and bell tower and see the other buildings repaired that Finguine left in ruins. Given the limitations of my position these last years, I was not able to do all. But at least we were able to keep the monks fed after years of forced hunger. They are very appreciative."

As Christmas drew near, a letter arrived from the deposed King Richard, who was still at Rothesay Castle on Bute. Donald had not heard from him for some time and was anxious to hear what he had to say.

King Robert's fears for the safety of his young son, James, have increased in light of Albany's recent actions. Looking forward to James' reign, the king has made the boy Earl of Carrick and given him lands in the southwest of Scotland, but the king worries Albany may seek to take the boy's life since Prince James is the only impediment to Albany's gaining the throne on the king's death. Hence, King Robert is planning to send the prince to France for the stated reason of giving him a better education. A ship is being fitted out to take the boy from St. Andrews where he is residing. Sir David Fleming and several nobles are to accompany him.

It is not a good time for ship travel, but the king believes this cannot wait until spring. Why he did not ask your help in this matter, I cannot say.

These are desperate times for King Robert whose health is not strong.

CHAPTER 18

Ardtornish Castle, Morvern, April 1406

DONALD, TOO, QUESTIONED why King Robert did not entrust Prince James to him. With hundreds of ships at his command, some of which sailed to France for trade on a routine basis, it would have been safer than taking an eastern route where pirates were known to ply the seas. His treaty with King Henry would have assured no attack would come from that quarter. Perhaps it was the fact the prince had been residing in the east, or the eastern route might have been the choice of the nobles who were to accompany him, but Donald regretted it. He believed Albany's ambition sought not only Ross, but the crown. And the only one standing in his way to the throne was the young prince.

Spring had just begun to awaken the land when Alex arrived at Ardtornish with urgent news. He greeted Donald and Mariota, and then blurted out, "Sir David Fleming, who was to accompany the prince, and his company were attacked and slaughtered by Albany's man, Douglas."

"Where?" asked Donald, stricken with the terrible news.

"On Long Hermiston Moor in East Lothian. Fortunately, the prince had been sent ahead to Robert Lauder's North Berwick castle with the Earl of Orkney, Henry Sinclair. Once it was known they were being pursued by Douglas, I am told Lauder had the prince rowed out to his castle on Bass Rock in the Firth of Forth."

Donald's heart sank within him. "The Bass castle is a bleak fortress on a rock that is home to gannets, hardly a fitting refuge for a future king, but at least Douglas and his army are not likely to attack them there. The rock is hundreds of feet high and surrounded by water. The prince should be safe until he can take ship for France."

"Sinclair and Lauder are good men," said Alex. "They will find a way."

"The poor lad," said Mariota. Turning her eyes on Donald, she said, "James is the age of our Angus, only eleven. Knowing his uncle seeks his life, he must be terribly frightened with his mother dead and his father far from him. I wish the king had sent him to us."

He nodded. "So do I."

Alex stayed for a time as they did business together and he reported on events in Lochaber. A month went by without further news, and then a letter came from the deposed King Richard.

Donald and Mariota were dining with Hector Maclean and John MacAlister, who, with great pomp, had recently been invested as the Abbot of Iona. Donald read Richard's letter aloud.

> As you know, King Robert gave his son, the prince, into the care of trusted nobles with orders to get him safely to France. All went awry when the Earl of Douglas and his men pursued the prince's company. In a desperate retreat, the prince was taken by Henry Sinclair to Bass Rock for safety. There, Sinclair made contact with a merchant ship from Gdansk, the Maryenknecht, and secured passage to France for the boy and himself. King Robert was much relieved when this news reached us.

Donald paused to see the relief on the faces of his wife and his guests. Then, he continued.

> But the boy was not yet safe. Off Flamborough Head on the

Yorkshire coast, despite England's truce with Scotland, English
pirates captured the ship. The pirates soon realized the important
passenger the Maryenknecht was carrying and took the prince to
King Henry.

When this news was brought to King Robert, we were sitting at
supper. As he listened to the messenger, his face grew pale and he fell
forward, senseless. We thought he had died. His servants carried
him to his chamber and laid him upon his bed. There he lay like one
dead. Indeed, he was so full of grief that he did not care to live.

I am sad to tell you that on the first day of April, the king passed
from this life. I think he died of a broken heart. He was a good and
gentle man, and we had come to be friends, but he was not a king for
these troubled times.

Donald hung his head. "Scotland has lost a king and a prince, and I
have lost an uncle."

Mariota, who was expecting their next child, laid her hand on his
arm, a comforting touch. "We must believe James will return. I will
pray for that end."

"I will pray for King Robert's soul," said John, "and for James'
return."

Hector scowled. "The time is coming when Albany must be dealt
with."

Donald exchanged glances with John. Both knew Hector was
right. "You speak truth, Nephew. There is no one to stop him now
that our uncrowned King of Scots is held prisoner in England."

"King Henry will use the boy for England's gain," said Mariota,
"but at least James lives. Think, Donnie, had Albany captured him, he
would be dead."

Donald nodded. "A small mercy." Mariota was always a source of
encouragement to him, a partner in all things. Even now, when she
was great with child, her thoughts were for the welfare of others.

"If you are willing," said John, "we could send a chaplain to serve
young James. He is our king and should have his own. A priest, well
chosen, would be a wise counselor in matters both secular and
spiritual as well as a comfort to him."

"A very good thought," said Donald. "Yes, we must do that, but before we take that step, I have an idea. Bypassing Albany, I would send you, Hector, my Lieutenant General and chief of the Macleans, to London to meet with our new king. I will send chiefs with you to show that the Lordship of the Isles claims James as our liege lord. Before you depart, I will send word to King Henry of my intention to do this and to seek a safe conduct for you."

"It will be my honor," said Hector. "A visit from some of his subjects might encourage the lad."

"Meantime," said John, "I will give some thought as to which of your new chaplains I would recommend is best to serve James."

Donald dispatched a letter to King Henry and then waited.

In early summer, Mariota delivered a healthy boy. They named him John, after Donald's father, John of Islay, and his friend, the Abbot of Iona.

Donald was pleased with his new son, a handsome child with large blue eyes, fair downy hair and a dimple in his chin.

As he gazed into the babe's face, Mariota said, "One more son for your collection, Donnie."

"Where did that dimple come from?" Donald inquired, amused.

"My father," said Mariota. "Or so my mother told me. My brother, Alexander, had one, too."

Baby John had many admirers among his siblings. Mari, their only redhead, at fourteen, doted on the child, like another mother. Anna at thirteen joined in, often helping the boy's nurse. At four, Aggie just stared into his cradle.

Sandy was unsurprising in his welcome. "Finally, a younger brother who can join me in battle." When Donald shot him a doubtful look, he added, "Angus can pray for both of us."

"Do not forget," Mariota told him, "wee John is your younger brother who must be protected and watched over."

With an air of reluctance, Sandy conceded. "All right. But when he grows up, he will take my orders, right?"

Donald laughed. "Only if you are not just chief but a wise leader who would never ask of your brothers or the lordship's chiefs something you would not do yourself."

Sandy sighed. "Yes, sir."

Donald was still waiting for news from King Henry when Willie's letter arrived later that summer. He and Mariota were enjoying a sun-filled day at Ardtornish, standing outside watching the eagles fish in the sound, as Donald read it to her.

I am certain you have learned of the capture of James Stewart, your new King of Scots. I had word from my sources as to what took place when James was brought before King Henry. I thought you would want to know.

The Scottish nobles who were taken with the boy fell on their knees, begging the king to set James free. They reminded Henry that the two kingdoms were at peace and to make James his captive was an act of war.

To this, the king laughed. "If King Robert had been truly friendly, he would have sent his son to England to be taught. For I know French indifferently well, and nowhere could he find a better master."

Had James been king of any country save that ruled by Albany, a great cry would have gone up and a demand for the young king's release sent immediately to England. But no objection or demand by Albany was received by King Henry.

This is, indeed, unfortunate, Donnie, but to encourage you, I believe the prince will be treated well and given a good education. He will be raised to excel in all knightly skills. King Henry's ego demands nothing less. Still, it would be good for you to call upon James when next you are in London. He will need to be reassured he has friends.

"I will send a reply," he told Mariota, "telling Willie we are sending Hector as soon as the good conduct is received." Donald was not surprised at King Henry's attitude and disregard of the truce between the two countries. Holding Scotland's young king as his captive was too great an opportunity to forgo. However, Willie's words of encouragement did take root. "When he arrives in London, Hector must meet with Willie and then call upon King Henry to inquire about James' situation."

Mariota nodded her agreement. "That would be good. We must

know how our young king fares. Every mother in Scotland will be worried."

It was the next summer, 1407, before all the permissions had finally been received and arrangements made for Hector to lead a large company from the Isles and Scotland's west coast to visit the young King James in London.

London, England, August 1407

THIS WAS NOT Hector's first trip to London. He had come once before with his uncle, Lord Donald, to meet with King Henry, but this was his first as head of a delegation from the Isles.

Donald had told him he would be allowed to carry no messages that were not first seen by King Henry, pursuant to Henry's order. Thus Hector carried many messages for Willie and the young King James but none were in writing.

With Hector was a large company, including several chiefs. Among them were Ferquhard Mackintosh, Chief of the Mackintoshes and Clan Chattan, Murdoch Mackenzie of Kintail, Chief of the Mackenzies, and Donald Dubh Cameron, Chief of the Camerons, the most dominant warlord in Lochaber. All save Hector had dark hair; all were muscular men, proficient at sword fighting. Together with Hector's men-at-arms, his chaplain and physician, and other retainers, they made an impressive sight as they rode their powerful horses through London's narrow streets.

As before, Hector wore the Maclean livery over his tunic, boldly displaying a silver tower on a field of blue. At his side was his great sword and on his head a blue felt hat with an eagle feather.

As they passed the people lining the street, Hector noted their faces displayed shock as if they were staring at giants. Hector wanted young King James to hear of their effect on the people of London so he would be proud of his subjects in the Isles and of the lordship that was loyal to him.

King Henry's man went before them, leading the company to the palace at Westminster where they would be lodged.

Ferquhard had not been to London before, as was evident by his reaction to the smells that rose to their nostrils. "The place stinks."

"Aye," agreed Hector, chuckling. "'Tis not Ross where your Castle Moy is located, nor," he said to Donald Dubh riding on his other side, "is it blue-green Lochaber."

They went first to their lodgings and then sent a message to Willie Thorpe who replied with instructions as to where he would meet them. Ensconced in a tavern's private room, Hector and the other chiefs with him took a seat before a table laden with victuals.

"I thought you might be hungry," said Willie.

"That was very kind," said Hector. "How are you, Willie?"

"I am doing well; business flourishes."

Hector knew Willie from his prior visit to London, and introduced the chiefs to Lord Donald's friend. "We will reimburse you for the cost of the meal as we eat much when our appetites are aroused."

Willie laughed. "I am not a poor man, and Donnie sent money ahead on your behalf. He is surely well-acquainted with your appetite."

As they spoke of the current situation, Hector inquired, "Is there any chance King Henry will allow young James to return with us? We can protect him."

"It is not protection King Henry worries about. It is keeping his leverage. As I told Donald in my letter, the king will not return your young king, at least not for some time. James is too great a prize and Henry's reign too insecure. Just after his capture, a delegation led by Sir William Graham of Kincardine went before the king, demanding James' release. They were not successful. But Lord Donald need not worry. The king will treat James kindly, doubtless raising him as a knight."

"An English knight," said Hector with a frown, as he glanced at his fellow chiefs.

Willie said, "If Albany seeks his life, he may be safer here. Better a living English knight than a dead King of Scots."

The other chiefs reacted with dismay, even though Willie's words were expected.

"We can at least let James know he is loved by his subjects," said

Murdoch Mackenzie.

Donald Dubh nodded. "After all, James' father was Lord Donald's uncle. They are kin, and both Lord Donald and James are being dealt with poorly by Albany."

Willie set down his wine. "James is kept in the White Tower where, I assume, you will be calling upon him. King Henry thought to move him to Nottingham Castle but was overruled by the council, which, along with parliament and Archbishop Arundel, effectively control the king."

Hector was puzzled. "Why do they control the king?"

"The concern is finances," said Willie, "and Henry still suffers ill health. He would campaign in Wales if he had his way, but the country lacks the money and Henry has no stamina for such a venture. In the few times he travels, Henry stops often at abbeys for rest. Hence, the king's eldest son, Henry of Monmouth, though he is only twenty-one, has gained great influence. He may attend your meeting."

The next day, Hector and the other chiefs were escorted into Westminster's throne room, where Henry received them. The king had changed much from the first time Hector had seen him. His robes and jewelry were as rich as before, but hung on a thinner body. He no longer had the appearance of a vigorous man. His dark eyes were sunken. His hair and beard were graying and his skin was pale, except for the red blotches that Donald had warned him about.

Standing to one side of the throne was a lean young man as tall as Hector, his face clean-shaven and his dark hair cropped in a ring above his ears. *The king's son.*

Hector was announced as "Hector Maclean of Duart, Chief of Clan Maclean, Lieutenant General of the Isles, and nephew and emissary of Donald of Islay, Lord of the Isles." The herald added, "General Maclean comes with other clan chiefs."

Bowing, Hector said, "Your Majesty."

Henry's gaze roved over the men of stature standing before him. Then his eyes fixed on Hector. "You have many titles, General Maclean, but one not mentioned, of which we are aware, is 'the greatest swordsman in all the Isles, perhaps all of Scotland', which says much for your skills."

"Thank you, Your Majesty." Hector wanted no flattery; he desired only to see Scotland's imprisoned king. "Lord Donald sends you his greetings." He then introduced the other chiefs and said, "We come at Lord Donald's request to inquire about our King James."

"The lad is well, as you will see. He resides in one of the upper floors of the White Tower. You may assure Lord Donald that we have arranged the best masters for the boy so that he will be educated in the same manner as our own sons."

"Lord Donald will be pleased to hear it." Because of Willie's words, Hector did not demand that James be released, though he was sorely tempted to do so. It was clear from the king's words that he planned to keep James for the foreseeable future.

"You may also tell Lord Donald that we will be sending emissaries again to him to make firm our alliance. I am forced to deal with Scotland's governor, but I have doubts about Albany. It may be that the Lord of the Isles would add the governor to the discussions with our emissaries."

Hector hid his surprise at the mention of Albany. "I am certain Lord Donald would welcome their thoughts."

Leaving Westminster, Hector and his company rode from the palace along the Thames to the Tower of London standing sentinel over the river. The quarters assigned to James were, as the king had said, high in the tower. They were furnished in modest fashion for his rank but adequate. There was a window from which he could look down on the castle's moat, and beyond, to the river.

As they entered, the boy turned from the window to face them. What Hector saw was a lad of thirteen of medium height with a well-proportioned body and strong limbs. His light brown hair fell just below his chin, which was free of any beard. He exuded nervous energy, leaving Hector with the impression of a caged animal.

Hector bowed before him, "Your Majesty, I am Hector Maclean of Duart, Chief of Clan Maclean, Lieutenant General of the Isles, and nephew and emissary of Donald of Islay, Lord of the Isles. He has bid me and these chiefs with me to come and pay homage to you, our liege lord, and to assure you of our devotion." Hector then introduced those who had accompanied them.

"I have been a captive of Henry's for more than a year," said James, his impatient tone suggesting they might have come sooner. "Can you do anything about getting me free of this prison?"

"Would that I could, Your Majesty. To the English king, you are a great prize, made more valuable with your father's death. He has plans to educate and train you as a knight, which tells me he intends to keep you for some while. Of course, Scotland must continue to work toward your release. We will make inquiries as to what is being done to secure it."

The boy took a seat and waited until Hector and the others found benches to sit upon. "Do you know why you were taken to Bass Rock?" asked Hector.

James lowered his gaze. "My uncle, the Duke of Albany, and his allies the Douglases, sought to capture me."

"Aye," said Hector. "Albany is a man of greed and ambition, not only your enemy, but ours. He would rob Lord Donald of the province of Ross that is rightfully his through his wife Mariota Leslie, daughter of the Countess of Ross. And he would rob you of your crown. As you know, he killed your elder brother, David, and I dare say he would take your life as well." A look of recognition appeared on James' face. The boy knew this truth. "Consider that you may, for the time being, be safer here. Since your father died, Albany rules Scotland as governor, not in your name but his own. Only you stand between him and the crown." Hector had thought of withholding that from the boy, but he needed to know if he did not already.

A furrow appeared on the boy's forehead. "Henry Sinclair, Earl of Orkney, who was with me when I was captured by the pirates, told me that. He is to be released as soon as hostages can be arranged." James frowned and looked to one side. "Albany will rue the day he sought to harm me. His son, Murdoch, is among the prisoners here that were taken at Homildon Hill. I am told Albany works for his son's release but not mine. I will not forget either father or son."

The determination on James' face was evident as he turned back to Hector and the other chiefs. "Before your capture," said Hector, "Lord Donald was asked by King Henry to be a part of the negotiations for the ransoms of the Scottish prisoners taken at Homildon Hill. It may be some time before those can be agreed upon as Scotland does not have the money needed. If he can, Lord Donald will secure your release, perhaps as a part of this."

James grew quiet then, though Hector could see the tension in his body had not subsided.

After that, the other chiefs shared what they could about the situation in Scotland and the Isles, assuring James that all the Isles and the Highlands were loyal to him.

As they got ready to leave, Hector said, "King Henry assures us you are well cared for. Is it true?"

"Like an animal on a tether," said James, "I am fed well but not often let out, though they say that will change. They can hardly teach me a knight's skills in this chamber."

Hector considered the impatient young king before him. "I have a message for you from your kinsman, the Lord of the Isles." James returned him an expectant look. "You are an intelligent young man. Bide your time and take advantage of all they would teach you, for one day, you will return to Scotland as her king and you must be ready."

Bowing, Hector and the chiefs departed.

Ardtornish Castle, Morvern, late August 1407

DONALD RECEIVED HECTOR'S report, satisfied his nephew had done a fine job acting as his emissary to Scotland's young king. "I am surprised and gladdened that King Henry would have his emissaries include dealing with Albany in our negotiations for the new alliance."

"It was the king's suggestion," said Hector. "I, too, was surprised. Apparently Henry does not trust the governor."

"Nor should he. Perhaps King Henry will be sympathetic to my claim to Ross. It would be good to have him as an ally."

In early autumn, a letter arrived from Willie Thorpe that provided much useful information.

You will be interested to learn that Albany's nephew, Alexander

Stewart, Earl of Mar, has been jousting in the north of England on a safe conduct from King Henry. It seems Mar no longer wishes to be seen as the Wolf's son, a Highland robber and leader of caterans. Now, he seeks to be known as a statesman and a knight of prowess in the tourney. One is tempted to think it a miraculous conversion.

There have been multiple letters exchanged between Albany and King Henry. Some correspondence deals with the truce between the two countries. But, in others, Albany argues for his son's release. In public dispatches, he lays equal stress on the release of his son, Murdoch, and James, yet in secret, he does nothing to secure the young king's freedom.

One rumor has it that the deposed King Richard lives in Scotland, and Albany and Henry have made a pact whereby Albany agrees to hold King Richard as long as King Henry holds James. If, indeed, by some miracle Richard lives, it would be ruinous for Henry if he were to be released. Many who dislike Henry would support Richard's return to the throne. And if James were to be released, Albany would lose his power.

"You never told Willie that Richard lives?" asked Mariota when he looked up from reading her the letter.

He shook his head. "The time didn't seem right, and I was unwilling at the start for my role in seeing to his safety to be revealed. When next I communicate with Willie, I will explain. Meanwhile, Alex tells me that Albany has moved Richard to Stirling Castle, which may mean we will receive fewer messages from him. More people will know of his existence, however, for Stirling is not as remote as Rothesay Castle on Bute."

Later that autumn when the leaves were turning red and gold and the days had grown shorter, Abbot John MacAlister came to Ardtornish for a visit. Donald was eager to hear news of Iona. As John stepped into the great hall, Donald could see he was unhappy. His dour expression was unusual for him, which told Donald something was wrong. "What is it?" he asked. "Come, sit with me by the fire and unburden your heart."

As they walked toward the fireplace where a fire burned steadily, Mariota came to greet John. She, too, noted his unhappiness. "What is it, John? What has happened?"

Once seated, and warmed by the fire and a goblet of wine, John said, "One of Wycliffe's followers, an English priest named John Resby, has been executed by burning in Perth for heresy."

Donald was stunned. "Who would do this and why?"

"Resby came to Scotland, why I know not, preaching the things Wycliffe taught, that the Bible, not the church, is the source of religious authority, that the doctrine of transubstantiation is not correct, that confession to a priest was not ordered by Christ and was not used by the apostles. And he challenged indulgences, saying they blaspheme the wisdom of God. There were more charges, forty in all."

"In short," said Donald, "he was teaching everything Wycliffe taught. But Wycliffe's followers have been around since before King Henry took the throne. In fact, his father, John of Gaunt, was a friend of Wycliffe. Why so severe a penalty?"

"Albany," said John. "He considers all of Wycliffe's followers to be heretics. He turned Resby over to the papal inquisitor at St. Andrews, Laurence of Lindores, the hunter of heretics. The inquisitor tried Resby, found him guilty and gave him to the secular authorities to be burned. Albany could have stopped it. He did not."

Donald took a deep breath and let it out, meeting Mariota's gaze. "The Roman church will tolerate no criticism it seems. Like the MacKinnon abbot, they would hold on to their wealth and power no matter what it costs the people or the good priests who serve them."

"I find it ironic," said Mariota, "that Albany, who freely engages in murder, would hold a man of God guilty who only wants the teachings of Christ to be embraced."

"I have no doubt we will meet Resby in Heaven," said John.

"And, unless he repents, Albany will surely burn in Hell," said Donald.

CHAPTER 19

Loch Aline, near Ardtornish Castle, Morvern, May 1408

MARIOTA WALKED ALONG the rocky shore of Loch Linnhe with her four daughters and Abby. High above them on the promontory stood Ardtornish Castle, a stone sentinel guarding the Sound of Mull. Abby strolled ahead with the youngest girls, Aggie and Marjory.

Sir Thomas, Mariota's ever present guard who had long ago become a dear friend, was not far away. He had a fondness for her handmaiden, who had grown more beautiful as the years passed. Mariota thought he and Abby would soon wed and was happy for them.

Her sons were elsewhere today. Sandy, now seventeen, was on Mull, hunting with Hector and his son, Lachlan, and Hector's younger brother, Neil. Donald often took his eldest son with him, but when he did not, Sandy could be found at Duart Castle with his hounds and the Macleans. Angus, now thirteen, was visiting the parish churches endowed to the abbey with his godfather, Abbot John MacAlister. Mariota's youngest son, John, just two, remained in the castle with his nurse.

Watching the sunlight flickering on the blue waters of the loch, Mariota's mind drifted to Donald and his trip to London. She could not help but wonder how he was. Would King James be pleased that Donald intended to take action against Scotland's governor? And what of King Henry?

"How long will Father be away this time?" asked Mari, her eldest daughter. At sixteen, she had grown into a beauty, her red hair darkening to a rich auburn. She had her father's blue eyes and a winning smile. All the unmarried young men who came to Ardtornish or Finlaggan with their noble fathers paid her much attention. Donald was considering a match with Alexander Sutherland, the second son of the Earl of Sutherland. Mariota thought her daughter would be pleased with her father's choice, for she had seen her daughter casting glances in the young man's direction.

"This will be one of his longer trips," she said to Mari. "He and your uncle, John Mor, will meet with emissaries for King Henry in Ireland and then travel to London to meet with our King James and King Henry."

"Do you worry about him?" asked Mari, her expression thoughtful.

"Your father? Of course," said Mariota, "but I knew when I married him that as chief of Clan Donald, he would have many duties that would take him away from home. Remember, too, your father is a skilled warrior and well-guarded. His galley's crew is the best in the fleet."

"Is it an important trip?" asked Anna. At fifteen, Anna most resembled Mariota with her light brown curls and hazel eyes. She was an intelligent and thoughtful girl. Donald was considering a marriage for her with Robert Lamont, the young Laird of Clan Lamont, but as they were related, a papal dispensation would be needed.

"Very important," said Mariota. Her gaze drifted to the bluebells blooming on the hillsides. Her younger daughters, Aggie and Marjory, six and five, were picking the flowers to make head wreaths. "Abby, make sure they stay free of the woods."

Abby turned and nodded.

"Why is it so important for Father to go now?" asked Anna.

"It's about Ross, isn't it?" put in Mari. "I heard Father talking to cousin Hector."

"It's more than Ross," said Mariota. How much should she tell her daughters? Deciding they would know soon enough, she said, "If my niece, young Euphemia fails, Ross is ours to claim. Your grandmother was the Countess of Ross. One day, Ross would be Sandy's. He would rightfully be the Earl of Ross. If your father is to stake his claim, it will help to know our young King James and King Henry agree he should do so. Ross is too large a province and too close to the Isles for the wrong man to control."

"Albany, you mean," said Mari.

Just then, Marjory spotted a mother otter with her pup in the kelp near shore and all the girls ran to see.

"Don't scare them!" Anna chided her younger sisters.

At Abby's insistence, the girls watched from a reasonable distance. "Look, Mother," said young Aggie, "the baby otter is sleeping on his mother's belly."

"That is how the mother otter keeps her pup warm," said Mariota. "She pulls the pup onto her belly. From there, he can nurse."

The rest of the morning was taken up with watching the otters and picking flowers. Mariota was glad she was spared from having to answer more questions. She worried about Donald more than she would say and didn't want her daughters to be afraid for him. He was a strong chief and an able warrior, but he was only a man, vulnerable to those who would willingly engage in evil. If the Duke of Albany would kill one of his own nephews and hunt the other to gain the throne, he would not stop at murdering Donald to have Ross.

Dunyvaig Castle, Isle of Islay, early August 1408

DONALD DINED WITH John Mor and his wife Margery at Dunyvaig the evening he and his brother returned from London. The next morning, he and John Mor took a walk along the shore, talking about the trip. "Considering all we had hoped to accomplish," said Donald, "I think our meetings in Ireland and London went well."

"There is no doubt King Henry sees you as a friend, even to the point of offering you ships and men should you need them against Albany."

"I was glad to accept the ships as I foresee a need for more galleys than even the lordship has, but I declined Henry's offer of men as I don't want England in the middle of the fight. My goal was to assure that Henry will not interfere."

"You achieved that. What about James? You two whispered much to the side when we met with him. Is he content with a move against Albany?"

"James hates Albany," said Donald, "which is not surprising given that the governor first hunted him and now does nothing to free him. Were I to act against Albany, I would have James' full support."

"But you have yet to speak of your plans."

Donald gazed east toward Kintyre, seeing not the peninsula but the future. "I will watch Albany carefully and should he move to eliminate my niece Phemie from inheriting Ross, I will make a last plea for him to recognize my claim."

"Surely you do not think he will grant you Ross?"

"No, but before I call the clans to battle, I must exhaust that possibility. And, as a last measure to assure the support of both kings, I would send a man to London to call upon them."

"Who would you send?"

"I have been thinking about that. I want a man Albany's spies would see as no threat, a man who could stay to serve King James." At his brother's raised brows, Donald said, "A priest, of course. John Lyon, whom I would send to be James' chaplain, was recommended by our cousin, John MacAlister. Lyon is a man of God, who is both well-educated, wise and gracious. I trust he will be a comfort and a councilor to James."

The hint of a smile crossed John Mor's face. "And a trusted messenger between England and Scotland?"

"Yes, that, too. Moreover, King Henry is not likely to oppose him."

"The way ahead seems clear," said John Mor. "You know I stand with you, Donnie, and when you call me to battle, I will not come alone. I will bring fighting men and galloglasses from Ireland as well as my lands on Islay and Kintyre."

Donald turned to the brother whose eyes were as blue as his own, his brother who once, years ago, had betrayed him. The one he forgave, who thereafter had remained always faithful. "It means more than I can say to have you with me."

Ardtornish Castle, Morvern, autumn 1408

THE NEXT DAY, Donald sailed north to Morvern and his castle on the Sound of Mull to pass a quiet autumn with his family. He was happy to inform Mariota that things had gone well. She never complained but he knew she worried.

While seeing to the business of the Isles, he kept his eyes on the rest of Scotland where Albany continued to rule as governor, seemingly content to leave James a prisoner in England.

In December, a large company was appointed by the Scottish Council to go to England to treat for the release of James, but the ambassadors never set out. It may have been, as Donald believed, a failure by Albany to take any action to see it through.

Meantime, at the suggestion of Donald and the Irish nobles appointed with him, King Henry had proposed a large ransom for Albany's son, Murdoch, but nothing came of it, in part due to the controversy over the Earl of Douglas. He had posted hostages for his own temporary release from prison in England, but had failed to return to London on the date set, angering King Henry. In all this, Scotland became disorganized with little accomplished. Even a needed tax was not authorized by Albany for fear he would lose popularity among the people.

Donald and other nobles looked to England to release James, but no progress was made. Donald wondered if King Henry would ever release the young king because of the pact he had made with Albany to hold James as long as Albany held Richard, still a prisoner at Stirling Castle.

The next year came and, in November, Alex brought Donald

news that Albany was moving forward with his plan to take Ross. As it happened, Donald was on Mull to grant his nephew, Hector Maclean, a charter for lands on the Isles of Coll and Tiree. The witnesses to the charter included Roderick, the young chief of the MacNeils of Barra, who had just become chief upon his father's death, and clergymen, including Michael, Bishop of the Isles, and two rectors of the churches of St. Columba on Mull and Morvern. In addition Donald had invited Lachlan, the current MacKinnon chief, who had come into Donald's favor.

Donald watched from the hill where Duart Castle stood as Alex left his galley on the shore and climbed upward. "I have news," said his brother as he drew near.

"I want to hear it," said Donald, "but first, we've a charter to execute." Then, with a smile, "I am giving Hector new lands."

"I am certain he deserves them," said Alex.

Alex greeted the bishop and rectors and nodded to the MacKinnon chief. To Hector, he said, "You do well as the Maclean chief, Hector. I am glad my brother is rewarding you."

Donald looked with approval at his general. "Hector is already constable of several of my castles, including Cairnburg in the Treshnish Isles, so that he serves well the lordship. He has earned a prize."

Hector inclined his head to Donald. "For which I am most grateful."

When the charter was duly executed, and the witnesses were congratulating Hector, Alex drew Donald aside. "As for my news...Albany is leaning hard on his granddaughter, Euphemia, to take the veil and give Ross to his son, John."

Donald let out a breath, resigned to all this meant. "So it has finally come. Albany moves ahead of my niece's action, knowing that if she succumbs to his pressure and takes the veil, she is considered dead under the law, and my claim to Ross, by right of my wife, becomes paramount."

"As you say, Albany surely knows this," said Alex.

"He does, and that is why we must act before he completes the theft. The Isles of Skye and Lewis are a part of Ross. And, it's not just

Ross. If Albany succeeds there, he will take more, perhaps the lordship itself."

"A worrisome thought," said Alex. "His agent Alexander, Earl of Mar, constantly contests our control over the area around the Great Glen, as his father, the Wolf did. I am forced to keep an armed force in Lochaber to thwart them. What will you do?"

"I will first send Chaplain John Lyon to King James and to King Henry that we might know for a certainty they will support us, not in arms, but in spirit. I want King Henry's neutrality if Albany asks for his help. Then I will formally make my petition before Scotland's General Council when they next meet in Perth."

John Lyon was dispatched to London and, soon after, sent word to Donald that he had the support of both kings. Donald then began to make plans for the coming fight and to speak to his chiefs about what they must do to prepare. An army had to be ready with weapons and training.

The Council met in July of the following year where Albany's son, John, appeared using the full title "Earl of Buchan". Listening to the Council, Donald knew the time to act was growing short.

In autumn, Donald's mother came to visit him at Ardtornish and brought Donald's youngest sister, Elizabeth, with her. He had not seen his mother for several years, not since she had complained about him to King Robert and to her brother, Albany. She was still a beautiful woman though her fair hair was laced with silver and her skin bore the signs of age. When he expressed surprise at her coming, she made it clear she wanted to patch up their differences. He soon realized why.

She was not well.

"I do not wish to go to my grave with ill will between us, Son. You have done well by your people. Your father would have been proud of you. It is time I said so."

Mariota had urged him to be conciliatory. "She is your mother, and Elizabeth is your sister. It is important for our children to know them."

He had to agree, seeing how his daughters, in particular, reacted to their grandmother and their aunt. Elizabeth had grown to be a comely young woman and his eldest daughter, Mari, was taken with her.

"I am glad you have come," he told his mother. "It is good for us to be reconciled and for you to know your grandchildren."

Donald had sent for John Mor and Alex so the family could be reunited.

John Mor was the last to arrive, having come from Antrim in Ireland. Donald met him at the shore as his galley was being beached. Before Donald could say anything, John Mor grinned. "I have a present for you, Brother. She's from Ireland and comes battle-trained."

"She?" His curiosity raised, Donald gazed beyond John, who stood alone with nothing in his hands, to the galley. Inside the hull of the galley in a horse sling, he glimpsed the head of a dark horse.

John called to his captain, "Have the men unload her." To Donald he said, "Her name is Morrigan, after the mythical Irish goddess of battle and war who incites warriors to brave deeds and can bring about victory over their enemies."

The magnificently caparisoned horse was led down the gang-plank. Her cover removed, Donald eyes grew wide as his gaze scanned her exceptional conformation. "She's a beauty!" Before him stood a dark dapple-gray horse whose head was nearly black. The silver dappling on her shoulders and thighs was striking. He ran his hand down her throat and then looked into her eyes, seeing her intelligence.

"I thought you would want her in the battle to come."

Donald placed his hand on his brother's shoulder. "I certainly do. Thank you."

"The Moors prefer mares to stallions in battle as they are calmer. Having been with Morrigan for some time, I can tell you it is true of her. She is also fearless."

Donald's mother stayed for a month, giving her children and grandchildren time to know her better. Then her health grew worse, and she took to her bed. Finally, nearing Christmas, she died with many tears shed at her passing. Abbot John MacAlister administered last rites, and they sailed to Islay, where they buried her on *Eilean Mor* in ground next to Finlaggan's chapel where the wives, sisters and daughters of other Macdonald lords were buried.

As they sailed back to Morvern, Donald said to his young sister, Elizabeth, "Stay with me and Mariota, Sister, and I will find you a good husband."

His fair-haired sister smiled up at him. "I accept your invitation, Donnie. It was in my heart to ask if I might."

With the coming of the new year, Donald turned his attention to matters in Scotland. King Richard finally managed to get a letter out of Stirling. In it, the deposed king told him that Albany was using flattery and threats to persuade Euphemia to join a convent and resign her rights to the Earldom of Ross. "If you wish to prevent this," Richard wrote, "the time is now."

In March of the next year, 1411, he and Alex attended the General Council's meeting in Perth. In attendance was Albany's nephew and Donald's cousin, Alexander Stewart, Earl of Mar, who had entered into a bond with the governor for mutual support. Albany had made Mar his deputy in the Highlands and commissioned him to lead an army of the counties of Aberdeen, Kincardine, and Forfar, and the citizens of the burghs of Aberdeen and Dundee. All this was alarming to Donald.

Donald asked for a hearing before the Council. The nobles remained silent when Donald pressed his claim to Ross, and Albany openly rejected the claim, denying Donald a hearing.

Donald replied, "I will either lose all or gain the earldom to which I have a good title!"

"Do it then," said Albany disdainfully.

Donald turned to go, saying to Alex, "I have waited as long as I could, hoping for another path. Now, I must summon the Isles, Ross and the Highlands to war."

CHAPTER 20

Finlaggan, Isle of Islay, May 1411

IN MAY, DONALD called the Council of the Isles to Finlaggan. Uppermost in his mind was the plan for the march into Ross. There was the route to consider, the battle formation, objectives and rules to be agreed upon and the galleys needed to transport thousands of men. Galleys supplied by King Henry were standing ready at Lagavulin Bay on Islay to be assigned to the chiefs whose own galleys would not meet the need.

As Donald was to claim the province of Ross as his own, he wanted no raiding there or any actions that would alienate the people who would otherwise rise to support him. Keeping thousands of men fed would be a constant challenge but he had a plan for that.

The chiefs arrived at Finlaggan with their families. It was late spring, a glorious time of year, when the hills around the loch were in bloom, but the usual gaiety was tempered with what lay ahead. Like Donald, none of them knew who might fall in battle. When they next met, some of their number would doubtless be missing.

A hunt for the red deer was to be held that afternoon with hounds and horses. Donald looked forward to that as a time of bonding with his chiefs.

The clergy came to Finlaggan as well, including his friend and cousin, John, Abbot of Iona, and Michael, Bishop of the Isles, who would pray over their decisions. The chaplains and physicians for each chief would accompany their march into Ross to attend the wounded and the dying. Donald was not so naïve as to think they would meet no resistance. Given Mar's arrangement with Albany, Donald expected it would be Mar he would face at some point.

"I would go with you," said John MacAlister. "You have chaplains, I know, but I feel a need to stand with you through this venture."

"Your presence would be welcome, John, and I think the clan chaplains would be encouraged by Iona's abbot being with us."

With everyone aware they would sail in the next few months, the tension in the air became tangible. There was excitement, too, as men prepared for war, buying swords and knives offered by the McEacherns of Kildalton, who were hereditary sword makers on Islay and horse masters to the Macdonalds.

The chiefs would ride into battle wearing chainmail and helmets, and armed with swords and dirks, but most of their army would be on foot, armed with swords, pole-axes, bows and arrows, dirks, and targes. Donald had recently purchased a bascinet and new mail, for it had been a while since he'd needed them.

The Fletcher family was busy making arrows for the archers. Sir Thomas' friend Gwyn Kimball, an archer of great skill, was serving with the MacInnes clan, the lordship's hereditary bowmen, who would have an important role in the battle to come.

Donald had just left his bard who was composing a lengthy poem to inspire the warriors before they launched into Ross. Always the Isles marched to war inspired by their bards.

Young men, wanting their first taste of battle, begged their fathers to be allowed to go. His own son, Sandy, was one of these.

Amidst all the activity, wives whose anxiety was clear on their faces, worried for their husbands and sons they might not see again.

As Donald was striding across *Eilean Mor*, the large island in the loch, he saw Mariota just ahead, speaking with several women, and knew the time had come for him to tell her. He waited until she spotted him and left the women.

"My love," he began, as she approached, "there is something I wanted to tell you before I mention it to Sandy."

She anxiously gazed up at him, her brow furrowed. "Tell me you are not taking our son into battle."

"It is my intention to take him with me."

"He is too young for battle."

"He is twenty, Mariota. Young, but still a man grown. I expect there will be others his age with us. Nevertheless, though he will surely object, I will keep Sandy out of the fray. But, as he will one day be Chief of Clan Donald and, if I am successful, Earl of Ross, he must witness what it cost the lordship to give him the title."

Her gaze flitted away. "I suppose you are right." Then she turned her green-gold eyes on him. "But promise me he will not fight. It is hard enough to face the dreadful possibility I might lose you. Think what it would mean if the lordship lost you both."

"I will see to it he does not fight. And, for that purpose, I would like to borrow Sir Thomas to act as Sandy's guard. There will be others assigned to his safety and yours, but since Sandy respects Sir Thomas, he will follow his orders. Abbot John wishes to go with me, and he, too, will be kept out of the battle and can remain with our son." He drew her to him and, holding both her hands in his, said, "Our cause is just, my love. I have tried for years to find a peaceful end to this and could not. We have the support of both King James and King Henry. Pray for us, that we might return to you."

Ardtornish Castle, mid-June, 1411

THE HEATHER HAD just begun to bloom when the fiery cross blazed through the Isles and the coast, summoning the clans to Ardtornish and to war. From every glen, isle and coast, the whole of Clan Donald and its allies rallied to the call.

They arrived by the thousands to gather beneath the unfurled banner of the *Rì Innse Gall*, or King of the Isles, the title their ancestor

Somerled first bore. Years ago, Donald had added to that saffron banner with the black galley the royal double tressure of the Stewart kings and the rising red eagle, wings spread and talons outstretched. The Hebridean Eagle had become the symbol of the chief and hence, Donald himself.

The first to arrive were the Macleans and the MacKinnons from Mull, currently obedient, and Alexander MacDonald, chief of the MacIains from Ardnamurchan. Then came Alex and Clan Chattan and Clan Cameron from Lochaber and the Macleods from the rugged hills of Harris and Lewis. The MacNeils of Barra heeded the call, led by their young chief Roderick, who had impressed Donald. The Macduffies of Colonsay, the lordship's recorders, came prepared to make a record of the quest to save Ross.

John Mor arrived, waving to him from the bow of his galley flying the pennon declaring him to be Lord of Dunyvaig and the Glens. Many other galleys followed in his wake overflowing with Irishmen, with bows and sparth axes, proud to accompany their lord into battle.

The waters of the Sound of Mull and the shores of Morvern overflowed with galleys flying colorful pennons of the clans. That night, the shores were dotted with hundreds of cooking fires and tents.

The next morning, standing with Hector Maclean, John Mor and Alex in front of the castle, Donald surveyed the multitude that had come. "How many do you suppose there are?" he asked, staring at the horde that had descended on Morvern.

Hector crossed his arms, looking every bit the general he was, his dark red hair lifted by the breeze. "The Macduffie has been keeping count. He says ten thousand."

Donald, too, had been observing the galleys unloading the day before to camp on the shore. "That is too many," he said. "Some are too young; some are young chiefs and lairds whose wives have yet to birth an heir. We must narrow the called to the chosen. I would send any home who are their family's sole support, who are really only boys, who would leave a wife with a young babe and any who are too old for the long journey at the end of which will be a fight."

"But that might eliminate hundreds," said Alex.

"Thousands," Donald corrected. "We have tomorrow to do it. Call the chiefs to me and I will explain."

By the next day when Donald dined in his castle with the chiefs, his brothers, and senior men from the Highlands, the army that would sail north from Ardtornish to Strome where they would head inland was down to six thousand six hundred men.

"I see your wisdom in those you have turned back," said Hector Maclean. "What remains are the choicest fighting men."

"And doubtless," said Callum Beg Mackintosh, "many others will join us once we step into Ross."

Donald agreed. Many from Ross would join them, as the province had always preferred to ally with the Lord of the Isles rather than the Stewarts. "I do not doubt that Walter Ross, Lord of Balnagowan, supports our effort to claim Ross," said Donald. "He is no friend of the Albany Stewarts."

"My own Mackintoshes of Badenoch will stand with us," said Callum. "And I expect to see Hugh Munro, Baron of Foulis, join us with his Munros. He, too, is a kindred of Ross."

Donald had great respect for Callum Mackintosh. He was young and short of stature, hence the nickname "Beg", but he was a strong chief. In addition, he was captain of the Clan Chattan confederacy and would draw his kindred to their cause and away from their Stewart overlords in the Highlands. "I would like you to lead one wing of our army, Callum."

"My pleasure," said Callum. "The right wing?" As this was the place of prominence, Donald was not surprised the Mackintosh chief had asked for it. With the strength he and his men would bring to the fight it was a reasonable request. Donald had anticipated it.

"My preference would be for Hector, my Lieutenant General, to have the right wing," said Donald, glancing at his nephew whose expression showed his pleasure, "but I would grant you a boon for accepting the left wing, Callum. The lands of Glengarry in Lochaber will be yours should you graciously yield the right wing to Hector." Donald had gained Alex's consent to this should the Mackintosh chief agree.

"I will gladly take the lands," said Callum with good humor, "and make the left behave as well as the right."

The men sitting around the table chuckled.

Pleased with what had been accomplished, Donald said, "It is my intention to command the main battle myself where I will keep you, Alex, and the Macdonalds and the majority of the Islesmen. If they agree, I would also keep with me the Macleods, John of Harris and Roderick of Lewis." The two men at the other end of the table nodded their approval. "As for you, John," he said to his brother, "I would put you in command of the reserve with your Irishmen and the lightest and nimblest of our force, to be joined by Murdoch Mackenzie and Donald Dubh Cameron, chief of the Camerons, and his son Ewen."

"It shall be as you say," said John. Of the others Donald had named, those who were present nodded their approval.

"Our captain, John Cameron of Lochiel, will also fight with us," said the Cameron chief, "though, given where our lands are, regrettably some Camerons may fight with Mar."

"Then we will have to win without them," said Donald.

That evening, Donald took advantage of the long summer day to walk among the campfires on the shores around Ardtornish and greet the men. He wanted to encourage them for the fight to come.

Up ahead, sitting on the grass with the Macleans, Donald spotted his son, Sandy, his fair hair reflecting the light from the campfire. Hector and his uncle, the Maclean of Buie, were lodged in the castle but Hector's eldest son, Lachlan, and Hector's nephews were here with the Maclean men.

Donald greeted the Macleans and then beckoned to his son. "Sandy, come walk with me. I would have a word…"

Knowing what he had to say would disappoint his son, Donald wanted to take him aside. "You will be going with us," said Donald, "but because you are heir to the lordship, you will not fight."

Sandy gasped. "What?"

"Were we both to fall, your brother John is too young to become chief and Angus is destined for the church. Your uncle, John Mor, assuming he survived, would become chief. It is my duty to the lordship to keep you safe."

Sandy looked aghast. "Then why take me at all?"

"When you are chief, you will understand. These thousands of men you see here have come at our call to save Ross for the lordship and Scotland for King James. Albany would have it all if allowed. One day, God willing, you will be not only Lord of the Isles but Earl of Ross. You must be a witness to what it cost to gain you that title. You must appreciate their sacrifice for some will surely die in the fighting. A commander must always consider the cost."

Sandy's expression turned somber. "I didn't think of that." A moment passed and then, with a sigh, he said, "Very well, Father, I will do as you say."

Donald put his arm around his son. "I know you wanted to fight, but sometimes duty calls one to refrain. And you will not be the only eldest son kept from the battle. I have asked Sir Thomas and our cousin, Abbot John, to stay with you as well as a few others."

Sandy nodded.

"I have no doubt when the time comes, Son, you will make a fine chief."

THE NEXT DAY, under a blue sky, Donald kissed Mariota and his children goodbye, and to the shouts of "Godspeed", climbed aboard his galley with Sandy, Sir Thomas and Abbot John.

Mariota had put on a brave face, sending him away with a smile. Knowing how difficult that was for her and the others left behind, he felt pride at her strength and how well she represented him with the other wives.

The fleet of galleys that sailed north that morning with pennons waving numbered in the hundreds. They were heading to Loch Carron, where many years ago Donald had beached his galley on the loch's northern shore and set out across Ross to Dingwall to meet his intended bride. This time, it would take longer, as he was leading thousands of men, most of them on foot, and with carts carrying food, weapons, supplies and servants. He couldn't help reflecting on how much had happened since that day long ago. Clan Donald had grown stronger, rivaling the lordship his grandfather, Angus Og Macdonald, had summoned to Bannockburn.

Among those sailing north behind Donald's galley was Allan MacDonald, 2nd of Clanranald and Moidart, and his brothers Donald and Dougall, Donald's kin from his father's first marriage. He highly valued their allegiance.

Arriving at Strome on the coast, they beached the ships on the grassy shore of Loch Carron, planning to set out the next morning. They had sufficient food for several days but would still need to hunt and fish and, where appropriate, raid. Donald had received firm assurances from the chiefs that their men would not plunder Ross. "Ross is part of the lordship," he reminded them, "and should be treated as such."

That evening, their campfires dotted the landscape, helping to keep the midges at bay. Donald thought it a good time to inspire the men for what lay ahead. He asked his bard, Lachlann Mòr MacMhui-rich, to read what he had written earlier as an incitement to battle. The bard positioned himself so his voice carried over the water as he spoke in a loud, stirring voice to the enraptured thousands.

O Children of Conn, remember

Hardihood in time of battle…

Be angry, audacious, agile, ambitious

Be bold, beautiful, brawny, belligerent

Be confrontational, courageous, clever, combative

Be deliberate, destructive, deadly, enduring

Be grim, gruesome, gymnastic, glorious

Be mirthful, mortally-wounding, mettlesome, militaristic

Be tight, triumphant, tenacious, tripping

O Children of Conn of the Hundred Battles,

Now is your time for honor

O raging whelps, O brawny bears, O splendid lions

O Children of Conn, remember

Hardihood in time of battle.

This was followed by a rousing tune on the pipes, inspiring all. A great chorus erupted as the men shouted the last line in unison, "Hardihood in time of battle!"

The next morning, Abbot John celebrated Mass and prayed for them before they marched into Ross. "Lead us to victory, Lord, for our cause is just."

They met with no resistance from the people of Ross, who came out in large numbers to welcome them wholeheartedly, preferring the Macdonalds as their overlords to Albany and his Stewarts.

Many from Ross' nobility joined them, for it was not just the rights of Clan Donald that Albany was ignoring but those of the kindreds of Ross.

Included with those who came forward were Walter Ross, Lord of Balnagowan, with his son John, and Hugh Munro, Baron of Foulis, Mariota's cousin, and his brothers Donald and Dougall. The Munros of Foulis were vassals of the earls of Ross. Thus, the two most powerful magnates in the earldom and their forces were now with Donald's army. Balnagowan possessed great influence as the male heir of the last native earl, and his support soon drew many to Donald's cause.

With the exception of Murdoch MacKenzie, all the northern lords joined Donald while he was still in Easter Ross. From six thousand six hundred, Donald's army had swelled with more arriving each hour, proud Highlanders ready to fight for the Lord of the Isles. "If it continues this way," said John Mor, "you will soon have ten thousand again."

Donald was not at all displeased with this result. It was good that the men of Ross should fight for their rightful lord.

As they approached Dingwall Castle, Donald's spies brought word that Angus Du Mackay, Chief of the Mackays of Strathnaver in Sutherland, meant to oppose him.

"'Tis said he is related to the Earl of Mar," said Alex, "and likely would resist us at Mar's or Albany's insistence."

Donald sat astride his horse on the grassy hillside, alongside his two captains and his brothers, looking down on the castle. Men-at-arms flowed out of the castle to join those already standing before it, weapons raised.

"Mackay can field four thousand men from Strathnaver," said Hector.

"That is not four thousand," said Callum Mackintosh, gazing at the army before them. "More like half that, I'd say."

Callum was right, but still, why sacrifice any? "I would prefer Mackay stand aside," said Donald. "He cannot defeat us and he will lose men he cares for. See if you two can persuade him to refrain so that we are not forced to join battle."

Callum and Hector walked their horses slowly down the slope to be met by the Mackay and what looked to be his brother and a few guards. A short discussion took place before Hector and Callum turned their horses back to Donald and the army waiting behind him.

"He is Mar's cousin," said Hector.

"So am I," said Donald with a smile.

"He was likely placed here by Albany," said Callum, "and will make no compromise."

"Very well," said Donald. "We attack, for we cannot gain Ross and lose Dingwall." Donald commanded his captains and his brothers forward. "For Ross and Alba!"

The battle cry was repeated, and with the pipes blaring and every clansman adding his own war cry, Donald and his captains rushed forward with the army following on their heels. Men swept past Donald, waving their axes and spears and swords.

The fighting was fierce and the clash of weapons and men's shouts loud, but it did not last long. In but a few hours, they had defeated the Mackay and taken the castle. Many of Mackay's men were slain, which Donald regretted.

Angus Du Mackay, his black hair and mail stained with blood and his face a mask of sadness, was led to Donald. "I would have had it otherwise," Donald told him.

"In retrospect, so would I," said the young Mackay. "My brother, Rorie, is dead."

"I regret your loss," said Donald, and meant it.

Donald directed his men to escort the Mackay to Dingwall's dungeon. "It's just for the night," he explained to the Mackay chief.

"Tomorrow, my men will escort you to the coast." To one of his guards, he said, "See he is taken to Mingary on Ardnamurchan's coast where my cousins, the MacIains will keep him until I return."

"Yes, my lord," said the guard.

Donald would advise Alexander Macdonald, chief of the MacIains who rode with him, before the evening was over. Murdoch Mackenzie, who had chosen the wrong side to fight on, was also taken prisoner at Dingwall but Donald considered him of so little consequence he didn't confine him to prison.

That night, the fires of Donald's army burned in the heart of Ross. Donald had no doubt Albany had been informed. Wanting to discourage raiding in the province, Donald was anxious to move on to Inverness, considered Albany's capital, where he expected to face Mar.

The next morning, assured that Dingwall Castle was properly garrisoned, Donald led his army twelve miles south to Beauly. There, he halted the advance to Inverness on the plains of Kilchirst, opposite the castle of Lovat. Hoping to find an ally, Donald sent a messenger to Alexander, Lord Lovat, explaining the injustice done him by Albany and asking for his assistance. Instead of encouraging Donald, Lovat sent a message back, saying he viewed Donald's effort as hopeless and, since the young king was a prisoner in England, dangerous.

Incensed, Donald shared this with his brothers and his captains and the chiefs who had gathered around him. "So, Lovat has decided to find an excuse to throw in with Albany," said Hector in disgust. "We might have known. The man has no backbone."

"He doesn't know us very well either if he thinks ten thousand of us are hopeless," said John Mor. "'Tis laughable."

Donald sent a stern reply to Lord Lovat and Hugh Fraser, Sheriff of Inverness, chiding them for opposing his rightful claim to the earldom of Ross. Still incensed at Lovat, Donald ordered his army to lay siege to Lovat's castle. However, the attempt to take it by storm proved fruitless. Donald deemed the castle sufficiently strong to resist them. Wanting to waste no more time, he raised the siege and allowed the army to pillage the surrounding countryside before proceeding east.

When they arrived at Inverness, Mar was nowhere in sight.

"Could it be," asked Callum Mackintosh, "that Mar is avoiding us?"

"His spies must have brought him word of our advance," said Donald's brother, Alex. "And behind all, Albany watches."

"It was Albany who ordered Mar to raise an army," said Donald, "which I presume he has done. We will continue east until we encounter him or reach Aberdeen." Since Donald controlled the Great Glen to the south and Urquhart Castle on Loch Ness, where Charles Maclean, son of the Maclean of Lochbuie, was constable, he knew he would get support from there, which he did with more fighting men arriving to join the cause.

Donald called upon the inhabitants of Inverness to join him, but they refused. He was disappointed but unsurprised. Inverness was a symbol of Albany's power. In retribution, he gave the army leave to sack the town, and set afire Inverness Castle and the oak bridge spanning the Moray Firth. The burning of the bridge was a signal to neighboring clans to come and join him, one they would not fail to recognize. Planting his standard in Inverness, he summoned all the fighting men of the north to him.

Those of the Clan Chattan confederation, who had yet to arrive, as well as the men of Clan Cameron saw the message and came in great numbers.

"We are all here now," said Donald Dubh, Chief of the Camerons.

"Aye," said Callum Mackintosh, "the Chattan confederation is here as well."

"If our army was not yet ten thousand before this," said John Mor, standing beside Donald as they surveyed the Inverness flames, "it surely is now."

They spent the night in Inverness, camped along the river, enjoying the food and wine the town had to offer. The next morning, they set out for Moray. He did not restrain the men from despoiling what was Albany's countryside, and they met little resistance. Though there had been no showing by Mar, Donald knew his chosen route would be watched by the earl's scouts. Donald's own men, scouting ahead, had yet to see anything of the earl.

As they proceeded east, Donald had Callum send messengers summoning all the fighting men in Badenoch between the River Deveron and River Spey. Donald's control over the Moray Highlands was central to his fight with Mar, which is why it meant so much to have Callum Beg, the chief of the Mackintoshes of Badenoch, as one of his captains.

Donald turned his army southeast, following the main road that ran north of the River Urie. It was in Strathbogie and Garioch, which belonged to the Earl of Mar, that Donald's Islesmen and Highlanders did the most damage. He had held them back in Ross, but he would not hold them back in Mar's territory. Instead, he allowed them to plunder for arms and provisions.

Donald was now headed to the strategic high ground of Inverurie. The summit provided a strong defensive position surrounded by farmland that led to the fertile plains of Aberdeen. As close as Donald's army would be to that town, Mar would have to face them soon or lose all.

Aware of this, Donald planned for it.

Two miles north of Inverurie, Donald drew a halt to his army's march at the village of Harlaw. He invited Abbot John and Sandy to join him that night to sup with his generals and chiefs. "We will dine on whatever the men's hunting has brought in and discuss the coming battle. Sandy, you should remain silent in the presence of such great men, but I trust you, John, will remind them to seek the Lord's blessing."

Once they were seated around the fire, Donald addressed his captains and the chiefs. "Tomorrow, is the 24th of July, the eve of St. James Day, which I believe is auspicious. Surely our young King James, when he hears of it, will think so, too. We will look for Mar that day or the next. Make sure your men are ready. Our scouts are out now."

"Will our positions be the same as you first laid them out?" asked Hector.

Donald nodded. "I see no reason to change what has worked well to this day. We will place our archers before us, except those Irish bowmen with you in the reserve, John. They are free to shoot as you direct and they find targets among the enemy."

"Why do you think Mar has yet to engage us?" asked Callum Mackintosh.

"Doubtless he is finding it difficult to raise volunteers to face ten thousand," said Alex with a smirk.

"You may be right," said Donald. "Mar is likely gathering his forces. He will not have as many men as we do, but he will have many knights, all well-armored. Our men are not lacking in courage or numbers, but they must be prepared to face a wall of steel. Avoiding the knights' lances and swords, they must pull them from their horses, or take the horses down. Once on the ground, the knights will struggle while our men will find the gaps in their armor and dispatch them with their dirks. It is best you explain this to any who have not faced a mounted, armored knight before."

The chiefs nodded, their expressions serious.

His brothers, too, indicated they understood. "My son, Alexander, and I will fight with you in the main battle," said Alex. "We are ready."

"My men are anxious to engage," said John Mor. "I have been drilling them as we crossed Mar's lands and my archers have been in constant practice. Then, too, the Irish have faced England's knights before."

Hector said, "My eldest, Lachlan, will fight with me in the right wing."

The evening concluded with Abbot John praying for them and for the coming battle.

Donald doubted if anyone in his army slept well that night. For his own part, he lay awake confessing his sins and asking God to take him should he die. He drew comfort from the monks at Iona who made regular prayers for him.

At first light, Donald's scouts returned with news. "My lord, Mar has set forth from Aberdeen," said one.

"How many?" asked Donald, peering into the dawn toward Aberdeen.

"Perhaps one thousand, my lord, or a bit more. They are led by the Earl of Mar with Sir Robert Davidson, Lord Provost of Aberdeen, and a troop of knights and men-at-arms in the vanguard, followed by Sir James Scrymgeour, Constable of Dundee, and Alexander Ogilvy, Sheriff of Angus, with the main body, including the Keiths, Forbeses, Leslies and Irvines, to tell by their banners. There are many knights wearing plate armor and mail-clad men-at-arms."

"Yet they are only a tenth of our army," Donald reminded him lest the young man lose heart. Donald thought about all those knights. Mar would think Donald's army weak because it lacked steel armor. But Donald thought of how that same armor would be a weakness. It would be a hot summer's day, and before long, Mar and his knights would be sweating beneath their steel plate. Fatigue would set in and they would be vulnerable.

After a word with his captains, Donald mounted his horse. Morrigan had served him faithfully and he silently thanked John Mor for his thoughtful gift. With his vanguard assembling behind him, Donald waited. Soon, he glimpsed Mar's smaller, well-armed force approaching with colorful banners waving, many of which Donald recognized. With the morning sun reflecting off their armor, they looked like they were headed to a tourney, not to war.

At the head of his men and, with his captains riding before the wings, Donald drew up his army to face the enemy.

Donald tightened his grip on his sword, his heart pounding in his chest. The air crackled with tension. On his command, the pipes sounded. War cries pierced the air.

Shouting his own war cry, Donald charged forward. Waving their swords, pikes, axes and spears, his army of Islesmen and Highlanders followed. Mar's army rushed toward them.

From Donald's archers, arrows flew over the heads of Mar's vanguard to fell some in his army.

With a thunderous roar, the clash of steel reverberated across the field as the opposing armies collided. When Donald's main force met Mar's armor and weapons, the momentum of their charge came to a halt.

Sir James Scrymgeour and his knights took advantage of the situation and pushed forward, leaving a trail of hundreds of dead and dying

Islemen and Highlanders. But for every man killed, another brave man took his place without hesitation.

Donald's blade flashed in the sunlight as he parried a vicious strike from an enemy warrior, the force of the impact sending a jolt of pain up his arm. With a burning desire for victory, he pressed on, weaving through the chaos. Sweat trickled down his brow, his muscles aching with every swing and parry. The din of clashing swords and the thud of bodies hitting the ground filled his ears, drowning out all other sounds.

His heart raced as he faced off against a skilled knight, their blades clashing in a deadly dance. Donald's mind calculated each move, each step, as he fought to outmaneuver his opponent. With a swift feint, he jerked Morrigan away from the enemy's strike and delivered a powerful blow to his side. The knight stumbled, nearly falling from his horse, blood streaming from his armor. Without hesitation, Donald moved on.

The battle raged, a swirling mass of violence. The ground beneath Morrigan's hooves was slick with blood. He had to guide her around the bodies strewn across the field. His muscles burned, his breath came in ragged gasps, but he pushed through, fueled by the knowledge he must win this day for the lordship.

As the sun reached its zenith, a surge of energy coursed through Donald's veins. He felt a flicker of hope, and knew that victory was within his grasp. With a rallying cry, he charged forward, his Islesmen and Highlanders at his side. Together, they formed an impenetrable wall, pushing back the enemy with every ounce of strength they possessed.

Sir James and his men gradually became exhausted. Surrounded, they were brought down from their horses and killed.

Donald's Islesmen, encouraged by the Constable of Dundee's fall, wielded their swords and axes with great effect, seizing and stabbing the horses, and pulling down their riders, killing them with their dirks. Donald fought with them, shouting commands when he glimpsed an opening.

Sir Robert Davidson with five hundred men-at-arms, including the principal gentry of Buchan, and the greater part of the burgesses of

Aberdeen, who followed their provost, were among the slain.

"Sir Alexander Ogilvy, Sheriff of Angus, and his eldest son, George, are dead along with seven knights," reported one of Donald's men.

Meantime, the Earl of Mar, wielding his sword at the head of his force, plunged into the field of blood, taking the fight to the heart of Donald's army. For hours, Mar fought but he failed to meet with success.

Hector Maclean's right wing drove Mar's left flank back to a large cattle fold, further down the hill not far from where Aberdeen's provost had fallen. Trapped, the mounted knights, overwhelmed by large numbers of fast-moving Islesmen and Highlanders, were mobbed and killed within minutes. Hector had caused Mar to lose almost the whole of his army.

Added to this, John Mor and his agile men from Antrim, Islay and Kintyre, came in from the rear, stinging Mar's men like bees, then flying away only to sting again. Their archers, too, did much damage.

The mounted men of Buchan who still lived harried Donald's left wing with their knights and men-at-arms slogging through the boggy wet ground that lay to the northeast of Harlaw. But Callum Mackintosh, effectively commanding the two thousand men in the left wing, including the Clan Chattan confederacy, intercepted them in the hill ranges to the north of Harlaw and brought them down.

As Donald surveyed the bloody battlefield, he saw many dead. Like Mar, Donald commanded the main battle from his horse, receiving a few wounds, none he deemed serious.

From his vantage, he witnessed the deaths of several he knew: two Munros, who fought with the men of Ross, the son of Macquarrie of Ulva, who was with the Macleans, and two Camerons. Allan of Clanranald and his brother Donald had shown great courage, distinguishing themselves, but sadly, their brother Dougall, who fought with them, was slain.

Though Donald believed the lordship would have the victory, he regretted the loss of every man. He dreaded the terrible task he would have when the battle was over of conveying the news to the mothers and wives, some of whom waited at Ardtornish.

Eventually, Mar's forces began to falter. Donald could see it in their eyes, the glimmer of fear and exhaustion. With a renewed sense of victory, he redoubled his efforts, his sword a blur of steel in the fading light.

Then he heard a shout from Sir Alexander Irvine, Laird of Drum, aimed at Hector Maclean. "Ha! Chief of Duart, follower of a rebel vassal, have I at length the satisfaction of seeing you within reach of my sword's point?" Sir Alexander was one of Mar's many cousins and one of his captains. Like Hector, he was a man of legendary prowess with his sword.

"Time-serving slave," shouted Hector, "you have, if it satisfies you, and if my steel be as keen as my appetite for your life, you will not have time to repeat your taunt."

The two men rushed at each other, brandishing their swords and clashing with great fury. Donald watched the fight unfold with growing alarm. Both men were already wounded when they began to fight, and now they inflicted more wounds on each other.

Donald rode his horse forward. "Hector will not thank you, should you interfere," said Alex, riding to his side.

His brother was right, but it pained Donald to see the two men slicing into each other. Blood ran freely down Hector's tunic and mail and his sword slowed in his attacks, as did Drum's. Such was the force of their fight, that they soon fell injured foot to foot on the field.

Donald dismounted and hastened to Hector, followed by Alex and the men of Clan MacInnes who were nearby.

Hector was still conscious when Donald reached him and spoke the words he knew Hector would want to hear. "My dearest nephew, you fought valiantly."

"Not so well as to defeat Drum," he said in a faint and halting voice.

"Drum lies here with you and will not rise."

With his faint breath, Hector said, "See to my son, Lachlan, and to my wife."

"You know I will," said Donald, squeezing Hector's hand.

The Maclean chaplain knelt on Hector's other side. With tears in his eyes, he pronounced last rites.

Hector's eyes closed, never to open again. It had been the ultimate test of a courageous warrior, one who never shied from battle. This fight, like so many others, Hector had won. And yet, this one he had also lost. Donald knew in that moment Hector's death would never leave him. And it contributed greatly to his wanting to end this now.

The MacInneses bore Hector's body from the field on their shields.

As Donald watched them go, he rose and told Alex, "I will take him back to the Isles and see he is buried at Iona."

"Aye, he would like that."

A message arrived from Alexander Seton, Lord of Huntly, who Donald knew to be a good man. He had been with Prince James when their ship was seized by English pirates and was taken prisoner but later set free. Donald quickly perused Huntly's message urging restraint in the following days. Donald tucked it into his tunic.

The light was fading and, while Donald could hear the sounds of sporadic fighting in various places on the wide battlefield, he knew it would end as darkness fell. The field lay littered with the fallen, a testament to the price paid for victory. Many would be buried here but some would be taken home to Ross and the Isles.

Donald stood amidst the chaos, bloodied but triumphant. The taste of victory was bittersweet, for the cost had been high, as he knew it would be. Yet, in that moment, he couldn't help but feel a surge of pride for his fellow clansmen and their unwavering courage. They had fought against knights in steel armor and won.

Except for those few still fighting, what remained of Mar's men lay wounded on the field, Mar with them, unable to continue.

"Do we pursue Mar's last breath?" asked Alex.

"No, leave him where he lies." Then, looking around him, he asked, "How many do you think we have lost?"

"Less than a thousand. We have the bulk of our army with us still. Mar's hundreds were decimated."

Abbot John and Sandy joined Donald and Alex and soon John Mor, too, stood among them with Donald's other captain, Callum Mackintosh. Donald thanked God they all lived.

"We have gained Ross," said John Mor, "and defeated Albany's army, and still have thousands to go on, should you command it."

"There has been enough killing," said Donald, "and the loss of Hector has been a grave one. Besides, the Lord of Huntly has sent me a message, acknowledging our victory and asking me not to plunder Aberdeen. I see no reason to do so. Our army has fields that will need to be harvested and families waiting for their return."

"Surely it was worth the sacrifice of these lives to assure the future of the lordship," said John Mor.

Without hesitation, Donald said, "Yes, and every man who fought here today would agree." Then glancing at Sandy, he said, "One day, my son will be Lord of the Isles and Earl of Ross. More importantly, the lordship is safe from the Albany Stewarts."

"I should think your restraint now will gain God's approval," said Abbot John. "If you will allow, I would say more." With Donald's nod, the abbot took from his robe his psalter Donald had seen him reading before. Opening it, he read,

> "I have pursued my enemies and overtaken them; neither did I turn back again till they were destroyed. I have wounded them, so that they could not rise; they have fallen under my feet. For You have armed me with strength for the battle; you have subdued under me those who rose up against me. You have also given me the necks of my enemies, so that I destroyed those who hated me."

"Which psalm is that you quote from?" asked Donald.

"The words of King David from the eighteenth psalm." John turned his eyes from Donald to gaze across the battlefield strewn with the injured and dead. "The words of that psalm have been on my mind today as I watched the battle unfold. Like you, David was at the height of his power and had engaged in battle with his enemies. God delivered him, as He has you, and thus David gave God praise."

"As will I," said Donald. "Will you pray for these wounded and fallen men and praise God for our victory?"

There on the field, with all bowing their heads, John prayed.

When he finished, Donald said, "We will take our army home."

Then, turning to his son who had remained silent, he explained his actions. "You may one day have such a choice to make, Sandy. Some would urge me to go on and plunder Aberdeen, but I do not think Scotland or her king would thank us for it."

"I see now why you wanted me to witness the battle. I understand the cost. And seeing Lord Hector die will help me mourn with my Maclean cousins."

As the light was overcome by darkness, what was left of the battle ended.

After they buried the dead, Donald ordered his army down the plateau to Inverurie, Mar's original muster point, where they spent the night and their wounds were tended. They dined on provisions from Mar's baggage train, abandoned with the defeat of his army.

As he and his captains discussed the battle, Donald happened to think of Hector's eldest son, Lachlan. He had not seen him among his men and wanted to pay his respects. "What of Lachlan Maclean?" he asked. "Has anyone seen him?"

"We think he must have been taken prisoner," said one of the Lochbuie Macleans. "His body was not on the field. His younger brothers were kept back at Duart so they are not here to ask."

"If Lachlan has not fallen," said Donald, "and we must hope for that, Mar must have had him taken to his castle at Kildrummy. It is imperative that we ransom him, for he is his father's heir and now chief of Clan Maclean. I will see to this myself."

From Inverurie, Donald and his captains led the army back to Ross where they received a great welcome. But they did not linger. Anxious to return his Islesmen home, Donald made his garrison at Dingwall strong, bid goodbye to the people of Ross, and departed the next day, exultant at their victory yet weary of a battle long in coming.

CHAPTER 21

Ardtornish Castle, Morvern, August 1411

NEWS HAD ALREADY begun to reach Ardtornish before Mariota spotted the returning galleys in the Sound of Mull. At a place called Harlaw in Aberdeenshire, there had been a great victory. All who waited at Ardtornish celebrated. For her own part, Mariota was relieved to hear both Donald and her son lived and were coming home. But many had died on that battlefield, so blood-soaked they were calling it "Red Harlaw".

The grievous report of Hector Maclean's death hit everyone hard, most especially Mary, his mother, and his widow, Anne Douglas. The younger Macleans who had been left behind wore solemn and sad faces.

Waiting with her arm around Mary in front of the castle, she watched the great fleet of galleys with billowing sails coming toward them. Mariota knew that Mary and Anne desperately wanted to see Hector's son, Lachlan, to be sure he lived, for there had been no news of him. Other wives and mothers had stayed at Ardtornish, unwilling to wait on their isles for their menfolk.

Donald's galley led the fleet down the sound. From where she stood, Mariota could see the hull of his galley held not only his horse but a body draped in an ivory silk pall with a long-shafted Celtic-ringed cross appliquéd in golden fabric.

"Bless him," said Mary. "He is bringing my Hector home to be buried."

Mariota squeezed her sister-in-law's shoulder. "Donnie would not leave him."

As Donald climbed down from the galley to the shore, Mariota and their children walked down to greet him and Sandy. She knew from her husband's somber expression he was feeling the weight of the deaths of those men who, like Hector, would not return.

With a smile on her face, she walked to him and wrapped her arms around him. "Welcome home, my love."

Sighing, he said, "The news is mixed, as I'm certain you have heard."

"Yes, we know about Hector. Mary and Anne are here." Seeing how weary he was, Mariota asked, "Do you want to come inside where you can tell us more?"

"First, I must address those who have waited." Abbot John and Sandy had disembarked and walked toward them to stand with Donald.

As more galleys landed and men flowed from them onto the beach, they were met by their families, some to great joy, others to sadness. Donald embraced Mary and then Anne. "I am so sorry. Hector fought bravely and led the right wing to victory. He was killed toward the end in a single combat with Alexander Irvine, Laird of Drum, a match each sought, valiantly fought. Both died of their wounds. Should you agree, we will take Hector to Iona and bury him with great honor."

Mary nodded, tears flowing down her cheeks. Hector was her eldest son and the clan's chief, loved and respected by all. His loss would be deeply felt in the Isles and beyond. When her tears subsided, Mary asked, "Where is Lachlan?"

"Taken prisoner by Mar," said Donald. At Mary's gasp and Anne's exclamation, he added, "We will ransom him. Do not worry. He will return."

Drawing hope from Donald's words, Mariota put her arm around Mary standing next to Anne.

Donald turned to address the crowd that had gathered. "As you will hear in more detail in the coming days, we were joined in battle in Aberdeenshire by the governor's army led by Alexander Stewart, Earl of Mar. We outnumbered them by a considerable amount, but they were mostly armored knights and well-trained men-at-arms. Our courageous Islesmen and Highlanders fought bravely, facing a wall of steel. Some sacrificed themselves to gain us the victory that is now ours. The province of Ross is won and the lordship is safe from the Albany Stewarts. You can be proud of your husbands, fathers and sons, for this is their victory, which will long be celebrated in Ross and the Isles."

Mariota observed the admiration shining in her son's eyes as Sandy listened to his father. Donald had been right to take him, for now he understood what every leader must. To risk the lives of others, a leader must have the strongest heart and, when the battle is over, bear the weight of all those who fall.

When Abbot John drew Mary and Anne aside, Mariota again suggested they go inside where she had wine and refreshments waiting. All who wanted to go with them were invited, but many decided to collect their families and return home. "We can celebrate the victory and mourn the losses at Finlaggan," she said to Donald. With their daughters and sons clustered around them, they walked slowly to the castle.

"I am returning Sir Thomas to your guard," said Donald, looking toward the knight striding from the beach, "which should please your Abby."

"It will, indeed. She has been worried."

Inside, Mariota watched Donald slump into a chair at the table in the great hall, to be joined by his brothers, some of the clan chiefs, and Abbot John. She and the servants served the men food and wine while she listened to their talk.

"What now?" asked John Mor. "Will Albany pursue us to the Isles?"

"He might," said Donald. "Vexed at his loss at Harlaw, he will want revenge. His pride has been wounded."

John Mor leaned forward. "Then let me be the one to repulse the governor. I have the men to do it and they are still eager for a fight. It would be my pleasure to see this done."

"My men of Lochaber can support you, John, if needed," said Alex.

Donald nodded. Mariota could see he was glad for his brothers' willingness to take up the cause. "Very well. Look for him to come to Argyll, though it may be some months."

"We will be ready to meet him," said John Mor, his smile eager.

"As for me," said Donald, "I must take Hector's body to Iona for burial in *Reilig Odhrain* to join the kings and chieftains buried there. Will you preside, John?" he asked his friend.

"It will be my privilege to honor in death a gallant warrior who served his people well in life. The monks, too, will join us."

"From Iona," Donald continued, "I would have my family and the Macleans return home, but I must go on to Mingary Castle on Ardnamurchan, where I have a meeting of some importance with a prisoner I took at Dingwall."

"The chief of the Mackays?" asked Alex.

"Yes. I have in mind an alliance with Strathnaver."

"If you can manage it," said Alex, "it would mean much by way of securing Ross, for he has at his command thousands of men, and his territory covers most of Sutherland."

Donald inclined his head to his brother. "My very thought."

That night, Mariota comforted her husband in the way she knew best, willingly giving him her body as she had given him her heart. Afterwards, he fell into a deep sleep. By the look of him, it was the first of its kind in many days. Listening to his soft breathing, she thanked God for bringing him home.

DONALD SAILED THE next day with three galleys to Iona. One he would take on to Mingary Castle; one would return to Ardtornish with his family; and the Maclean galley would carry Mary, Anne and the Macleans back to Mull.

Mary and Anne sailed in his galley with Hector's body. As they glided over the blue waters, his crew sang the song that had been sung many times before when great men and kings were brought to rest on the sacred isle.

Softly glide we along, softly chant we our song,
For a chief who to resting is come;
Oh, beloved and best, thou art fairing out west,
To the dear isle Iona, thy home.

Calmly there shalt thou lie, with thy fathers gone by,
Their blood mingled deep with thine own;
Ne'er again to awake, till the last morn shall break,
And the trump of the judgment is blown.

Donald stepped from his galley to the shore of Iona with Mariota at his side. The isle had always brought him peace with its blue-green waters lapping at the white sand beaches and the ever-present breeze that stirred the soul, whispering of days long passed. It had been a hallowed place long before Columba made it his home. Sixty kings were buried in the graveyard at *Reilig Odhrain*. And, one day, Donald's body would be laid to rest in St. Oran's Chapel to join those of the Lords of the Isles who preceded him.

The monks of Iona welcomed him, his family and the Macleans and those with them into the abbey. It would be a brief but significant stay in order to show Hector the honor he deserved.

In consultation with Mary, he ordered a stone cross to be carved by the O'Brolchan family of high artisans and masons who served the Lord of the Isles. It would mark Hector's grave, a cross that would give witness to Hector's faith. The next morning, they carried his body from the abbey church, where it had rested for the night, to the place where other Macleans were buried.

Abbot John, in his remarks at the graveside, spoke of man's mortality and eternity that lay beyond the grave. All were deeply affected. And then, speaking from a familiar passage, he said, "We do not grieve like the rest of mankind, who have no hope. For we believe that Jesus died and rose again, and so we believe that God will bring with Jesus those who have fallen asleep in him, including our Hector. According to the Lord's word, we who are still alive, who are left until the coming of the Lord, will not precede those who have fallen asleep. For the Lord Himself will come down from Heaven, with a loud command, with the voice of the archangel and with the trumpet call of God, and the dead in Christ will rise first. After that, we who are still alive and are left will be caught up together with them in the clouds to meet the Lord in the air. And so, we will ever be with the Lord. The Apostle Paul told us to encourage one another with these words, and so we shall. You will see Hector again."

When the burial was accomplished, the mourners traveled over the ancient stone path, the Street of the Dead, back to the abbey.

"Hector would have loved that ceremony," said Hector's mother. "I thank you, Donald, for the honor you have paid him." Anne walked at Mary's side, silently weeping, comforted by one of the Maclean women.

That evening, they dined and toasted Hector, remembering his great exploits. At one point, Donald drew his friend, the abbot, aside. "I would like to do something for the abbey as a token of my gratitude to God for the victory he has given us."

"A good thought," said John. "What do you have in mind?"

"Might we seek a relic of St. Columba from where his bones lie in Ireland that I might cover it in gold and silver and present it to the abbey?"

"An elaborate gift, to be sure, and a worthy one. The saint's relics are at his home in Derry. With our connections to Ireland, we might well obtain the arm and hand bones and have them brought to Iona where our artisans can fashion the gold and silver covering. I know the Bishop of Derry, Donnell MacCawley, and can reach out to him. If we are successful, on St. Columba's Feast Day next June, such a magnificent gift could be displayed for all to see. The clans would consider it a sign of God's blessing."

Donald wanted to do this, not only to show his gratitude, but also to bestow a gift on the abbey that would bring it esteem. "If you will make inquiries, I want to proceed."

John agreed and the following day, Donald sailed to Ardnamurchan and Mingary Castle, taking only his guard with him. The castle stood above the shore of Kilchoan Bay, looking across to the Isle of Mull. Its location allowed the MacIains to control the entrance to Loch Sunart and observe shipping across the Sound of Mull.

As his crew beached the galley, and he climbed down to the sand, a sea eagle flew across his path, its high-pitched rapid call piercing the air. The eagle was the symbol of the MacIain clan, and Donald took it as a sign that portended a good result from his visit.

He had only learned after the battle at Harlaw that his cousin, Alexander MacDonald, chief of the MacIains of Ardnamurchan, had been killed, a great loss to the clan and a personal loss to Donald. Alexander's son, John, who was Sandy's age and one of his friends, now led the clan, and greeted Donald as he strode to the castle door.

"I am sorry for the loss of your father," Donald told him. "He was a great leader and will be sorely missed by all in the lordship."

"Thank you, Lord Donald. It will take some time to get used to his absence." Then turning to the matter for which Donald had come, he said, "We have your prisoner. Do you wish to speak to him?"

"Yes, if I might see him in private?"

John directed him to a small chamber off the great hall. "I will have him brought to you. He is in good health."

Angus Du Mackay's appearance was notably better than the last time Donald had seen him after the battle at Dingwall. Since then, he had bathed, his black hair had been combed, his beard neatly trimmed and his clothing restored.

"I trust you have been well cared for by my relations?"

"Yes, they have been most gracious," Angus said, taking a seat across the table from Donald. "What do you intend to do with me?"

"I would rather we were friends than enemies, Angus. It would benefit both the lordship and Strathnaver were we to join our interests."

"I can see how it might. What do you have in mind?"

"An alliance, one that would bind us together for generations."

"You have me intrigued. What do you propose exactly?"

"To begin, I would invite you to return with me to Ardtornish where there is someone I want you to meet." Angus Du's dark eyes fixed Donald with a steady gaze. "My youngest sister, Elizabeth, is a comely lass and unwed. The granddaughter of King Robert the Second, she will make some powerful chief a worthy bride."

"Ah, ha!" said the Mackay chief. "You plot to join Strathnaver to the lordship!"

"I but conceive of a partnership that would bring much to both our realms and offer you a most excellent bride, one who I treasure as a beloved sister. Moreover, to the man she marries, I will bestow lands."

Angus appeared to consider the offer. "I confess you tempt me." Then, inhaling deeply and letting out the breath, he said, "Very well, I would meet this sister of yours."

Donald believed once Angus had seen Elizabeth, he would be unable to resist the offer to bind himself to the Macdonalds, and he trusted his sister would be impressed with this young chief. "Good, then we sail this day. Should you be wondering, I have said nothing to my sister about this or of your coming, so that you might be free to decide for yourself."

By the time Donald arrived at Ardtornish with his guest, the Macleans had returned to Duart and only his family greeted him. Along with Mariota and his children, his sister Elizabeth came. Seeing her through Mackay's eyes, he knew he had not been wrong in describing her as comely. Her fair hair and blue eyes were a stark contrast to the dark-haired Mackay, who bent his head over her offered hand. "My lady, I am delighted to meet you."

For her part, Elizabeth, a wise young woman, gave Donald a knowing look and smiled sweetly at the Strathnaver chief. "And I you, Lord Mackay."

Over the next several days, Angus and Elizabeth came to know each other, taking walks along the shore within sight of the castle. Donald was pleased to see their affection growing. In the afternoons, Mackay hunted with Donald and Sandy and then dined with the family each evening so that he was more than a guest by the end of his time at Ardtornish.

When Angus finally indicated he was ready to leave, a proposal of marriage had been made to Elizabeth, and she was inclined to accept. "He is a good choice for you," Donald told her. "A respected chief with much power in Sutherland."

Donald offered galley transport to Angus to return him to Strathnaver.

The young chief said, "I must assure my clan I am alive and well, but I will return before the end of autumn with some of my clansmen to claim my bride."

"We will plan for the wedding," said Donald, pleased that the alliance was assured. Donald shook Angus' hand as he turned to board the ship that would take him home. "This will be a good alliance for all."

Shortly after this, Donald received a letter from the dethroned King Richard, who was still at Stirling Castle. He congratulated Donald on the victory at Harlaw. "I could not be more pleased," he wrote. "Albany is storming around the castle when he is here shouting his anger at his loss. He scolds the Earl of Mar for his defeat." The governor had yet to send soldiers into Argyll but Donald knew it would happen soon.

Meantime, Donald sent a messenger to the Earl of Mar, who had apparently recovered from his wounds, asking to ransom Lachlan Maclean. In his note, he said, "As you know, Hector Maclean fell at Harlaw. Lachlan, his eldest son, is now chief of the Macleans. He is much loved and needed by his people. I will pay his ransom. Only return him to his family and to the lordship."

He received no reply through the rest of that year. But in the early spring of 1412, Lachlan suddenly appeared on Mull with a large retinue. When word reached Donald, he and Mariota sailed the short distance across the sound to meet him. Mary greeted them on their arrival. "You will not believe what has transpired!"

Standing with Lachlan was a young dark-haired lass, who it turned out, was Mar's daughter, Margaret, born of his second marriage. It seemed Lachlan had met her while imprisoned at Kildrummy. A love had grown between them, and she had become Lachlan's bride.

While the young woman was speaking to Mariota, Donald drew Lachlan aside. "You have taken Mar's own prize," whereupon Lachlan smiled and handed Donald a message.

"From Mar, my lord." Donald opened the folded parchment, which read, "No ransom need be paid."

Standing there with his new bride, the red-haired Lachlan looked very much like Hector. Though Lachlan's demeanor was more subdued than his famous father, Donald thought he would be a good chief and serve well the lordship. And so, celebration came to the Macleans, softening the tragedy of Hector's loss. While Donald could smile at this turn of events, he would always miss his nephew, a man who left a bold impression on all who knew him.

That same spring, Albany sent a force into Argyll, seeking revenge for his defeat. As John Mor had promised, he came with his men from Antrim, Islay and Kintyre and promptly turned them back, defeated. For a short while, Donald knew peace. But in Ross, discontent reigned due to Albany's attempt to take control without the support of the key nobles.

It seemed to Donald and the nobles of Ross that Albany intended to base his Ross operations from Inverness Castle, which he was rebuilding. This proved to be the case as the months wore on.

Albany extended his power into Ross through punitive military measures, carried out by his captains, who attempted to pacify the earldom through intimidation of the Ross kindreds. The strategy failed. As a result, Donald continued to exert authority in Ross, and Mariota spent much time at Dingwall that had once been her home. With Angus Du Mackay as Donald's brother-in-law and ally, his control was especially strong in northern Ross.

Unwilling to let matters rest, Albany continued to pressure Euphemia, Alexander Leslie's daughter and Mariota's niece, to give up her rights to the earldom and enter a nunnery. In furtherance of this, he set up his son, John Stewart, Earl of Buchan, to obtain Ross as his second earldom. Buchan did not long attempt to claim the title as the people of Ross accepted Donald as their rightful lord.

By June, with John MacAlister's help, Donald had obtained the arm and hand bones of St. Columba and the Iona artisans had encased them in silver and gold at Donald's expense. On St. Columba's Feast Day, he gifted the reliquary, a thing of dazzling, wondrous golden beauty, to the abbey in a great ceremony that was widely attended by those in the lordship. Scores of galleys were beached on the shores of the small isle, as many pilgrims were drawn to the event.

In the ceremony, Abbot John came through the archway in the carved and richly decorated rood screen, past all the choir monks singing St. Columba Feast Day chants. Holding the golden hand and arm aloft, the candlelight glinting on the polished metal, he blessed the congregation and said, "This gift is a benediction by St. Columba himself, who resides in Heaven with God." All those in attendance rejoiced.

Donald was filled with regard for John's role in restoring the abbey and bringing honor to Iona after the MacKinnons had sullied it. As the abbey founder's heir, he rejoiced that he could bestow this gift, for it represented Clan Donald's continued commitment to preserve Iona's spiritual legacy.

In the spring of the next year, King Henry the Fourth died, replaced by his son, Henry the Fifth, the tall youth whom Donald had met in London. The change of monarchs marked the passing of an era in Donald's mind.

The payment of the ransom for the noble Scottish prisoners taken at the Battle of Homildon Hill, so long at issue, was finally agreed to, and with this, the prisoners were released, all save Albany's eldest son, Murdoch.

Donald hoped this release of prisoners was a sign that Scotland's young king would soon be released. Sitting by the fire one evening with Mariota, discussing what lay ahead, he said, "This will mean a change for Scotland. King James will not defer to his kin, the Albany Stewarts, who he holds responsible for his long imprisonment. I foresee turbulence ahead."

Mariota returned him a fond gaze, the firelight making her eyes glisten. "When it comes, my love, with God's help, we will weather it together."

AUTHOR'S NOTE

Even before Donald was born, his father, John of Islay, Lord of the Isles, had effectively recreated the kingdom of Somerled, whose story is told in *Summer Warrior*. Donald's life justified his father's decision to name him the successor to the lordship and chief of Clan Donald. He was bold, dauntless and astute, a true descendant of Somerled, who had fiercely maintained his Isles' independence. Like his father and grandfather, Donald was also a man of faith who loved God.

That Donald would resort to war to claim what was rightfully his (by right of his wife) is in keeping with the culture of the day. "At all levels of the church hierarchy across Europe, from pope downwards, the 'defenders of the faith' frequently sought recourse to the battlefield to air grievances, redeem pride and foster might." (A.T. Lucas, *The Plundering and Burning of Churches in Ireland*, 7th to 16 Century). But he did so only after trying to find satisfaction through his rightful claim.

To say Donald had the victory at Harlaw is an understatement, as many sources attest. It has been a constant frustration to me how many websites and sources suggest Donald was "surprised" by Mar's forces and that Donald "lost" the battle. That is just not believable. Both armies had spies scouting ahead so Donald was not surprised. At Harlaw's conclusion, the Lord of the Isles still had at least 9100 warriors on the field while the Earl of Mar and the men he had left were lying on the field wounded. It is believed Mar started with around one thousand men and half were slain. (Keith Norman Macdonald, M.D., in his book *Macdonald Bards*, says Mar's men were "cut to pieces".)

As for Donald, even assuming 900 of his remaining 9100 men were wounded, with 8,000 fighting men remaining, he could easily have taken what was left of Mar's army and marched on to Aberdeen. As Donald J. Macdonald said in his book, *Clan Donald*, at p. 86, "That Macdonald of the Isles at the head of 8000 clansmen, or even half that number, retreated in dismay before a wounded leader lying prostrate on the field of battle surrounded by a mere handful of men, most of whom were crippled with wounds, cannot easily be believed by any unprejudiced person." Hence, another explanation for Donald's return to the Isles must be found, and I have tried to present one that is logical given what I know of the man.

The nearest contemporary record is found in the *Irish Annals of Connacht* where, under the year 1411, it is stated, "Mac Domnaill of Scotland won a great victory over the Galls of Scotland." The 2011 article by Iain G. MacDonald, *Donald of the Isles and the Earldom of Ross: West-Highland Perspectives on the Battle of Harlaw*, is excellent and records the victory.

The book *Bludie Harlaw* by Ian Olson discusses some of the primary sources that touch on the battle, though the author gets Clan Donald's history wrong in several places. The *McKean Historical Notes*, relating to the MacIain MacDonalds of Ardnamurchan, compiled by Fred G. McKean, 1906, at p. 38, refers to the *Annals of the Old Abbey of Inis-Macreen* and mentions the "great victory" of the Macdonald of Scotland in 1411.

According to Donald Gregory, whose manuscripts are cited in the *Highland Papers* for May 1914, "Macdonald enjoyed the Earldom of Ross all his lifetime without any competition or trouble...but as long as the king was captive in England, the Duke of Albany the Regent used all his power to oppose him and impair his greatness, being vexed he lost the Battle of Harlaw." (Highland Papers, vol. 1, at p. 34).

It is thus an accurate statement to call Donald "the Hero of Harlaw", as I do. It is why he is known to this day as Donald of Harlaw. There are those who say otherwise despite the glaring facts of the rout of Alexander Stewart, Earl of Mar. "In short, the upshot of the battle of

Harlaw is thus wittily summarized," said Patrick, Earl of Tullibardin, as he and other noblemen were speaking of the battle, "We know that Macdonald had the victory, but the governor had the printer!" (*Macdonald of the Isles* by A.M.W. Stirling, 1913, at p. 88.)

As my story shows, Donald did, indeed, forgive his brother, John Mor, for his betrayal and rebellion, and John Mor rewarded him with loyalty. He was at the head of the reserve at Harlaw and "contributed largely to the victory of the Lord of the Isles." (*Clan Donald* by Rev. A. MacDonald, vol. 2, 1900, at p. 496). When the Duke of Albany afterwards gathered a force and followed them back into Argyll, it was John Mor who came forward to repulse the governor.

The Lowland chronicler Walter Bower, Abbot of Inchcolm, writing in the mid-fifteenth century, saw Harlaw as a struggle between the burgesses of Aberdeen and the gentry of Buchan and Mar and the "wild and rapacious men of the Isles and Ross in the service of the Lord of the Isles". However, one must consider that the abbot had a profound personal dislike of the culture and society of Gaelic Scotland and Ireland. Moreover, he was wrong. Donald of Islay was an educated man and a man of faith who was ever in the company of priests, while the Earl of Mar, who had acquired his title by rape and murder, was the illegitimate son of Alexander Stewart, Earl of Buchan, known as the Wolf of Badenoch. Mar raided with his father and their caterans with impunity and was known to engage in piracy. He may have raised his status when he acquired Mar, but he was a cateran at heart.

Because you might ask, my research into the dethroned Richard II indicates that he died at Stirling in 1418 and his ashes lie there. The details of his escape, his coming to the Lord of the Isles and his residing with King Robert in the historical record were such that I was persuaded it might have happened just that way.

By the seventeenth century, Harlaw was cemented in tradition as a great victory for Clan Donald, and an aggressive campaign for control of the Highlands. In a Gaelic verse of 1678 to Sir Donald Macdonald of Sleat, Iain Lom, the bard of Keppoch, speaking of Donald, described Harlaw as "a famous expedition and that more than half of Alba was under your sway".

It was due to Donald's Gaelic loyalty to king and kingdom that, in the aftermath of Harlaw, he never considered staking a claim for the crown of Scotland, though he could have done given his royal pedigree and the empty throne. His forbearance helped ensure the continued stability of Scotland's kingless realm. Perhaps that and his relationship with the imprisoned James I explain the king's subsequent actions upon his return to Scotland in 1424. Donald had died the year before but James placed Donald's son, Alexander, Lord of the Isles, on the panel that judged the Albany Stewarts. Robert Stewart, the ruthless Duke of Albany, had died in 1420, but the others, including his heir, Murdoch, were soon eliminated.

By then, Donald's son, Alexander, was using the title Earl of Ross, inheriting the support of the earldom's nobility that his father enjoyed. King James did not take issue with this. As for Donald's claim to the title,

> "Since his claim to the Earldom of Ross in right of his wife was, subsequent to his death, virtually admitted by King James I, and as Donald was actually in possession of that earldom and acknowledged by the vassals in 1411, he may without impropriety be called the first Earl of Ross of his family." (Id. at p. 89.)

As my story makes clear, Donald was a lover of the church and the clan's ecclesiastical seat at Iona, which, as patron, he maintained, as did his forefathers. To Donald, it was both his right and his duty. His lifelong friend and cousin, John MacAlister, with Donald's help, became the Abbot of Iona and supervised some of the abbey's restoration. Before Donald died, being assured of his heir, Alexander, he took the brotherhood of the Benedictine order at Iona. The Lords of the Isles who followed Donald dedicated themselves to rebuilding and restoring Iona's abbey, such that by 1495, its church was elevated to the status of the Cathedral of the Isles.

Donald died in 1423 on Islay, years before Mariota. He was the last Lord of the Isles to be buried in St. Oran's Chapel on Iona, interred in the same tomb as his predecessors, as was the lordship's custom. (You can experience the ceremony in *Bound by Honor*.) In attendance would have been Mariota and their children, including his son and grandson (both named Angus), who would later become Bishops of the Isles. Abbot John MacAlister, his friend and partner for thirty years, had died two years before him.

Donald's son, Alexander Macdonald (nicknamed "Sandy" in my story) carried the titles Lord of the Isles, Earl of Ross, and Justiciar of Scotia. Under Alexander, the power of Clan Donald would reach its zenith, both secular and ecclesiastical. With Ross and all of the Isles under his control, Alexander's power was even greater than that of his ancestor, Somerled. Alexander was effectively King of Western Scotland—not just the Isles and the Western Highlands—and on equal terms with King James I.

Coming next: Book 4, *Born to Trouble* (Sandy's story). For notices of future releases, follow me on Amazon. You can also sign up for my infrequent newsletters on my website. I give away a free book each quarter to one of my new subscribers. And, should you be on Facebook, do join the Regan Walker's Readers group.
amazon.com/Regan-Walker/e/B008OUWC5Y
www.reganwalkerauthor.com
facebook.com/groups/ReganWalkersReaders

For pictures of the places and castles and characters in my story, see the Pinterest storyboard for The Clan Donald Saga. It's my research in pictures.
pinterest.com/reganwalker123/the-clan-donald-saga-by-regan-walker

AUTHOR BIO

Regan Walker is an award-winning author of Regency, Georgian and Medieval novels. She has six times been nominated for the Reward of Novel Excellence (RONE) award. Her novels *The Red Wolf's Prize* and *King's Knight* won the RONE for Best Historical Novel in the Medieval category. *The Refuge: An Inspirational Novel of Scotland* won the Gold Medal in the Illumination Awards. *To Tame the Wind* won the International Book Award for Romance Fiction and Best Historical Romance in the San Diego Book Awards. *A Fierce Wind* won a medal in the President's Book Awards of The Florida Authors & Publishers Association. *Rogue's Holiday* won the Kindle Book Award for historical romance. *Summer Warrior*, book 1 in The Clan Donald Saga of historical fiction, won first prize in the Chaucer Awards for Pre-1750s Historical Fiction, and *Bound by Honor*, book 2, won the Gold Medal in the Readers' Choice Book Awards.

A lawyer turned writer, Regan's years of serving clients in private practice and several stints in high levels of government have given her a feel for the demands of the "Crown". Hence her novels often feature a demanding sovereign who taps his subjects for special assignments. The Clan Donald Saga, her newest venture into historical fiction, is close to her heart as she is a part of Clan Donald. The series tells the stories of the Lords of the Isles the great sea lords who ruled the Hebrides for hundreds of years. She has made several trips to Scotland as a part of her research.

Regan lives in San Diego with her dog "Cody", a Wirehaired Pointing Griffon, who is dearly loved.

BOOKS BY REGAN WALKER

The Agents of the Crown series (Regency):

Racing with the Wind
Against the Wind
Wind Raven
A Secret Scottish Christmas
Rogue's Holiday

The Donet Trilogy (Georgian):

To Tame the Wind
Echo in the Wind
A Fierce Wind

Holiday Novellas (related to The Agents of the Crown):

The Shamrock & The Rose
The Holly & The Thistle
The Twelfth Night Wager

Medieval Warriors (England and Scotland 11th century):

The Red Wolf's Prize
Rogue Knight
Rebel Warrior
King's Knight

The Clan Donald Saga (begins in the 12th century):

Summer Warrior
Bound by Honor
The Strongest Heart

Inspirational

The Refuge: An Inspirational Novel of Scotland

www.ReganWalkerAuthor.com

Made in United States
Orlando, FL
08 November 2023

38735274R00174